# PILLOW TALK

Will watched Maggie cross the room in long-legged strides. She certainly didn't look ready to apologize for anything. As she passed the bed, she scooped up a pillow without even pausing.

Will set his glass down. "Maggie, what—"

"You big oaf!" She swung the pillow with all her force, hitting his shoulder. "You should know me better than that. How *dare* you think so little of me?"

She hit him with the pillow again. "Of all the conceited, self-absorbed, addlepated fools—what makes you think what happened in there was about *you?*"

She swung the pillow a third time.

"Enough of this!" he bellowed, catching the cushion in mid-swing and tossing it aside. What the devil was she fuming about?

"Maggie, I don't understand. I—"

Before he could finish, she took his right hand in hers, and slowly lifted it to her face, brushing her cheek softly with it, her eyes never leaving his. "Then try to understand this."

Very deliberately, she kissed the top of his hand, then uncurled his fist, bringing his scarred palm to her mouth, anointing every inch with her warm, soft lips. Still holding his gaze with her own, she placed seductively lingering kisses on each finger, even the scarred stump.

# A WILL
## OF HER OWN

# WINNIE GRIGGS

LEISURE BOOKS          NEW YORK CITY

A LEISURE BOOK®

January 2004

Published by

Dorchester Publishing Co., Inc.
200 Madison Avenue
New York, NY 10016

ISBN 0-8439-5302-0

The name "Leisure Books" and the stylized "L" with design are trademarks of Dorchester Publishing Co., Inc.

Printed in the United States of America.

Visit us on the web at www.dorchesterpub.com.

*To all of the following, my most sincere gratitude:*

*To Joanne Rock, Beth Cornelison and Connie Cox, for coming to my rescue with the very generous gift of their time and talent when I needed last-minute help streamlining this story.*

*To Catherine Mann and Sue Morgan, for their truly insightful feedback on the first draft of this book.*

*To Laura Wallace, for answering my countless questions about the English peerage and forms of address.*

*And last but not least, to my wonderful editor, Kate Seaver, whose suggestion for 'one little change' made all the difference in the world.*

# A WILL
## OF HER OWN

# Prologue

"Well, well, Lilly, I see you *are* here. This is twice in as many days you've managed to surprise me."

William Trevaron straightened from the bow he'd offered his former fiancée and her mother. After what had transpired last night, he was in no mood to exchange pleasantries with the lethally attractive Lilly this morning.

Especially not here, in the presence of his grandfather.

How *dare* the brazen witch dart into his grandfather's study to tell her tale before Will could speak for himself?

Had she really thought she could turn his grandfather against him? If so, she underestimated the bond between the two men.

Will leaned against the mantle and gave his grandfather a casual nod. "Good morning, sir. I assume Miss Radwin spared me the disagreeable task of informing you of our broken engagement."

His Grace, the duke of Lynchmorne, enthroned behind his massive mahogany desk, pinned Will with a quelling look. "Don't be flippant, William. Miss Radwin has made serious accusations against you, accusations I find it difficult to credit."

1

Will stiffened. He hadn't been addressed in such a tone since he'd left Eton. Something was amiss here—something more than the fact that he'd cried off his engagement to Lilly.

Then Will took in his grandfather's appearance, and his concern deepened. All the Trevaron men were imposing— even at sixty-two the family patriarch was no exception. But today the duke's imperious demeanor seemed oddly askew. There was a brittleness about him, an uncertainty Will had never seen before.

Will's anger kicked back in, stronger now. Whatever Lilly had said this morning had put those flags of color in the duke's cheeks and the flicker of doubt in his usually steady gaze.

Her betrayal of *him* was bad enough. If she had been so ill-advised as to aggrieve his grandfather, she would soon regret it.

Will glanced at the angel-faced viper he'd nearly shackled himself to. She appeared more the distraught mourner than the scheming hussy he now knew her to be. Why the deuce would such a vain creature hide her much-vaunted beauty behind a veil?

She bloody well wasn't grieving from a broken heart. More likely, she found herself unable look him in the eye after what had passed between them last night.

Whatever deep game she played, she had best tread carefully. He and his grandfather were daunting enough separately—together they were formidable, indeed.

"And what has Miss Radwin accused me of?" Will heard the silky menace in his voice. Lilly would *not* make a pawn of his grandfather, no matter what contemptible scheme she'd concocted.

Lilly twisted a handkerchief. "Please, Will," she implored brokenly, "I didn't want to—"

"He can't hurt you anymore." Lady Blom took Lilly's hand, eying Will as she would a loathsome insect. "You

A WILL OF HER OWN

know quite well what this is about, you brute. You doubt-less thought it would be your word against Lillith's, but in that you were mistaken. Lift the veil and hold up your arm Lillith."

Will snapped upright as she revealed an ugly discoloration on her cheek. "Lilly, what happened? Did someone—" He started forward but halted as she shrank from him. His sympathy turned to wariness. He would do well to remember that last night she'd demonstrated just how foreign the concept of honor was to her.

Lady Blom's lips thinned. "Don't pretend surprise. There can be no doubt who is responsible for *these*."

She held up Lilly's arm, revealing bruises on the delicate alabaster wrist. Though fainter than the ghastly marks on her cheek, the shape proclaimed that it had been caused by the grip of a large hand. A grip that lacked its fourth, smallest finger.

A hand identical to the one at the end of Will's right arm—the mark of failure he'd borne for eight years now.

Will stared blankly at the damning marks, then guilt sliced through him. Of course—he'd grabbed her when she tried to slap his face the second time.

But what the devil had marred her face? Had someone dared strike her? What sort of craven bastard would do such a thing?

"Oh, Will, I know you didn't realize what you were doing." Her hand gingerly touched her cheek. "You were so deep in your cups . . ." Her voice trailed off as tears filled her violet eyes.

Deep in his cups? He'd been sober as a vicar's wife. Surely she wasn't accusing *him* of this atrocity. "See here—"

But Lady Blom's parental fury drowned out his protest. "Don't dare defend him, Lillith." Outrage lent shrillness to her voice. "Anger and drinking do *not* excuse such brutality."

3

Enough was enough. He would accept censure for the bruise to her arm, but Lilly was mad if she thought he would tamely—

His former fiancée's lips curved in a vindictive smile.

With all eyes on him, Will was the only one who saw her expression. Only *he* saw her mouth silently form the words, "*You promised*," before she transformed back into the fragile victim.

With a sickening lurch, he recalled his promise—that he would support whatever story she cared to contrive in order to lessen her embarrassment over their broken betrothal. But this—

Would Lilly dare to use his generosity to silence him?

"Well," the duke demanded, "what is your answer to this?"

Will hadn't moved since that first, unguarded half step in Lilly's direction. His mind reeled at the depth of her treachery, her antipathy.

Flexing his disfigured hand, fighting the memories it evoked, he wondered how his own well-meant actions could have turned on him so horribly once again.

This time, though, it would end differently. This time, he was no fourteen-year-old boy facing the nightmare alone.

Will turned to his grandfather, certain he would find evidence of the trust and support that had always been there, that had gotten him through the darkest period of his life.

Instead, impossibly, he saw doubt in the older man's eyes, in the way he braced himself to receive a blow. The duke absently fingered the miniature of his mother that rested on his desk, an unconscious gesture at odds with his normally controlled manner.

This was absurd, obscene. Lilly's treachery had wounded his pride, but it was as nothing to this. That his grandfather should credit her claim even for a moment, sliced through Will with an almost physical force.

Honor was the guiding principle of the duke's life, and of Will's—the notion of a man's word being his bond, of never taking advantage of those weaker or less privileged. Never in Will's twenty-two years had he given his grandfather cause to believe him capable of straying from that code.

Devil's teeth, this was too much. Surely honor would not be served by keeping his promise under such circumstances? Not when it had been given to a creature who twisted it so vilely. Will opened his mouth to defend himself, then clamped it shut again.

He *had* given his word—to whom was immaterial. He would not lower himself to Lilly's level by throwing his principles to the wind. And, by Jove, why should he have to? Was Grandfather's faith so thin that it would crumble at the first real test?

Will straightened. "If you choose to take Miss Radwin's word over what you know of me, then so be it. I will not stand here and bandy words over this." He felt a muscle twitch at the corner of his mouth. Would his grandfather understand the message conveyed in that statement?

The duke released the miniature and slammed his fist on the desk. "Confound it, Will, that's not an answer." His voice thundered across the room. "Deny these charges here and now so we can be done with this whole damnable mess."

It said something about his grandfather's state of mind that he would use such language in the presence of ladies. But neither man turned at the startled gasps from across the room. Instead, their gazes locked in a stubborn test of resolve.

Will refused to flinch, willing his grandfather to read the truth in his face.

The moment stretched out unbearably. With each heartbeat of silence, something inside Will hardened and shriveled, until it formed a tight knot pressing painfully against his breastbone.

At last he could bear it no longer.

He drew his shoulders back. "What passed between Miss Radwin and myself last night is a private matter. I cannot say more on the matter." *You should trust in me*, he silently raged, *in who you* know *me to be*.

But he no longer believed that was possible.

"There!" Lady Blom crowed. "That's as good as a confession. What do you intend to do about this, Your Grace?"

Will's jaw clenched as he watched his grandfather's shoulders sag, saw his eyes dull in weary disappointment, saw him absently finger the small portrait once more.

How could he have been so wrong about a man he'd looked up to his whole life? It was almost a relief when the duke broke his gaze from Will's and turned to the ladies.

"I will do all in my power to ascertain your daughter does not suffer from the vulgar curiosity of the public over this matter. I shall also settle a sum on her that will provide a comfortable dowry, should her affections turn to another."

The duke's brows drew down and he was again the brook-no-arguments aristocrat. "My only stipulation is that details of what passed between them last night never leave this room."

Will swallowed several choice oaths. The truth of what had happened last night had never *entered* this room.

But Lilly's mother nodded. "Of course. You may count on our discretion. Isn't that so, Lillith?"

"Yes, I could never—" The Jezebel's voice broke on a sob.

"Spare me your concern." Will barely glanced at Lilly. Her vengeful theatrics were no longer of much concern to him.

"If you ladies will excuse us," the duke's tone made it clear they were dismissed, "my grandson and I have matters to discuss."

He glanced at the miniature again, then speared Will with a glare. Both men held their silence as the women exited.

Then, as the door closed behind them, the duke sagged back, bitter disappointment etched in his face. "How could you?"

The words, with all they implied, clawed at Will's gut. "I have said all I can." One last time, he hoped his grandfather would hear the message in his words.

"You don't even have the decency to feign repentance," the duke bit out.

It was true then. Impossibly, his grandfather accepted Lilly's story. Will commanded his breathing to hold steady, his expression to remain impassive, the bile not to choke him.

Steel returned to his grandfather's backbone and fire to his eyes. "The thought of what you did to that fragile creature, no matter the reason, disgusts me, makes me ashamed of our familial connection. I can neither forget nor forgive such an atrocity."

This time Will *did* flinch.

His grandfather's next words fell with the finality of a gallows weight. "I no longer count you a member of this family. You are henceforth banished, not only from my presence, but from Lynchmorne Hall and every other property of my holdings."

Will's hands fisted with painful intensity and he had to lock his jaw to prevent a cry of protest. He had to get out of here, needed time to absorb what had just occurred. The man whose respect meant so much had just tossed him out as if he were a piece of offal.

"I'll take this as my cue to leave, then, Your Grace." With a mocking bow, Will strode from the room.

Closing the door behind him, he sagged against the frame, his anger-fueled energy deserting him. Surely this was a nightmare he would awaken from soon. Not since he'd watched his mother's life being squeezed away had he felt so alone, so betrayed.

Notes from an indifferently played piano brought his head up.

Jenny.

Telling his little sister good-bye would be difficult—for both of them. He couldn't explain this, even to her.

Will struggled against the urge to howl in anger and frustration. How could his whole life, his whole foundation, have changed in the space of a few minutes?

He moved stiffly toward the music room. Best to get this over with quickly.

He had been naïve to think those close to him would believe in who he was. More fool him to have made himself so vulnerable.

Never again.

Suddenly, Will wanted a great deal more distance—both from his grandfather and from his old life. From here on out, he'd have to prove himself on his own, and that was fine with him.

Self-reliance ridded him of the problem of future betrayals.

# Chapter One

*Clover Ridge, Virginia 1830*

". . . twenty-eight, twenty-nine, thirty!"

Maggie Carter opened her eyes, then planted her hands on her hips. "Now where could those children have gotten off to?"

Her lips quirked in a smile as she heard muffled giggles from a bush to her right. The sound of Beth's laughter again, after weeks of mourning, warmed Maggie as nothing else could have.

This outing was just the tonic her stepchildren needed. For now, on this glorious May afternoon, they could pretend all was as it should be.

"What do you think, Tully? Do we check in the trees first or down by the pond?"

The gray feline at her feet greeted the question with a sneeze, then went back to grooming his paw.

Maggie walked past the scraggly bush, ignoring the glint of sunlight on blond curls, giving the five-year-old a chance to bolt for "home" if she wanted to take it.

The two boys were another matter entirely. Owen might only be a year older than Beth, but he was a cunning imp, a scamp quite equal to the challenge of besting her at a game of hide-and-seek if she let down her guard. And Cal, at age nine, would be highly insulted if she gave any indication that she was "letting him" get away.

Rustling from above hinted at where her quarry could be found. "Sounds like a mighty big squirrel nesting in this tree." She shaded her eyes and studied the branches overhead. "You may as well come down, Owen—I've got you."

Beth, ever faithful to her brothers, erupted from her hiding place. "You can't catch me," she squealed, and sprinted for the picnic blanket.

Willing to be distracted, Maggie gave a whoop of surprise, lifted her skirt, and gave chase, deliberately stumbling a bit until Beth was safely "home." Before Maggie could regroup, Owen dodged around her and stepped triumphantly on the cloth as well.

Beth jumped up and down, clapping her hands. "We made it! We made it!" She gave Maggie a saucy grin. "Now you have to find Cal or you're going to be 'it' again."

Maggie tossed her head and pushed up her sleeve in mock-determination. "Oh, I'll find him, all right." She straightened Beth's pinafore then waved toward the picnic basket. "Why don't you two set out the food? We'll eat as soon as I tag Cal."

Maggie winked. "I didn't have time to count the cookies, so if there are a few missing when I return, I'll never know."

Finding Cal took less time than expected. She'd only walked a few minutes into the sparse copse of trees when she spied him sitting on a large rock, scratching in the dirt with a stick.

He looked up when she approached, his expression solemn, troubled. He scooted over, making room for her.

"Did you get tired of playing?" Maggie asked, giving him an opening to share his thoughts.

Cal only shrugged and continued scribbling aimlessly. This time she let the silence draw out.

Finally he straightened. "What's going to happen to you?"

The knot in Maggie's chest drew tighter as she touched the amber broach at her throat. Stubborn, direct, protective Cal. His father's death was barely six weeks behind him and now he was losing his home, his father's legacy to him.

But his concern was all for *her* fate.

She placed a hand on his knee and forced a smile. "Don't you worry. I'm certain I'll find other accommodations before the month is out. I'll be all right." Maggie prayed she sounded more confident than she felt. Giving up these children was the most heart-wrenching thing she'd ever had to do. But what choice did she have? She had no means to support them herself.

Cal's hands fisted. "It's not fair!"

Another piece of Maggie's heart splintered. *What have we done to you, Cal? You're too young to sound so bitter.*

"Look at me." She waited until his gaze met hers. "No one planned this. It just happened. We must accept that and move on." She smiled encouragingly. "I understand Boston is a grand place, with lots of things to see and do. And your Uncle Henry and Aunt Imogene will take good care of you all."

The boy seemed unconvinced. "Why can't you come with us?"

She adjusted the collar of his shirt. "Your Uncle Henry has no obligation to look out for me, and it wouldn't be proper to ask him to bear the added expense. Besides, I'm a grown woman and quite capable of looking out for myself."

"Will we ever see you again?"

She squeezed his shoulder. "God willing, someday. But whatever happens, we can keep in touch through letters."

11

"You can't hug someone in a letter."

With a sharp intake of breath, Maggie crushed the boy to her. She fought to speak words of comfort through the strangling lump in her throat. "Know that I am hugging you and Owen and Beth close in my heart every single night." She couldn't take much more of this before her control broke, and she refused to burden her stepson with the memory of her hysterical sobbing.

She released him and brushed a lock of hair from his brow. For once, Cal allowed her the tender gesture without squirming.

"Now," she said with a cheerfulness she didn't feel, "no more gloomy talk. We're having a picnic. It's a lovely day, there's a basket full of scrumptious treats, and we're all together."

*For perhaps the last time.*

The words hung in the air as if she'd said them aloud.

Tomorrow her brother-in-law would arrive, and he would carry these precious sweetlings away. They would be gone from her life with no guarantee the four of them would ever be reunited.

Maggie fingered her broach again, trying to draw the strength from it to hold her tears at bay.

She forced a brisk smile. "Come along. Owen and Beth are waiting. If we don't hurry, there'll be no cookies left."

That evening, after the children were tucked in bed, Maggie sat at the desk in her bedchamber. A deep, burning sense of betrayal welled inside her. She struggled to tamp it down, to re-armor herself with her protective mantle of calm reserve.

Her husband was dead. She should be mourning his loss, not burning with resentment.

Why had he hidden this situation from her? The extent of his debts—her debts now—was staggering.

Heaven above, how could she find herself in this situation *again*?

Maggie rubbed her temple. She shouldn't be so surprised Joseph hadn't discussed the true state of his affairs with her. She'd known all along he thought her more ward than wife. In his mind, even wheelchair-bound, he was more able to deal with such matters than a "mere girl." Undoubtedly he'd thought he could turn things around eventually.

Well, she'd fended for herself before, she could do so again.

But the children . . .

Maggie set the pen on the inkstand and drew her shoulders back. Enough of this. Joseph's brother had agreed to take them in for as long as necessary. The three would be well cared for.

Refusing to give way to self-pity, she returned her attention to the stack of letters she'd penned, letters to all whose horses were stabled here at Clover Ridge or who might have an interest in purchasing new stock. Everything would have to be claimed or sold before month's end—before the creditors stepped in.

Maggie stared at the letter on top, the one addressed to Will Trevaron. It had been nearly two years since she'd seen him. Would he come himself or would he send someone else to retrieve Orion? After all, he was a wealthy man now, the owner of a thriving shipping company.

Strange how their paths kept crossing during the years since she'd first met him. Her lips curved in a reminiscent smile. He was an interesting man, one who made her feel—

A tentative knock shifted her thoughts back to the present.

"Yes?"

Almost before the word left her lips, the children and Tully crowded through the doorway.

"What are you doing up? You should be asleep." Her voice lacked any hint of sternness. Truth to tell, she was glad to see them. Sitting on her bed, she patted the mattress in invitation. They immediately clambered up to join her.

"We wanted some time to say good-bye on our own," Cal explained. "Before Uncle Henry and Aunt Imogene arrive."

"Please come with us," a tearful Beth pleaded.

"Don't cry, Sunshine," Maggie crooned, gathering the little girl into her lap. "We've been through this before. I can't go with you. But you'll live in a grand new house. Your cousins Annabelle and Fredrick will be there, and so will Cal and Owen."

"I don't want to live in a grand house with cousins I don't know. I want to stay with you."

"Just think of the great adventure you'll have, all the new things you'll see and the people you'll meet." Maggie tapped her stepdaughter's nose. "And I expect you and your brothers to write me long letters and tell me all about it. Promise?"

Beth hiccupped and nodded.

"Don't you want to be our momma anymore?" For all his bluster, Maggie could see Owen was close to tears himself.

"Oh, Owen," she hugged the boy to her as well. "Don't ever doubt I love you, and how proud I am to be a part of your family. But there isn't a place for me in your uncle's home." For three years she'd been their stepmother and she'd grown to love them as if they were her own. How could one just stop being a mother?

"It's not right for you to be all alone." Cal slid from the bed and stood in front of her. "So we've all decided."

The other two nodded agreement, though Beth sniffled loudly.

Cal bent down and picked up the cat. "We want you

14

to have Tully. He'll keep you company, and we'll feel better if we know you have him with you."

Maggie didn't know what to say. The cat was a beloved family pet. He had belonged to Joseph's first wife, the children's real mother, and carried a special place in their hearts. She couldn't accept such a precious gift.

Then she looked at their earnest faces and knew she couldn't turn it down.

"Oh, children, this is the most wonderful thing anyone has ever done for me. Thank you all so much."

Later, after the children had returned to their rooms, Maggie plopped on her bed and stared numbly at the closed door. Then her control crumpled, and she buried her face in her hands.

Would she ever see them again after Henry carried them off?

Curling her fingers around the amber broach, she silently vowed that she would find a way.

*Crane Harbor, Virginia     Two days later*

With a string of oaths that would have made an east-end dock worker proud, Will crumpled the letter from his grandfather. The tersely worded missive was nothing short of a summons, and a bloody insulting one at that. No one had dared address him in such a manner in a very long time. Six years, in fact.

Six years since he'd last set foot on English soil.

Six years since he'd stalked out of his grandfather's study.

Six years since he'd had any communication with the man whose approval had once meant everything to him.

And *this* was what his grandfather had broken the long silence for—to make it bitingly obvious how little his opinion of Will had changed during that time.

Disappointment twisted Will's gut. He should have known better than to think it would be an olive branch.

His grandfather would *never* discern the truth—something Will should have come to terms with years ago.

He thought he *had* come to terms with it—more fool him.

He leaned back and took a deep breath. Reining in his anger, he mentally digested the news that had prompted his grandfather to dispatch the letter. Will hadn't known his uncle and cousin well, so word of their unexpected demises within a month of each other produced only stirrings of sympathy for the wives and daughters they left behind.

That fate had conspired to make him his grandfather's heir mattered to him even less.

His grandfather apparently thought it significant enough, however, to demand Will return to Lynchmorne forthwith. Phrases from the letter sliced through Will's determined detachment, mocking him with evidence of the older man's disdain:

   *. . . the reason for your exile is not widely known . . .*

   *. . . give up those Yankee, merchant-class ways . . .*

   *. . . arrange a suitable match to re-establish your place in society . . .*

No acknowledgement that Will had come into his own, had built a formidable shipping empire, had acquired a wealth to rival his grandfather's.

Well, so be it. Will wouldn't even grace the letter with a reply. Let his silence speak for him instead.

He flexed his right hand to ease the sudden cramping. Even though the disfiguring scars had healed long ago, he still felt occasional twinges when he was tired or tense.

Or when the memories of that nightmare night surfaced.

With his other hand, Will flung the crumpled wad across the room. Then he stood and grabbed his coat.

He needed fresh air and action. A walk down to the docks should satisfy both needs.

He jerked the door open to find his business manager standing with fist raised to knock.

Ian Spencer took one look at Will and his freckled face split in a familiar grin. "I hope whatever put you in such a pleasant mood has nothing to do with me or the new shipping contract. Ellen has threatened to come down here herself and have words with you if I'm forced to work late again tonight."

Will managed an answering smile. They both knew Ian's wife was too sweet-tempered to follow through on that threat. "I think Ellen would be grateful to me for keeping you out of her way so much this past week."

He clapped the younger man on the shoulder. "Don't worry, I've already reviewed and signed the Johansen contract. In fact, you can go home early this evening if you like."

Ian's smile widened. "If you expect me to protest that I've too much to do, then you've confused your priorities with mine."

When Will didn't rise to the teasing, Ian held up a couple of packets. "These just arrived. Do you want to look at them now, or shall I set them on your desk?"

In no mood to handle additional correspondence, Will nodded toward his desk. "I'll read them later. If anyone needs me, they can find me checking on the *Lady Jen*."

Ignoring Ian's worried frown, Will marched past him and out of the building.

But he couldn't ignore the feeling of old wounds reopening.

The next afternoon, Will slowed his horse to a walk as he neared the arched entrance to Clover Ridge. Maggie Carter's letter, though not a happy one, had come at a fortuitous time. The two-hour ride from Crane Harbor had given him opportunity to think matters over in regard to his grandfather, to temper his anger of yesterday with a more coolly reasoned logic.

Not that he wasn't still angry, but much of that anger was now directed inward. How could he have allowed his grandfather's contempt to drive him from England, from his sister, for so long?

Jenny was seventeen now. Next year she would enjoy her first London season. And all he had to mark her progress from gangly schoolgirl to near womanhood were the letters they'd exchanged.

What a self-righteous fool he'd been to permit such a thing.

Perhaps it *was* time he returned, time he laid a few ghosts to rest. After all, whether he wished it or not, he was heir apparent, and that carried responsibilities both to the family and to those dependent on the Trevarons for subsistence. He also wanted to get reacquainted with his sister before she set her cap at some young jackanapes and started a family of her own.

Yes, the more he thought on it, the more certain he became that returning to England was the proper course of action.

But he'd do it on his own terms.

Will was proud of what he'd achieved, and not at all ashamed that he'd had to roll up his shirtsleeves and work beside these resourceful Americans to accomplish it. The devil take anyone who thought he'd apologize for the path he'd taken. If his grandfather wanted the heir close by, he'd have to accept Will as he was, newly acquired "merchant-class" ways and all.

Will passed inside the gates and returned his thoughts to more immediate matters. Staring up the drive at the sprawling house and well-groomed lawn, he patted the neck of his mount.

He'd stabled horses at Clover Ridge ever since Maggie married Joseph Carter, just so he'd have an excuse to visit occasionally. But he'd gotten lax about taking advantage of that privilege.

How was the redoubtable Maggie faring? Her letter had given very little information, other than, due to the death of her husband, Clover Ridge holdings were being liquidated. The lack of information was not surprising. She'd never been particularly forthcoming on matters of her personal situation.

Had she been properly provided for, or was the sale of the estate a sign she faced a less-than-secure future? Was she receiving the counsel she needed to handle such weighty matters?

It would be difficult to get straight answers from the starchy young lady herself. But Will knew of another, quite reliable source.

He turned his horse toward the stables.

Fifteen minutes later, Will marched toward the house, a grim set to his jaw. He'd gathered enough information from the gossipy groom to get a good picture of Maggie Carter's situation.

Confound it all! How the deuce had matters gotten to this stage without his knowing? What had it been—a year? fourteen months perhaps?—since he'd last checked on Maggie's situation? Everything had appeared in proper order then.

Well, he was now in a better position to help the stubborn young woman than he had been on the last two occasions she'd required assistance. This time, he'd make certain her future was more permanently secured.

It was the least he could do for the Lady Samaritan who'd once saved his life.

On learning Maggie was in the garden, Will insisted he could find his own way.

His steps quickened as he approached her sunlit retreat. It surprised him how much he looked forward to seeing her again. He shouldn't have waited so long.

Had she changed since he'd seen her last?

How would she greet his reappearance into her life?

With her back to him, the newly widowed Maggie didn't notice his approach, and Will took the opportunity to study her.

She wore somber widow's garb, but if the manner in which she attacked the hapless weeds was any indication, widowhood had not daunted her spirit.

Hatless, she wore her hair in that tight bun she favored. She likely thought the style prim—in truth it only served to make a man itch to remove the pins and see what those tresses looked like loose and free. Today, as if to tease him, a few curls had escaped to beckon invitingly as they tickled her nape.

Maggie had always been a paradox to him. Only seventeen, she had not yet been married when he first met her. A tall, dark-haired girl with clear green eyes, she seemed much too solemn for someone so young. And much too proud to have been raised to be a servant.

For all her youth, she had defied her employer to come to the aid of a stranger. That act saved his life and, in the process, cost her her only source of income. She had shown admirable determination to do what she felt right, no matter the cost. She'd sat with him during his convalescence, never displaying so much as a jot of regret for her actions. She also had proved herself to be a girl of extraordinary intelligence and wit.

Those same qualities, though, had confounded him ever since. Her refusal to accept payment had forced him to stand aside while she made her own way, though he *had* managed to give fate a nudge here and there when her situation became desperate.

Well, things had changed since the last time she'd needed his assistance, and this time he would make her see reason.

A movement in the nearby shrubbery brought his

thoughts back to the present. A large gray cat stepped out into the sunlight and Will's nose wrinkled in disgust.

He *detested* the useless, bothersome creatures.

Biting back an oath, Will realized the feline carried a dead mouse in its mouth. With a flourish, the animal dropped its gruesome treasure on the ground in front of his mistress.

Devoutly hoping Maggie wouldn't swoon, Will braced himself for an unpleasant bout of hysterics.

# Chapter Two

Maggie planted the small spade in the ground and re-moved her garden gloves, glad for the distraction.

"Why thank you, Tully." She scratched the victorious hunter behind the ears. "What a very thoughtful, clever cat you are." Her voice caught on the last word, and she swiped at a stray tendril of hair with the back of one hand. At least there was no need to guard her emotions from the cat.

She had escaped the much-too-empty house, hoping to find solace here in the garden. Today, however, the looked-for peace was difficult to grasp.

Heaven help her, she missed the children. She felt as if a piece of herself had left with them.

Maggie's hands trembled as her thoughts echoed Cal's— it *wasn't* fair!

The children were gone—she might never see them again.

Clover Ridge would be placed on the market within the month.

She was on her own. Again.

"Mrs. Carter."

Maggie let out a squeak and her heart lurched painfully

as she twisted around to see who had approached with such stealth. A paralyzing heartbeat later, she recognized the large man looming over her.

Her momentary panic gave way to pleasure. "Mr. Trevaron!"

*He'd come!* It was as if she'd somehow conjured up the white knight from her most secret daydreams.

That fanciful thought was followed by a dose of reality. He'd come about the horse, of course, not to slay her dragons.

*Had he recognized her initial recoil? Her current pleasure?*

But his expression reflected only polite concern. "I apologize if I startled you."

Strange how his deep, rich voice, enhanced by the timbre of a British accent, always gave her a tingly feeling. Of course, her parents had come from England, moving to Virginia shortly after they married. No doubt that was responsible for her reaction.

A perfectly innocent association.

He reached down to help her rise, offering his left hand with practiced ease while keeping the other inconspicuously fisted at his side. Maggie had always wondered how he'd come by those scars on his palm, how he'd lost that finger. But she'd never had the courage to ask such a personal question.

Accepting his assistance, she stood and brushed at her skirt, using that as an excuse to take a half step back. She didn't like feeling crowded, even by her white knight.

She'd forgotten how tall Will was. Few men could make her feel short, but the top of her head barely passed his chin.

In truth, his lips were level with her forehead.

Chiding herself for that betraying thought, Maggie caught his sideways glance toward the grisly little corpse at her feet, and smiled. "I hope Tully's offering doesn't offend you. It's just his way of trying to cheer me up."

Will's lips twitched. "Not at all. I just confess to being surprised by your unruffled reception."

Relieved to find him amused rather than shocked by her unladylike reaction, Maggie wrinkled her nose. "It *is* rather gruesome, isn't it? But it would have offended Tully if I'd rejected his gift. He's a proud creature, you know."

The cat eyed them with a superior air, then stalked away, the picture of haughty indifference.

Will escorted her to a stone bench and Maggie deliberately returned to the reserved tone that had become second nature to her. "I apologize for receiving you so informally. Someone should have notified me of your arrival." Aware of the smudges on her cuffs and the gritty feel of dirt on her face, she lifted her chin a bit higher to compensate.

"Think nothing of it." Will sat on the other end of the bench, leaving a respectable distance between them. "Your housekeeper seemed busy, so I offered to show myself out here."

"How considerate of you." Strange. She was both grateful and a bit disappointed that he hadn't sat closer.

"I want to express my condolences on your loss," he said somberly. "I didn't know Joseph well, but he seemed a good man."

"Thank you." She was keenly aware that he had placed his hand on the cool stone of the bench near her own.

"I wish to also thank you for looking out for my interests in the matter of Orion at such a time."

He had the most incredible gray-blue eyes. They were like quicksilver, so changeable, so compelling—

Maggie blinked and looked down as she folded her hands in her lap. She must be more overset than she'd thought to allow herself to be so distracted.

"No need to thank me," she said, picking up the thread of the conversation. "It's my duty to ascertain everything is in order before we settle the estate."

When he didn't respond immediately, she looked up again. And met a probing, intent gaze.

"So, you *are* handling this matter on your own."

A shiver of awareness whispered through her.

When she nodded, he raised a questioning brow. "I understand Clover Ridge itself is being placed on the market."

Maggie shifted and offered a rueful smile. She didn't want her bleak prospects to intrude on this pleasant interlude. "I fear this place is too big for me to run alone."

He responded to her smile with one of his own. "I think you underestimate your abilities." A flash of sunlight burrowed through the tree branches, picking out the chestnut in his dark brown hair, turning his eyes from grayish blue to pure silver.

He leaned forward slightly, but his expression was determined rather than affectionate. "I don't mean to be indelicate, but I *am* aware that you are having financial difficulties. I would like to offer my assistance, if I may be so bold."

Maggie's fanciful distractions evaporated with a snap. How lowering to realize that word of her financial straits had reached all the way to Crane Harbor—and to Will.

He bridged the distance between them to touch her arm. "Please, allow me to repay the debt I owe you. I assure you—"

Ignoring the offered comfort of his touch, Maggie withdrew her arm. They had been through this before. She *thought* he understood. "That debt was repaid years ago, sir, when you located a position to replace the one I'd lost. It's an insult for you to think I would ask for more."

He'd only come because of that too-long-held sense of duty. She'd been a fool to attribute any other motive to him.

Frustration etched lines near the corners of his mouth. Why were her eyes so drawn to his features today?

"Mrs. Carter." He spoke as if to an obstinate child. "You must be aware I hold you in the highest esteem and intend no insult. Your selfless attitude is admirable, but a trifle impractical." He paused, seeming to search for the proper words.

Maggie was sorely tempted. It would be so nice to lay her troubles on his very broad shoulders. She couldn't ask him for money—it would take a small fortune to pay her debts and still keep Clover Ridge. But would it be so terrible to ask his help in finding a comfortable place of service? He was so much better connected than she. Perhaps he—

"I'm not sure if you are aware of this," he said, intruding on her thoughts, "but fortune has smiled on me since we last discussed this subject. I now have more money than I could ever hope to spend. I say this not to brag, mind you, but to have you understand that it would be no hardship to provide you with a stipend. And it would bring me a great deal of comfort to know that you are not without the means to support yourself."

Would he make a kept woman of her? Or, more likely, relegate her to the role of pensioned servant. How *could* he?

Maggie focused on her affront—much safer that than to dwell on the sting of shattered illusions. "Mr. Trevaron—"

He forestalled her refusal with a raised hand. "There is something else you should know. I will be traveling to England soon, and may be away for quite some time. I won't be nearby to lend assistance should your situation grow truly desperate."

Will was going away! Maggie's anger melted, puddling into dismay. The thought that she would likely never see him again was yet another loss to add to her growing list.

His expression softened. "Now, will you give over and do me the honor of accepting my assistance?"

He still didn't understand. Truth to tell, she would be hard pressed to put her feelings into words. Contradictory as it seemed, refusing to let him pay her was a purely selfish act. As it stood now, she felt noble. Her rescue of him was one thing she could look back on with pride, something she had done at significant personal cost. If she accepted payment for her actions, she would feel forever diminished.

Besides, he didn't know the extent of her troubles. Even if she accepted a stipend from him, she was certain he did not intend to provide a sum sufficient for her to live on.

Not trusting herself to meet his gaze, Maggie watched a leaf drift to the ground. "Thank you for your concern. But I assure you, I have everything under control."

They sat frozen as she held her breath, wondering what he would say next. She tried to convince herself she didn't care if he thought her unreasonable. Better that than to have his pity.

The moment stretched on interminably, the only sound that of insects buzzing and the wind rustling the bushes.

Then Tully sprang onto her lap, breaking the spell.

Will stood, seeming eager now to put some distance between them. Had she insulted him?

"My apologies, madam, for distressing you." His manner was now quite formal. "I'll leave you to your gardening and be on my way. Again, my sincere condolences on your loss."

He sketched a short bow. "If you should change your mind concerning my offer, please don't hesitate to send word."

Maggie stood, taking comfort from Tully's purring warmth. "You are most kind." She tried to match the formality of his tone, not sure if she was sorry or relieved to see him go.

He produced a smile designed to reassure her all was

well. Or was she just reading into it what she wanted to see?

"Don't bother to show me out, I know the way."

Maggie released a sigh as he disappeared around the corner of the house. She hadn't handled that well. He'd truly meant to be helpful. As he would to any poor wretch in need.

And that's what really stung.

Will was a chivalrous white knight, yes, but one who regarded her as a trial to dispatch on his quest, not as his lady fair.

She might yet have to swallow her pride and ask for his assistance in finding a position. But only as a last resort. Demeaning one's self in front of the man you harbored romantic daydreams about took a stronger constitution than she possessed.

She'd been taken with Will from the moment he'd looked up at her with pain-fogged eyes, apologizing for soiling her dress with his blood. His stoic refusal to complain during his recovery had deeply touched her seventeen-year-old heart. From then on, Will Trevaron had been the standard she measured other men by.

Setting Tully down, Maggie collected her gardening tools.

She wasn't seventeen any longer. It was past time she abandoned her foolish daydreams of the dashing Mr. Trevaron. Quite likely even *he* couldn't live up to the image she'd formed.

Still, how did one let go of such pleasurable fantasies? What would it be like to be courted by a man such as Will Trevaron? The very thought sent a shiver fluttering through her.

Straightening, she caught sight of her black skirt and chided herself again. She was newly widowed, for goodness sake. Such thoughts were inappropriate at any time, but now, especially, they were almost obscene.

Maggie resolutely turned her thoughts to her current situation. She had to think, had to plan for her future.

Her time was almost up.

As Tully stropped himself against her ankle, a steely determination settled deep inside Maggie. Never again would she trust others to look out for her future, no matter how much they professed to love her, no matter how sincerely they claimed to have her best interests at heart.

Her parents had loved her. But it hadn't mattered in the end. When her father died, everything Maggie held dear had gone with him, leaving her little more than the clothes on her back. Though raised in relative comfort, she'd found herself forced to go into service at the age of sixteen.

Mr. Peabody had seemed a godsend when he offered her a position caring for his mother. Instead, Maggie had been left with a legacy of nightmares that plagued her still.

Joseph, too, had promised to take care of her. Yet Joseph's death had thrown her out on the street again. Worse yet, *his* abandonment had cost her the children.

No, she was done with looking to others to provide for her security. Somehow, she would find a way to take charge of her own life. And she would find a way to reclaim the children.

She would go into service again, of course. As the daughter of a physician, she had certain skills that lent her an advantage in that area. Querying Dr. Huxley about which of his patients might need her services, however, had netted depressing results. There had to be another way.

She just had to find it.

Will slowly walked back to the stable. The woman was impossible! Why did she find it so difficult to accept his aid?

For a moment, when she shared that smile with him, he'd felt a tug of something—sympathy? attraction?—

# Winnie Griggs

from her. It had disappeared quickly enough when he'd offered assistance.

Perhaps he'd been too heavy-handed. Not that subtlety had ever garnered better results with the stubborn lady in need.

Well, devil take her pride. Whether she wanted his help or not, she would receive it. He wouldn't depart for London until he was certain her future was comfortably secured.

And he knew just how to handle it.

Leaving Clover Ridge, Will rode into the nearby town of Preston, to the office of the Carter family's solicitor.

When he explained his plan, Mr. Martin appeared skeptical. "Mr. Trevaron, what you propose is admirable, but I don't think you realize exactly how much money is involved."

Will leaned back in his chair, eying the older man with a confident smile. "I assure you, money will not be a problem."

The solicitor sat up straighter, a speculative gleam in his eye. "Even so, Mrs. Carter would never believe such a tale. She had me review the accounts numerous times, looking for a way to hold off the creditors. She even studied them herself. Mrs. Carter was quite determined."

Will tried not to smile. That was his Maggie—thorough and always ready to take matters into her own hands. "I'm certain you can convince her." He nodded in concession. "I know Mrs. Carter is an intelligent woman, but it's my observation that women in general don't comprehend enough about business and finances to be able to question such matters effectively."

"Mrs. Carter is not the sort to let a thing rest until she's gotten to the truth of it."

Will dismissed his concerns. "She may have questions, but I'm certain she'll be so happy for the unexpected deliverance that she won't examine the source too closely."

30

Before the solicitor could raise further objections, Will lifted a peremptory hand. "Be creative. Have her believe it's a forgotten investment, or a special account that just came to light. I'm sure you'll find a way to allay her suspicions."

He leaned forward. "However, under no circumstances is she to know the funds came from me. Is that understood?"

"I'll do my best."

Will departed feeling quite pleased with himself. He had finally discharged his debt to Maggie. Assuming she didn't make any disastrous investments with her new-found funds, she would be comfortably situated for the rest of her life.

He shook his head over the solicitor's concerns. Maggie would no doubt suspect something wasn't just as it seemed, but after considering her options, she'd surely accept her windfall at face value.

After all, she was a woman without the protection of a husband or father.


Three days later, Will leaned back in his desk chair, easing his leg into a more comfortable position. Though only bruised in yesterday's dockside accident, his thigh still protested angrily when jarred. Of course, he was luckier than the man who'd stood next to him. Pete would be bed-bound for several weeks yet.

His business manager looked up as he dipped his pen in the inkwell. "That leg still bothering you?"

Will waved a hand, dismissing Ian's concerns. "I just needed to stretch it out a bit. I'm fine."

"Are you sure you shouldn't have the doctor look at it again? Dodging that runaway horse this morning couldn't have done it much good."

"I said I'm fine." Will sat up straighter. "Now, tell me where we stand on the *Lady Jen*."

31

Ian turned back to the papers they'd been working on. "With this added incentive we're offering Mitterman, I think we can count on the *Lady Jen* being seaworthy by the end of the week."

Will nodded, pleased that matters were falling into place so well. Now that he'd made up his mind to return to England, he found himself impatient to get on with it.

Fighting the urge to grimace, he eased his throbbing leg slightly to the left.

"You know," Ian said thoughtfully, "that's two bouts of bad luck you've encountered this week. My Gran used to say these things occur in threes."

"Don't tell me you're a superstitious man." Will didn't attempt to hide his amusement.

Ian's grin proved he took no offense. "Laugh if you wish, but were I you, I'd take extra care the next few days."

Will shook his head and turned the discussion back to the business at hand. "Tell me, how do you—"

A commotion in the outer office interrupted his question.

"Here now, Miss," someone exclaimed. "You can't just barge into Mr. Trevaron's office—"

The door swung open to admit a militantly determined-looking Maggie Carter with an indignant junior clerk at her elbow.

"It's all right, Jack." Will halted the clerk's sputtering with a raised hand. He stood, smothering a wince as his leg twinged angrily. "Mrs. Carter is always welcome here."

Her demeanor didn't soften at his conciliatory words. In fact, if the tightness of her jaw was any indication, her temper actually raised a notch.

So, her snit was over more than just his clerk's attempt to bar the door. That could only mean one thing. Ian's warning about a third disaster was about to bear fruit.

The business manager gathered his papers. "I believe I

can finish these in my own office. I'll leave you to your guest."

Will mentally commended Ian on exercising the better part of valor. But he kept a pleasant smile on his face as he greeted his stormy-eyed visitor. "Please, have a seat." He gestured toward a comfortably upholstered chair.

"No, thank you." Maggie's blistering gaze never wavered from his. "My business won't take long."

How could he feel at once singed by the fire in her eyes and chilled by the ice in her tone? Even the broach on her collar appeared to glare accusingly at him.

"And just what is your business with me, madam?"

"I came to deliver this." She tossed a document on his desk as if it were a gauntlet.

He picked it up, glanced down, then jerked his gaze back up to hers. "What the deuce is this?"

"The deed to Clover Ridge."

He made an impatient gesture. "I see that. Why are you giving it to me?"

"Because you bought and paid for it."

"I most certainly did—"

"Please, sir, don't further insult me by pretending you had nothing to do with the monies that magically turned up this week." Maggie's raised brow dared him to deny her accusation.

Will decided it would be best to say nothing.

She nodded. "I thought as much. The estate's creditors pounced on the money, so most of it has already been spent."

Satisfaction snickered through Will. His plan had worked. Even if she wasn't pleased with his methods, she was no longer in danger of being tossed from her home.

"Since your money paid the debts," she continued, her tone dousing his smug assurance, "I can only assume you intended to purchase the estate."

She tugged her glove more firmly onto her wrist. "You'll

find the deed transferred in your name, all legal and proper." Eying him as a governess would a recalcitrant charge, she folded her hands primly together.

"You know it was not my intent to purchase Clover Ridge." Realizing he'd raised his voice, Will took a deep breath. "I have no use for such an estate. Besides which, it is your *home*."

"No longer. If you don't care for Clover Ridge, I suggest you sell it. It matters not to me. Now, good day to you, sir."

Will swore under his breath as the woman had the audacity to actually turn her back on him. "Hold a minute."

She turned, her frown eloquently proclaiming her impatience.

He moved around the desk. "Please, have a seat so we may discuss this."

Maggie's stiffness eased slightly as her brow wrinkled in concern. "You're limping."

"Just a little accident at the docks. Nothing of import." At least one good thing had resulted from that mishap. Her sympathy had distracted her enough to halt her precipitous exit.

"Have you had a doctor look at it?"

"Yes. And he assures me I'll be back to normal in less than a week." Will deftly led her to the chair as he spoke and she sat primly on the edge.

He leaned back against his desk, watching her gather that air of hauteur around her again. But Maggie's mask had slipped enough that he now saw the hurt and uncertainty in her eyes as well. And that pained him more than her outrage had.

He chose his next words with extra care. "I owe you an apology for the manner in which I handled matters. At the time, I thought it the best way to insure your welfare while sparing your feelings. I see now that I was wrong."

Maggie nodded, her spine poker-stiff. "Yes, you were."

Her face hardened. "Every man seems to think he can take whatever action he pleases in regard to a woman, so long as he can convince himself it is for her own good. My father, employers, Joseph—all of them let me down in this regard."

Will was caught off guard by the bitterness of her tone.

She fiddled with her broach—that amber amulet he'd never seen her without—and pinned him with an icy stare. "I thought you, at least, were above such deceptions, would deal with me honorably. It was disappointing to have been proven wrong."

That brought Will up short. Questioning his honor was a bit strong. After all, he *had* only been looking out for her welfare.

His jaw worked for a moment, then he sketched a stiff bow. "Once more, you have my apologies. I won't make such a mistake again."

Maggie inclined her head. "Apology accepted." She shifted in her chair, then managed a smile. "I *do* understand that your actions were well-meant and not malicious, and for that at least, I thank you."

How bloody generous of her. He reached behind him on the desk and retrieved the document she'd flung at him earlier. "Now, how do we resolve this matter to both our satisfactions?"

Her lips pursed in an uncompromising line. "It would be both inappropriate and unprincipled of me to accept so extravagant a gift. I just could not do so and ever hold my head up again."

Will refused to be swayed by stirrings of sympathy, or any other emotions her meadow-green eyes evoked. He knew he would react the same way in her place, but confound it all, he was a man—he had many more options open to him. For a woman in her position to put such store in salvaging her pride was both foolhardy and futile.

"Then consider it a loan," he pressed. "You can pay me

back a little at a time, on whatever schedule you can manage."

Her smile turned challenging. "We both know I could never repay such a sum. Calling it a loan would not change the nature of the transaction—it would still be a gift."

She stood and again tugged the string to her reticule. "And unless I felt there was a real chance I could give you value for your money, we come back to the fact that I cannot accept it. I'm sorry to have interrupted your business. Please make my apologies to the young man who exited so precipitously earlier."

This was absurd. He refused to be the person who tossed her out of her own home. "At least promise me you'll remain at Clover Ridge for a while longer." He saw the hesitation in her expression. "Just for a few weeks, until you've had time to find suitable arrangements elsewhere."

After a moment, she nodded. "Thank you. That's most generous." And without another word, she left.

At least she had given him time to come up with another solution to this problem that only grew larger with every attempt he made to fix it.

"Is your lady friend gone?"

Will looked up to see Ian in the doorway, watching him with a knowing grin.

"Yes." Though it seemed a part of her lingered—a hint of flowery scent, the echo of her voice, the accusing flash in those honest-as-springtime eyes.

How could he assuage Maggie's pride and satisfy his debt to her at the same time? He raked a hand through his hair. The woman would have him pulling it out before this was over.

Aware that Ian still watched him, Will swallowed the string of oaths burning his tongue. He didn't have time to deal with Maggie's melodramatic sensibilities. There was still a number of pressing matters to attend to before he sailed for England.

Why couldn't she just accept his help and be done with it?

It would serve her right if he did as she asked. After all, he'd made a good-faith effort and been rebuffed. If Maggie Carter was too proud to accept his money, that was her choice.

Perhaps he could find her another position, as he had with Joseph Carter. Not that it would be likely to lead to a wedding again. That had merely been a lucky happenstance.

But would she accept even that much help from him at this point? Irritated by the whole impossible situation, Will returned to his desk and slammed the ledger closed.

"I believe that's enough for today," he told Ian. "Have Jack deliver the addendum to Mitterman first thing tomorrow."

Ian nodded. "Of course."

After Ian made his exit, Will crossed his arms and frowned at nothing in particular. What should his next move in this campaign to aid Maggie be? One thing was certain, it would require a defter hand than he'd used thus far.

Her starchy streak of independence was so typical of Americans. You'd never find a proper Englishwoman, at least not one of his acquaintance, acting in such a manner. Maggie's spirit would be admirable if it wasn't so bloody irritating.

She'd given him part of the answer. He had to find a way to have her believe he needed her assistance. It would have to be a matter of enough import for her to feel she had repaid the debt.

He couldn't sail for England until he'd settled the matter. Not unless he took her with him.

His lips curved in a wry grin as he thought of his grandfather's reaction should he show up with the thoroughly American, solidly "merchant class" Maggie on his arm.

Then he sat up straighter.

Now *that* idea had interesting possibilities.

# Chapter Three

Later that evening, Will locked up the offices, turned down the lamps and climbed the stairs. He allowed himself the luxury of limping now that he was alone.

During the lean years, he'd converted the attic office into modest living quarters and learned to survive without the convenience of servants.

He now owned an elegant home just outside of town, but he still spent many of his nights here. Not only was it more convenient, but he'd grown accustomed to it.

He threw his coat over a chair. How could the proud, independent-minded woman who'd stormed into his office today bear to contemplate a future as a servant in another's household?

When he made his next move in their chess match, he had to be certain it was check and mate. He could not contemplate her living the kind of existence she faced otherwise.

Abruptly, he moved to the basin and splashed water on his face. Unfortunately, it only washed away the grime of the day—not the memory of the hurt he'd seen behind the magnificent outrage in Maggie's eyes.

He reached for a towel. The sordid tale of his banishment was key to gaining her acceptance, but it was also strong incentive for her to reject him. He had to wager that her circumstances would tip the scales in his favor.

A vision of her backing away in disgust and fear skittered through his mind, and he flung the towel aside. There was no help for it. He had to make this one last attempt to repay Maggie before he sailed, no matter the risk.

Will forced himself to plan his strategy as he would any business campaign. By the time he stretched out on his bed, he thought he had figured out exactly what line and tone to take.

But an edgy feeling gnawed at him, kept sleep at bay. After staring at the ceiling for what seemed hours, he tossed aside the covers with a growl of disgust.

Ten minutes later he was prowling the streets. The cane he carried was as much weapon as aid for his injured leg— the waterfront streets could be dangerous this time of night.

A murky mist shrouded the nearly deserted streets, wrapped clammy fingers about him. The gloomy atmosphere suited his mood.

His thoughts turned again to his plans for Maggie's future. Was he doing the right thing, the honorable thing? Was he going into this merely to satisfy a debt of honor?

Six years ago, when she had come to his rescue, she'd been barely seventeen. Remarkably mature and spirited perhaps, but a mere child nonetheless. In addition, he had been new to this country, still full of the pompous attitudes his upbringing had instilled in him. Maggie had, after all, been a paid companion.

Yes, he'd felt gratitude and admiration for her. But over the years he'd continued to see her in the light of a young girl who needed a benign benefactor, a guardian angel of sorts.

That's not what he'd seen today. Somehow, when he

wasn't paying attention, the girl turned into a woman—a woman full of starch and fire. Nor was she a servant. She was any lady's equal, no matter what situation circumstances might place her in.

If nothing else, six years in this country, being forced to prove his own worth, had taught him the foolishness of judging a person by the title he or she carried.

Here in the dismal solitude of the waterfront fog he could be honest with himself. What she'd stirred in him today could in no way be called benign or angelic. Some part of him celebrated this turn of events, felt a spark of excitement at the idea of binding his and Maggie's futures together.

Will turned up his collar to ward off the damp night air.

The question was, would she feel the same?

Maggie let Seraph have her head, encouraging the mare to a full gallop. It was exhilarating to feel the air whip her hair, to let her body thrum with the pounding of hooves, to see the trees at the edge of the meadow blur into a green cloud.

For this space of time, the world was as it should be—only this wonderful, invigorating here and now, where she was mistress of her fate and free to fly.

When she reached the far end, Maggie slowed the mare enough to turn, intending to continue the run in the opposite direction.

And just like that, the thoughts she'd worked so hard to hold at bay, pounced, stole her smile.

Discovering the source of her new-found monies had ignited tinderbox feelings of betrayal. In her mind, Will's actions had merged with those of the other men who had caused her such painful disappointment and shame in the past.

The urge to rail against the smug assumption that men

were superior creatures, that it was their right to play fast and loose with the destinies of women in their care, had exploded inside her, left her determined to fight back any way she could.

The startled chagrin on Will's face when she flung the deed on his desk had been most satisfying. By the time she exited, however, she'd regretted that she hadn't let her emotions cool before she acted.

Will had been manipulative, true, but at least he'd been trying to *give* her something, not take something away. He hadn't deserved the full brunt of her anger.

Had she been a fool to refuse his offer? If she'd accepted, she could even now be awaiting the children's return. She missed them so much, especially at night when it was time to tuck them into bed with stories, and lullabies, and hugs.

Hang her stubborn pride—it may have cost her her only chance to be with them again.

Maggie leaned forward, ready for another run, hoping to regain her former sense of exhilaration and freedom. But the sight of a rider near the tree line caught her attention.

The rider raised a hand in greeting, and even from this distance she recognized him. *Will!*

A sizzle of pure pleasure pulsed through her a half-second before she remembered the last time she'd seen him.

Was he here to make yet another attempt to convince her to accept his help? If so, what would she do? What *should* she do? How much humble pie should she eat to get what she yearned for?

Trying to still the fluttering in her stomach, Maggie altered Seraph's course, and prepared to face her would-be savior.

Breathless—from her invigorating ride, of course—she knew she presented a disheveled appearance. On the other hand, Will looked magnificent, sitting his horse with an arrogant grace that seemed as much a part of him as his strong chin and discerning gaze. Just watching him set her treacherous mind drifting toward forbidden territory.

Why did he have to be such an arresting figure of a man?

And why was she so distractingly aware of it?

As she neared, Maggie retreated into her safe, reserved façade. "Good day to you, sir."

"And to you." His horse took a dancing step to one side, and he controlled the powerful roan with a barely perceptible movement. "I apologize for interrupting your run. They told me at the stable where to find you."

His smile invited her to relax, but she resisted. Letting down her guard would be dangerous, in more ways than one.

She patted the mare's neck, noticing how Will's unreadable eyes shone with that silver cast again today. "I just wanted to say good-bye to Seraph, here. We're old friends."

He drew his horse alongside hers. "She's a fine looking bit of horseflesh."

"I'm glad you like her," Maggie responded with a sideways look. "As she comes with Clover Ridge, she is yours now."

Will didn't respond as she'd expected. Instead he nodded. "That's what I've come to discuss. I think I've found the solution to our problem."

"Have you?" What sort of scheme had he concocted this time?

"Do you mind if we walk while we speak?"

At her nod, Will dismounted quickly and moved to assist her. His leg seemed to have improved but there was still a slight catch in his stride, a barely perceptible limp. She wondered again how he had injured himself.

Distracted by that question, Maggie didn't realize what Will was about until he placed his hands at her waist.

Alarm crackled through her, remembered fear setting her pulse pounding. Her vision blurred and she felt an overwhelming urge to struggle, to escape Mr. Peabody's imprisoning hold.

"Are you all right?"

The fog cleared and it was Will's hands on her, not Edwin Peabody's. She blinked, seeing the concern furrowing his brow.

Heaven help her, she'd done it again.

*Compose yourself. Smile.*

*Pretend you didn't just panic like a child facing a bugaboo.*

"Of course," she replied, finally remembering his question. Forcing herself to relax, she placed her hands on his shoulders.

Will lifted her from the saddle as if she were weightless, a novel experience for someone of her height. Though his strength was evident, she felt no threat in his touch now.

After all, this was Will.

Maggie's churning senses sharpened, focused, as he held her, as her body slid against his. Suddenly her head was spinning for an entirely different reason.

The scent of leather and horse and salty air, and something so uniquely *Will*, swirled around her. The tingle of well-muscled strength harnessed to hold her with gentle control, the firmness of his chest brushing against her own, combined to make her feel so very feminine. A tremulous breath escaped before she could call it back, and his eyes changed from silver to storm-gray.

He paused, holding her suspended, staring into her eyes. Her breathing stopped for that endless second. A giddy fluttering stirred deep inside her.

Then her feet touched the ground and the spell was broken.

Maggie stepped back, seeking both physical and mental distance. "Thank you." Without waiting for a reply, she took Seraph's reins and began walking.

It wouldn't do for him to see how rattled she was.

Will caught up and matched his steps to hers. Remembering his injured leg, she forced herself to set a sedate pace.

He made no move to touch her again. Maggie wasn't sure if she was relieved or disappointed. She slid a quick glance his way, but his expression revealed none of her own agitation.

Hadn't he been affected at all?

Well, she'd be hanged if she would show any sign *she* had felt something out of the ordinary either.

"How is your leg?" she asked, breaking the silence.

He waved away her concern. "Good as new."

*Liar.* There was that masculine pride again. But she let it pass. Instead, she turned the focus back to his reason for coming here. "You said you'd found a solution to our problem. Might I ask what problem you were referring to?"

"The problem of how to convince you to accept my help."

Maggie mentally prepared herself. *Whatever offer he makes this time, accept it. Even if his scheme is hopelessly transparent, thank him. No matter how galling it is to accept his charity, smile sweetly.*

She would do almost anything to get the children back. That was all that mattered. "I'm listening."

"The other day, you said you would accept my assistance if you felt you could offer something of like value in return."

That wasn't the opening she'd expected. "And you think you've found a way for me to do that?"

"I don't *think* I've found the answer—I know I have. It only remains to be seen if you will accept my proposal."

The note of challenge in his voice tilted her chin up. *Remember, be pleasant.* "If you wanted to pique my interest, you've succeeded. I can't imagine what I could give you that would equal the value of Clover Ridge."

Will took Seraph's reins. "First, let me tell you a story." Leaving the horses to graze, he seated her on a nearby log.

He stood in front of her with his hands clasped behind his back. "I've mentioned that I will return to England soon."

Why did he have to remind her of that?

"What I want to tell you now is why I left in the first place, and why I've stayed away—until now."

Maggie sat up straighter. This conversation was taking a very unexpected, and interesting, direction.

"Six years ago," he began, "I stood accused of a dishonorable, unforgivable act. As a result, my grandfather banished me from his presence and his holdings."

The faint pulse of a tic at the corner of Will's mouth alerted her that he wasn't nearly as dispassionate about that event as his tone indicated.

"Recent events have forced Grandfather to invite me back into the fold. The invitation, however, was grudgingly tendered. He does not hold me in any higher esteem now than when he tossed me out six years ago."

She watched him pluck a stem of grass, and wondered what thoughts he hid behind those shuttered eyes.

"The thing is, I have a younger sister who still resides with Grandfather. I find that I *would* like to visit Lynchmorne again, both to see her and to stand on home soil once more. Besides, there are family obligations awaiting me that I can't ignore."

Family obligations? What did that mean?

He twirled the bit of grass between his fingers and thumb. "However, I intend to return on my own terms. There will be no donning of sackcloth and ashes."

"I understand," she said dryly. Did he realize he'd just articulated her own sentiments about accepting his largesse?

He smiled, as if reading her mind. "I thought you might."

Maggie ignored the tingle his smile gave her. "Mr. Trevaron, this is all very interesting, but I am still waiting for you to explain what it has to do with me."

Will seemed not to have heard her question. "Among the more unappealing plans my grandfather has laid out for my return, is that he search out a suitable wife for me, one who would be willing to overlook my many faults, and who would enhance my respectability through association."

An unpleasant jolt shot through Maggie, startling her with its intensity, and her hand crept up to her broach. The thought of Will married to someone else was . . . Well, she didn't care for it one bit.

If he asked her to play lady's maid to his new wife she didn't think she could bear it.

Will flashed her a mirthless smile. "I have no interest in marriage to any woman Grandfather selects for me."

He straightened, and the glint of challenge had returned to his expression, along with some other emotion she couldn't read. "Although I do wish to start a family of my own. But, because of the dishonor associated with the circumstances of my banishment, I gave up hope that I would find a lady of intelligence and principle who would agree to join her life with mine."

His eyes darkened and she'd swear his gaze probed deep into her very soul.

"Until now," he said levelly.

# Chapter Four

As his words sank in, Maggie stiffened. He couldn't mean—

She'd braced herself for an offer of genteel employment—but this! A chaotic mix of emotions tumbled through her in the space between one heartbeat and the next—doubt, hope, confusion, exultation, panic.

Heat rose in her cheeks. Merciful heavens, had he guessed about her foolish daydreams? Would he dare use such knowledge to gain an advantage? "Sir, if you think to mock me . . ."

He raised a hand. "I assure you, I'm quite serious."

His words and earnest expression did little to allay her suspicions. "What you suggest is preposterous."

"Not at all." His gaze never wavered from hers. "Like most men, I have a desire to establish a family, to see my line continue. But as I said earlier, my circumstances are such that only the most mercenary or undesirable of women would care to link their name with mine."

Maggie narrowed her eyes. "And just which category do you place me in?"

*Hold onto the anger.*

*Don't think about that flash of yearning his words jolted from deep inside you.*

48

"Neither." His tone was matter-of-fact. They could have been discussing the horses. "That is one of the things that makes you uniquely suited to fill my need, to repay my *largesse* as you phrased it, with something of like value. You're respectable and your character is above reproach." He smiled wryly. "I, of all people, know you won't be motivated by greed."

Perhaps not greed in the sense he meant. But to get the children back . . .

"Besides," he continued with a wolfish grin, "returning with a solidly American wife on my arm will convey to my grandfather more clearly than words that he no longer controls my actions."

How flattering—he wanted to use her as a red flag. "Is that supposed to make me more amenable to your proposal?"

He shrugged. "What this will say to my grandfather is only a happy coincidence. The main issue is, I want a wife, and you have it in your power to give me what I want."

He was serious—he truly *was* asking her to marry him. It was absurd. But just the thought of being wed to Will—oh my.

Maggie's pulse raced as her mind presented the possibilities.

She forced her thoughts back to a more pragmatic path. "How do I know this isn't another of your grand gestures, an elaborate deception for you to fulfill your supposed obligation to me?" For some reason, that point mattered a great deal.

He met her gaze levelly. "Let me lay that thought to rest. Yes, I feel a degree of responsibility to you because of what you did for me six years ago. And yes, I would go to great lengths to discharge that obligation. But the story I told you is absolutely true. And I would not ask you to marry me unless I thought we would suit."

What did that mean exactly? "Suit?"

"Yes. We are both past the point of looking for romantic entanglements in a marriage partner. I'm too cynical for such idealistic notions."

Was he trying to convince her or himself? If he was truly as pragmatic as he'd have her believe, he wouldn't feel so strongly about the rift with his grandfather.

"As for you," his gaze was approving, "you've wed once before for reasons of practicality, so you, more than most, would be more focused on the business rather than fairy-tale aspects."

Maggie mentally winced. So much for thoughts that he saw her in lover-like terms. She again pushed aside personal feelings.

If she accepted, she would be trading the dominance of an employer for that of a husband, but that was no different than the choice most women faced. And while Will made it abundantly clear this would not be a love match, she did trust him to treat her fairly and with a measure of friendship.

And he offered a reprieve from something she dreaded. To never again have to go into service. To never again have to swallow her pride and dignity to please a despotic employer. To never again find herself in a household where she constantly looked over her shoulder.

More importantly, though, he was offering her the thing she wanted most—the means to reclaim her children.

Or was he? How *did* he feel about children—specifically raising another man's children? So much depended on that answer.

But first, she had to make sure she knew just what sort of tangle she was getting herself in to.

Will saw past the banked fire in Maggie's eyes and the proud tilt of her chin to the trepidation she did her best to hide. He supposed she wasn't happy with the idea of marrying him—Lilly had made it scathingly clear the only thing to recommend "a maimed brute of a man" such as himself to a woman of delicate sensibilities was his money and position.

"A woman of delicate sensibilities," however, was not how he would describe Maggie. The words practical, intelligent and generous came more readily to mind.

At the moment, vibrant, stubborn and proud could be added to the list. Which was fine with him. He'd already tried his luck with a fragile English hothouse blossom. This earthy American wildflower was much more to his liking.

She made as if to rise, and he stepped forward to assist.

His thumb brushed her sleeve as he steadied her, and he found himself itching to stroke the warm, pulsing skin beneath the fabric. The firm yet pliant feel of her arm reminded him of the surprisingly trim waist he'd grasped when helping her dismount. Will suspected there was a more femininely rounded figure than he'd ever imagined beneath the unflattering dresses she wore.

Why would Maggie go to such lengths to hide her attributes? It would be an interesting question to explore. Perhaps—

Maggie firmly withdrew her arm as soon as she was upright, her manner alerting him that he still had some convincing to do.

She took a half step back, the distance allowing her to meet his gaze on more even terms. "This trip to England— is it merely for a visit, or do you plan something more permanent?"

Will took her question as a sign she was at least considering his proposal. "England is my home. I have obligations there that I've neglected for too long, and more responsibilities have been added recently."

He brushed an insect from his sleeve. "That's not to say, however, that we could not return for periodic visits if you should desire to do so." There, that was reasonable enough.

To his relief, she nodded. Another hurdle safely crossed.

Then she met his gaze, a hint of challenge in her expression. "You omitted one very important point from your story. What did you and your grandfather have a falling out over?"

His gut clenched reflexively. The moment he'd been dreading had arrived. He had to tell her of his alleged crime.

Honor demanded no less.

Seraph drifted closer and Maggie turned to stroke the mare's nose. But not before he saw the hint of softness in her expression, a willingness to believe him the injured party.

He clasped his hands behind his back again, knowing his story would likely change that. How could he expect her to see through his words to the truth, when the man who'd raised him had not?

His only hope was that she would believe in who he was *now*, and that, even after hearing his story, she would find his offer more appealing than her alternative.

Will forced himself to speak evenly. "Six years ago I was engaged. During a weekend gathering at my grandfather's home, my fiancée and I had a falling out. By the time the row was over, we were no longer engaged."

She turned to face him, her brow drawn down in uncertainty.

Will forced the next words out. "The next morning, Lilly presented herself to my grandfather with a badly bruised face and arm, and accusations that I had savaged her during our argument." And his grandfather had *believed* her.

His jaw tightened as the color drained from Maggie's face. She staggered, as if he'd delivered a physical blow.

One hand reached for Seraph's bridle to steady herself while the other felt for the amulet at her throat.

He reached out to help. When she stepped back, a look of revulsion on her face, another part of Will's soul withered.

He withdrew his hand and braced himself for her response. Would she dissolve into hysterics? Or simply flee?

But she drew a shaky breath and took control of herself with visible effort. "Were you guilty?" Her voice was almost steady.

The years rolled away and he heard his grandfather pose that same question. He again felt that gut-roiling sense of betrayal.

"The marks on her wrist were incriminating," he bit out. "It left no doubt in the mind of anyone who saw them just who had been responsible." Flexing his right hand, Will displayed the missing digit.

Years ago he'd made a point of learning Lilly's secret, of discovering what brute had been responsible for her injuries. And he'd not even had the satisfaction of calling out the bastard. Because it hadn't been a person—it had been a piece of furniture. The little cheat had tripped on her way back to her room that night and knocked her face against a table corner. She'd used her own clumsiness to ruin his life.

Remembering Maggie, Will moderated his tone. "For what it's worth, you have my word you will never suffer physical harm at my hands."

Even to his own ears, the words sounded hollow. If only he could tell her the truth. But he was as bound by his oath today as he had been all those years ago. Would this hell Lilly's accusation relegated him to follow him his entire life?

"What did you argue about?"

Again, she caught him off guard. No one had ever asked that question. Why was Maggie the only one to show interest in this facet of what had happened that night?

As he noted the wide eyes in her pale face, Will thought she'd never looked braver, never looked more untouchable.

*How much should he say? How much* could *he say?* He decided this question, at least, he could answer without compromising his promise. "I caught her in the embrace of her lover."

Though it cast him in the unflattering light of a cuckold, it felt good to finally say those words aloud. Was his explanation enough to set her at ease?

Maggie's lips tightened and he caught a flicker of something—anger? sympathy? Clenching and unclenching her hands at her side, she stared at him with a haunted expression, with eyes that guarded their own secrets.

Time to end this discussion, before she gave him the "no" he was sure would be forthcoming with her next breath. "Unfortunately, I haven't the time to let you ponder the matter over long. I sail for England in two weeks and there's much to be done before then, especially if I am to take a wife with me."

Still she said nothing. What emotion was she holding in?

He tried again. "All that I ask is before you give me your answer, compare what I'm offering to your alternatives."

He straightened. "As I said, you must decide quickly, but don't answer now. Why don't I take Orion for a run while you collect your thoughts?"

Maggie stared at him, her color high and her lips compressed in a thin line. Her fingers toyed with that damnable broach again, as if it were a talisman to protect her from evil. He thought for a moment she would reject him out of hand.

But at last she gave a curt nod.

As he took Orion's reins and mounted, he felt tension radiating from her in waves. She held herself poker-stiff, refusing to meet his gaze. Was she truly afraid of him now? That thought stung more than he would have thought possible.

This had been a mistake. He should just end it now.

Before he could say anything, Maggie turned her back on him. With a smothered oath, he turned Orion's head and galloped off.

Hearing Will ride off, Maggie allowed herself to breathe normally again.

To be at the mercy of someone so big and powerful—

She shivered and tasted bile rising in her throat. Memories flooded back, threatening to overtake her with nightmare vividness. She wrapped an arm around Seraph's neck, drawing on the mare's warmth, grounding herself safely back in the present.

Any man who would maul a woman was lower than a slug, was the vilest, basest of creatures, was . . . Words escaped her as her heart pounded painfully in her chest. Not again, not ever again.

But this was *Will*. He wasn't like that. It didn't make sense. Her mind couldn't reconcile what she knew of him with the villain he'd painted himself to be.

Would a man capable of such savagery have concerned himself with her welfare long after she insisted he need not worry? The very fact that he had confessed proved him honorable. If he'd kept silent she would never have been the wiser, at least not until it was too late.

Maggie stroked Seraph's nose. She wanted to trust Will, wanted to believe his promise that she would come to no harm at his hands. She wanted it with every fiber of her being.

Perhaps he was no longer the same man he'd been then. Or perhaps what had happened all those years ago had been an aberration fueled by extraordinary provocation. Still, even if he *was* a changed man, the knowledge of what he'd done couldn't help but complicate matters between them.

It all came down to how much she trusted her own instincts. But how much of her judgment was clouded by the fact that Will had been the Prince Charming of her fantasies?

What if she were wrong?

He'd once lashed out at a woman.

While inexcusable, it had obviously affected him greatly. He'd said he would never do such a thing again, and she certainly would not give him the kind of provocation this other woman had.

She was willing to take a chance with her own future, but she could not risk the children. Before she brought them to Will's household, she would be certain he could control his temper.

To be reunited with them again . . .

She squared her shoulders. A chance such as this was not likely to come her way again. It only waited for her to step up and grasp the prize. He'd called this a business partnership—so be it. She had listened to his terms. Now she had a few of her own to set. Will needed to understand he was acquiring a partner with a mind of her own.

Maggie ran her thumb over the face of her broach as she gathered her thoughts. Will would be back soon and this called for clear thinking and delicately crafted strategy.

Five minutes later she watched as Will approached. Her heart thudded painfully in her chest as she contemplated the interview to come, but she hoped she had succeeded in schooling her expression into a calm, confident facade.

My, but he did look magnificent astride a horse. All that harnessed power and grace of movement. It was enough to distract even the most cool-headed miss.

*Remember—that same power can hurt as well as protect.*

Maggie held perfectly still as he dismounted. *Think of*

*yourself as a queen awaiting a petitioner.* She was pleased that she controlled her impulse to fidget. She *could* handle this.

*This* man might soon be her husband.

*Don't think about that now.*

He halted in front of her and executed a short bow, his expression unreadable. "Have you reached a decision?" The words were clipped, almost brusque.

Maggie inclined her head. She kept her hands hidden in the folds of her skirt, afraid their annoying tendency to tremble might give her away.

"After due consideration," she began, "I've decided your proposal has merit."

A spark of surprise flashed across his features, and she felt a trace of unladylike satisfaction. It seemed the oh-so-confident Will Trevaron was not nearly so sure of himself—or her—as he'd appeared.

"But before we can come to an understanding," she cautioned, "there are a few stipulations I would make."

He had already recovered his control, and now his eyes narrowed suspiciously. "And those are?"

*Don't weaken. Make him discuss this on your terms.*

*Take a deep breath. Focus. You can do this.*

"I want the deed to Clover Ridge put solely in my name—entailed so that it will fall to me, no matter what may happen in the future." Maggie had trouble holding his gaze—she felt so tawdry, so mercenary.

Heaven help her, if she had this much trouble with her first demand, how would she deal with the rest of the conversation?

Will drew his brows down. "I thought it understood—Clover Ridge is to be yours." Then he frowned. "However, it won't serve my purpose for you to stay here while I return to England."

"I have every intention of accompanying you," she said steadily.

Before he had time to wonder at the stir of relief her words evoked, she spoke again.

"I do, however, want to have a place to return to should I ever have need of it. If I should end up . . ." she paused, and her color rose, "on my own again, I would find myself not only alone, but alone on foreign soil. I want to know, without doubt, that I have a safe haven to return to."

Was she questioning his ability to provide for her? "You have no need of such precautions. I am *not* Joseph. Even if something should happen to me, your allowance would continue, and my family would see to your welfare."

Her eyebrow quirked up. "As they've seen to *your* welfare these past six years? As Joseph's family saw to mine?"

Devil take it, he'd given his word. "Do you find it so difficult to trust me to provide for your needs?"

"I believe that you have every *intention* of doing what you think best," she temporized. "However, I believed the same of others in my life only to find myself disappointed."

There was his answer. Just like his grandfather had before her, she judged him and found him lacking.

Did Maggie have any idea what it did to a man's pride to have a woman speak of how she would handle matters should he fail her?

A muscle pulsed at the corner of Will's mouth—once, twice—then he tightened his jaw before it could betray him further.

He shrugged as if her words had not opened old wounds. "As I said earlier, the money is yours to do with as you please, so long as you carry out your end of our bargain."

Her face wiped clean of emotion. "And what exactly is that?"

"I beg your pardon?"

Though Maggie's expression remained impassive, Will saw her hands move up to her broach.

"What *exactly* is involved in my end of the bargain?" A strange tension thrummed in her voice.

Hadn't they covered that already? Why was she so edgy? "You agree to marry me and accompany me to England. You stand by my side when I confront Grandfather. Afterwards, you help establish a household I can invite my sister and business associates to."

His answer didn't seem to satisfy her. She stared at him, as if trying to discern something from his expression. Then she shifted again and brushed at her skirt.

"What I wish to know, sir," she said without quite meeting his gaze, "is what *wifely* duties will be expected of me."

# Chapter Five

Will barely managed to keep his mouth from gaping open.

Had he understood her question? He'd praised the Americans for their frankness, but this was a bit much coming from a lady.

Saints above, just by asking the question she evoked images and thoughts that were highly inappropriate for this discussion.

He had assumed that if she agreed to his plan, the marriage would be fully consummated. To be honest, he had even allowed himself fleeting thoughts of how he would enjoy fanning that spark of passion he suspected lurked below her reserved façade.

But was that what *she* wanted? He bloody well didn't care to have a reluctant martyr in his bed.

Will stared at her, trying to read her thoughts. Her cheeks were aflame and tension vibrated from her in discordant waves.

Maggie had always seemed ready to face life's challenges head on, but now she stared at him with white knuckles and a vulnerable air, as if prepared for a weighty blow.

The fact that she'd made it obvious she didn't trust him to look out for her still galled. But this—

Was the thought of their being intimate so disturbing to her? He had come to believe she felt some pleasure in his company, some warmth toward him. What had changed that—the thought of being touched by his disfigured hand? Or the sordid tale he'd recounted earlier?

He *had* vowed to repay his debt to her, he reminded himself, and if this was the only way he could do it, then so be it.

Will eased the tautness in his jaw. "If you refer to our private life," he bit out, "I have neither the desire nor the need to force my attentions on an unwilling partner."

*Even if it kills me to hold back.*

A wince flitted across her face. Will wasn't sure why, and at the moment didn't much care. "Once we've re-opened Briarwood and set up our household, I'll no doubt spend much of my time in London, establishing a second business office for Wind Dancer. You'll be free to arrange your days as you please."

"Briarwood?"

After all he'd just said, *that* was her response?

He did his best to swallow several choice oaths. "Briarwood is the family estate I mentioned earlier," he explained through clenched teeth.

"I see." She folded her hands in her lap. "I presume this estate is of sufficient size to house a large family."

Was Maggie now saying she *wanted* children? An image of her holding their babe in her arms flashed across his mind, startling him with the fierce stab of longing it evoked. "Of course."

"Good." Her hand went to that bloody broach again. But the only hint of emotion on her face was a darkening of her expressive eyes. "As my second stipulation, I would like your word that, after an appropriate settling-in period, say six months, if I should decide to pursue guardianship of Joseph's children, you will not oppose me."

A visceral reaction roared through Will. After all but

denying him any chance at a legitimate heir, she had the temerity to request he raise another man's children. The frustration and affront to his manhood he'd kept in check the past few minutes threatened to slip the bonds of his control.

Recognizing the longing in her eyes, longing for someone other than him, only fanned the flames of his frustration higher.

Then he swallowed another oath. Was he actually jealous of the affection she felt for her stepchildren?

Self-disgust cooled his ire. "Agreed."

His acquiescence was rewarded by a muffled sigh, as if she'd been afraid to breathe while awaiting his answer.

"Thank you." Her relief was evident in the tremulous quality of her voice, in the brilliance of her smile. "I promise—"

"Don't thank me yet." He wasn't altruistic enough to let her off so easily. "I have my own stipulation to add to yours."

Wariness returned the tension to her countenance.

Will held her gaze. "I said earlier that I would make no unwelcome advances toward you."

Surprise flared in her eyes, and she drew up as taut as a sail in a stiff wind.

By the saints, was she *that* put off by him? "You understand that I will, naturally, desire an heir at some point."

A stain of pink crept into her cheeks.

He strove for an offhand tone. "There's no need to rush into the matter. We can wait for an 'appropriate settling-in period,' I believe you mentioned six months." He shrugged. "Once I have my heir, of course, there will be no need for me to bother you further, if it is your desire to avoid such intimacies."

Her troubled expression grated on his conscience. He dropped his relaxed pose. "As I said earlier, I have no desire to bed a martyr. Will this be a problem for you?"

To his relief, his bluntness returned the steel to her backbone. "The role of martyr is not one I care for. Rest assured, I *will* carry out my end of the bargain." Her haughty tone was at odds with the slight trembling of her hands.

"Very well. Is there anything more you wish to discuss?"

She shook her head. He had finally rendered her speechless.

"Then we are agreed. I'll turn the matter of Clover Ridge over to my solicitor as soon as I return to Crane Harbor. I will, of course, have him consult with your own solicitor."

She tucked a wisp of hair behind her ear. "I will let Mr. Martin know to expect it."

Why did it bother him that she treated this affair so matter-of-factly, when that was exactly what he'd said he wanted? "In the meantime, I'll procure the marriage license. I'm sure you agree, under the circumstances, a small ceremony is in order?"

"Of course." The words were spoken with perfect aplomb.

"Then I will send a carriage for you in eight days. We'll be wed in ten, and sail shortly thereafter."

"I'll be ready," she assured him.

Will retrieved the horses' reins. "Then I believe we are done here."

During the return to Crane Harbor, Will found his thoughts poor company. Now that Maggie had agreed to his plan, he had second thoughts about the matter. Especially with the stipulations she'd added.

How had he managed to shackle himself to a woman who didn't trust him, had only agreed to provisionally allow him to bed her, and expected him to take another man's children under his roof?

Slowly, his glum thoughts turned to self-mocking amusement. All she had done was take him at his word, and approach this as a business arrangement. If she'd tipped the scales a bit further in her own favor than he'd planned, it only said something for her intelligence and resolve.

Not to mention courage. No matter how composed she'd seemed, he knew portions of their interview were uncomfortable for her.

The more he saw of Maggie Carter, the less sure he was that he knew her at all. Conflicting images flashed through his mind.

Flushed and breathless from her ride one minute, cool and reserved the next.

Tossing the deed to Clover Ridge at him defiantly, then coolly requesting he transfer it back as her bride price.

Prim and proper as she stated her terms, then boldly inquiring about his expectations on their marital relations.

He shook his head. Figuring out just how her mind worked was going to be an interesting exercise.

He'd been right about her lack of foolish romantic notions.

But that might well be the only thing he'd gauged correctly.

Maggie trudged up the stairs to her room.

It was done. In ten days time she would be Mrs. Will Trevaron. Afterward she would leave America, perhaps forever.

There was so much to do.

She should inform Mr. Martin about her reacquisition of Clover Ridge. She should pen a letter to the children and Joseph's brother, informing them of this new turn of events.

But her treacherous thoughts kept returning to one point.

*Will wanted an heir.*

For a moment, Maggie thought she would be ill.

It wasn't that she didn't want children—God only knew how *much* she wanted to cradle her own babes in her arms.

It wasn't even her fear of disgracing herself—although that was part of it. As long as she wasn't caught unawares when he came to her, she was fairly certain she could control her reaction, could get through the encounter without panicking.

It was just that, heaven help her, she wanted more. She remembered the tenderness between her parents, the love they had for each other that was evident in every look, every word.

Maggie's lip trembled as she again heard Will's tone when he spoke of "bothering her with such intimacies." Instead of a tender lover, she would face a husband looking only to fulfill an obligation. Their physical union would be nothing more to him than a means to continue his family line. He truly *did* intend for their relationship to be "strictly businesslike."

*Dear Lord, please don't let me disgrace myself.*

Maggie tightened her jaw. Rather than wallow in self-pity, mourning the loss of something she'd never had, she should look at the good things to come.

She would never need to go into service again. There was a strong possibility that before the year was out she would have her stepchildren back. And, regardless of his feelings toward her, Will would see that she one day had a babe of her own.

What more could she want?

Will roused reluctantly, wanting to hold on to the last wisps of a very pleasant dream about his future wife. He blinked irritably at the moonlight streaming in from the window. Something had awakened him, but what? The sound of yowling from beneath his window solved the mystery.

Cats! With a string of oaths, he turned over, wishing the noisy tom and all his kin to perdition.

The moment he shut his eyes, however, wisps of his interrupted dream floated back, and he was suddenly wide awake.

Blast and double blast! What the devil was he doing dreaming of a flushed and willing Maggie lying next to him in a satin covered wedding bed? Wasn't she satisfied with disrupting his waking hours—did she have to invade his slumber as well?

Not that the dream meant anything. Except that Maggie Carter was a deuced attractive woman under that prim armor of hers.

Punching his pillow back into shape, Will resolved to put all thought of the contrary widow from his mind. But the more he tried to banish the dream images, the less success he had.

Finally, for the second time that night, he flung the covers aside, dressed, and headed down the stairs. If he wasn't going to sleep, he might as well get a bit of work done.

Will paused on the second floor. He hadn't bothered with a lamp—there was more than enough moonlight to see by. But that smell, like smoldering coals in a distant grate . . . If someone had left a lamp burning, he'd have the man's hide come morning.

Following the scent, Will neared the door to the outer stairway. Perhaps it was coming from outside after all. Still—

He stepped out, testing the air. Yes, it was stronger out here. Not a clerk, then. But it was much too close to ignore.

Will started down the stairs, determined to locate the source. Drifters and drunkards sometimes set fires in alleyways to warm themselves on damp nights. More than one building had been damaged because these fires were carelessly laid.

A low-lying fog skulked about the alley, hugging the building, thickening as he watched. If there was a fire out here, it wasn't large enough to penetrate the murky curtain. Will wrinkled his nose. The odor was definitely stronger now.

Then he caught sight of the broken lock on the first floor storeroom, and thoughts of a possible fire were pushed aside. Normally, the room only held tools and spare dry goods. But just yesterday, Edwin Tern had leased the room to store several kegs of whiskey while his own storeroom was being repaired. If word had gotten around, there was no telling—

Before Will could finish that thought, the storeroom door buckled and, with a shudder, burst into flames.

"Everybody out!" Will barely recognized the raspy bark as his own voice.

Help had come running as soon as he sounded the alarm, but it was obvious it was a losing battle. Even now, flickering blades of flame sliced through the smoke here in the front office.

They'd managed to get most of the files and ledgers out, but this would be the last trip inside. Gathering an armload of documents, he turned to follow the men who'd braved the fire to help him. Then he paused and turned back to his private office.

Cursing his own foolhardiness, Will coughed his way blindly through the thickening smoke. He found his desk by the simple expedient of banging his knee against it. An inkwell crashed to the floor as his hand swept the desktop and finally curled around the miniature of Jenny. Nearly doubled over from racking coughs, he fumbled for the lower right-hand drawer. He yanked it open, then scrabbled for the treasure he kept there.

With a triumphant surge, he stuck the box under his arm. Taking a precious, lung-protesting moment to get his bearings, Will plowed forward, dodging ever-greedier flames, and followed his internal compass to the exit.

Lunging out of the hellish interior, he braced a hand against his thigh, gulping in lungfuls of soot-tinged air.

*Keep moving, keep fighting. Don't think of the loss.*

"Let me take those, Mr. Trevaron." Jack stood over the pile of salvaged documents, like a pirate guarding booty.

It took Will a moment to realize the apprentice referred to the papers he still held. Drawing another lungful to clear his head, Will nodded and handed them over.

"And the box?" Jack asked.

Will hesitated, his hands tightening around the cache of letters and drawings from Jenny.

Seeing the puzzled look on the lad's face, Will thrust the box toward him. This was no time for sentimentality.

Meeting Jack's gaze with eyes that still burned, he waved toward the disorganized pile of ledgers and papers. "Keep a close watch on those."

*Stay in control.*

*Think of what needs doing now.*

*Count the loss later.*

He spied the familiar face of one of his crewmen. "Zeb!" Will tucked the miniature into his pocket as the old salt hurried over. "Find a wagon and get it here as quick as you can."

Barely waiting for the Zeb's nod, Will turned back to Jack. "When he returns, load these papers up and take them to Mr. Spencer's place." His gaze narrowed. "Make sure not a scrap gets lost. And take particular care of that box, understand?"

"Yes sir. You can count on me."

Will nodded. "I know I can, Jack. Now—"

"Let me go," someone yelled. "I've got to get in—"

That was Ian's voice. Was he seriously trying to fight

his way into that inferno? Well, the young fool would have to forego whatever prize he'd left inside. There was no way in Hades Will would let anyone back in that death trap.

Will barreled around the building, ready to do battle.

Ian struggled to pull free of two burly dockworkers. "Let me go, you barnacle-crusted heathens. I have to get in there."

The normally easygoing fellow struggled like a madman. "I'll have you flayed and used for fish bait," he yelled. "I'll have you castrated, and feed the puny leavings to the pigs. So help me I'll use your—"

Who would have guessed Ian had such passion in him—not to mention such a colorful vocabulary?

"Are you daft?" Will grabbed Ian's collar and leaned forward until they stood nose to nose. "After all that's happened today, there's no way I'm going to cap it off by telling Ellen her fool of a husband got himself killed running into a burning building."

The men restraining Ian stepped back. To Will's surprise, rather than arguing further, Ian grabbed him in a bear hug.

"Will! You made it out!"

Will frowned. "Made it out? What—" Then realization struck and he pushed Ian back. "You were going in after *me*?"

Ian's sheepish expression confirmed his suspicion.

Will was stunned. Ian had been ready to risk his life . . .

Behind them, the roof collapsed in a thunder of crashing timbers and snarling flames. Men scrambled to get out of the way. Sparks and ash rained down as if spewed from a volcano. For an eternity of seconds, chaos reigned.

Then Will saw the flaming debris jump greedily toward the building next door. "The Craymore warehouse," he yelled, swatting at sparks that landed on his clothing like fireflies. He spared a quick glance back at Ian, trying to convey his thanks with a gaze and a quick squeeze of the shoulder.

Then he took command, barking orders at the men scrambling away from the blaze. "Refill the buckets. We've got to douse those flames before they spread."

The Wind Dancer office was a lost cause. But there was still a battle to be fought. It would take every man here, and a huge dollop of luck, to keep the fire from spreading.

Will ran his hand wearily through his hair as the sunrise smeared itself across the horizon. After an intense, uncertain battle, the blaze had been reduced to smoldering rubble. Miraculously, there were no serious injuries.

They'd contained the fire, preventing its spread to nearby structures. It was difficult for Will to savor that victory, though, as he studied the charred ruins that had been the Wind Dancer office.

This had been more than a place of work, more than a residence. It had become his refuge when he first arrived here. He'd spent countless late-night hours working at his scarred desk, building Wind Dancer into what it was today. The thought that he could no longer return *here* was unsettling.

"All things considered, we came out of this okay." Ian clamped a hand on Will's shoulder.

Will frowned, then gave a reluctant nod. Ian was right. It could have been much, much worse. Like so many others around him, he had a few burns and scrapes to show for his efforts, and the activity hadn't done his bruised leg any good.

But, under other circumstances, he would have been asleep in his bed at the time the fire spread. Would he have awakened in time to escape?

Ian flashed a crooked smile. "If you don't mind my saying so, you look like an overworked chimney sweep. Why don't you come back to my place where you can clean up and catch a bit of sleep? You've got several busy days ahead of you if you're going to set sail for England in a couple of weeks."

Stopping in his tracks, Will put an arm out. "You can't really think I'll leave you to sort out this mess on your own."

He glared at the younger man, almost angry that Ian would think such a thing. "First, we have to explain to Tern about the whiskey that just went up in flames. Then we'll have to find a temporary office and start rebuilding immediately."

Will rubbed his neck wearily. "No, I'll delay my departure. It's been six years. Another month won't make much difference."

"There's no need to put your trip off." Ian's jaw thrust forward. "Unless you're thinking I can't handle this on my own?"

Will rolled his shoulders. "Of course you can. You just shouldn't have to."

But Ian stood firm. "If this had happened a month from now I would have had to anyway. Go ahead with your plans. And don't worry. Knowing you, I imagine you'll still find time to get your hands dirty with this job."

Will started to argue, then reluctantly acknowledged the truth of Ian's words with a tired nod. As the two headed to Ian's house, Will glanced sideways at his companion. "I haven't thanked you yet for rushing to my rescue as you did."

Will was more touched by the gesture than he cared to admit. He considered Ian as much friend as business manager, but he hadn't ever done anything to inspire the kind of loyalty the young man had demonstrated earlier.

Ian shook his head ruefully. "Some hero I turned out to be. I should've known you wouldn't wait for a rescue party. Good thing you woke in time."

Will dusted soot from his sleeve. "Actually, an infernal

71

cat woke me and I couldn't get back to sleep. I was already on my way downstairs when I smelled the smoke."

"Seems to me you should be singing that cat's praises."

The very idea drew a snort of disgust from Will.

Ian grinned, then sobered. "Any idea how the fire started?"

Will suddenly remembered those first seconds when he'd stepped off the stairs. "Devil take it! How could I have forgotten? The lock on the storeroom door was broken."

Ian's brow furrowed. "Do you think someone set the fire deliberately?"

"Anything's possible. We've made some enemies; dissatisfied customers, rivals, dismissed employees. But I can't imagine anyone with a grudge this big." Too tired to think it through, Will shrugged. "More likely someone wanted Tern's whiskey, thieves already drunk enough to fumble and drop their lamp."

He rolled his shoulders again. "I'll talk to the constable as soon as I've cleaned up. We'll see what he can come up with."

They continued in silence for a few minutes, then Ian cut him a sideways glance. "So, did your trip yesterday fare well? Did you settle matters with your lady friend to your satisfaction?"

Will smiled wryly. "I'm not sure yet. But you can congratulate me. I'm now engaged to be married."

Ian stopped dead in his tracks. "You're *what*?"

"Mrs. Carter has agreed to marry me."

Ian took a few quick steps to catch up to Will. "This is rather sudden isn't it?"

"Yes, but well thought out, nonetheless. We both agree it is the best course of action."

Ian's frown drew furrows in his forehead. "You make it sound like one of your business deals."

Will quirked a brow, surprised Ian hadn't let the matter

drop. Did the young man harbor a sentimental streak? "Isn't a marriage just a business deal between the two parties when you cut away all the romantic nonsense?"

"It's a lifetime partnership," Ian responded. "And that so-called 'romantic nonsense' can make the difference between one that thrives and enriches, and one that withers and embitters." He gestured, giving his words added emphasis. "Lord man, look around. You've seen it happen yourself."

Will repressed his amusement. Ian's passion and idealism were sincere, even if misplaced. "Don't worry, Maggie Carter is a sensible woman." *Sometimes too much so.* "Besides, we both have something to gain and very little to lose in the bargain."

Ian relaxed with a self-conscious smile. "It's really none of my business. I just hope you've thought it through."

Will nodded. "Of course. The marriage itself should change my life very little. She'll be free to run my household as she wishes. Otherwise, I intend to carry on as always."

Ian laughed outright at that. "Which only proves you have no idea what you're getting yourself in to."

Will didn't dignify that with a response. Despite Ian's doubts, he knew exactly what he was doing. And the thought of having Maggie Carter in his life held a growing appeal for him.

When Will's carriage arrived on the appointed day, Maggie was ready. Her only baggage were two small trunks. One contained her modest wardrobe, the other a few personal treasures—favorite books, handmade keepsakes from the children, her father's medical bag.

And, of course, there was Tully on the seat beside her, unhappily caged in a roomy carrier. Not that he stayed there long. Shortly after the carriage set out, she succumbed to his indignant stare and let him take a more befitting seat—her lap.

She massaged him gently behind his ears, smiling as his eyes closed to contented slits. "You and I are embarking on a grand adventure," she told her blissfully purring companion. "A whole new world is opening before us."

For the first time since her parents' death, Maggie felt in control of her destiny. Will appeared willing to treat her as an equal in this partnership they'd arranged. Clover Ridge was hers now, a formidable buffer against any future calamity that might threaten her financial security.

Best of all, she would soon be reunited with her children. She had posted separate letters to them and to their uncle earlier this week, announcing her upcoming marriage. Henry had likely rejoiced at the news she wanted to reclaim the children within the year. He had taken them in more out of duty than any true desire to have them.

As for the children, she hoped they understood, and wouldn't view this as an insult to their father's memory.

When they finally reached the outskirts of Crane Harbor, Maggie placed Tully back into his carrier, trying with little success to still the nervous fluttering in her stomach.

Will had told her she would be staying at the home of his business manager, Ian Spencer. Sure enough, when the carriage stopped in front of a modest townhouse, Maggie saw a familiar-looking gentleman step out onto the small porch. It was the red-haired man she'd seen in Will's office the day she'd visited.

With him was a plump brunette with a sweetly pretty face, undoubtedly his wife.

Then she saw Will stride to the carriage, and her attention focused fully on him. A tingle shimmered through her as she realized again that within a few short days this impressive figure of a man would be her husband. He might not have any of the more tender feelings for her that she longed for, but they were friends, and a woman could do worse in a husband.

She vowed again that she'd do her best not to let him down.

Opening the carriage door, he executed a short bow, then gave her his hand. "Welcome to Crane Harbor. I trust you had a comfortable trip."

"Yes, thank you." Maggie felt a sudden shyness. Attempting to hide her nervousness, she turned to lift Tully's carrier from the seat beside her. As she stepped from the carriage, Will reached to take it from her.

"Let me get that, and then—"

Abruptly, his arm halted and his nose twitched as if he'd smelled something vile. "A cat! Don't tell me you expect to take this creature with us."

Frowning, Maggie drew herself up. "I most certainly do. The children entrusted Tully to me and I will not leave him behind."

"Out of the question. I refuse to travel with a feline."

Maggie stiffened, ready for battle. "You *refuse*?"

# Chapter Six

Will's violent sneeze interfered with whatever response he'd been about to make.

Maggie refused to feel any sympathy for him. Tully seemed just as incensed. Letting out an ear-splitting yowl the cat landed a wicked-looking scratch on Will's hand.

"The devil!" he dropped the cage without ceremony.

Concerned for her pet, Maggie retrieved the carrier. Luckily, it had remained latched. "It seems Tully returns your sentiments," she announced with asperity.

"It certainly does." The laughing comment had come from Mr. Spencer.

Maggie's cheeks burned as she realized she'd been standing on the sidewalk, arguing like a fishwife. What a terrible first impression to make on her hosts.

As if just remembering their presence himself, Will waved his uninjured hand in their direction. "Maggie Carter, I'd like you to meet Ian Spencer and his wife, Ellen."

"My apologies, Mr. and Mrs. Spencer, I didn't mean—"

Mrs. Spencer batted her husband's arm affectionately, then stepped forward. "Don't let these menfolk rattle you, dear," she said warmly. "I know you must be tired from your trip. Come along and we'll get you *and* your pet settled in comfortably."

Maggie gave Will a haughty look. "As soon as my trunks are brought up, I will retrieve my medical bag and see to your hand."

"Please don't bother yourself, madam." Will was all chilly politeness now. "It is only a scratch."

"Still, it should be looked after properly." Chin high, she turned to follow Mrs. Spencer inside without waiting for a reply.

Maggie didn't speak until she was alone with her hostess. "I appreciate you opening your home to me, Mrs. Spencer. I hope my presence won't cause you or your husband any undue hardship."

"On the contrary, we are looking forward to your stay." She slid Maggie a smile. "And please, call me Ellen. I confess, I've been riddled with curiosity about the woman who finally snagged Crane Harbor's most eligible, and entrenched, bachelor."

The words were said with such friendly humor, Maggie found herself unable to take offense. Instead, she said ruefully, "That was not an auspicious start to my new life, I'm afraid."

Her hostess made a non-committal sound. "Mr. Trevaron obviously doesn't care for cats," she added dryly. Then she gave Maggie a knowing smile as she opened a door on the second-floor landing. "Just make certain you continue to stand your ground."

Maggie set Tully's carrier down and looked around. "Oh, what a lovely chamber. And fresh flowers—how thoughtful."

"Thank you. The flowers are from my own garden."

Ellen turned as someone came up behind her. "Good, here are your trunks." She waved a hand. "There's a basin of fresh water and a clean cloth on the washstand. Take your time freshening up. Join us in the parlor whenever you're ready."

"I won't be but a minute," Maggie assured her. "I really

do want to tend to Mr. Trevaron's scratch." She winced as the cat let out an indignant yowl. "And I should take Tully for a walk."

Her hostess tutted away such concerns. "One of the staff will be glad to take your pet out for a spell."

Maggie hesitated, then decided it might be better to get Tully out of the house while she and Will settled the matter of his accompanying her. "Thank you, that would be most kind."

She opened a satchel and pulled out a leash. "Whoever opens the cage should be careful. Tully won't be in a pleasant mood. And please make sure the leash is securely fastened to his collar. He can be quite cunning when he wants to get away."

Ellen laughed outright. "Sounds like the perfect pet for Will Trevaron."

Maggie bit her lip. "Oh dear, perhaps I *should* take care of this myself."

"Don't be silly. We'll manage famously."

The matter taken out of her hands, literally, Maggie spent a few minutes freshening up, then dug out her medical bag.

Squaring her shoulders, she stepped into the hallway and headed downstairs. Following the sound of voices, she located the Spencers and Will, seated in a comfortable-looking parlor near the foot of the staircase.

Pasting on a smile that she hoped displayed more confidence than she felt, Maggie joined them.

"There you are," Ellen welcomed her as Mr. Spencer and Will stood. "I hope you found everything to your liking."

"Yes, thank you." Even though Maggie refused to glance at Will, she was acutely conscious of his commanding presence.

"Good. And I trust you'll let us know if you should require anything during your stay." Her hostess stood and turned to her husband. "There's something I wish to discuss with you concerning the household accounts. I'm sure our guests will excuse us for a few minutes."

Though no one was fooled by Ellen's heavy-handed attempt to give her and Will a bit of privacy, Maggie was grateful nonetheless. She'd never been one to put off unpleasant matters. The quicker attended to, the quicker put behind you.

As soon as the Spencers exited, Maggie set her bag on a table and met Will's gaze. "I'll have a look at that cut now."

He silently offered his hand and, as she took it, she once again felt that tingling sensation wash through her. Forcing herself to concentrate on her task, she examined the cut. "It's not as deep as I'd feared, and you've done a good job cleaning it. I don't think stitches will be required."

"Then it's your opinion I'll live?" he asked solemnly.

Unaware that she'd been thinking aloud, Maggie looked up quickly. She was relieved to see the smile in his eyes.

Releasing his hand, she took a deep breath. "Mr. Trevaron, I'd like to apologize for my earlier behavior. I should have checked with you before I brought Tully along. It's just—"

He forestalled her explanations with a resigned sigh. "Mrs. Carter, please don't say any more. We both know I overreacted. I suppose I should offer an explanation."

He paused, and Maggie had a sudden inkling that offering explanations was something he wasn't in the habit of doing.

Will flashed a self-mocking smile. "You see, it's not just that I dislike cats. I also have an unfortunate physical reaction to them as well. My eyes get watery, I sneeze, and if exposed for long periods, I break out in an unfortunate rash. It's very hard on one's dignity, I assure you."

Maggie was immediately sympathetic. "Oh, I had no idea! Of course I'll send Tully back to Clover Ridge. I was selfish to have taken him with me just because he is a link to the children. Tully will be happier there than in some unfamiliar place."

Will made a sharp gesture. "Such self-sacrifice is really unnecessary. The animal seems important to you, so of course you must bring him along. Just keep him away from me."

Disconcerted by his tone, Maggie was nevertheless relieved by his offer. Sensing he wouldn't appreciate effusiveness, she made do with a simple nod and a thank-you.

Then she turned the subject. "If you have a moment, I would appreciate some discussion on what plans you've made."

"Of course." He waited until she took a seat. "We will be married in a small ceremony tomorrow. The following day we will board the *Lady Jen* and set sail for London."

He smiled proudly. "The *Lady Jen* is Wind Dancer's newest ship, and I'm sure you'll find the accommodations quite comfortable." He gave her an unreadable look. "We will, of course, have separate cabins."

Was that a concession to her, or his own preference?

"I've sent word ahead to have Briarwood made ready," he continued. "We'll spend a few days there to let you become familiar with your new home and staff before proceeding on to my grandfather's estate."

Will straightened. "We can continue this later if you wish. I have a business matter I must attend to."

He smiled companionably, and Maggie was struck again by how charming he could be—when he wasn't being insufferable.

"I've made an appointment for you with a dressmaker for this afternoon," he added. "She's agreed to set her other work aside to prepare a new wardrobe for you before we sail. Ian's wife will escort you. Feel free to purchase whatever other furbelows you need as well."

There he went, making decisions for her again. "That is quite impossible," she said firmly.

He frowned. "I don't—"

Had the man no sense of propriety? "It would be most improper for me to accept so extravagant and personal a gift from you before we wed. Thank you for the generous offer, but I will do quite well with what I have for now."

"We will be wed tomorrow," he insisted. "I am but purchasing your trousseau. And I assure you this offer was not prompted by motives of generosity. You may be quite willing to 'make do' with what wardrobe you have, but I am not. When you step onto English soil, it will be as my wife. As such, there is a certain standard I will expect you to maintain."

He eyed her critically, as if she were some scraggly, matted-fur stray that had shown up on his doorstep.

Her soon-to-be-husband gave his cuff an impatient tug. "I have no desire to show up in London with a wife on my arm who displays the fashion sense of a charwoman."

Mortified, she rose with stiff dignity, one hand toying with her broach. Was her appearance really so abhorrent to him? "Thank you for shedding the proper light on the situation. Of course it will be done as you say. If you will excuse me, I shall waste no time in carrying out your wishes."

Will watched her retreating back and decided perhaps he'd been a bit too harsh. But blast it all, why couldn't the woman just accept a gift with a gracious thank-you instead of getting all prim and huffy? And he would truly like to see her decked out for once in clothes that were more frivolous than serviceable. "Mrs. Carter."

She halted, though she didn't turn around.

He took a deep breath, reminding himself of all he owed her. "I'm sorry if my bluntness offended you. But surely you realize that in your new role as the marchioness of

Rainley and the future duchess of Lynchmorne you will be subject to the scrutiny of . . ."

Her gasp as she whirled around halted his apology.

"Marchioness . . . future duchess," she echoed weakly, sitting down with a thud.

Amused by her melodramatic reaction, Will raised an eyebrow. "Of course. Did I fail to mention that my grandfather is the duke of Lynchmorne? I've recently become the heir apparent. It's the main reason he's offered the olive branch."

As she continued to stare at him, he added, "The role of Grandfather's heir carries with it the courtesy title Marquess of Rainley. As my wife, you will be addressed as Lady Rainley."

"But, I had no idea . . . I don't think I could possibly—"

Devil take it, she wasn't just being melodramatic. Maggie was genuinely aghast. You'd think he'd told her he was penniless! "Not thinking of reneging on our agreement are you?"

She speared him with an accusing glare. "Not at all. I gave my word. But it was too bad of you, sir, not to give a full accounting of what role I was stepping into."

Before he could form a response, she whisked from the room.

As Will took his leave of the Spencers, he wondered what had come over him. He wasn't usually riled so easily. The starchy Maggie could be irritating, true, but he had displayed better control under more trying circumstances.

Perhaps it was because her reactions constantly surprised him. It kept him off balance—a most uncomfortable sensation.

Most women would be delighted to acquire a new wardrobe and to join the ranks of England's social elite. Yet both of these had elicited strong negative reactions from his future bride.

Maggie became more of a puzzle to him with each en-counter.

Maggie sat in the swaying carriage, Tully safely enthroned on her lap. She was doing her best to ignore her less than serene thoughts as she smiled at her companion. "It is most kind of you to put aside your own activities to ac-company me today."

Ellen gave her a mischievous smile. "I wouldn't dream of passing up a chance to visit Madame LeBlanc's estab-lishment. She is the most sought-after dressmaker within a hundred miles. Most ladies feel pampered if they can boast purchasing one or two of her creations in a year. And you are to have a whole wardrobe!"

This enthusiastically delivered bit of information did little to brighten Maggie's mood. Of *course* she was getting an extravagant trousseau. Apparently there was nothing too good for the wife of a marquess.

"I'm sure Madame LeBlanc does lovely work," Maggie replied agreeably. After all, Ellen was not to blame for any of this.

Will was titled! Heaven help her. What did she know about negotiating the social mores of the British aristoc-racy?

She wouldn't put it past Will to have deliberately with-held this information from her until today. He had told her how his grandfather felt about Americans, but not this.

Men!

Well, he could dress her up in all the fine clothes money could buy, but he would still end up with plain and simple Maggie Carter.

Tully let out an indignant yowl, and Maggie apologet-ically loosened her hold.

"You know, your Tully would have been perfectly safe if you'd left him behind," Ellen said. "Mr. Trevaron is at the office, and my housekeeper has a fondness for cats."

"He probably would be more comfortable there," Maggie agreed ruefully. "I do appreciate your offer. And I'm not concerned about Mr. Trevaron's response. Once we discussed the matter, he withdrew his objections." She would give the devil his due, even if he *was* overbearing and insufferable.

"My concern is that Tully is used to country living," she explained. "At Clover Ridge he came and went as he pleased. I don't want to bother your staff with guard duty."

"So, you convinced Mr. Trevaron to accept your cat, did you? And he seemed so opposed to the idea."

Some of Maggie's outrage eased. Will *had* shown an unexpected ability to compromise in that matter.

Was she being too harsh in her assessment of him? For some reason she found it difficult to remain objective where Will was concerned.

By the time they arrived at Madame LeBlanc's, Maggie's optimism had resurfaced, and she and her companion were chatting as if they were old friends.

Stepping inside the shop, however, Maggie stopped in mid-sentence. "Shop" was much too mundane a word for this place—it had the solemn dignity of a church sanctuary.

The richly textured, jewel-toned fabrics on display dazzled the eye as would finely crafted stained glass, and the silk-lined display cases were suitable for the most precious of relics.

The heavy velvet drapes along the back wall were doubtless meant to shield the inner sanctum from view of the common masses.

Four slender chairs with tapestried seats awaited any who dared to sit amidst these august surroundings, and a lavish carpet, so sumptuous it invited one to bend over and caress it, covered the center of the floor.

"May I help you?" The thickly accented question startled Maggie. Where the room had seemed abandoned a moment ago, a stately, olive-skinned woman now stood before the velvet curtain. No doubt she'd entered while Maggie gaped at her surroundings like a bumpkin.

The woman, obviously the high priestess here, made no further move to greet them. Instead, she studied Maggie with a critical eye, as if noting and mentally cataloging each physical flaw. "You must be Monsieur Trevaron's fiancée."

Her tone raised Maggie's head—not to mention temper—a notch. She'd had enough set-downs for one day.

"I am." Maggie placed every ounce of American spunk in her tone that she could draw on. "This is Mrs. Spencer. I assume you are Madame LeBlanc?"

The aristocratic seamstress inclined her head. "Monsieur Trevaron indicated you were in need of a new wardrobe." A contemptuous glance at Maggie's dress made it obvious she agreed. "My staff is at your disposal for the next two days. How does madam wish to proceed?"

"Madame LeBlanc," Maggie responded in an even tone, "it is my fiancé's wish, as well as my own, that I do him justice when we arrive in his home country." Maggie tossed her head. "If you and I reach an understanding, I will consider any suggestions on design and color you wish to offer. But understand now that I will have the final say in what is purchased."

She pointed to an elegant creation, prominently displayed. "I will have none of the excessive ruffles and frills such as fashioned on that gown. I prefer a simpler, more subtle style."

She gave the string of her reticule a firm tug. "If you are willing to work within these limits, then let us get on with this. If not, I must make other arrangements."

By the time she finished her little speech, Madame LeBlanc's assistants were peeking out in open-mouthed surprise. Obviously, the dressmaker was usually treated with a great deal more awe.

With a mental wince, Maggie remembered she wasn't alone. She hoped she hadn't completely mortified Ellen Spencer. Nothing for that now, however.

To her surprise, Madame LeBlanc relaxed and smiled broadly. "Ah, if monsieur has seen you thus, with your back straight and your eyes flashing emerald sparks, then it is no wonder he has finally succumbed to Cupid's call."

Maggie blinked, nonplused by this unexpected reaction. She turned sharply when she heard a muffled giggle from the woman beside her, but Ellen met her gaze with an innocent smile.

"You have misunderstood." The seamstress recaptured Maggie's attention. "I do not disapprove of you, only the garment you are wearing. Bah! It does not deserve to be called a dress."

Her hands, which moved constantly as she spoke, waved toward Maggie's dress. "Why do you hide your form behind such shapeless rags? You must put yourself in my hands. You will not be disappointed." She gave a knowing smile. "And neither will Monsieur Trevaron, I assure you."

The diminutive designer clapped her hands. "Now, there is much to be done."

As she spoke, the modiste ushered Maggie to a dressing room at the rear of her shop. Before she quite realized what was happening, Maggie had stepped out of her dress, and madam's assistant was taking her measurements. That done, she was once more clothed and led back to the front of the store.

Ellen entered enthusiastically into the selection of this new wardrobe. Her companion and Madame LeBlanc debated the various merits of fabrics, colors and styles. They consulted Maggie only once or twice, and then with the air of it being an afterthought.

In amused exasperation, she finally gave up and left the two women to make the selections. So much for her determination to stay in charge of this expedition.

Maggie did put her foot down, however, when the purchases seemed to be getting out of hand. "Ellen," she said sternly, "I believe six dresses will be quite enough, four for day wear and perhaps two gowns for evenings. I would not wish to take advantage of Mr. Trevaron's generosity."

Ellen, in the process of debating with Madame LeBlanc the relative merits of the green taffeta as opposed to the rose brocade for dress number ten, looked up, her eyes glinting with determination. "Now, Maggie—"

Madame LeBlanc intervened. "Monsieur Trevaron gave me instructions to provide you with a full wardrobe." She placed a hand over her heart. "I have given my word, madam."

Her stern tone was wasted on Maggie.

"Nevertheless, I will accept no more than six." Maggie felt decadent agreeing to even that many.

"Such a stubborn lady." The seamstress gave a melodramatic sigh. Then she brightened. "Very well, let us look at what accessories madam will require to complete her wardrobe."

A short while later, Maggie found herself exiting the shop with Madame LeBlanc's assurance that she would have everything completed before they sailed.

"I do wish you would reconsider," Ellen said as they stepped onto the sidewalk. "I'm quite certain Mr. Trevaron intended for you to be more extravagant in your purchases."

Maggie's stomach already churned with guilt over those two extra gowns she'd ordered. She waved her a hand. "Extravagant is exactly what I was. I can't imagine needing more than six new gowns all at once."

"Oh Maggie," Ellen's tone held a note of affectionate exasperation, "life in London society will be so different from what you are accustomed to. I assure you—Oh dear."

Ellen paused, a chagrined expression on her face. "I forgot my reticule inside. Check on your cat. I'll be right back."

Maggie nodded, but as she moved toward the carriage, something in a shop window caught her eye. Impulsively, she stepped back. "If Mrs. Spencer returns before I do," she told the coachman, "please tell her I'll only be a moment."

When Maggie stepped back onto the sidewalk, she found Ellen waiting. Her companion's eyebrows rose in question when she saw the package Maggie carried. Carefully wrapped in brown paper and twine, Maggie knew the contents were intriguingly indiscernible.

"It's a peace offering of sorts." For some reason, Maggie was uncomfortable confessing what she'd done. Ridiculous to be so self-conscious. The ring she'd worn on a chain had been hidden beneath her bodice, so Ellen would not notice its absence.

*Forgive me Joseph, but I would soon have put it away at any rate, and it was all I had to barter with.*

As the carriage lurched forward, Ellen reclaimed Maggie's attention. "I hope you don't mind, but I need to stop at the Wind Dancer office to speak to Ian. It's not far out of our way and I won't take but a few minutes."

Making a non-committal sound, Maggie set her package on the seat beside her. She opened Tully's carrier and pulled him onto her lap, using the activity to cover her lack of enthusiasm. She was in no mood to face Will just yet.

To her surprise, when they passed the spot where his office had stood, there was nothing but a charred ruin. "What happened?"

"There was a fire just over a week ago. They only managed to salvage their files and a few personal items."

"How awful! Was anyone hurt?"

"Thankfully no, at least not seriously. They're working

out of a temporary office until they can rebuild."

They reached their destination a few minutes later. "You go on," Maggie told Ellen. "Tully is in need of a bit of exercise."

Ellen gave Maggie a speculative look. Then she nodded. "I'll give Mr. Trevaron your regards if I should see him."

Telling Ellen not to rush on her account, Maggie clipped a leash on Tully and set him on the ground. The feline sat on his haunches, eying her with a look of affronted majesty.

That was just too much. Maggie placed a fist on her hip. "One aristocrat in my life is quite enough, thank you very much. If you want to go for a walk, you'll do it on the end of this leash. Otherwise you can climb right back into the carrier."

Tail swishing in challenge, Tully met her gaze without blinking for a long moment. Then he stood, turned with an audible sniff, and moved away, head and tail held equally high.

Maggie's pleasure in that small victory lasted all of two steps. She tried to ignore the feeling that she was behaving like a coward, but wasn't succeeding.

"Ellen saw right through me," she told a disinterested Tully. "She believes I'm avoiding Will—which, of course, I am."

Why did she always turn from self-confident woman to bumble-headed ninny when Will was involved? She should just go inside, and if she encountered Will, there was no reason they couldn't behave civilly to one another.

Maggie tugged the leash. "Come along, time to turn back."

Tully, however, had other ideas. Before Maggie realized what he was about, the resourceful feline slipped from his collar and streaked down a narrow lane beside the Wind Dancer building.

"Tully! Come back here!" Maggie clamped her mouth

shut, realizing calling the cat would do no good. With a frustrated huff, she started after the runaway.

The lane was little more than an alley between buildings, but Tully was nowhere in sight. Bother that cat, where had he gotten himself off to?

She reached the far corner of the building and paused. An alley intersected the lane, and this one had a different feel.

The space was narrower, with shadows that shifted and odors that wrinkled her nose. Her heart thudded uncomfortably at a sudden clattering from the farther recesses. Surely that had only been natural settling of the haphazardly stacked debris?

Nevertheless, Maggie could well imagine unsavory creatures scuttling among the clutter and grime. Tully or no Tully, she had no intention of entering that noisome jumble.

Perhaps she should go back and get the coachman to help her.

Really, Will should be more meticulous in keeping the area around his office orderly. Even if this was only a back alley—

A flash of movement among the drunkenly scattered boxes and barrels startled a squeak from her. Several erratic heartbeats later, she realized her errant feline had jumped atop a splintered crate.

"Tully!" Relief mingled with exasperation. "Come here you wretched animal. You've caused enough trouble for one day."

But the cat merely stared, eyes gleaming balefully through the gloom, his tail slowly swishing from side to side. When further coaxing had no effect, Maggie finally gave in and marched toward her recalcitrant pet, holding her skirts above the litter-strewn ground, muttering dire threats the whole time.

As if he'd only been waiting for her approach, Tully

turned and jumped away from her, next to a pile of discarded rags.

"Whatever has gotten into you?" Maggie resisted the urge to stomp her foot in frustration. "Just wait 'til I get my hands on you, you thankless feline. You'll be lucky if I don't lock you in your cage for the rest of our stay. I declare—"

Peering over the stack of debris, Maggie jerked to a stop, her hand flying to her throat. Tully wasn't standing guard over a pile of rags at all.

Will, unconscious and deathly pale, lay on his side in a dark pool of blood.

# Chapter Seven

Maggie yelled for help as she knelt beside Will's crumpled form. *Dear God, no—please don't take Will from me, too.*

A sob of relief escaped as she saw the rise and fall of his chest. Murmuring a quick prayer of thanksgiving, she tried to push back the paralyzing panic.

*Get hold of yourself.*

*Remember your training.*

She took a steadying breath and examined Will as dispassionately as she could. His breathing was shallow and ragged, his pulse barely detectable.

*Dear Lord, there's so much blood!* It was everywhere, staining his clothing, her hands, pooling beside him.

"Please God," she prayed desperately. "Help me to help him."

Maggie's head turned at the sound of a door opening. "Help me!" she yelled. "Mr. Trevaron's hurt." Then as a young man sprinted toward her, "Send for a doctor. Tell Mr. Spencer what's happened. I need clean cloths—as many as you can find."

The lad stood staring, mouth agape. "Hurry!" she shouted.

He started, swallowed hard, then fled back inside.

Maggie took another deep breath. Ever so gently, she rolled Will on his back. A blood-soaked rip in his clothing indicated the injury was high on his chest, near his left shoulder. Pushing aside his coat, she ruthlessly ripped open the already ruined shirt.

Her heart lurched at the sight of the ugly, gaping wound.

*Don't swoon. Hold on until the doctor arrives.*

*Will needs you.*

That last thought stopped the dizzy spinning around her. Every second counted. But where to start?

Panic rose again like bile, paralyzing her, trapping her breath only to release it in ragged gasps.

*First, stop the bleeding.*

Maggie could almost hear her father's firm, competent voice guiding, steadying her. With hands that trembled only slightly, she cleared her mind of everything but the task at hand.

Tearing strips from Will's shirt, she formed a makeshift pad and did her best to staunch the flow of blood.

Sounds intruded and she realized a crowd had formed, its numbers swelling by the minute.

"He's dead!" someone shrieked. "Mr. Trevaron's dead!"

Maggie fought the urge to scream out her own fears. "Stop that! He is *not* dead." She glared at the crowd. "Don't just stand there. Prepare a place inside, away from this filth. Find a litter. And see what's keeping the doctor."

Several men rushed off, hopefully to do her bidding. She waved the others away. "If you aren't going to help, back away and give me room."

"Let me by!" Ian Spencer plowed through the crowd. "What's going on? Someone said Will's been hurt."

"He's wounded." Maggie struggled to keep her voice calm while every nerve screamed for action. Each of her senses strained for signs that Will still lived.

Mr. Spencer sucked in a breath. "Is he—"

The last thing she needed was a hand-wringer, someone who'd just ask questions and get in her way.

"He's alive, Mr. Spencer, but only just." Already her hands were at work, brushing a sticky lock from Will's brow, seeking signs of other injuries. "He's lost a great deal of blood. I have some medical skills. I'll do what I can until a doctor arrives." She paused, meeting his gaze with a stern look. "But if I'm to keep him alive I need action, not questions."

He stiffened at her tone, then nodded. "How can I help?"

Maggie released a breath, grateful for his quick understanding. She only hoped his trust was not misplaced.

"My medical supplies are at your home," she instructed. "In a satchel near my bed. I'll need them as soon as possible."

"Of course." He stood as if jerked up by a string. "I'll send for it at once."

Trying to block out the smell of blood and the sounds of the crowd, Maggie examined Will's much-too-pale face. The gash near his left temple painted a ragged line on his ghostly white face. Thankfully, the ugly cut had nearly stopped bleeding.

Someone handed her cloths just as Mr. Spencer returned.

"Ellen is sending for your bag and preparing Will's room." He knelt across from her. "What else can I do?"

"Take these cloths and fashion a fresh pad." She watched him do as she asked. "When I remove this one, replace it with yours. Make certain you apply firm, steady pressure. Ready?"

At his nod, Maggie removed the blood-soaked cloths, wincing again at the sight of the hellish wound that oozed precious life from Will's body. A second later, Mr. Spencer applied the fresh bandage, hiding the atrocity from sight.

"Thank you." Maggie sat on her heels and watched,

making certain he applied the proper amount of pressure. Satisfied, she began checking for other injuries. She gently lifted Will's head and laid it in her lap. *Where was that doctor?*

Maggie ran a hand over his head. She offered a silent prayer of thanks when she found no further injury.

She brushed his cheek with the tip of her forefinger. He deserved to know how much his kindnesses, his friendship, meant to her. How just knowing him made her life brighter.

*You will get better. I won't allow the last words we exchanged to be those of sarcasm and frustration.*

If only he would open those silver-gray eyes, even if just to frown up at her. . . .

"We're ready."

Maggie started and looked around. Two sturdy men stood behind her bearing a litter. "Of course." She shifted, making room for them to set it beside Will. "Careful you don't jostle him. Mr. Spencer, keep steady pressure on that pad."

Maggie bit her lip, forcing herself to step aside, though she itched to push them away, to do it all herself. Each jarring movement they made threatened her control. Fear roiled her insides as the pad pressed to Will's chest darkened.

*Hold on, Will, please. The doctor will be here soon.*

As they crossed the debris-strewn alley, Maggie took one of Will's hands, trying to lend him her strength, needing the physical contact to bolster her own courage.

Ian Spencer barked orders, ensured doors were opened and the way was cleared as they negotiated the maze of halls. "Jack," he called to a familiar youth, "warn my wife we're coming."

He shot Maggie an apologetic look. "Ellen grows faint at the sight of blood. It's a weakness she abhors."

At the moment, it was a weakness Maggie could empathize with.

When they reached their destination, she was pleased to see there was actually a bedroom here. "Wait." At her command, the men immediately halted. "I need a knife or scissors."

Someone stepped forward and produced a pocketknife. "Here, Miss, will this do?"

Maggie studied the well-honed edge. "It'll do just fine. Jack, is it?"

"Yes ma'am."

"Well, Jack, I need you to very carefully cut away Mr. Trevaron's outer clothing."

The youth's Adam's apple bobbed convulsively. "Beg pardon?"

Maggie's own face warmed, but this was no time to be missish. "We need to remove these filthy clothes from Mr. Trevaron before we place him in the bed."

"Jack," Mr. Spencer commanded, "take my place." As soon as they swapped places, Will's friend took the knife. He paused, eying Maggie. "Would you care to join Ellen in the outer office? I can have someone call you when we have him settled."

Maggie shook her head, hoping she wasn't shocking Will's associates, but she had more important things to worry over. "For now, think of me as Mr. Trevaron's physician."

He gave her an unreadable look, then went to work. Quicker than she would have thought possible, he was done.

Maggie refused to be distracted by the sight of Will's manly form. It wasn't as if she hadn't seen him thus once before.

*And in a few choice dreams since.*

For now he was only a patient, one in dire need of her

help. She cleared her throat. "Gently now, transfer him to the bed."

With the help of Jack and a few others who'd been crowding the doorway, that task, too, was accomplished quickly. By the time they had Will settled, Maggie's medical bag had arrived.

"What else do you need?" Mr. Spencer stood at her elbow, looking to her for further direction.

Heaven help her, could she deal with such grievous injuries? Maggie fought to think dispassionately about what she had to do, but this was *Will*.

If he should die . . .

A shudder shook her. No time for hysterics. A deep breath for fortification, a tilt of the chin for show. They couldn't wait for the doctor.

"Open the curtains wider and light a lamp—I'll need plenty of light. Have the basin of water replaced as often as possible. And please, keep everyone out but the doctor."

Seeing Mr. Spencer's relieved nod, she washed the blood and grime from her hands, then instructed him to do the same.

Digging deep inside herself for the resolve to face the task ahead, she removed the blood-soaked pad. *Where was that doctor?*

Mr. Spencer held the basin while Jack kept her supplied with fresh water and clean cloths.

As she carefully cleaned around the wound, Maggie was relieved to discover the bleeding had nearly stopped. But the injury was a bad one, deep and ugly. Maggie swallowed against the bile that rose in her throat as she studied it more closely.

"It's not a gunshot wound," she told her helpers. "There's no need to dig for a bullet." Her stomach roiled at just the thought of attempting such a thing.

At last Maggie admitted that she had done all she could.

Straightening, she rolled her shoulders, then washed her hands. "Mr. Spencer, if you'll lend a hand, we'll secure a fresh pad with some strips around his torso."

"Pardon me, ma'am." Jack stood at the foot of the bed. "The doctor's with another patient across town. Says he'll get here as soon as he can. I thought you'd want to know."

*As soon as he can—that could mean anything.*

Maggie didn't care how selfish the thought—nothing was more important right now than saving Will. "Thank you, Jack. Please make sure he is informed the situation is critical."

As soon as they finished bandaging Will's chest, Maggie turned her focus to the gash on Will's head. This one was shallower than she'd feared. It probably happened when he fell.

She looked across the bed to Mr. Spencer. "You'll find a needle and thread in my bag. Have someone boil it, then soak it in whiskey if you have any."

He bent over her bag. "What are you planning?"

"I'm going to stitch this cut on his head. And you're going to assist me." She noted the tightening of his jaw, but he made no further comment, and neither did she. By the time she had the cut cleaned to her satisfaction, her implements were ready.

"Now, Mr. Spencer, I need you to keep Mr. Trevaron's head perfectly still once I get started."

Maggie concentrated on her task with exhausting intensity. She looked up only once, when Mr. Spencer made an inadvertent movement, and was surprised to see how pale he'd become.

After she completed the stitching, she studied her work with a frown. "I don't think that'll leave much of a scar."

"I'd think a scar is the least of Will's worries at the moment," Mr. Spencer said dryly, handing her a cloth.

She took the rag, and dabbed her sweat-moistened face.

"My apologies. I'm afraid I sometimes talk to myself while I work."

"No need to apologize, ma'am. You seem to be handling the situation with remarkable resolve. Will's a lucky man." Then, before she could comment, "What's the verdict?"

"The best answer I can give is that if it's in my power to save him, he'll live. But I honestly don't know if that's enough." She could hear the worry and strain in her voice, despite her efforts to conceal it. "I'm anxious for the doctor to arrive. For now, we'd best check for other injuries."

With Mr. Spencer's help, she meticulously examined Will's scalp, torso and limbs. She could feel Mr. Spencer's gaze on her as she worked. She refused to look up, afraid to see censure for her boldness, but neither did she halt her examination. She did, however, move quickly over some of the more intimate areas.

Maggie had just finished gently flexing his ankles when Jack finally ushered the doctor in.

"Mrs. Carter, this is Dr. Lawson. Dr. Lawson, this is Mrs. Carter. She's been taking care of the doctorin' while we waited for you to get here."

"Has she, now?" Dr. Lawson's tone was frosty at best.

Mr. Spencer frowned, but Maggie had dealt with this attitude before. Acting defensive would serve no purpose, and Will's well-being mattered more than her pride.

"Good day, sir. You are a most welcome sight." At his nod, she calmly launched into the facts she thought would be most helpful to the physician. "Mr. Trevaron was discovered in the alley behind this building about seventy-five minutes ago. He was unconscious and bleeding from a wound near his left shoulder. There is also a small gash on his forehead. I have found no other injuries on his person."

She took a breath. "In the time since we first discovered him, we've done what we could to stop the bleeding and make him more comfortable. I used tincture of marigold to clean the wounds. I also stitched the gash on his forehead."

Her words were acknowledged with a curt nod, and the doctor waved her aside as he began his own examination. With Mr. Spencer's assistance, he unwound the bandages from Will's chest.

After studying the wound in silence for several minutes, the doctor turned to Maggie. "We'll need a poultice of milk and linseed meal prepared as soon as possible."

Maggie nodded and stepped out of the room to find Ellen waiting in the hallway.

"I heard," Ian's wife said. "Milk and linseed meal—I'll have it fetched at once."

Returning, Maggie could read nothing from the doctor's expression. Her throat burned from the effort not to ask questions. Her thumb traced endless circles over her broach.

*Please tell me it's not as bad as it looks.*

While they waited for the poultice, the doctor moved his focus to the gash on Will's head. Again he held his own counsel, not volunteering an opinion on the patient's condition. To Maggie the examination seemed to take an agonizing eternity.

Finally he turned to her with a bow, his demeanor friendlier than before. "My apologies, ma'am, for my earlier brusqueness. It's been my experience that amateurs often do more harm than good to a patient, regardless of how well-meaning they are."

Dr. Lawson returned his instruments to his bag. "But you've handled this quite well, given the circumstances. I doubt I could have done better myself."

Maggie ignored his apology and praise, pressing on to more important issues. "But what do you think his chances are?"

He met her gaze evenly. "I imagine you know the answer as well as I do. He's lost a great quantity of blood, and that knock on the head hasn't helped any."

He studied Will, an assessing light in his eyes. "He's a big man, strong and fit, which will help his chances. But I don't hold with dangling false hopes. I'm afraid it isn't promising."

No! Will was *not* going to die! She wouldn't let him. "Thank you for your honesty doctor, but I happen to believe in miracles. What can I do to help him fight this?"

The doctor snapped his bag shut. "Get as much liquid in him as possible if he regains consciousness. If he makes it through to morning, his chances for recovery will go up considerably."

Jack entered the room then bearing a bowl. "Mrs. Spencer said I was to bring this to you straight away."

"Ah, the poultice." The doctor applied the medication-soaked pad to the wound.

At last he was done. "Change the poultice at least twice daily, and check closely for signs of infection."

He moved to the door. "Now, you seem to have this situation in hand, so I'll leave it to you and see to my other patients who aren't lucky enough to have a private physician. I'll check back with you in the morning if you like."

"Yes, please. And thank you for coming when you did."

When he'd gone, Maggie mechanically began cleaning the instruments she'd used during her examination, avoiding any direct glance toward the nearly lifeless form on the bed. Suddenly she was trembling so hard she could no longer control her movements. The scissors she held clattered to the floor.

"Mrs. Carter!" An alarmed Ian Spencer was at her side immediately, helping her to a nearby chair.

"I'm sorry," she said weakly. "I'll be fine in a minute."

*Take deep breaths.*

*He's strong. He'll pull through.*

"Sit and rest. Jack and I can clean this up." Mr. Spencer's brisk words intruded on her thoughts. "It's a wonder you remained such a pillar of strength as long as you did."

"More like a pillar of mush right now." Maggie brought herself back under control. But she didn't try to stand.

"An understandable reaction to all you've been through." Mr. Spencer touched her shoulder, then he straightened. "I hate to add to your distress, but I need to ask a few questions."

She nodded. "Of course, but you heard the doctor. There's no way to tell what his chances are. All we can do is pray."

He shook his head. "You misunderstand. I want to ask about the circumstances surrounding your discovery of Will. Did you, for instance, see anyone else in the alley?"

"Why, no I—" Maggie's hand flew to her mouth. "Good heavens, of course. I've been so worried about his injuries, I never stopped to think how he got them. Someone *stabbed* him!"

She shuddered, searching Mr. Spencer's face for answers. "But why? Who would do such a thing?" She fought the urge to look over her shoulder, to demand he bolt the door.

Should they set a guard outside this room?

"As for why, I assume someone was after his purse," he answered grimly. "As for who, it could have been any one of a number of thieves who haunt the waterfront."

He gave her a bracing smile. "Now, other than what you already described for the doctor, is there anything else you can recall that might tell us what happened? Start with how you came to be in that alley, and exactly what you saw there."

Maggie's brow furrowed as she tried to remember. "My cat slipped his leash and I followed him into the alley. I found him sitting on a pile of rubble. When I got closer, I saw Will."

She shivered. "He was just crumpled there, laying in a

pool of blood." Would she ever forget the horror of that sight?

Her gaze met his. "I'm sorry, I just didn't pay attention to anything else after that."

"That's all right." He patted her hand. "Your quick actions have kept Will alive so far, and that's what counts." He straightened and moved toward the hall. "I think I'll take a look around anyway, just to satisfy myself."

He paused at the door. "I imagine the constable will be around soon, if he's not here already. He'll want to speak to you, but I'll try to head him off until tomorrow."

Maggie was touched by his concern. "That's very kind, but if the constable wants to speak to me, I'd as soon get it over with."

"Very well. But as soon as that's done, I'll have someone escort you and Ellen back to the house so you can get some rest."

Did he actually think she would leave Will's side? "Thank you, but I plan to stay just where I am. These next hours are critical, and I want to be close by if I should be needed."

She held up a hand at his protest. "There's no point arguing. Unless you intend to use force, I'm not leaving."

As if that settled matters, she firmly changed the subject. "Please have some broth prepared and brought in. If Mr. Trevaron regains consciousness, I'll try to get him to drink a bit."

She glanced down at her skirt, stained by the dirt of the alley and Will's blood. Fighting the queasy roil of her stomach, she tightened her jaw. "I would be most grateful if you could have someone fetch me a change of clothes."

"Of course." He stepped back into the room. "At least let me make you more comfortable. Sit yourself here, and let everything else be," he said pushing a padded armchair near the bed. "Your only job is to watch over Will. Understood?"

She nodded. He really was a very nice man.

"Is there anything else you need?"

Maggie had already turned her attention back to Will. "No, thank you, I'll be fine. But please, let whomever this room belongs to know we may need it for quite some time."

Mr. Spencer's lips quirked up in a smile. "Since the room is Will's, I don't think that will be a problem."

"You mean he lives *here*?" Maggie looked around the neat but small room. It was starkly furnished and contained few personal items. Why would a man of Will's means choose to live like this?

"He had a more comfortable set of rooms at our old office that he used when he stayed in town. After the fire he just set this up as a temporary replacement until he left for England."

Will's friend moved toward the door. "Oh, Ellen asked me to tell you not to worry about your cat. One of the clerks helped her capture him, and the animal is on its way back to our house."

Guiltily, Maggie realized she hadn't given Tully further thought since she'd made her horrific discovery in the alley. She made a silent apology to the cat, then promptly emptied her mind of everything but Will.

Reaching out, she gently clasped his hand between both of hers, as if she could transfer her strength to him by touch and sheer force of will. He *would* live.

The alternative was too awful to contemplate.

Maggie sat by Will's bedside all through that first night. By morning Ian gave up suggesting she return to his house to rest, and had a cot brought in.

She allowed the others to relieve her for short periods of time, but it was grudgingly done. More often than not, she made do with naps in the chair beside Will's bed.

This was familiar, yet so different from that first encounter six years ago. Though seriously injured then, he'd been conscious most of the time and not in any real danger of dying.

She hadn't even been responsible for his medical treatment, since he'd been under the care of a local physician. Her main task had been to make certain he got the rest he needed—no easy feat since he was one to be testing his limits.

She'd done her best to keep him entertained during his convalescence—read to him, played chess with him, and even made idle conversation when all else failed. At times it had been a test of wills, but she had managed to prevail, at least long enough for him to mend properly.

And between his sheer contrariness and her force of will, she planned for them to prevail again.

For three days Maggie struggled to keep Will alive. When his brow burned, she applied cool cloths. When he flailed, she made sure he didn't hurt himself. And at least once every hour she patiently worked, drop by drop, to get the fluids his body desperately needed past his parched lips.

She talked to him when they were alone, by turns coaxing him to fight and berating him for putting her through this. She knew he couldn't hear her, but she needed to say it out loud.

Keeping it bottled inside hurt too much.

Dr. Lawson tried to prepare her for the worst, but Maggie refused to give up. Only in her weakest moments did she admit that she might be motivated by something deeper than friendship. Being with Will, even when they sparred, ignited a spark in her, a sense of rightness she'd never experienced with anyone else.

The thought of never feeling that way again was unbearable.

# Chapter Eight

Will woke slowly, reluctantly.

Pain. Fiery pain. Each breath jabbed a hot poker in his chest.

*Hold still, don't move.*

He needed water. His mouth was parched, his throat burned.

Will pried his eyes open. The room spun sickeningly.

*Fight the nausea. Look for water. Focus.*

He turned and glass shards splintered in his head.

A raspy groan clawed its way from his throat.

A heartbeat—or was it an eternity?—later, someone lifted his head, brought a cup of blessedly cool water to his lips.

*More pain. Damn, even swallowing hurts.*

But he would endure it for the chance to indulge in that blessed liquid.

Three sips, then coughs wracked his body, painted his world red with pain.

A cool cloth wiped his brow, a soft crooning offered comfort.

Had an angel been sent to rescue him from this hell?

*Focus again. Look through the haze.*

Was that Maggie? Or was he dreaming of that other time?

She turned and suddenly it wasn't Maggie at all but Lilly, her bruised face accusing him yet again.

Not an angel, then. He'd been sentenced to hell.

Will closed his eyes. Better oblivion than this.

When Will opened his eyes, the room was in shadow. The only illumination came from a bedside lamp and the glow of embers in the grate. He still hurt like the devil, and his skin was clammy as a waterfront fog, but that mind-dulling haze was gone.

The memory of his earlier nightmare returned, and he warily shifted his gaze, not sure what he would see.

Relief washed over him, and a self-mocking amusement at his own foolish imaginings. The apparition his pain-clouded mind had conjured was gone now, leaving Maggie in its place.

Other memories returned in disjointed flashes. He'd been hurt. Stabbed. In the alley behind the building. Falling. Pain exploded in his head.

Then—nothing.

Had the bilge scum who attacked him been caught?

His head throbbed in protest, and he let the questions go.

Instead, he focused on Maggie. Watching her soothed him. She was reading by that dim lamplight, a frown of concentration creasing her brow.

As if sensing his gaze, she looked up. Her expression brightened, flooding her face with pleasure and concern.

"Welcome back," she whispered, laying the book aside.

Will had only a moment to appreciate the picture she made, to savor the warmth of her tone. Then her face turned more fully to the light, and he sucked in a strangled oath.

She was immediately at his side. "Easy. Don't try to

move. Dr. Lawson left drops to help lessen the pain."

"Your face." Will's voice was a painful rasp.

Her hand cupped over the ugly purple mark below her left eye.

What the devil had happened? Had she arrived before his attacker ran off? Had the same brute done this to her?

That bastard better pray Will never laid hands on him.

Maggie dropped her hand, and with a brisk *tsk*, turned to the bedside table. "Nothing for you to worry over— you've got your own healing to do." She measured liquid into a spoon. "Take this." She eased the spoon between his lips. "You need plenty of rest if you want out of that bed anytime soon."

Setting the spoon aside, Maggie poured a glass of water. "Drink this up and I promise to have some nice warm broth for you next time you open your eyes."

"I don't wa—"

As if she hadn't heard, Maggie sat on the edge of the bed and gently lifted his head.

Damn, he was weak as a day-old pup. He drank from the glass she held to his lips, but his gaze never left her bruised face.

Maggie, however, kept her gaze on his lips.

Why wouldn't she look him in the eyes?

"Tell me what happened," he demanded when he'd finished his drink. But it was hard to sound commanding when your voice came out as a whispered croak.

"We're not certain." She set the glass down, then stood and tucked the blanket back in place. "All we know is you were stabbed and robbed. But—"

"No." He winced at the jolt of pain brought on by his own movement. "Your face." Why did his tongue feel so thick?

"We'll discuss that later. You just rest now." Her words seemed to come through a tunnel.

"Blast it . . ." He paused, hearing the slur in his voice,

having trouble forming words. He shook his head to clear it. A mistake as fire knifed through his body.

What had she given him? He tried to command his eyes to remain open but they refused to obey. Maggie had won for now. But if she thought he would drop the subject, she was . . .

Once again, when Will roused, time had leapt forward. A slit in the curtains let in a cheery ray of sunlight.

The bedside chair was empty. Where was Maggie? He felt a momentary panic, as if something precious had been lost.

"Good morning."

He turned to find her on the other side of his bed, and his world righted itself again.

"You're looking better today," she said with a smile.

Did he? He felt like he'd been keelhauled, then hung from the yardarm for good measure. "How long have I been lying here?"

"A little over four days now. You gave us quite a scare."

"Four days! Devil's teeth!" He tried to sit up, but the throbbing in his shoulder caught fire, sucked his breath away.

"I'll thank you not to swear," Maggie said primly. She helped him settle back among the pillows. "And no sudden movements, please. You'll reopen the wound and bleed all over everything again. We've nearly run out of clean bed sheets."

"Your sympathy overwhelms me," Will grumbled. He wasn't accustomed to being in such a helpless position, and he didn't like it. It seemed the height of injustice that this was the second time in their short acquaintance she'd seen him this way.

Maggie moved the covers aside to check his bandages, and he became acutely aware that he was wearing nothing *but* the bandage from his waist up. Maggie, however, seemed unbothered by the prospect, a thought that only deepened his frown.

She made quick work of her inspection, then smoothed the covers. "I don't believe you've done any damage to yourself. But we'll see what the doctor has to say when he comes by." She stepped back. "Now, I'll get you a glass of water, then see about that broth I promised you."

Will bore the ignominy of having her help him drink the glass of water with what dignity he could muster, then flopped back on the pillows. Plague take it, he couldn't swat a fly in this condition. "Did they catch the bas—, er, bounder who did this?"

She shook her head. "No. It appears no one saw or heard anything. The authorities hope you can identify the villain."

"No." He grimaced in self-disgust. "I let him sneak up on me and never got a good look. I suppose he stole my purse?"

"Yes. I'm sorry." She moved to the window and spread open the curtain. When she turned to face him again, Will met her gaze head on. "What happened to your face?"

He realized from the startled flash in her eyes that he'd spoken more harshly than he'd intended. But he wanted to make sure he got a proper answer this time.

"A bit of clumsiness," she said, her tone carefully off-hand.

She was hiding something. "That's not an answer."

"Don't get all in a twitter. It's not as bad as it looks."

Will took exception to that. He'd never been in a twitter in his entire life.

"It's *your* health we must worry about." She plumped his pillow.

Distracted by having her bend over him, Will was struck by the intimacy of that gesture. As if she were already his wife.

Then he remembered their engagement was a sham,

one he'd all but forced on her. "Playing the devoted fiancée role with unexpected fervor, I see."

A moment of resounding silence echoed in the room as she froze in mid-movement.

Blast! Why had he said that? He wasn't in the habit of taking his frustration out on innocents. Will's mind scrambled for some way to recall the words, to smooth over his rudeness.

Too late. Her spine stiffened and her face shuttered. "I see by the return of your temper that we can expect a full recovery. As for my role in seeing after you, you only chose to awaken during my shift. Ian and Ellen have taken turns, as well."

If she'd intended to make him feel a churl, she'd succeeded. Why in the world had he ever thought her reserved? This woman could hold her own in any verbal battle.

She stepped away from the bedside. "If you'll excuse me, I'll see that someone brings your breakfast." Then she pointed a finger at him as if he were a recalcitrant schoolboy. "And if you try to so much as sit up on your own before then, you're a bigger fool than I would care to be associated with."

Before he could respond, she spun on her heel and stalked out, closing the door with exaggerated care. He got the distinct impression she'd exerted extreme effort not to slam it.

A few minutes later, Ian burst into the room. "Maggie gave me the good news, but I had to see for myself. Lord, Will, you gave us quite a scare. Of course, I should have known you were too obstinate to let a knife-wielding cutpurse do you in."

"I prefer determined to obstinate." Will grinned a welcome, then winced as he tried to sit up.

"No you don't," Ian ordered. "I gave Maggie my solemn vow not to let you move about. She'll have my head on a platter if you start bleeding again on my watch. And I also promised to keep this visit short so you can get your rest."

"Rest!" Will snorted. "It seems I've been doing nothing *but* resting for the last four days. Besides, I'll be the judge of what I can and can't handle."

Ian grinned, then turned serious. "So what happened? Did you get a look at the coward who stabbed you?"

"No more than a glimpse," Will said in disgust. "I'd just come from the Silver Sail and was headed for the back door to the office when I heard a pile of crates come crashing down. Someone cried out for help and I went over to investigate."

His frown deepened. "It was a ruse, and I walked right into it, just like an untried youth on his first visit to the city. I didn't even realize it until I felt the knife go in."

Ian's lips compressed in frustration. "And you didn't get so much as a peep at the man."

"Just a vague impression that he was tall and slim and smelled of cheap whiskey." Will shifted uneasily. "Ian, perhaps you ought to watch your back for the next few days."

His friend raised a brow in question.

"It's probably coincidence." Will almost felt foolish for his impulsive warning. "But I don't like that this followed so close on the heels of the fire. We should take precautions, just in case someone is trying to exact some sort of vengeance on us."

Then he remembered he had responsibility for another now. "In fact, it wouldn't hurt to do a little checking on the passengers and any new crew members of the *Lady Jen*."

Ian nodded grimly, but before he could say anything, they were interrupted by a knock at the door. A servant entered with a tray. "Mrs. Carter said I was to feed you, sir."

Will took a close look at what she carried. "Broth! Bah,

take it away and bring me something more substantial."

"Oh, no sir, I couldn't do that. Mrs. Carter said all you was to have today was broth." Then she smiled brightly. "But you can have as much as you want, and tomorrow it'll be gruel."

He'd be hanged if he'd be treated like a milksop. "Blast it, I don't care what Mrs. Carter says, I want real food."

"Mrs. Carter's only thinking what's best for you, sir." She cast a pleading glance Ian's way.

Will wasn't accustomed to having servants argue with him. "Since when is Mrs. Carter an expert on what's best for me?"

He spied Ian's expression and turned his glare in that direction. "I'll thank you to wipe that grin off your face."

Ian's grin only broadened as he took the tray from the flustered servant. "Here, let me have that. I solemnly promise to see that he eats every bit."

Then, as Dorrie fled, he turned back to Will. "You may as well drink this. If Maggie says broth is all you'll get today, you can rest assured that that's all you'll get."

He set the tray on the bedside table. "That's some lady you have there, by the way. You might have finally met your match."

"Seems like you two got to know each other rather well." Hearing that peevish tone in his own voice further soured Will's humor. It goaded him that Ian and Maggie had gotten on a first-name basis with each other, an intimacy he had yet to reach.

"Not jealous, are you?" Ian was definitely amused now.

Surely it *wasn't* jealousy spurring his irritation? No, it was only the impropriety of Ian's familiar form of address.

"Don't worry," Ian assured him with a grin. "Maggie is absolutely devoted to you."

"Devoted to what our alliance can do for her, more likely."

Ian frowned. "You didn't use that tone with her I hope?"

Whose side was Ian on, anyway? "I thought you were against this marriage?"

"Now that I've met Maggie, I've changed my mind." Ian paused, raising an eyebrow. "In fact, seeing as she's responsible for saving your life, you ungrateful wretch, I'm starting to believe *you're* not good enough for *her*."

What the devil did he mean by that? "Saved my life?" *Again?*

"Didn't Maggie tell you?" Ian grimaced. "No, of course she wouldn't." He pointed the spoon at Will. "She's the one who found you lying in a pool of your own blood amid that rubble."

Will suddenly felt lower than a snake. "What was she doing in the alley? That's no place for a lady." If she'd arrived a little earlier, she might have been attacked herself. At that thought, a cold shiver slithered up his spine.

It also reminded him of the bruise on her face. "What—

"She was looking for her cat." Ian answered Will's earlier question, stepping over his next. "She took complete charge of the situation. Before you could say 'Jack be nimble,' she had you moved in here, stripped down, and ready for the doctor."

He snapped open the napkin with a grin. "She then proceeded to bandage you up, stitch that gash on your head and check you, head to toe, for other injuries."

Will groaned, realizing just how churlish his earlier behavior had been. As Ian's last words soaked in, he gave his friend a sharp look.

Ian's wicked grin confirmed his worst fears. "That's right. Your body now holds few secrets for your future wife."

Blast, this got more humbling by the minute! "Where the devil was the doctor while all this was going on?"

"Across town with another patient. When Dr. Lawson saw what Maggie had done, he gave it as his opinion that if she hadn't acted so quickly and done everything exactly as she did, you'd have been dead in less than an hour."

Ian was serious, Maggie had actually saved his life. Again. "This is becoming a habit with her."

Will hadn't realized he'd said the words aloud until he saw Ian's startled frown.

"What do you mean?"

"I never told you about the first time I met Maggie, did I?"

"No, but now that you've brought it up, and with such an intriguing preface, I'm not leaving the room until you do."

Will grinned. "It's not a particularly flattering story. It happened shortly after I arrived here and took over Wind Dancer. Do you recall the business trip I took to Calfair, trying to encourage Tipperman to do business with us?"

Ian nodded, slipping another spoonful of broth into Will's mouth. "Isn't that the trip where you took ill and came back some weeks later with your arm in a sling?"

"That's the one. But there was a bit more to it than that."

"I wondered at the time." Ian grinned. "But you know me, never one to pry."

Will snorted, but let that pass. "I felt something was wrong when I left Tipperman's, but I shrugged it off as having gotten hold of a bit of bad meat."

"It was more than that, I take it," Ian prompted.

"Yes. I became lightheaded and at some point realized I'd developed a fever. Then my horse shied—not sure at what. But in my condition it didn't take much to unseat me."

"That's how you broke your arm."

Will nodded. "I blacked out. When I came to, my arm was on fire and either the fever or the fall had me seeing double." He paused for another spoonful. "I'm not sure how long I lay there until another rider came along. I thought I was saved."

Ian raised a brow. "But you weren't?"

"The man was a thief, a scavenger come to pick the bones clean." He shook his head in disgust. "He took my money, my horse, my pistol, my hat—even my boots. And I couldn't do a bloody thing to stop him."

Ian made a sympathetic noise. "So, where does Maggie come into your story?"

"After the bottom-feeder left, a carriage came by, but didn't stop. I think I might have passed out again. The sound of a second carriage roused me. I pulled myself up to get the driver's attention. And it worked. But someone inside told the driver to move on, that my trouble was none of her affair."

Ian frowned. "Surely that wasn't Maggie?"

"Oh, no. Another voice protested that they couldn't possibly leave me lying there without doing something to help."

"Ah—*that* was Maggie."

"Exactly. I later discovered she was the other woman's paid companion. While the harpy ordered the driver to move on, Maggie came to my aid." He smiled, remembering how she'd ignored the grime and his disreputable appearance to kneel at his side.

"What happened next?" Ian prompted.

"The carriage drove off, but not before Maggie solicited a promise from the driver to send someone back. She stayed with me until help arrived, sat in the back of the buckboard with me all the way to the doctor's house, then helped nurse me until I was back on my feet."

He gave Ian a direct look. "She was only seventeen at the time, and did that for a stranger, knowing full well that her defiance would cost her her only means of support."

Ian gave a low whistle. "And you waited until now to marry this woman."

Will smiled. "You forget, for most of the past three years she's been married to another man."

"Even so, I think fate is trying to tell you something, and in a not-too-subtle fashion."

"More of your superstitions?"

Ian only shrugged. "Call it what you like." Then he smiled. "I hope you were an easier patient the last time around."

"Can't imagine being of much trouble to anyone in the shape I'm in," Will grumbled. He *hated* this weakness, this inability to even so much as feed himself.

Ian sobered. "That fever spun you in and out of delirium, gave you a madman's strength at times. When that happened, you were difficult to handle, even for the indomitable Maggie."

Will's stomach lurched with a sudden thought. "That bruise on Maggie's cheek—how did she get it?"

Ian shifted uncomfortably. "I don't—"

"I want a direct answer."

After a moment of strained silence, Ian nodded. "Very well. During one of your more vigorous deliriums, Maggie attempted to restrain you." He sent Will a sympathetic glance. "I walked in just in time to see you knock her to the floor."

The ground shifted under Will as he bit off an oath.

He'd hit her!

No wonder she evaded his questions.

Ian set the bowl aside. "Good grief man, you were delirious. No one holds you accountable, least of all Maggie."

Will barely heard Ian's words. He felt turned to stone. How could he have done such a thing? He'd promised her she'd never suffer physical harm at his hands.

He'd broken his word.

This time, he was guilty.

# Chapter Nine

Will flinched as Maggie chose that moment to return.

The bruise on her cheek glared accusingly, convicting him of his vile action. To repay her kindness with such treatment was worse than reprehensible. It was unforgivable. It was brutish.

It was all his grandfather thought him to be.

"Mr. Trevaron," she said with a frown, "you appear to have overextended yourself already."

Will, still reeling from the knowledge that he'd hurt her, made no rebuttal.

Her gaze sharpened as she moved closer, lines of worry etching her forehead. "You mustn't try to do too much too soon."

Without waiting for his response, she turned to Ian. "If you have a moment, I'd like a word with you, please."

"I believe that's my cue to leave." Ian touched Will's shoulder briefly. "It's good to have you back."

Will ignored Ian, focusing on Maggie with clenched-jaw intensity. How could he right the wrong he'd done her? "Mrs. Carter, we need to speak."

She paused. "Of course, but first—"

"Now." She stiffened and he moderated his tone. "Please."

She seemed primed to refuse. Finally, she gave a short nod.

As the door closed behind Ian, Maggie moved stiffly to stand beside the bed. "Is there something I can help you with?"

Will silently cursed his inability to sit upright. Why had he been so churlish earlier? He hated that wary look in her eye.

"Ian explained how you acquired that bruise." The words were ballast weights pressing on his chest. "I gave my word to never do you injury, and I've broken it. Therefore, I release you from our bargain. Of course, Clover Ridge is yours regardless."

Her lips thinned primly. "Ian shouldn't have said anything. I got in the way of a delirious patient, nothing more."

He detected no hint of hesitation. Relief surged through him. "Nevertheless, I gave my word. If you wish to part company with me, I won't stand in your way."

Her expression softened. "Mr. Trevaron, I appreciate your sense of fair play." Her chin raised. "However, please credit me with the same integrity. You have not broken any promise. For me to leave would be the same as reneging on our agreement."

A woman who understood nuances of honor and intent? "Very well. We'll proceed as planned. But I no longer consider you bound by our agreement. You may change your mind at any time between now and the wedding without fear of argument from me."

She shook her head. "You are a stubborn man, but we'll leave it at that for the time being. Now, get some rest."

He watched her leave, a smile tugging at his lips. She'd had the gall to call *him* stubborn. It was a bloody good thing she hadn't taken him up on his offer—he was beginning to feel life without Maggie would be much too bland.

Maggie stepped into the hallway and leaned against his door.

Did Will truly think he'd broken his word because of something he'd done in a fever-induced delirium? Or was he having second thoughts about marrying her?

Whatever his reasons, Maggie was determined to see this through. Her future and that of the children depended on it.

She pushed aside her disquiet and searched out Ian. He was in his office, as promised. "There's a matter I need your guidance on," she said, taking a seat. "The *Lady Jen* is to set sail tomorrow, but Will still needs several days of rest before he can even attempt to travel."

Ian smiled. "Since the *Lady Jen* is a Wind Dancer ship, arranging for a delay shouldn't be a problem. How soon do you think he'll be ready to travel?"

"I imagine it'll be at least three days."

"I'll speak to the captain and have him inform the other passengers. Don't worry yourself any more over this matter."

"There is one other thing." Maggie leaned forward. "I've never been aboard a ship before. I'd like to take a look at our accommodations so I'll know what to expect."

"Of course. I'll escort you myself."

She felt a thrill of anticipation at the idea of visiting the ship. "I'd like to wait until Dr. Lawson has had a chance to examine Will, but after that, the sooner the better."

"Then we'll plan to go this afternoon." He raised an eyebrow in challenge. "That is, if you'll agree to accompany me back to the house where you can freshen up and rest properly first."

Maggie smiled. She'd gotten to know both of the Spencers as they'd shared the vigil at Will's bedside. The friendship they had forged was now quite precious to her.

"Thank you. I'd be most pleased to accept that offer." The thought of soaking in a tub of hot water was quite seductive. She'd made due with a rag and basin for the past few days.

But first she had to make sure the right person was set to watch Will in her absence. It would need to be someone who wouldn't cower or give in when he tried bullying his way into doing more than was good for him.

And she knew just the person.

Will shifted irritably, staring at the door as if he could will Maggie to walk through it. The sun was nearly set and he hadn't seen her since this morning.

Instead he'd spent most of the day under the watchful eye of Ellen Spencer. For a small woman with a sweet disposition, she was quite adept at getting her way. Somehow, he'd ended up swallowing mugfulls of the detested broth, staying flat on his back when he wanted to sit up, and generally being mollycoddled.

It wasn't that she was forceful—just the opposite. Any time he tried to go against some inane request, she assumed that childlike, wounded kitten look that made him feel like a cad.

Will had drifted off to sleep thinking how much he'd prefer to face a wildcat like Maggie any day.

He'd awakened to find himself blessedly alone. For the last ten minutes, he'd mulled over some of Mrs. Spencer's seemingly random chatter. It seemed his future bride had stayed by his side almost constantly the entire time he'd been unconscious.

So why had she tried to make him believe differently?

A light tap at the door interrupted his musings. At his "Come in," the object of his thoughts entered the room.

He sat up straighter. "There you are. I was beginning to feel you were deliberately avoiding me." Then he took a second look. Rather than the drab, nondescript dresses she usually wore, she had on a light green gown that fit her most becomingly.

As she crossed the room, he took in her trim waist and the smooth expanse of skin exposed at her neckline. Strange, he'd never noticed how creamy, how *touchable*, her skin was.

Oh, yes, a most becoming frock indeed.

"Not at all," she said, answering the question he'd almost forgotten he'd asked. "I was running a few errands. Ellen tells me you've had a good day."

Before he could form a response, she placed a hand on his forehead, studying his face with those luminous green eyes of hers. Her touch warmed and comforted and felt oh so right.

"Splendid. There's no sign of a fever and your color's good." The smile she gave him was dazzling. It made him feel that merely by recuperating he'd given her a gift. "We should be able to let you move about for short periods in just a few days."

Will dragged his thoughts back to the conversation. He had fences to mend and needed his wits about him to do it properly.

"Thanks to the fine care I've been receiving." He intended to be fit enough for more than sitting in a chair by then, but he didn't want to get diverted into an argument with her right now. "Please, have a seat. I'd like to talk with you for a bit."

Tension dimmed her smile as she sat and smoothed her skirt. Will mentally grimaced, realizing she expected him to give her an additional dressing down.

He gentled his voice. "I wish to apologize for not showing proper gratitude this morning. It seems I'm in your debt. Ian, the doctor, and most especially Mrs. Spencer, have all gone to great lengths to explain how you saved my life."

"Nonsense." She relaxed and flashed a teasing grin. "In fact, if you want to give proper credit, you must look to Tully."

Will had been momentarily distracted by the reappearance of her dimple, but her outrageous statement reclaimed his attention. "The cat? You can't be serious."

"Oh, but I am." Her earnest expression was belied by the amused gleam in her eyes. "Tully led me straight to you. If he hadn't, you wouldn't have been found until it was too late."

Will dismissed the cat with a wave. "Be that as it may, I understand it was your expertise and quick thinking that actually saved my life. Again. For that I wish to thank you."

Not giving her time to respond, he turned the subject. "So, how did you spend your day?"

"Ian took me on a tour of the *Lady Jen*. I've never been aboard a ship before."

Jealousy knifed through Will. *He* wanted to be the one to share her firsts. "And what did you think of her?"

"She's a beauty." Maggie paused a moment, worrying at her lower lip, reaching for her broach.

A tell-tale signal something was bothering her.

"However," she said, "I requested a change to our accommodations."

"What kind of change?" The guilty look on her face did nothing to ease his wariness.

"I requested a door be set into the wall between our cabins."

"You did *what*?" She'd had the cheek to request structural changes to his new ship? "And what did the captain say to this?"

"He was a tad hesitant at first, but once Ian helped me convince him that you would have no objections, he agreed."

So, she'd managed to wrap the captain around her finger just as neatly as she had Ian. It's a good thing he, at least, was immune to her wiles.

And now that he'd recovered from his outrage at her

audacity, Will saw some interesting advantages to having private access between their cabins.

No point letting her believe she could get away with taking such liberties all the time, though. "And what made you think I would have no objections?"

"Now, Mr. Trevaron, you—"

But he halted her with a single word. "Will."

She blinked. "I beg your pardon?"

"Call me Will. We are, after all, soon to be married." He held up a warning hand. "Don't tell me it wouldn't be proper, not when you and the Spencers have already dispensed with such formalities." He still smarted over the fact that Ian had achieved that intimacy first.

"Very well, but shouldn't I call you William?"

Will frowned. "Now where did you pick up on that?"

"It was on the deed to Clover Ridge—William Anthony Trevaron. I think it is a wonderful name."

Will raised a skeptical eyebrow. "And I suppose Maggie is your full given name? Not short for something else, perhaps?"

She had the grace to blush. "Actually, it's Margaret."

"Margaret," he repeated thoughtfully. "I like it."

Catching the teasing glint in his eye, she smiled back. "Maggie suits me much better."

"I think Margaret suits you quite well. It sounds strong and dignified, while also carrying a hint of feminine softness."

She gave a flustered laugh, a sound that teased a smile to Will's own lips. Were they actually flirting?

"Such eloquence. I do believe there's the soul of a poet lurking somewhere inside you, William." She drawled his name, her eyes sparkling with humor and her elusive dimple coyly accenting her smile.

Will, appreciating the picture she made, decided he didn't care what she called him, so long as she looked at him that way. "The new dress looks quite fetching on you," he said impulsively, hoping to keep that smile on her face a bit longer.

"Since you bought and paid for it, I'm glad you approve."

*Uh-oh.* That wasn't the direction he'd intended to take this conversation. Her chin had that militant tilt to it again.

Then her expression softened. "But thank you, for both the compliment and the gown. It's been a while since I've had anything so lovely to wear."

"My pleasure," he said, meaning every syllable of it. "This mode suits you much better than your normal attire."

Will groaned inwardly, realizing how that had sounded. It must be the loss of blood still affecting him. He normally wasn't so clumsy with words. "Maggie, I—"

"Don't apologize." Her tone was serious, but to his relief, he spied a twitch to her lips. "I spent a great deal of time cultivating the appearance of someone with—how did you put that?—oh yes, 'all the fashion sense of a charwoman.' I can't very well complain that you found it convincing."

Will winced. The words sounded so much ruder when parroted back to him. "Why would you intentionally make yourself—"

"Unattractive?" she finished sweetly, and he winced again.

She shrugged. "When one goes into service, beauty is not necessarily a desirable quality. In fact, the less remarkable one is, the better it is all the way around."

A shadow crossed her face as she touched the broach. "It is considered an asset to be able to fade into the background and still carry out your given duties."

Will didn't like to think what that must have been like for the independent-minded Maggie. "Surely, once you married . . ."

She smiled as if he were a naïve child. "I started out

helping care for him after the accident that left him crippled and widowed. It was only later that he proposed marriage. He spent most of his time mourning his first wife. I didn't think it appropriate to wear bright clothes."

Did she have any idea how poignant a picture her words painted? But she didn't seem to want sympathy. Instead, she stood with a brisk, let's-talk-about-something-else smile. "Dr. Lawson asked me to change your bandage every day and to check for signs of infection."

"Of course." He remembered his earlier feeling when she'd placed her hand on his forehead. Thinking of those same hands ministering to him more intimately stirred a sense of eager anticipation. He struggled to sit up, not wanting to appear completely helpless.

She was at his side immediately, easing him up and propping pillows behind him. "If you'll raise your arms slightly, I'll get this bandage off and we'll have a look."

As her fingers brushed his flesh, Will decided that perhaps there was something to be said for appearing helpless after all.

In fact, from this vantage, he found much to recommend his sitting back and admiring the view, as well as enjoying the touch of her hands on his skin.

Remaining passive, however, just might be the death of him.

Maggie found changing Will's bandage, now that he was conscious, both easier and more difficult than before. Easier, of course, because he could hold himself upright and she didn't have to do any awkward maneuvering of his limp form.

More difficult because she was now acutely aware of his presence as a vital male, not just as a patient. His broad, well-muscled chest, bared before her, seemed to epitomize masculine virility, vibrant with heat and life. Her fingertips tingled where they met his flesh.

As she bent to her work, his warm breath whispered against her cheek, startlingly intimate.

Maggie reached around him to pass the bandage behind his back, very nearly embracing him. She tried to ignore the tingle of awareness that intimate contact evoked.

Then his breath caught in a sharp hiss.

Had she hurt him? Maggie looked up—and was caught by the fire in his gaze. Neither moved, not even to breathe. Their faces were inches apart, her hands still wrapped around him.

Tearing her gaze away from the disquieting effect of his silver sorcerer's eyes, her eyes were drawn to the sight of his mouth. *What it would be like to kiss those lips?*

Mesmerized, she leaned closer, her own lips parted. She shivered as she felt him gently stroke her arms.

Then he gripped her upper arms as if to draw her closer and the world turned upside down. The sensual warmth evaporated, leaving in its place a bubble of panic that rose in her throat, threatening to choke her.

"Let me go!" She jerked away, taking a hasty step back.

He released her at once. As the fog of past demons cleared, she saw confusion and a wounded look in his eyes. A second later that emotion was replaced by something cold and hard.

Heaven help her, what had she done? What must he think of her? How could she explain?

Maggie tried to still her racing pulse, to overcome her shaken embarrassment. "Mr. Trevaron . . . Will . . . I mean . . . I don't . . . that is, I'm not sure what came over me."

Realizing she was babbling, Maggie took herself firmly in hand. Words wouldn't fix this. She had to finish her work and exit as quickly and gracefully as possible. "Please excuse me and I'll have you out of this bandage in just a second."

"Of course."

Winnie Griggs

His flint-like tone did little to restore her composure. With cheeks that were uncomfortably warm, Maggie again bent to her task. This time her movements were brisk, impersonal, and she carefully avoided any unnecessary contact with his bare skin.

Inside the stone prison that was her face, her eyes ached with unshed tears for that cherished closeness she'd just lost.

Will fought to keep his expression shuttered during the agonizingly long minutes it took her to finish her ministrations. He wanted to send her away, to be alone with his thoughts.

But that would be cowardly and ungrateful.

The intimacy of her accidental embrace had ambushed his senses, sending a flash of liquid fire surging through him that had been as intense as it had been unexpected. When she'd leaned toward him, her gaze filled with awakening passion, he'd been only too ready to answer her unspoken request.

The touch of his hands, however, had broken the spell. The tactile reminder of his deformity had been enough to cool her ardor. Devil's teeth, had that been revulsion in her eyes?

Fool! Would he never learn the lesson Lilly had done her malevolent best to teach him? His touch was not one a woman would ever welcome.

"Let's have a look at that wound," she said as she removed the bandage. She examined him with an air of detached politeness. As soon as she was done, she didn't so much exit as flee, promising to have his supper brought in soon.

Will stared at the door long after it closed behind her. So, Maggie felt friendship for him, and perhaps something warmer. But she obviously did not relish anything of an intimate nature.

128

Well, a businesslike arrangement was what he'd promised her, and it looked like he'd have to live with exactly that.

But what of their agreement that she would provide him an heir? Would she feel differently after the six month "settling in period?"

Because, no matter how "brave" she tried to be, he could never bed a woman who was repulsed by his mere touch.

The rest of the day passed with the same teeth-grinding slowness. Maggie didn't return—instead Dorrie brought his supper in. He thought perhaps his bride-to-be would step in before retiring for the night, but he drifted off without so much as a glimpse of her.

Later, Will roused from a fitful sleep. His wound ached as if branded with hellfire. Not that he minded. He preferred the ache to the dreams he'd been having tonight. That look on Maggie's face as she'd jerked away from him this afternoon was carved into his mind so deeply it had followed him into slumber.

A storm rumbled outside his window, a fit companion for his gloomy thoughts.

A moment later he realized he wasn't alone.

# Chapter Ten

His senses sharpened and his pulse quickened as he prepared to face another attack. He might be down but, by Jove, he wasn't completely helpless.

The shadowy figure was brought into sharp relief by a lightning-streaked backdrop.

*Maggie!*

What the deuce was she doing in his room this time of night?

"I'm sorry if I woke you." The apology was uttered in a near-whisper.

She stood looking out the window with her back to him. How did she even know he'd wakened?

"I couldn't sleep and thought I'd check in on you." A long thick braid hung down her back, catching bits of light from his bedside lamp. It enchanted him with its sinuous shape and its unruly strands that mocked her attempt to confine them. It was the kind of hair that tempted a man to loosen it, to watch it fall free around her shoulders, to see her dressed in it, and nothing more.

He struggled to get his thoughts back under control as she turned to face him. But he needn't have worried, her attention was still focused on the weather outside rather than on him.

She rubbed her arms as if to ward off a chill. "The storm seems to be dying down now, don't you think?"

He murmured an agreement, alerted by something in her tone. Why did she seem so uneasy, so tense? Was it the storm, or what had passed between them this afternoon?

She finally turned toward him. "Is there anything you need before I let you get back to sleep?"

*Nothing that you're willing to provide.*

Will chided himself for that stray thought. A certain resonance in her voice, the stiff way she held herself, all added to his sense that something was wrong. He needed to focus on *that*, not his own base urges. "Don't go just yet."

She'd paused at his words, but in the shadowy darkness of the room he couldn't see her expression. "Don't be foolish." Her I'm-the-doctor tone was back in place. "You need your rest."

Even through her firm protest, he detected a remoteness, as if she gathered her inner resources tightly to herself.

"I'm not tired," he coaxed. "And since you woke me, you owe me the distraction of your company."

She hesitated. At last her sympathy won out over her reluctance, as he'd known it would.

"Very well, but just for a little while." She turned up the wick on the lamp and settled in a nearby chair.

"Shouldn't you be at Ian's house?" Will asked. Then he frowned. "Surely, he didn't leave you out here alone."

She shook her head. "Of course not. Jack has been spending the night in the front office since your injury, and Dorrie is keeping me company in the next room." She gave him a hint of that teasing smile he'd grown so fond of. "So you need have no worries for your reputation."

Were they to be friends again, then? Pretend this afternoon had never happened?

She shifted as lightning flickered in the distance. Why was she still so tense, so distracted? Whatever it was, it seemed to be related to the storm.

Before he could comment, a booming crash rattled the windows and a flash of lightning illuminated the room.

Maggie's reaction, though soundless, was nonetheless disturbing. She shuddered violently. Her eyes squeezed shut as her whole face tightened, and she gripped the arms of the chair with knuckle-whitening ferocity.

Ignoring the pain in his shoulder, Will reached out a hand, his whole one, closing it over hers. "Are you all right?" He wanted to *make* it all right for her, to slay whatever dragons had invaded her enchanted garden.

Her eyes flew open. The vulnerability mirrored there was gone in a flash. "Forgive my theatrics." She gave a self-deprecating smile "Night storms have an unfortunate affect on me. I'm something of a coward where they're concerned."

"There's nothing to forgive, and those weren't theatrics." There was more awry here than fear of storms. "You're a lot of things Maggie, but a coward isn't one of them. What's wrong?"

Detaching her hand from his, she moved to the grate. Keeping her face averted, she stirred the coals with a poker. A tremor fluttered her shoulders. "If I fall asleep during a thunderstorm I inevitably get nightmares."

She straightened and came back to his bedside. "You're wrong about me not being a coward." Her face tightened in a brittle smile. "Rather than face the bad dreams, I keep myself awake, roaming the halls or reading a book. Anything to hold the monster at bay." A muscle in her jaw tensed and she reached for her broach. "For all the good that does."

Those last words were whispered with such bitterness, Will reached for her hand again. "There's nothing cowardly in that. It's sound strategy for dealing with a powerful enemy."

She relaxed and finally focused fully on him. Her lips turned up in amusement. "You make it sound like I'm waging war."

That was better. She had her color back and the bruised look was gone from her eyes. "In a way, you are," he agreed. "Sit down again, and I'll see that you don't wage it alone tonight."

Her expression softened into gratitude. "Thank you. But I'll be fine now, and I insist that you get some rest."

He wasn't ready to let her go yet. "That's a rather unusual broach. I notice you seldom go without it."

Some strong emotion flitted across her face, there and gone before he could decipher it.

"It belonged to my father. He used it as a watch fob."

There must be more to it. "So it's not a family heirloom? There's no special story surrounding it?"

Maggie's lips twitched into an amused smile. "Disappointed? Were you looking for a bedtime story?" She settled back in the chair. "Very well. There is, in fact, a legend surrounding this broach, one with all the elements of a fairy tale."

She unclasped the ornament, cradling it in her palm. "This piece of jewelry has been handed down to the women in my mother's family, in an unbroken chain, for hundreds of years. Each mother gave it to her oldest daughter when the girl reached womanhood."

"But you said it belonged to your father."

She waggled a finger at him. "Be patient and all will be explained. First, we must travel several centuries back."

Will leaned against his pillows, pleased with himself. Not only had he managed to distract Maggie from her demons, but he also had succeeded in keeping her with him a bit longer.

And listening to her tell a story was a treat he remembered well from that time six years ago.

"The story goes," she continued, "that the first of my ancestors to possess this was the wife of a knight who fought in one of the Crusades. She was deeply in love with him and couldn't bear the thought of a long separation. So she begged him to take her with him, pleading with such heart-rending emotion that he finally agreed. But her husband did not love her with the same intensity, and while they were in that far-off land, he betrayed her by consorting with an exotic beauty."

Will found himself caught up in the cadence of her voice, the evocative expressiveness of her face and hands. She could weave word-spells as well as the most talented of ancient minstrels.

Maggie's sigh was bittersweet. "Heartbroken, she sought the aid of a sorceress. The young wife didn't wish for retribution, mind you. She still cared deeply for her husband. She only wanted the pain to go away."

Maggie lifted the broach. "It was this wisewoman, this reputed sorceress, who gave her the amulet." She handed it to Will. "If you look closely, you'll see a small insect trapped inside, perfectly preserved in every way."

Will held it up so that the light from the lamp shone through. Sure enough, what he'd taken for a flaw was a tiny, ant-like creature.

"This wisewoman told my ancestor that a female has very little to truly call her own—all her worldly possessions are in truth the property of her father or husband. What she *does* have complete mastery over, however, are her heart and her spirit—those two things only. If she wishes to protect herself from hurt, she must guard those well. Never should she entrust them entirely to another's care, no matter how tempting the desire."

Maggie spread her hands. "My ancestor, of course, asked how that could be possible. After all, one cannot dictate to the heart. But the woman told her that the broach had great powers, powers fueled by a woman's will."

Maggie leaned forward and to his eyes seemed to take on the personality of that sorceress.

"If her will was strong enough, as long as she wore the broach, the essence of her heart and spirit would be sealed inside along with the tiny guardian, and no one could touch that part of her, no matter what else he might take from her."

Maggie leaned back. "From that day forward, the crusader's wife was never without the broach. Discovering she was with child, she traveled back to her homeland, and took care of her husband's estates and raised his daughter while he continued to fight his holy wars. It is said that she was beloved by her people and well respected for her wisdom and justice."

Maggie held out her hand and Will returned the broach. "When her daughter reached womanhood, the mother passed the amulet to her, along with its secret. She had the girl vow never to reveal the story to any but her own daughter, and only when the time was right to pass it on."

She fastened the broach back onto her collar. "And so it passed from mother to daughter, and each generation kept the secret and drew strength from it."

"Until your mother," he prompted.

Her lips curved in a tender smile. "Yes, until my mother." Her finger traced circles over the face of the amber jewel. "Mother had an unhappy life before she met my father. She fell deeply in love with him and he, unlike the crusader, returned her love in equal strength. In fact, he gave up all he had—his family, his home, his friends— in order to marry her."

Maggie's hands fell to her lap. "After they wed, mother broke with tradition and told him the legend. She then presented the broach to him as a wedding gift, telling him she no longer needed it—that *he* would guard her heart and her spirit."

Maggie's eyes lost that faraway look as she met his gaze. "So you see, just like a true fairy tale, it has a happy ending."

Will studied her face. "And do *you* believe this broach has some sort of mystical power?"

She laughed and waved a hand. "No doubt it served a purpose, helped the girls feel a sense of control over their fates that they might not otherwise have had. Other than that, it's a wonderfully rich, inventive legend—nothing more."

Yet she never seemed to be without it.

Maggie *tsk*ed. "Listen to me, nattering on when you need to rest." She twitched his bedcovers. "Off to sleep with you, now."

He watched her close his door behind her with quiet dignity.

She'd told him to sleep. How the deuce was he supposed to do that when he couldn't forget the sight of her heart-aching vulnerability?

He finally understood her attachment to that blasted broach. It wasn't because it had belonged to her father, though that was probably what she told herself. Some part of her had latched on to the legend. For some reason she wanted that distance, that protection from hurt, the talisman symbolized.

What or who had done this to her?

He mulled over the telling bit of information she'd revealed about herself. How many more secrets was she holding onto?

And what would it take for her to hand that amulet over to him as her mother had to her father?

Maggie slipped another pin into her hair, firmly anchoring the chignon at her nape. It had been three days since Will's fever broke, and he'd made remarkable progress. He was still mostly bedridden, much to his very vocal frustration. But he was already issuing orders from his bed as if it were his office.

Yesterday Dr. Lawson had allowed him to get up and walk across the room, with assistance from Ian. Will, of course, had stretched that walk to include a short foray into the outside hall. By the time he was back in bed, he had lines of pain etched in a too-white face, but had said only that he was ready to have another go at it after a short rest.

Maggie feared they would have trouble keeping him down now.

And today he would marry her.

She winced as she jabbed the next pin in a bit harder than she'd intended.

Were they really going to go through with this? Would it change their relationship?

Silly—of course it would. How could it not?

But in what manner?

They no longer shared that warmth, that connection they'd shared before that unfortunate near-embrace. After she'd intruded on him the night of the storm they'd been carefully pleasant to each other, but that wasn't the same thing.

Not at *all* the same thing.

She would be a candidate for Bedlam if she had to go through the entire voyage cooped up in those two small cabins with this wall of cool politeness between them.

And it was all her fault. Which meant it was up to her to make it right.

She gave her hair one final pat and studied her reflection, pleased with the way the looser hairstyle softened her face. She'd never be considered beautiful, but at least Will would have no reason to apologize for her appearance today.

Maggie stood and smoothed her skirts. With the exception of the extravagant ball gown Madame LeBlanc had insisted she must have, this was the most elegant of her new dresses. The soft pongee fabric was a deep shade of rose with lighter accents at the hem and neckline. Delicately figured posies adorned the bodice, and the froth of lace on the sleeves was the finest Maggie had ever seen. She felt like a princess ready for the ball.

She glanced at the clock and grimaced. All this primping had taken more time than expected. It wouldn't do to be late on this, of all days.

Snatching up her gloves, she took one last look in the mirror as she tugged them on, then headed for the door.

But as she reached for the knob, she halted and spun on her heel. Will's wedding gift!

Before she had taken two steps, though, a knock had her turning back to the door.

*Who could that be?*

The Spencers had both gone down to the Wind Dancer offices earlier. Ian to handle a bit of business, and Ellen to keep an eye on Will so Maggie could take a nap and bath without worrying.

She opened the door to find Mrs. Hudgins, the housekeeper, standing in the hallway. "Pardon me, ma'am, but there's a gentleman here to see you. Says his name is Mr. Henry Carter."

*Henry? What would—*

Maggie's hand flew to her throat. *The children! Oh, please, God—don't let it be bad news.*

"Where is he?"

"He's waiting in the front parlor."

Barely waiting for the housekeeper's answer, Maggie lifted her skirts and raced down the stairs.

"Henry!" She charged into the parlor, too worried to stand on ceremony. "What is it? Are the children all right?"

Joseph's half-brother didn't answer right away. Instead

he stood with hands clasped behind his back and stared at her disapprovingly. "Your husband is buried less than three months and already you have shed your widow's weeds."

Maggie stopped short at this verbal slap in the face. Her nails bit into her palms, but she refused to make herself accountable to a man who had not taken time to attend his brother's funeral because of "pressing business matters."

"How I choose to mourn Joseph's passing is not your affair. Now, I ask again, how are the children?"

Henry's lips thinned at her tone. "The children are in good health, if that is your concern."

It was all Maggie could do to keep her knees from buckling as relief washed over her.

"As for their behavior, they are turning my household inside out. Did you teach them nothing about discipline?"

Maggie's hackles rose, but she kept a tight rein on her temper. After all, her darlings would be in Henry's charge for several months yet. "They are lively and spirited, yes," she temporized, "but they are also considerate and well-behaved."

"Well-behaved—bah! Elizabeth whines constantly about missing you and her father, Owen is a young hooligan, and Calvin is forever telling me how much he dislikes city life."

*Take a deep breath. He is providing a roof over their heads and sustenance for their bodies.* "Surely you can understand that it will take them time to adjust to their new surroundings. After all, they've lost so much in such a short period of time."

Henry gestured impatiently. "They've had a month—that's plenty of time. It's not as if I've locked them in a dungeon."

He grasped the open edges of his coat. "My home is situated in one of the finest areas of Boston. Calvin goes to the same school as my Fredrick, and Owen and Elizabeth share Annabelle's governess. They have their own rooms and nice clothes to wear." His expression soured. "Clothes, by the way, which *I* provided to replace that ragtag attire they arrived in."

He leaned forward, glaring at her. "And how do they repay my generosity? With tantrums and sulks. They are driving my wife to distraction and are a bad influence on my children."

Maggie could feel her carefully held control slip. No one, *no one*, talked about *her* children that way. "See here—"

"No—you see here." Henry pointed an accusing finger her way. "When I agreed to take on Joseph's children, I did so because you had no means to support them. That has now changed. Therefore, I insist you take them back into your care at once."

Blast Henry. She just needed a few months to make certain they would be safe. "I can't, not immediately. If you would—"

His lips twisted into a sneer. "Afraid your new husband won't take you if you have a passel of ragamuffins tied to your apron strings? Well, that is your concern, not mine. Either you take them now, or I'll pack them off to a boarding school. I won't have my household disrupted for another day."

That was too much. Even without his threat, Maggie would not leave her precious sweetlings in the hands of such an unfeeling cad, especially not when she would be an ocean away.

She drew herself up. "How quickly can you send them to me?"

"They are already here," he said smugly.

Maggie wasn't certain she'd heard correctly. "Here? But—"

"They're waiting outside in the carriage."

A white-hot bolt of fury blazed through her. "Of all the insensitive, mean-spirited actions. How *dare* you treat those children in such a fashion? Would you leave your own son and daughter in a carriage outside while you stand in a comfortable parlor and decide their fate? If so, I can only pity them."

Henry sputtered a response, his face turning an alarming shade of red. But she spun on her heel before he'd gotten so much as a word out.

She yanked the cord near the door and the housekeeper appeared almost immediately.

"Mrs. Hudgins, there are three children in the carriage outside. Please find someone to help me with their luggage and have rooms made ready for them." She mentally apologized to the Spencers, but felt certain they wouldn't mind. "As soon as their bags are unloaded, Mr. Carter will be leaving."

Without a backward glance for *that man*, she marched toward the front door, her feet moving faster with each step. It was only now sinking in—the children were here!

It felt like an eternity since they'd been together. She couldn't wait to see them, to hug them and hear all that had happened since she was with them last.

Apparently, the children were as eager as she. No sooner had she stepped outside then they came tumbling out of the carriage.

Cal took a minute to steady Beth, so it was Owen who reached Maggie first. She stooped down as he enthusiastically hurled himself into her arms. "Are you surprised to see us?"

"I certainly am. But it's a happy surprise." She squeezed him tight, reveling in the squirmy, little-boy feel of him.

"Momma, Momma!" Beth flung her arms around Maggie, demanding a portion of attention for herself.

"Hello Sunshine." Maggie included the little girl in her

embrace, ignoring the sound of Henry stomping past them.

"I missed you so much." She kissed the top of Beth's head, letting the hair tickle her nose, inhaling deeply of the child's memory-evoking scent.

Cal stopped in front of her and Maggie looked up, ready to include him in their reunion hug. But he just stood there, feet planted firmly, a fierce expression on his face.

"Hello Cal." She extended an arm for him to join them.

When he remained where he was, she stood, keeping Owen and Beth close on either side of her. "It's good to see you again."

He didn't smile. Instead, he jerked his head toward the carriage. "Are you going to let *him* take us back to Boston?"

Maggie felt Owen and Beth look up at her, waiting anxiously for her answer. But her focus was on Cal, staring past the grown-up resolve in his expression to the afraid-of-being-abandoned-again boy.

She quickly reached over and placed a hand on his shoulder. "Oh Cal, no. No one is ever going to take you from me again."

Without another word, he launched into her embrace, wrapping his arms around her waist in a fierce bear hug.

Her children were back.

By the time Maggie refocused on her surroundings, the carriage had driven off, leaving the children's trunks and baggage piled on the sidewalk.

Henry hadn't wasted any time. Well, good riddance.

Maggie stepped into the role of mother again with relish. "All right, let's gather up your belongings and head inside."

It took several trips, but they made a game of it and all the luggage was finally transferred to the front hallway.

"The rooms are ready, ma'am." The housekeeper stepped from the stairway onto the ground floor.

"Thank you." Maggie put her hands on Cal's shoulders.

"These are my stepchildren." Ignoring the woman's obvious surprise, she proceeded to introduce each of them in turn.

"Mrs. Hudgins," she said when that was done, "would you please send word to Mr. Trevaron? Offer my apologies for the delay, inform him that I will be about thirty minutes more and that I will explain everything when I arrive."

She turned the children toward the parlor. "Come along and let's have a little chat." She prayed for the right words to both set their fears at rest and to explain the situation.

Beth and Owen flanked her on the settee and Cal sat in a nearby chair.

Maggie took a deep breath. "Did you get the letter I sent?"

Cal nodded. "Yes. You're getting married again."

That was her Cal, direct and to the point. But how did he and the other two feel about her upcoming nuptials?

"That's correct. But I want you all to understand that this doesn't mean I cared any less for your father."

"We know," Owen assured her. "We already talked about it."

"You did?"

"Uh-huh." Owen nodded vigorously. "Cal explained this was much better than you having to work as a housekeeper or such."

Beth snuggled close. "It's like when Daddy married you after our first Mommy died, so we could have someone else to love us."

Maggie flashed Cal a grateful smile. How could a nine-year-old be so wise?

"Is this Mr. Trevaron a good man?"

"Yes, Cal, Mr. Trevaron is a very good man." Every instinct she possessed told her this was true, no matter what he'd said about his prior life. "I've known him for a number of years. Not only has he always been gentlemanly, but he's helped me out of difficult situations a time or two."

"And how does he feel about our coming to live with you?"

*That's a very good question.*

She wrapped her arms around the two younger children and squeezed them to her. "How could he help but like you? You're my children, so of course you will come with us."

She hadn't exactly answered Cal, and his expression told her he realized that. But Owen spoke up before his older brother could continue with his pointed questions.

"Are we really going to sail on a ship across the ocean?"

"That's right, all the way to England."

"Do you think we'll meet up with pirates?" His tone indicated excitement rather than fear.

"Eeeew!" Beth made a face. "I don't *want* to meet pirates."

"Don't worry, Bethy, I'll protect you." Owen stood, chest puffed out, and swished an imaginary cutlass through the air. "Just give me a sword and I could fight ol' Blackbeard himself."

"I want to fight pirates, too," Beth declared, in a reversal of attitude.

"Girls can't fight pirates." Owen's sneer would have made any buccaneer proud.

"Can too!" Beth scrambled to her feet and faced her brother with pudgy fists on her hips.

"Beth, Owen, that's enough." Maggie hid a smile, the sound of their bickering like music to her ears after their long absence. "No one will be fighting pirates on this voyage."

With a very feminine sniff, Beth plopped down onto the settee. Then she fingered the fabric of Maggie's dress. "You look very pretty today, Momma. Are you going to a party?"

"Actually," Maggie answered, "today is my wedding day."

Surprise flared in Cal's eyes, but it was Beth who spoke up. "It is! Oh, can we go? I've never been to a wedding before."

Maggie reached a quick decision. "Of course you can come, Sunshine. You should all be with me on such an important day."

Maggie stood. "Now, let's get you into your best clothes as quickly as we can. We're already late for the ceremony."

As they filed out of the room, Cal touched her arm. "Are you sure you want us to be there? I can make Beth understand if you'd rather go on alone."

Sometimes she wished Cal wasn't so alarmingly perceptive.

"Nonsense," she reassured him. "Having you there will make my wedding day that much more special."

Assuming there still *was* a wedding after she sprang this latest surprise on her husband-to-be.

# Chapter Eleven

Where was she?

Will refrained from looking at the clock again. Hang it all, this was their wedding day!

She'd sent word she would be thirty minutes late, but that deadline had come and gone and there was still no sign of her.

Thanks to Ian's help, Will was fully clothed for the first time since he'd been laid low. He bloody well wasn't going to go through his wedding ceremony lying in bed like some invalid.

But he hadn't counted on being up this long. His shoulder throbbed, his energy flagged, and the armchair he sat in was fast becoming a torture device.

If Maggie didn't arrive soon, he might have to lean on his best man to make it through the ceremony.

Ian stood to one side, chatting with the Reverend Stilton, while Ellen fussed with flowers she'd brought to brighten his room. All three were trying to act as if nothing was amiss.

Were they feeling pity? Did they assume he had been jilted?

Will refused to believe they could be right.

It wasn't so much he didn't think it possible Maggie had changed her mind. Devil take it, with the way they'd both been carefully *not* noticing the tension humming between them it was quite possible she'd decided to cry off.

But he had a bone-deep certainty that she wouldn't just bolt without a word. He'd told her once he didn't believe her to be a coward, and he still held to that. She would have the pluck to tell him of her decision to his face. It wasn't like her to draw the agony out in this manner.

Which meant something had happened.

Had the string of bad luck that dogged him lately found her? His gut tightened as any number of horrific possibilities crossed his mind. A tumble down the stairs. A carriage accident.

Damning the weakness that made him unable to go look for her himself, Will opened his mouth to send his best man in his place.

"Ian, I need you to—"

Before he could finish his request, the door opened. And there stood Maggie, looking none the worse for wear. In fact, her composed demeanor was marred only by the flush of her cheeks, a shade rosy enough to rival the color of her gown.

She smiled into the room at large, and he was instantly on the alert. Something was wrong. He could sense it in the way she held herself, in the way she avoided his gaze, in the way she toyed with her broach. "My apologies for keeping you waiting."

He heard the tension underlying the politeness of her tone.

Without further explanation, she turned to Ellen. "May I have a word with you, please?"

Will's temper rose. How dare she treat him so cavalierly! She'd better have a dashed good reason for her behavior.

He studied the byplay between the two women, trying

to decipher Maggie's mood. She seemed composed—too composed. Which meant she was nervous. Something was definitely afoot.

Ellen's eyes widened in surprise as Maggie said something else and pointed toward the front office. With a quick nod, Ellen turned to her husband. "Ian, would you come with me?"

Ian looked uncertainly from his wife to Will.

"Go ahead." Will waved Ian toward the door but never took his eyes from Maggie. "I believe my bride-to-be and I have some matters to discuss."

Maggie nodded. "Yes, we do. Reverend, if you don't mind leaving us for a few minutes?"

"Of course." The clergyman nodded solemnly. "Take whatever time you need. One mustn't enter into matrimony lightly."

Will ignored the sympathetic look Rev. Stilton sent him. His gaze finally connected with Maggie's, and what he saw there sent a blade of ice through his chest.

She was still fingering her broach and had that resolved look in her eyes. So, she *had* decided to terminate their arrangement.

He fought to keep his expression impassive, to suppress the burning in his gut. He refused to examine what emotions fueled that roiling fire.

Confound this wretched injury! It tied him to this chair when he wanted to lunge to his feet, to face her as a man while they had this discussion, not some weak-limbed invalid.

Instead, she moved closer, towering over *him*.

Lord, but she looked magnificent—regal bearing, crying-to-be-touched hair, kissable lips—and eyes that reflected disquiet and determination.

He sat up straighter, ignoring the twinge in his shoulder. "Have a seat before you force the gentleman in me to do something ill-advised, like try to stand."

She smiled at his weak attempt at humor, then pulled another chair up and settled stiffly on the edge of the seat. If he extended his arm he could touch her.

"How are you feeling?" She studied him as if she expected him to fall over at any moment.

He was not in the mood for pleasantries. "Well enough to discuss whatever it is you have on your mind," he said tersely.

She took a deep breath. "Henry Carter visited me today."

Will blinked. That wasn't the opening he'd expected. "Who is Henry Carter?"

"Joseph's half-brother, the one who took in the children."

Will struggled to make the connection. The children were obviously all right or she'd be much more distraught.

"I wrote to him about our upcoming marriage and our trip to England," she continued. "I thought he should know how to reach me if something should happen to one of the children. And about the possibility of my sending for them later."

Was that it? Was this Henry contesting her claim to the children? Relief flooded Will at the thought that she'd delivered a dragon he could slay for her. "Maggie, if your brother-in-law is attempting to keep you from the children, we'll fight him. I have access to some of the finest lawyers, both in this country and in England. He won't prevail, I promise you."

The smile she gave him was so dazzling he almost didn't catch her next words.

"That won't be necessary. Henry isn't fighting me on this."

*What?* Will tried to clear the fog from his brain. Had she been testing him, or had he misunderstood the last few seconds of conversation? "I don't—"

"Quite the contrary. Henry is wiping his hands of the

children. He came here to deposit them on my doorstep. Or rather, on the Spencers's doorstep."

"You mean they're here, in Crane Harbor?" Will felt thick-witted—not sure he was following the conversation properly.

"I mean they're *here*, in this building." She leaned forward and placed a hand on his arm. "You truly won't mind if they come with us now rather than my sending for them later?"

Hang it all—what had he gotten himself into? How old were these children, anyway? He and Maggie weren't even married yet and already she was asking him to take on a brace of urchins.

Besides, bringing her nursery along would divert Maggie's attention from him—something he'd planned to have exclusive rights to during the voyage.

This wasn't what they'd agreed to. If the uncle didn't want them, there were other options they—

Will's mental objections ground to a halt as he saw the desperate hope glimmering in her eyes, the way she braced herself for his answer. He wasn't proof against her obvious yearning. Despite reservations, he nodded. "Of course they must come with us—they are your children."

She squeezed his hand as she sprang up. "Oh, Will, thank you. This is the best wedding gift you could have given me."

He'd never been the recipient of a smile such as the one she focused on him—a mixture of pure, blinding joy, affection and gratitude. It tugged at him, warmed him, made him feel a hero and a fraud at the same time. He knew deep inside that he'd never done anything in his life to earn such a look.

Then she did something completely unexpected. In a quick movement, as if on impulse, she bent over and graced his cheek with a kiss, murmuring a soft, "You're a good man, Will Trevaron," as she did so. That brief, chaste contact of her lips on his skin, of her warm breath near his ear, set his blood on fire and made his body hungry for much more.

She gave his hand a final squeeze as she straightened, then released it.

Had she felt what he had, or was the color in her cheeks due simply to her pleasure over having the children with her again?

"I'll call everyone back in," she said, her ready-to-take-charge demeanor surfacing. "You can meet the children and then we can proceed with the ceremony. I'm sure Rev. Stilton has other things to get to today."

And before he could utter another word, she'd whisked from the room.

Will drew his first clear breath since she'd entered. His pulse slowed to something approaching its normal rhythm, and his whirling thoughts steadied.

What was wrong with him? It had only been a smile and a kiss, after all. And not even a proper kiss, at that—just a peck on the cheek. It must be his weakened condition playing havoc with his normally staid reactions.

That and the way she'd looked. By the saints, if she wasn't a vision to behold in that gown. Its fitted bodice and flared skirt accentuated her curves provocatively. Not to mention the creamy expanse of skin at her neckline.

But it was more than the dress—it was the confidant way she carried herself and the graceful way she moved. And while not classically beautiful, her features were so arresting and so undeniably Maggie.

Will mumbled a few choice oaths. There he went again, rhapsodizing over her like some inept poet or mooncalf.

Maggie returned, rescuing him from his own thoughts, and ushering three children before her. "Children, I would like you to meet Mr. William Trevaron, the man I am going to marry."

Will straightened, pleased by her choice of words.

"Will, these are my dear stepchildren." She started with the older boy. "This is Calvin, aged nine. He's taken his role as man of the family quite seriously these past few months and has been a real source of strength for all of us."

"It's good to meet you, Calvin."

"Thank you, sir." Calvin's tone and nod were respectful. But there was an assessing look to the boy's expression, as if he were trying to make up his mind about this new man in his stepmother's life. Did he resent the fact that there would now be a new "man of the family?"

"This is Owen," Maggie said, moving on to the other boy. "He's six and has more energy than a room full of puppies."

"Owen."

"Hello, Mr. Trevaron. Did you really get stabbed?"

"Owen!" Maggie's tone was censuring, but fond exasperation was buried in it as well.

Will's own lips twitched at the boy's ghoulish curiosity. It seemed Owen didn't share his brother's reserve. "Yes I did. Foolishly careless of me, I'm afraid."

"Owen," Maggie warned as the boy opened his mouth for what was undoubtedly another inappropriate question.

The youngster took one look at Maggie and snapped his mouth closed, though his expression was far from repentant. Will foresaw some interesting times ahead with this one.

Maggie placed her hand on the little girl's shoulder. "And this bundle of sunshine is Elizabeth, aged five."

"Mistress Elizabeth, it's nice to make your acquaintance."

The child giggled as she sketched him a charming curtsey. "I'm not Mistress Elizabeth, I'm Beth." Then she stared adoringly at him with bright blue eyes that he knew would be some young buck's undoing one day. "Thank you for marrying my momma so we can all be together again."

How the devil was he supposed to respond to a remark like that? He shot Maggie a quick look and noted her flaming cheeks.

A strangled cough from across the room reminded Will they had an audience. He spotted Ian, trying hard not to laugh, and Ellen watching with a misty-eyed smile. Rev. Stilton stood patiently, watching the whole proceeding as if this were the most normal setting in the world for an upcoming wedding ceremony.

Will shot Ian a warning look before turning back to Maggie's stepdaughter. "You're quite welcome, Beth. But bringing you all together is not the only reason I'm marrying your mother."

"Oh, I know," the girl agreed with a bright smile. "People get married 'cause they love each other. Just like the prince and princess in that book Momma reads to me."

This time the strangled cough came from Maggie. "Reverend," she said hastily, "I apologize for taking up so much of your time, but I believe we are ready to begin now."

"Very well." The reverend began issuing instructions as if he were a stage director and they the actors. "Mrs. Carter, take your place next to Mr. Trevaron. Children, you stand beside your mother. Mr. and Mrs. Spencer, the other side of Mr. Trevaron."

Will retrieved the cane that he'd placed beside the chair, and carefully rose to his feet. His legs felt a bit rubbery, but he willed them to hold firm. He saw the protest form on Maggie's lips, and then she paused and gave him a smile.

Pleased that she understood, he crooked an elbow.

As she stepped beside him and placed a hand on his extended arm, she met his gaze with a tentative, uncertain expression. Had Beth's artless comments unnerved her?

As the ceremony began, Will felt his strength return.

The physical contact with Maggie invigorated him, gave him an extra dollop of energy.

The heat of her hand radiated through his sleeve, up his arm, and through his chest, until his whole body felt warmed by it.

With a sense of exultation, he repeated the vows that would bind him and Maggie together for a lifetime.


"What do you mean, there's not another cabin?" Maggie stared at Ian, certain she had misunderstood.

Ian spread his hands. "I'm sorry, but every cabin on the *Lady Jen* is already spoken for."

Maggie massaged her temple, trying to ease the throbbing. So much had happened today it was no wonder her mind rebelled. The preparations for her wedding, the confrontation with Henry, the reunion with the children, the marriage—

The marriage. Something soft and warm as a kitten uncurled inside her. Mrs. William Anthony Trevaron.

They were married. Really and truly married.

She and Will were bound together for life now, just as surely as if this had been the love match she'd always dreamed of.

The sparkle of the elegant square-cut emerald Will had placed on her finger less than an hour ago caught her eye. She tilted her hand just so to get a better view. It was perfect.

How had he known what size to purchase?

"Ahem."

Maggie dropped her hands to her lap, heat rising in her face.

"As I was saying," Ian's voice vibrated with barely disguised amusement, "you'll have to make do with just the two cabins. There's no other choice."

"But—"

"Maggie, each room normally sleeps three people.

There are five of you—you'll be fine." Though Ian's expression remained matter-of-fact, the roguish gleam in his eye intensified. "Of course, some of you will have to double up in the larger bunks."

Maggie held her tongue, refusing to play the blushing bride. She and Will had entered into marriage as a business arrangement, and that's the tone she would maintain. At least in public.

This situation merely needed a bit of reasoned logic to resolve the matter. Will, of course, would require a lower bed to himself. His injuries precluded his climbing into an upper berth or sharing his bed with anyone.

Maggie hurried past that thought.

She and Beth could share the lower bed in the adjoining room. That left Cal and Owen to take the upper berths. Owen would be better in her room, Cal in Will's, for several reasons.

Maggie shifted in her chair as her conscience prickled. Was she considering what was best for all concerned, or only what would best maintain her own equanimity?

Less than a week ago they'd thought Will at death's door. Though he grew stronger daily, he still required a great deal of care. In fact, she insisted someone watch over him at night, though he grumbled over her "mollycoddling." Even Dr. Lawson had warned her to be vigilant during the days ahead for signs of renewed infection or vapors of the lung.

Sending Cal to share Will's room instead of assigning herself that spot was not only impractical, but just plain cowardly. There was no reason why she shouldn't share Will's room. No reason at all. They were married, so there was nothing the least bit shocking or improper about the notion.

And it wasn't as if she'd be sharing his bed.

Maggie shifted. Why did that image keep popping into her head?

She owed it to Will to put her missish notions aside and treat him as she would any other patient.

She nodded. "Very well. If that's all there is, then we shall make do." She stood and Ian quickly followed suit.

"I'm sure you'll manage famously," he said. "Now, what else can I do for you?"

"Nothing, thank you." Maggie moved to the door. "I'll check on Will, then relieve Ellen from her child-caring duties."

"Don't feel the need to rush. I'm certain Ellen is enjoying their company."

Maggie smiled her good-bye, then started down the maze of hallways that would eventually lead her to Will's room.

Her husband's room.

A little shiver tickled its way up her spine.

What would he think about sharing a cabin with her on the long voyage? After all, it was he who had arranged for separate accommodations. Suppose that had been his preference? Would she be trespassing on his privacy?

Maggie hesitated outside Will's room. As soon as the nuptials were complete, she had asked Ian to help Will undress so he could return to his bed. Despite Will's protest that he was "just fine," the tinge of white around his mouth worried her enough that she'd read him a lecture on the danger of overdoing things so early in his recovery.

In truth, she felt responsible for the obvious strain on his constitution. She had kept him waiting today without telling him why. Then she'd thrown the children at him with little warning.

No wonder the man appeared to be holding himself together by sheer willpower.

Should she risk waking him? If she didn't look in she would worry all evening about how he fared. Surely she could take a quick peek to reassure herself without disturbing his slumber.

Stepping inside, Maggie shook her head in exasperation. He slept, yes, but he obviously hadn't paid attention to her strictures. He was only semi-reclined, and a newspaper lay on his chest, gently rising and falling with each breath he took.

Maggie crossed the room and gently removed the newspaper, placing it on the bedside table. Then she drank in the sight of him, studying his features in a way she didn't dare when he was awake. She enjoyed watching him sleep, took guilty pleasure in allowing herself a slow perusal of his appearance.

The pinched look was gone now, and his color was good. At least she could rest easy on that score. His face was so hard, so chiseled when he was awake. In sleep it took on aspects of both vulnerability and a noble strength that tugged at her heart. The rhythmic sound of his breathing, strong and even, was the sweetest music she'd ever heard.

Ah, and that recalcitrant lock of hair that always fell into his face—that was what she liked most. That disobedient curl gave him just a hint of boyishness that he would never countenance when awake. Her hand itched to lift it from his brow, to twine the dark, silky strands through her fingers.

And why shouldn't she? After all—she was his wife now. That entitled her to take a few liberties, did it not?

As if it had a will of its own, Maggie's hand moved toward that tantalizing tendril, hesitated, then ever so gently fingered her prize. The lock was as silky as a spaniel's coat and seemed almost alive as it curled itself around her index finger. Little firefly sparks of awareness flickered through her, spurred by the surprising intimacy of that simple contact.

An intoxicating sense of daring built inside her. That kiss she'd given him today—her boldness had embarrassed her, but she certainly felt no regrets.

Would he waken if she planted another soft kiss on his cheek?

Just a tiny one.

A chance to feel the sensual rasp of his face against her lips again. To inhale the scent of sandalwood and cloves and the indefinable something that was uniquely Will. To see if that tingle would travel all the way down to her toes once more.

Maggie leaned forward, moistening her suddenly dry lips.

Was she really going to do this?

# Chapter Twelve

Will roused from a light slumber to the feathery touch of fingers in his hair.

*Mmmm, that's nice.*

He pried his eyes open, and his mood changed from a hazy pleasure to instant arousal. Maggie bent over him, so close he could feel her breath on his cheek. Her pose revealed a creamy expanse of skin below her throat that absolutely begged for a lover's attention. The increased tempo of her breathing played counterpoint to his own rapid pulse.

*I'm still asleep. This has to be a dream.*

It didn't matter. Whether this was real or a dream, he sure as Hades wasn't about to let the moment slip away. If he held himself perfectly still, could keep his breathing even—

Her tongue darted out to wet her lips and he lost the battle. A hissed intake of breath escaped before he could call it back.

Maggie froze, her face inches from his own. Then her gaze collided with his, a startled flash of guilt coloring her face.

If he didn't do something quickly, she would pull back, was already poised to do so.

"We need a kiss to seal our wedding vows." He hoped Maggie would credit the huskiness of his voice to his recent slumber.

Her breath left her in a warm little puff that caressed his cheek. The scent of lemon and jasmine and sunshine—the scent of *Maggie*—wrapped around him like a siren's song.

Triumph flooded his veins at her tentative, consenting smile.

But he wanted more. "A new groom deserves a kiss on the lips rather than the cheek, don't you think?"

Surprise, and something akin to desire, darkened her eyes. With difficulty, he swallowed a groan. Ever so slowly, she closed the distance between them and brushed his lips with hers.

That simple, chaste contact hardened his body and set the pulse pounding in his ears. Those sweet lips were like fresh-picked plums, warm, ripe and ready to be savored. He had an urgent need to throw his arms around her, to crush her to him and deepen the kiss until she was breathless and panting for more.

Only the knowledge that the touch of his mangled hand would break the spell kept his fists anchored at his sides.

When Maggie's lips moved reluctantly—or so he hoped—from his, she didn't back away. Her eyes searched his, as if seeking something there.

Was it approval? If so, she most definitely had it.

Missing the contact of her skin on his, Will gently stroked the edge of her jaw with the back of his fingers.

So soft. So firm. So vibrant.

Her eyes closed, and an exquisite tremor fluttered her shoulders. Such an arousing picture of innocence and passion.

Hang it all, this was their wedding day. It didn't matter what plans they'd made or how dispassionate their arrangement, she deserved better than this.

She deserved a flower-bedecked cathedral, followed by extravagant festivities—not a sickroom.

She deserved a groom to stand at her side and proudly show her off to the world—not some propped-up invalid.

And tonight she should lie in his arms—not in a house several miles away.

What would it be like to stroke her body the way he now stroked her face? To loosen that passion he'd only caught glimpses of, passion she kept trapped below her calm façade?

For one precious moment longer she allowed his touch, actually seemed to lean into it. Then she opened her eyes and slowly straightened. "Are the vows sealed to your satisfaction now?" Her smile was soft, teasing.

Satisfaction was not exactly what he felt. "Sealed all tight and proper." Will was pleased his voice sounded so normal.

Maggie fiddled with a bottle on his bedside table, her cheeks a becoming shade of rose. "I'm sorry I disturbed your slumber."

"I'm not." She disturbed him, but not in the way she meant. Will sat up, ignoring the twinge of pain, trying to turn his thoughts to less arousing territory. "Where are the children?"

"Ellen took them with her. I wanted to check in on you one last time before I joined them."

"I'm glad you did." A definite understatement. But he wasn't ready for her to go yet. "How do they feel about traveling to England?"

"They're very excited." She sat in the chair next to his bed. "If you're up to it, I need to speak to you a moment."

As soon as Will saw her teeth nibbling that luscious lower lip of hers he raised a brow. What bad news did she have to deliver this time? "Of course. Is something wrong?"

Winnie Griggs

"Oh, no," she reassured him quickly. Then promptly spoiled it with an added "Well, not exactly."

"And what is this 'not exactly wrong' news?" He wasn't truly concerned. He was too busy admiring the flush of her cheeks and the distracting way her bodice moved when she was agitated.

"It's about our sleeping arrangements."

His gaze flew to meet hers. She definitely had his full attention now. "Sleeping arrangements?"

"Yes, on board the ship, I mean. I checked with Ian, and it appears the *Lady Jen* is fully booked. There's no additional cabin for the children."

"I see." He knew how *he'd* solve that problem, but knowing Maggie, she'd already planned the whole thing out.

Which of the boys would be sharing his room? He wasn't sure if he'd prefer the impish Owen or the ready-to-judge-him Calvin. Was there some way he could convince her to—

She took a deep breath, then drew her shoulders back. A move Will approved of wholeheartedly.

"I've decided, since you will still require regular care for some time after we set sail, it would be best if I share your room, and the children take the other cabin."

Will blinked, wondering if he'd heard right. Maggie was *volunteering* to share his cabin for the long voyage to England?

It seemed his blasted infirmity had yielded a happy bonus.

She stared at him, an uncertain expression on her face.

It took another heartbeat for Will to realize she was waiting for his response. "Given the situation," he said carefully, "I agree this is the best solution."

He had the devil of a time swallowing his grin—especially given the delicious possibilities spinning through his mind.

"Very well." Her expression reflected relief and a flicker of something else he couldn't quite define.

She stood, giving him a businesslike smile. "We'll consider the matter settled. Now, I'll let you rest."

Rest—hah! The sensual images her visit had stirred were anything *but* restful. They would, however, be pleasant company in her absence.

A moment later, Maggie stood outside Will's bedchamber, and leaned against the wall.

She'd kissed him!

Full on those firm, commanding, sensual lips.

And he'd kissed her back!

She'd felt no panic, no urge to escape, no unpleasantness whatsoever. Quite the contrary.

Maggie touched her lips, remembering the pulse-stirring warmth of that contact.

Oh my! It had been . . . stimulating. Her cheeks burned. Strange to view herself in such a wanton light. For years she'd believed she would never be able to welcome a man's touch.

Of course, this wasn't just any man, this was Will.

Her husband.

Perhaps, in time, this marriage could develop into something much more than either had bargained for.

Maggie straightened and started down the hall. There were several matters that required her attention before they boarded ship—especially now that the children were coming along.

She had purchases to make, packing to do, rules to lay down. Tomorrow would be a very busy day.

But Maggie had an extra spring to her step and irrepressible smile on her lips as she made her way to the waiting carriage.

"Maggie, for the last time, please step aside so we can be on our way." Will was determined to walk out of the office—he would not bear the ignominy of being carried.

His overly concerned wife glanced to Ian, standing at his side. "Would you please talk some sense into him?"

"My mind is made up, Maggie." Will stood toe to toe with her. "I am quite capable of walking to the carriage."

She rolled her eyes and finally stepped aside. "Oh, for heaven's sake. Standing here arguing is not doing you any good. We'll do it your way."

As if there'd been any doubt.

She extended her arm, her expression making it clear she intended for him to lean on her should he need extra support.

Will took her hand and tucked it on his arm. He was done with having her mollycoddle him.

By the time they reached the carriage, though, each step sent a little bolt of pain through his shoulder.

He allowed Ian to hand Maggie in first. Then, as his friend climbed up beside the driver, Will pulled himself into the carriage with white-knuckled effort.

He dropped heavily on the seat beside Maggie, doing his best to breathe with some semblance of normalcy. After his earlier boasts, he'd as soon endure the rack as admit that the walk had left him winded and sore.

Leaning back, he found himself the subject of scrutiny from the three youngsters sitting on the seat opposite.

"Does your scritch-scratch hurt?" Beth asked with wide-eyed sympathy.

*Scritch-scratch?* "It's getting better every day."

Owen leaned forward, and there was none of Beth's sympathy in his expression. "Momma said Tully can't ride in here with us because being around him makes you ill. Is that right?"

"Yes." Will bit out the answer as the carriage jerked forward. He *would not* allow himself so much as a wince.

Not that he'd fooled Maggie. She linked an arm through

his, providing a steadying force as the carriage continued its less-than-smooth progress.

He slid a quick glance her way, fully expecting to see a touch of I-told-you-so righteousness in her expression. Instead, he saw only her usual air of calm competence.

His conscience pinched that he had been so shabby as to think she would gloat over his condition. He lightly squeezed her arm to convey his appreciation.

Then he turned back to the children, ready to give Owen an explanation. His gaze, however, snagged on Calvin's.

The oldest of Maggie's stepchildren studied him with an unblinking stare, his expression neither approving nor disapproving. The lad seemed to assess him, reserving judgment as he weighed Will's actions and responses.

Receiving such scrutiny from a mere boy was unnerving.

"It's not only Tully I have this problem with," he explained to Owen. "Being near *any* cat sets me sneezing and itching."

This time Maggie gave *his* arm a squeeze, her expression softening. Was that admiration lighting her eyes?

So—his stoic march to the carriage had garnered only reproof, but his unmanly confession earned her regard. Would he ever understand the way a woman's mind worked?

"But you're a grown man," Owen protested. "Tully's just a cat."

"Now Owen," Maggie interjected. "Do you remember last spring, when we had that picnic by the far pond? You came back with a rash that was itchy and bothersome for nearly a week."

The boy's wrinkled-nose expression made it obvious he remembered the incident all too well.

Will's amused smile was wiped clean, however, as the carriage turned a corner. Though he attempted to brace himself, he swallowed an oath as his wretched weakness forced Maggie to bear a measure of his weight. Blast it all, he was doing a lamentable job proving himself recovered.

Maggie gave no sign she'd noted anything out of the ordinary, but a flicker in Calvin's expression indicated *he* had. Will definitely wasn't winning points with the boy.

"That rash was caused by nothing more than a small plant," Maggie continued. "It's the same with Mr. Trevaron and cats."

That put a more charitable expression on Owen's face.

"But Tully doesn't *mean* to make you sneeze," Beth interjected anxiously. "You won't send him away, will you?"

Devil's teeth, did the children think him an ogre? Then he remembered that that was exactly what he'd intended to do when Maggie first arrived with the furry nuisance.

"Of course not. Your mother explained what a special animal Tully is. I wouldn't dream of separating you from him." Will looked at each of them in turn. "But I need you to help keep Tully and me apart. Can I rely on you for that?"

Beth and Owen gave enthusiastic yeses, Calvin a reserved nod.

It was a start.

Maggie opened the door to the children's cabin, giving Will an assessing look as he and Ian moved to the next one. Boarding the ship and negotiating his way to the passenger section had taken its toll on him.

Not that she thought she would ever hear him admit as much. "Mule-headed stubbornness," she mumbled as he met her gaze.

As soon as she entered the cabin, Maggie turned to the wall it shared with the room Will had entered.

Good. The door had been installed just as she'd asked. She tried the knob, finding it turned with ease. The door-

NAME: _____

ADDRESS: _____

_____

_____

TELEPHONE: _____

E-MAIL: _____

_____ I want to pay by credit card.

__ Visa           __ MasterCard           __ Discover

Account Number: _____

Expiration date: _____

SIGNATURE: _____

*Send this form, along with $2.00 shipping
and handling for your FREE books, to:*

Historical Romance Book Club
20 Academy Street
Norwalk, CT 06850-4032

*Or fax (must include credit card
information!) to: 610.995.9274.
You can also sign up on the Web
at www.dorchesterpub.com.*

Offer open to residents of the U.S. and
Canada only. Canadian residents, please
call 1.800.481.9191 for pricing information.

way was narrow and a few inches shorter than she, but it would do.

Will was easing onto the edge of the bed with Ian's help as she looked in. And that was exactly where she planned to see her foolhardy husband stay for the remainder of the day.

"Ian," she said pointedly, "would you help Will remove his boots? He won't require them any more today."

The fact that Will didn't argue was telling in itself.

Maggie turned back to find the first of the bags had arrived.

"Please put Tully's cage under that window, out of the way," she instructed Cal.

Then she smiled at Beth. "Sunshine, talk to Tully and keep him calm. Just don't let him out before I say so. All right?"

The little girl nodded, and plopped cross-legged on the floor. In seconds she was cooing her own peculiar brand of soothing nonsense to her incarcerated pet.

Maggie turned to the boys. "I need you two to help sort through the baggage. Have the porters put your and Beth's things in here. Send everything else next door. Can you do that?"

"Yes ma'am."

"Thank you. I'll be right through here, checking on Mr. Trevaron. Call if you need me." She paused in the doorway. "Oh, and Cal, when you see the satchel with my medical supplies, send Owen over with it."

Maggie stepped into the adjoining cabin to find Will already bootless and recumbent.

Ian straightened with a smile. "I should be going." He shook Will's hand with a cocky grin. "Don't worry about Wind Dancer. I know you think you're indispensable, but we'll manage for the next few months without you looking over our shoulders."

Will answered with a weak harrumph. "Just try not to muck up the contract files too badly."

Ian rolled his eyes. "Listen to him. If he didn't have me to keep things straight, we'd never find anything." Then he sketched Maggie a bow. "It's been a true pleasure to make your acquaintance. I'm happy to see Will has finally met his match."

Maggie reached for Ian's hand and gave it a quick squeeze. "Thank you for all you've done for Will and for me. And give my regards to Ellen, as well."

Ian grinned. "Don't take any humbug from your patient." Then with a quick salute for Will, he exited, followed by the porters who'd delivered the last of the baggage.

Before Maggie could say anything, Owen stepped into the room. "Here's your medical bag." He set it at her feet. "Can we let Tully out of the cage now? He's fussing something fierce."

"All right. But before you do, make certain both doors are closed so he doesn't escape."

"Yes ma'am!" Owen sped back into the other room, closing the door behind him with a pronounced thud.

Maggie turned to find Will staring at her with disquieting intensity. Was he as aware as she of the fact that they would be sharing this confined space for the next several weeks?

"How are you feeling?" she asked, breaking the silence.

He shrugged and then winced. "I've been better."

She nodded but refrained from saying anything.

Will was not so reticent. "Come now," he teased. "Surely there's an I-told-you-so lurking behind that sanctimonious expression."

Maggie's irritation eased, but not her concern. She tried to maintain a stern façade, but her *humph* wasn't very convincing, even to her own ears. "You must take things slowly if you wish to make a full recovery before we reach England."

She raised a brow in challenge. "Unless, of course, you *want* to be at half-strength when you face your grandfather again."

That wiped the smile from his face. "Of course not."

"Then listen to your doctor." She moved closer. "Now, let me help you out of that shirt so I can look at your chest."

Maggie realized how that indelicately worded sentence sounded about a second before Will's lips curved in a slow, heated smile.

The flame that leapt in his eyes set something as thick and hot as molten amber flowing through her veins. And, like an insect trapped in that amber, for a moment she couldn't move, couldn't even breathe.

Will's flagging energy revived considerably as he enjoyed the blushing confusion in Maggie's expression.

"That is, so I can make sure your wound hasn't reopened."

"Of course." Will sat up straighter, a smile of mock-surrender on his face. "I'm yours to command." He unfastened the top button of his shirt.

The focus of her gaze on his chest as he released each button nearly undid him. Watching *her* watch *him* was an unexpectedly arousing experience. And it wasn't just her expression. Even a blind man would notice the banked desire sizzling in the air between them.

Only when he had the shirt completely open and started to shrug out of it did she blink and look up.

"Here." She stepped forward. "Let me help you."

Will was certain he could manage quite well without her aid, but he wasn't about to refuse her offer. Not when it meant having her close to him, touching him, *undressing* him.

As she bent over him, Will took the opportunity to lean

into her, to "accidentally" brush against her, to breathe softly into her hair. Triumph surged through him at the signs she was as affected by the contact as he—small catches in her breathing, trembling of her fingers, the rosy color warming her cheeks.

Could he entice another kiss from those luscious lips?

Before he could act on that thought, Owen opened the door and stuck his head inside. "Momma, I can't find my tin soldiers."

Maggie started guiltily. "Owen Matthew Carter, how many times must I tell you to knock before opening a door?" Her tone was firm but not censorious.

Will, feeling less charitable, swallowed several choice oaths at the boy's timing.

Owen hung his head. "I'm sorry."

"That's all very well." Maggie waved him back into the other room. "But you need to show me how to do it properly."

"Yes ma'am." Owen drew back and shut the door. A second later there was a heavy knock.

"Come in." Maggie stood patiently as Owen stepped back in.

"Much better. Now, your soldiers are in the large tan—"

"Beth, grab Tully!" Cal's cry was followed by a streak of gray fur bolting through the doorway.

Owen dived for the animal and missed. Cal and Beth followed suit, and before Will could take a breath, his room was filled with scrambling children and a frenzied cat who seemed to be everywhere at once. Maggie's repeated call for order went unheeded as the youngsters tried to capture their energetic pet.

"Enough!"

At Will's stern command, all movement ceased. Even Tully, who'd had the temerity to jump onto his bed, paused and gave Will a curious look. Will took the opportunity to use his discarded shirt as a net to trap the animal.

He lifted the squirming bundle, his arm extended, and winced at what the animal's claws were doing to his shirt. "Calvin, take this and your siblings back into the other room, please."

Will felt the familiar tickling in his throat just before a sneeze exploded with enough force to twinge both his injury and his dignity. "*Now*, if you don't mind," he added firmly.

With a quick glance Maggie's way, the boy took the bundle, then shooed the other two children back into the adjoining cabin. The click of the door was echoed by another sneeze from Will.

Why couldn't the children have had a dog?

He looked up to find Maggie watching him, her expression a mixture of apology and sympathy.

So much for the building passion that had glowed there just a moment ago. "Does that door have a lock?" he asked sourly.

Her amused smile did nothing to improve his mood. "Don't worry, I'll have a talk with them. It's just the excitement of the trip and the enclosed space that has them so . . ."

"Unruly?" he supplied when she paused.

"Exuberant," she corrected. Then she put on her brisk, take-charge expression. "Now, let's get this bandage off and make certain you haven't done any damage with this day's activities."

Will raised his arms and sat tamely as she unwound the gauze strips. Before the children's invasion, he might have tried wrapping those arms around her. Ever since he'd enticed that chaste kiss from her on their wedding day, he'd wondered what it would be like to share a true lover's kiss with her, to taste fully of her sweetness, to duel with that siren tongue that teased him unmercifully whenever it moistened her lips.

However, the moment for that had passed.

If it had truly ever existed outside his own desires.

# Chapter Thirteen

Maggie examined Will's wound, trying to ignore his half-naked body, tantalizingly available for her scrutiny, as well. This was going to be a long trip in very close quarters. She had best learn to control her wayward thoughts here and now, or she would have a very uncomfortable time of it.

Still, ever since that kiss two days ago, she'd day-dreamed about doing it again, fantasized about taking it further. . . .

Heavens! Where *was* her self-control?

"It appears you haven't done any permanent damage." She forcibly turned her thoughts back to practical matters.

"Glad to hear it."

Maggie ignored the amused drawl in his voice. "However, I think it best you take it easy for the rest of the day." She gave him a stern look. "I don't know if you truly understand how close you came to not making it at all." She still shuddered when she thought of how tragically this could have ended.

"On the contrary," he said, "I'm well aware of how close I came to dying and whom I have to thank for my survival."

His words, and the intensity of his gaze, sent delicious tingles up her spine to tickle the nape of her neck.

Then he offered a teasing grin. "I mean Tully, of course."

Maggie bit back a laugh. "I see. That explains why you just booted him out of your cabin with such ceremony."

He nodded. "Due to his bravery and prowess I've elevated him to the role of guard cat. Guarding the children, of course."

"Of course. Now, shall I fetch your nightshirt?"

Will raised a brow. "I don't own one."

"Oh." Maggie let that sink in. He had slept bare-chested since the accident, but she hadn't realized . . .

Just how *did* he normally sleep?

She met his gaze and saw a wickedly amused glint in his eye. Had he guessed her thoughts? What if he asked her to—

"Maggie," he said in a tone of gentle amusement, "why don't you look in on the children while I prepare for bed?"

With a quick nod, she all but fled the room.

The children looked up at her precipitous entrance.

"Is he very angry?" Owen asked.

It took Maggie a moment to remember the incident with Tully. "Of course not. We just need to remember to keep Tully away from him. With his injury, he doesn't need an attack of the sneezes."

"Did he hurt his scritch-scratch?" Beth asked worriedly.

"No, sweetheart. But Mr. Trevaron's scritch-scratch is still healing, so we must be careful." *Time to change the subject.* "Let's get you all settled in, shall we?"

Maggie looked around the room. "Cal, you'll sleep on the top bunk. Owen and Beth, you can each have an end of the lower one."

"How come Cal gets to sleep up there?" Owen protested.

"Because I'm the biggest," Cal answered smugly.

"But—"

"Don't argue Owen. Cal's right. He's the oldest."

"Where will *you* sleep, Momma?"

Beth's question sent warmth inching into Maggie's cheeks, especially when Cal and Owen's gazes latched onto her as well.

"I'll be in the room next door," she answered, bending over a trunk. "That way I can take care of Mr. Trevaron and still be close by if you need me."

"Does that mean you'll get to sleep on top?" Owen asked.

She nodded.

"But ladies shouldn't climb." Owen's tone was solicitous. "I can stay with Mr. Trevaron and you can sleep with Bethy."

Maggie smiled. "That's a most gentlemanly offer, Owen. But you don't know how to take care of an injured man, so I'm afraid Mr. Trevaron will have to settle for me."

She turned to Cal. "While I tend to Mr. Trevaron, I'll be counting on you to look after things in here."

Cal nodded self-importantly. "Yes ma'am."

She looked at his siblings. "And I expect the two of you to mind your brother. Understand?"

She received a quick, "Yes, Momma," from Beth and a less enthusiastic nod from Owen.

Ignoring the looks that passed between the brothers, Maggie set to work. By the time she finished, the ship had left harbor.

Their trip had begun. "What do you say we explore a bit?"

Her proposal received an enthusiastic round of yeses.

"Can Tully come too?" Beth asked.

Maggie nodded. "Of course. But let's keep him on a leash."

Once the cat was properly tethered to the end of Beth's wrist, they stepped out into the passageway. Following a queue of other passengers, they made their way to the promenade deck. Maggie's first view of the open sea was breathtaking. The vastness of the ocean, which seemed to merge with the sky itself, made her feel very small and insignificant.

The children experienced the same awe, though they displayed it differently. Maggie had to grab Owen's shirt-tail to keep him from racing to the railing, while Beth clutched at her skirts.

Cal, on the other hand, stood with feet braced and hands on his hips, staring around him for all the world as if he'd come home. When he turned to Maggie, a new fire gleamed in his eyes.

"Someday," he said with absolute certainty, "I'm going to captain a ship like this one."

Staring into his face, Maggie believed him.

Keeping the children close, she escorted them for several turns around the deck. She wanted them to drink their fill of fresh air and open space before returning to the small cabin.

The wind tugged playfully at their hair and clothing as they exchanged casual pleasantries with the other passengers. A festive air prevailed, as if they were all guests at a party.

Maggie enjoyed watching people and guessing their history. One pair, in particular, caught her eye. The two older women, though obviously traveling together, seemed oddly matched.

One was tall and slender, had the posture of a general and wore a flamboyant turban. The other was of medium height, plump, and seemed to favor frilly clothing more suited to a schoolgirl.

The taller of the two stopped in front of Maggie. "I'm Lady Maude Blendell and this is Miss Abigail Landry." Her accented voice, while not harsh, had a you-*will*-pay-attention quality.

Before Maggie could respond, Lady Maude pointed a gold-tipped walking stick her way. "And you must be Mrs. Trevaron."

Flustered, Maggie wondered if she should introduce herself as Lady Rainley. Or would that be rude?

She settled for a deferential nod. "Yes ma'am. And these are my children—Calvin, Owen and Elizabeth."

Lady Maude received the children's greetings, then turned back to Maggie. "I understand your husband is responsible for our delayed departure." She obviously believed in being direct.

"I apologize if you were inconvenienced." Maggie adopted a polite but unintimidated tone. "Mr. Trevaron met with an accident and was unable to travel before today."

Lady Maude waved her apology aside. "A few days makes little difference to me. I merely wanted to hear about the attack. It's been all the talk for days. I understand you single-handedly rescued him from a band of cutthroats."

Maggie heard the children's surprised intakes of breath, and Owen's reverently uttered, "Cutthroats?"

She laughed, resisting the urge to roll her eyes. "Nothing could be farther from the truth. I assure you, I'm no heroine."

Lady Maude *tsk*ed. "A shame." Then she tapped the deck with her stick. "Stroll with me and you can explain what happened."

Maggie obediently fell into step beside the aristocrat, allowing the children to follow behind with Miss Landry. Lady Maude's idea of a "stroll" resembled a military march.

With imperious prompting from her inquisitor, Maggie gave an edited account of what had happened that awful day.

Lady Maude smiled approvingly. "You are mistaken my dear—you are most definitely a heroine. You were not too missish to take charge when the situation called for it. I hope that young buck of yours appreciates those qualities in a woman."

Not sure how to respond, Maggie turned the subject. "So, did you ladies enjoy your trip to America?"

"Yes, thank you, it was quite pleasant." And without further prompting, the woman launched into a description of their numerous trips around the world.

Maggie smiled as she thought of describing these two to Will.

Which reminded her, it was time to check on her patient.

"It has been most pleasant chatting with you," she said. "But it's time the children and I return to our cabins."

As they walked away, Owen swaggered beside Maggie. "If I had been there, I would have fought off that cutthroat."

Beth's eyes widened. "But the bad man might have hurt you."

"Not me," Owen boasted. "I would've been too fast for him."

He pranced around, making sweeping gestures as if brandishing a sword. And promptly barged into a gentleman walking past.

"Whoa, there." The man caught Owen before he could fall.

"Excuse me." Owen scuffed his toe on the deck. "I didn't—"

"No need to apologize." He gave Owen a wink. "I can see you had your hands full battling a hoard of marauding pirates."

Owen grinned. "Weren't pirates. It was a cowardly thief trying to slit our throats."

"Owen, that's quite enough." Maggie drew Owen to her side. "I hope you'll excuse my son. He's a bit on the energetic side."

"No harm done. I fought many a brigand in my youth."
He executed a dapper bow. "Simon Cassidy, at your service."

Mr. Cassidy was tall, with a winning smile set in a handsome face. Smooth was the word that came most readily to mind when Maggie looked at him.

"It's a pleasure to meet you. I am Mrs. Trevaron, and these are my children, Cal, Owen, and Beth."

He nodded to the children, then raised a brow. "So, *you* are the famous Mrs. Trevaron. I trust your husband is doing well."

Maggie hoped everyone hadn't heard the same outlandish version of the tale Lady Blendell had recounted. "Yes, thank you."

"Having such a redoubtable heroine on this voyage will definitely make the time pass more agreeably."

She gave him a polite smile. "It's kind of you to say so. But I assure you, I am no heroine, redoubtable or otherwise. Now, if you will excuse us, we were just returning to our rooms."

Will sat up straighter as he heard the light knock. "Come in." It was about time—it seemed hours since Maggie had left.

She stepped in and closed the door. "How are you feeling?"

His shoulder burned and he felt as if he'd run twenty miles uphill. "The mattress must be stuffed with rocks."

Maggie raised a brow. "If it makes you feel better to grumble, go right ahead. I promise to make sympathetic noises as I unpack and put away our things."

Was she making fun of him? Will's glower faded. "Don't you know humoring a person is only effective if he doesn't realize what you're about?"

Her lips twitched into an approving smile. "If you

promise to be civil, I'll tell you about the other passengers I've met."

"How can I resist such a tantalizing incentive?" he queried dryly. Actually, she could just read the passenger list and he'd listen, so long as she kept bustling about. Did she realize how enticing she looked as she bent over trunks and cupboards?

Maggie smiled over her shoulder. "Lady Maude and Miss Abigail are wonderfully eccentric ladies. And Mr. Cassidy is quite dashing. But if you'd rather I not discuss—"

"By all means," he interrupted, "tell me about your new friends." He was especially interested in hearing about the *dashing* Mr. Cassidy.

Maggie grinned as if she'd read his thoughts, then turned back to the trunks. She related in excruciating detail all she'd learned about the pair of female world travelers. When was she going to move on to that Cassidy fellow?

He was on the point of raising that very question when she lifted something out of a trunk with a triumphant, "Aha!"

She spun around, her eyes sparkling with an anticipatory gleam. "I was beginning to fear I'd left this behind."

The "this" she referred to was a rectangular bundle wrapped in a fancy scrap of fabric and tied with a velvet ribbon.

"And just what is this treasure that had you so worried?"

She approached his bedside. "It's your wedding gift. What with the excitement over the children's arrival, I didn't have an opportunity to give it to you sooner."

She'd bought him a wedding gift? Will accepted the package, strangely touched by the unexpected gesture.

Was it just a token she'd purchased as a nod to convention? Or had she selected something more personal?

With mounting curiosity, he untied the ribbon. The

wrapping slipped away into a soft puddle of cloth, revealing a flat box of polished wood.

Will opened the hinged lid and lifted an intricately carved ivory sculpture.

The figures were of a dragon and dragonfighter in mid-battle. The dagger-clawed beast towered over the man—twice again as tall, fierce, menacing, and powerful. Lunging toward his prey, the monster's roar of victory was almost audible.

The warrior, on the other hand, was no triumphant St. George. He had dropped to one knee, and his left arm dangled uselessly at his side. His shield lay on the ground beside him, and he wore no armor. Though he held an upraised sword at the ready, his defeat seemed imminent.

But there was something about his defiant pose, some nuance the artist had imbued in that nearly fallen figure, that gave the impression of determination through weariness, of a resolve that would never allow him to give up. A closer look showed the sword positioned to pierce the dragon's heart as the beast descended.

So, there was hope for this dragonfighter, eternally poised on the fine line between triumph and defeat.

Will blinked. How long had he sat staring at the piece?

What had Maggie seen when she purchased this—a maimed, defeated, would-be hero, or an embattled defender, braced to grasp victory from the jaws of defeat?

Or had she merely thought it an interesting bauble?

Will looked up to find her chewing her lip uncertainly.

"I hope you like it," she said with a nervous smile. "There was something about it that drew me when I first saw it."

"The workmanship is exquisite," Will agreed, watching her face. "A true gem."

She stroked the sword-wielder's back with the tip of her index finger. "He has a certain quality to him, don't you think?" she asked dreamily. "That of someone you can trust to stay the course, to fight against injustice no matter the cost." She sighed. "Honor and courage are his only armor."

She gave a self-deprecating smile. "You must think me a sentimental goose."

"Not at all." Will held her gaze, looking for some sign that there had been a message in those words. Dare he hope she saw something of him in that image?

"Is there a dragon you need me to slay, Maggie?"

He didn't realize he'd said those words aloud until he saw surprise flare in her eyes.

Something akin to yearning flickered in her face. Then her hand moved to her broach and her expression shuttered before she offered a teasing grin. "Now you're the one being fanciful."

She pointed to the ivory carving. "Shall I put it away?"

He carefully replaced it in its case, then handed it over. Had he imagined that look of naked vulnerability clouding her face? Much as he liked the gift she had given him, he would have preferred she mimic her mother and turn over the broach.

"Pack it carefully. I plan to give it a place of honor at Briarwood."

Her face softened at his words.

"I'm sorry I don't have anything to give you in return."

Bent over a trunk, she glanced back with a quick laugh. "You've already given me so many wonderful gifts—Clover Ridge, the chance to have the children with me, an elegant wardrobe." She closed the trunk and moved on to a larger one. "My little token is paltry in comparison."

But those had been undertaken as calculated business transactions, not as gifts. He should have—

"Oh my!" Maggie stared down into the trunk.

"What is it?" Will asked the question a heartbeat before he realized what she'd stumbled on. He braced himself, not certain what reaction he'd get from his mercurially tempered wife.

"Someone else's trunk was mixed in with ours." Maggie lifted a velvet gown of midnight blue. "Another passenger is undoubtedly bemoaning the loss of her things."

Will watched her reverently smooth the lush fabric, then return the gown to the trunk with obvious reluctance. Perhaps this would turn out positively, after all.

"Shall I report it to the captain, or to someone else?" she asked as she closed the lid.

"Neither. That trunk is in the right room."

She frowned in confusion, then suspicion. "What did you do?"

Will shrugged and then winced. But there was no sympathetic softening in her expression as she waited for his answer.

"After our conversation about my purchasing you a new wardrobe, I thought that perhaps you would be . . . *reticent* to order a complete trousseau. So I paid a visit to Madame LeBlanc before your arrival and made certain she understood my wishes."

"So I had no choice from the outset." The tilt to Maggie's chin would have done a queen proud. "Why even bother to send me to her shop in the first place?"

Will sighed in exasperation as her hand moved to toy with her broach. "Of course you had choices. I told Madame LeBlanc she was to defer to you in matters of style and color." He tried a coaxing smile. "Besides, she had to take your measurements."

When she still didn't unbend, he raked a hand through his hair. "Deuce take it, Maggie, it's a *gift*. Just as the ivory sculpture you gave me a moment ago was a gift."

To his relief, the stiffness eased from her shoulders. "I'm sorry," she admitted, lacing her fingers together over her skirt. "You're right. I did overreact. It's only that I . . ."

"Don't like to feel indebted to anyone?" he finished for her.

She nodded ruefully. "Exactly." She gave him an almost-believable smile. "The gowns are lovely, thank you. They will go a long way toward making me presentable to your family."

Is that what she thought had prompted his gift? Perhaps that had been a small part of it. The thing was, he found himself wanting to give her nice things, to see her draped in pretty clothes and bright colors, because that was what she deserved.

But not at the cost of her smile. "Maggie, I don't for a moment want you to feel you are in any way 'unpresentable.' I like you as you are. If you don't feel comfortable with the gowns, then don't wear them."

His mouth quirked in a smile. "I would, however, prefer you not be clothed in mourning when I introduce you as my bride."

This time Maggie's answering smile was genuine. "I'll keep that in mind."

She swiveled around as a loud clattering from the children's room claimed her attention. "Excuse me," she called over her shoulder, already striding to the adjoining door.

Will heard disclaimers from the two youngest that "it" had been an accident—whatever "it" was. He leaned back as Maggie disappeared through the door.

What had caused such a strong reaction to his gift? Why that look of yearning when he spoke of slaying her dragons? That telling reach for her broach worried him. Something in her past had left deep scars.

And he intended to find out just what that something was.

Will watched Maggie at work. Weariness enveloped her like a cloak, but she doggedly continued to ply her needle.

The children had been tucked in two hours ago. How

much longer before she found the courage to prepare for bed?

She peeked sideways at Will, and his lips twitched. "Give it up, Maggie. I've slept half the day. You won't outlast me."

She tilted her chin. "I have no idea what you are referring to. If you'll excuse me, I think I'll prepare for bed now."

Flouncing across the room, she gathered what he assumed were her sleeping garments. Then, with a last nervous glance his way, she stepped behind the privacy screen.

The rustling sounds stirred images of her slipping out of her clothes, her hips shimmying as the skirt puddled to the floor. That vision alone was enough to fire his blood.

The dress appeared over the top of the screen, and he pictured her standing in nothing but her chemise. When the chemise followed, Will felt sweat bead on his forehead. If she'd been trying to seduce him she couldn't have done a finer job.

He heard further rustling, and pictured her slipping into her nightshift. How would she look when she stepped out? Surely Madame LeBlanc had designed appropriate nightwear for a new bride.

Things got very quiet, but she remained behind the screen. The waiting was exquisite torture. When at last he heard movement, his whole body went on the alert.

Almost defiantly, Maggie stepped out into plain view.

# Chapter Fourteen

What the devil was she wearing? It looked like a pair of trousers, tailored to fit someone her size, and topped by a shirt that came to mid-thigh. Constructed from a sensible cotton fabric, it was a far cry from the gauzy confection he'd pictured.

Maggie bit her lower lip as she eyed him. "I had Madame LeBlanc construct this when I realized what our sleeping arrangements would be. I thought it would be easier for me to climb into bed above you wearing this than a traditional shift."

Will swallowed with some difficulty as her artless comment conjured up wild images he knew she couldn't possibly have intended. If this kept up he'd need a dunk in the sea to get himself back under control.

She smiled nervously, then sat with her back to him and pulled the pins from her hair. He watched, fascinated, as the doe-brown mass tumbled down her back in sinuous waves.

She shook her head, fanning out those impudently wavy tresses, then began to rhythmically brush them from scalp to tip. The sight mesmerized him, made him want to comb the vibrant tendrils between his bare fingers, to bury his face in that softness, to tickle her naked flesh with the feathery ends.

The sensual torture drew out unbearably, but he was sorry to have it end. Laying her brush down, she tamed the flamboyant mass into a braid with quick efficiency, then turned down the lamp. With a soft "good night," she climbed into the upper bunk.

Ten minutes later, Will could tell by the sound of her breathing that Maggie was asleep.

His lips curved in an appreciative smile as he remembered how she'd looked as she'd stepped from behind the screen—her cheeks stained with an appealing blush, her eyes gleaming like liquid emeralds in the lamplight, her chin tilted defiantly.

She'd looked nothing short of magnificent.

If her intent in wearing that boyish garment was to make herself less alluring, she'd failed miserably. But, of course, she hadn't had the advantage of his view.

Her proud posture and slightly heaving bosom had drawn attention to her ample endowments. And when she moved, the fabric clung to her curves in a superbly eye-pleasing manner.

But saints alive—those trousers! Seeing Maggie's deliciously long legs delineated so nicely had made his mouth go dry, had coiled the tension in his body, had set his thoughts racing in a forbidden direction. Spying her naked feet and trim ankles hadn't eased his discomfort one bit.

When she passed between him and the lamp, his body had reacted with a force that rocked even him. Bless Madame LeBlanc! The fabric of Maggie's unconventional night garb became almost sheer, outlining her form in exquisite detail. It was all he could do to swallow the groan rising in his throat. Luckily, the bedcovers had shielded his reaction from her view or she would undoubtedly have bolted from the room.

Wounded or not, given the tiniest bit of encouragement, he would have had her in his arms, in his bed, in a heartbeat.

Will stared at the bottom of Maggie's bunk, listening to her breathe. Would she sleep so soundly if she knew his thoughts?

She was so seductively close, separated from him only by a promise.

How would he endure this assault to his resolve night after night, knowing he was unable to act on the desires she stirred in him? Could he make her burn for him the same way?

He had six months to try.

Maggie regulated her breathing. There was no point letting Will know she was still awake, still unsettled from his hot-eyed scrutiny. Even though she'd avoided looking at him after that single glance as she stepped into the open, she had felt the heat from his gaze sizzle across the room to scorch her flesh. The nape of her neck had tingled as if she were prey being stalked.

For perhaps the hundredth time since she had agreed to this marriage scheme, Maggie considered telling Will her own sordid history. She never could quite go through with it, even after all he had told her about his own past. It was one of those pieces of herself she kept locked away.

Despite what he thought, she was a coward, plain and simple.

Her last thought as she finally drifted off to sleep was that, if she could ever trust anyone enough to bare her secret shame to, it would be Will.

Maggie stepped from the children's room, surprised to find Will sitting on the edge of his bed, fully dressed except for his bare feet. Apparently yesterday's exertion hadn't set his recovery back by much. "You seem to be feeling better today."

"I'm getting dashed tired of the role of invalid." He shrugged, albeit stiffly. "I thought I'd throw it off today."

Having to depend on someone else to care for his needs chafed, did it? Maggie could sympathize with that.

And she had just the diversion to offer him. "If you're feeling up to it, I was wondering if you might provide a little lesson on protocol."

Maggie hid a smile at his knitted-brow grimace.

"Protocol?"

"Yes. During my meeting with Lady Maude yesterday, there was an awkward moment when I wasn't certain how to address her or how best to introduce myself. It occurred to me that I should become better acquainted with proper forms of address in your world before I find myself immersed in it."

Will stroked his chin. "I see. Easy enough to do. The best approach, I believe, is to use my own family as an example."

"Wonderful." Maggie felt a stir of anticipation at this promised glimpse of Will's family. "Let me gather the children."

A question flickered across his face.

"Since they are to become part of your world as well," she explained, "they can benefit from this discussion as much as I."

Will nodded. "Just keep that dratted cat out of here."

Once she'd gathered everyone and firmly closed the door on a curious Tully, Maggie pulled a chair up near Will's bed. The youngsters sat on the floor nearby.

"Mr. Trevaron is going to tell us about his family," Maggie explained. "I want you to pay particular attention to how we should address them. People do things differently in England."

She turned to Will, yielding him the floor.

He cleared his throat somewhat officiously. "We'll begin with Grandfather. He is head of the family, and was christened Benjamin Albert Trevaron. His predominate title is His Grace, the duke of Lynchmorne. He also carries a number of subordinate titles, which I will speak of in a minute. The important thing is, he is never addressed by his surname. You would address him simply as Your Grace, especially in public."

"And what do you call him?" Maggie asked. Surely, immediate family members did not hold to such formality.

A trace of cynicism tainted Will's smile. "Depending on the situation and tone of the discussion, either Grandfather or Sir."

Maggie wondered how she would get on with this man who had left such deep scars on Will.

"Grandfather has one sister," Will continued. "Her given name is Roberta. Since she never married, she is formally addressed as Lady Roberta Trevaron."

"And this is by virtue of being the sister of a duke?"

"No, it is because Aunt Robbie is the *daughter* of a duke."

Maggie wrinkled her nose. "Isn't that just semantics?"

"Not necessarily." Will held up a hand. "Let me proceed and you'll see what I mean."

Maggie nodded, hoping he was right.

"Grandfather had three sons. The oldest, my uncle Charles, automatically took the highest of Grandfather's subordinate titles at his birth. So he became Marquess of Rainley. He would be addressed as Lord Rainley, not by his surname of Trevaron. Likewise, his wife would be addressed as Lady Rainley."

So that meant, at least in England, she would not be Mrs. Trevaron.

"Grandfather's other two sons are my father, Lawrence, and my uncle Osgood. As younger sons, they would simply be addressed as Lord Lawrence Trevaron and Lord

Osgood Trevaron." He smiled. "Or, less formally as Lord Lawrence and Lord Osgood. But never as Lord Trevaron, since the style of lord, in their case, simply indicates the status of their father."

This was more complex than she'd realized. How much of the discussion were the children following?

"Now, for the next generation. uncle Charles had three children. My father had myself and Jennifer. Uncle Osgood had one son, Alexander."

Maggie felt a twinge of jealousy. She'd never had siblings, grandparents, aunts, uncles, cousins in her life—all those ties he mentioned so casually.

"Since Charles was a marquess," Will continued, "his children all carry courtesy titles." He paused and spread his hands. "On the other hand, Jenny and I, along with our cousin, Alex, carry no titles. We are simply addressed as Mr. or Miss."

Owen drew his brows down. "That doesn't seem fair."

"It's neither fair nor unfair," Will replied. "It's simply a matter of birth, like having green eyes or brown hair."

His expression sobered. "When my uncle Charles died, my cousin, Thomas, assumed the rank of Lord Rainley. Unfortunately, Thomas passed away, as well. Peerages, almost without exception, pass through the male line. Since Thomas had no sons, the title would fall to the next male in line of my grandfather's heirs."

He paused and looked at the children expectantly.

"That would be your father," Cal answered.

"Yes." Will gave the boy an approving smile. "Except my father died over fifteen years ago."

That caught Maggie's attention. Fifteen years ago—he would have been little more than a schoolboy.

"My father died, too." Beth stared at Will with a sympathetic, we-share-a-loss expression.

Maggie's insides warmed at the way Will's own expression softened. "I know, poppet, and I'm sorry."

Then he looked around. "So, who becomes Lord Rainley?"

"Your other uncle?" Owen ventured.

"No. He is also deceased, but even were he alive, the title would not go to him. It passes down through the duke's oldest sons, as long as there is a male in direct line."

"So that means *you* are Lord Rainley," Cal said slowly. Then he turned to Maggie. "And that would make you Lady Rainley."

Maggie couldn't tell whether Cal was pleased or upset.

"Very good, Calvin," Will said. "And someday I may be duke. However," he turned to Maggie, "even so, my sister will remain simply Miss Jennifer Trevaron, until she marries, at which time she will take her style of address from her husband."

Maggie nodded. "That's why you said your aunt's title came from her relationship to her father rather than to her brother."

Owen frowned up at Maggie. "Does that mean we have to call you Lady Rainley instead of Momma now?"

Maggie reached down and tousled his hair. "Of course not. You three had best continue to address me as Momma or mother if you know what's good for you."

Beth faced Will. "Does that mean we should call you Poppa?"

Maggie was caught off guard by the question. Her gaze shot to Will's, and she saw uncertainty flicker in his expression.

She should rescue him, answer Beth's question herself. But her mind refused to provide the words.

Will looked at Beth's innocent, little-girl face, and felt at a loss. Just how the devil should he answer that question?

Calvin, however, stepped in. "Don't be a goose, Beth. Just because Lord Rainley married Momma doesn't mean he's our poppa."

# A WILL OF HER OWN

Will noted the stilted emphasis the boy put on his title. Was it because he was unused to that form of address, or because he disapproved? Whatever the reason, he gave the boy a look of approval. "That's correct. I would never presume to try to take your father's place. However, I *will* promise to take care of you as I believe he and your mother would wish."

Then he turned to Beth. "As for what to call me, 'sir' will do for now, unless it is a very formal occasion."

He saw Maggie execute a subtle nod of approval, and was relieved. "I think that is enough about my family for one day. We can speak of this more later, if you like."

As the children stood, he gave them one last bit of advice. "The easiest thing to do, if you are uncertain how to address someone, is to remember how they were introduced to you. You can't go wrong using that form of address."

"Go on and check on Tully," Maggie told the children. "I'll be along in a few minutes."

Good—he would have her to himself for a while. Will thought fast, trying to come up with a possible distraction. He was determined to keep Maggie with him as long as possible.

Thirty minutes later, she sat across the table from him, studying the chessboard with a frown of concentration. While he waited for her move, Will looked around the room.

The connecting door stood open, the unfortunate Tully having been relegated to the confines of his carrier.

Beth sat on the floor by the table, playing with a rag doll. Owen orchestrated battles nearby with an army of painted tin soldiers. And Calvin leaned back against the door jamb, half in one room, half in the other, with a book propped on his knee.

Will hadn't found himself part of such a domestic scene

in many years. He hadn't realized how much he missed it.

"There!" Maggie reclaimed his attention as she moved her remaining bishop. "Check."

He pretended to study the board. Having anticipated her move, though, he already had his next one planned out. "I believe you owe me a bit of a history lesson."

"A history lesson?"

"Yes." He glanced up. "I told you about my family. I believe it only fair I hear about your."

She shrugged. "There's not much to tell. I'm an only child. My parents moved here from England before I was born and I only know bits and pieces about the families they left behind."

"You have relatives in England?" Perhaps that would provide added incentive for her to settle happily there.

"I'm not sure. My parents didn't keep in touch with their families after they moved to America." Maggie raised a brow. "Are you stalling because you can't figure out your next move?"

Something in her tone warned him she wasn't interested in pursuing this discussion. He'd have to come back to it later, perhaps when they were alone.

"On the contrary." Will moved his rook and smiled. "I believe that's check and mate."

She stared at the board, then sat back with a look of amiable chagrin. "It seems the first match goes to you, sir."

As she cleared the board, Maggie dropped a pawn. Will bent to retrieve it, but Beth was ahead of him.

The child held out the piece, then paused as she frowned over his disfigured hand.

Will stiffened, waiting for her reaction.

Beth gazed up with a look of sympathy. "Does it hurt?"

Nonplussed by her concern, Will shook his head. "No, it healed a long time ago." At least physically.

She looked back at his hand. "Will the finger grow back?"

He sensed Maggie's dismay at the child's artless questions, but he was glad she held her tongue. Refreshing to have someone treat his mangled hand as a mere curiosity.

"No, I'm afraid not."

"Oh." The child sat back and hugged her doll. "I'm sorry."

Will's heart warmed to the child. Yes, this one would definitely be a sought-after miss when she grew up.

And he would be responsible for her. "Thank you."

Owen looked up, taking an interest in their conversation. "How did it happen—wolves, highwaymen, pirates?"

Will froze for a moment as the memories flooded back. His finger wasn't all he'd lost that night. His scars were fitting payment for such a tragic failure.

"Owen, I don't think—"

Will shook off the morbid thoughts. "Nothing so exciting, I'm afraid. It happened in a carriage accident."

Maggie sensed Will's hesitation, noted the self-revulsion cross his features. He wasn't telling the whole story, but now was not the time to dig deeper.

Nor did she want the children to do so.

"After I put away this chess set," she announced, "I think we should spend a bit of time catching up on our lessons."

Her words were greeted with a chorus of groans. "Let's have none of that, now. We haven't done any schoolwork since you returned from Boston."

Then she smiled. "But first, why don't we give Tully a reprieve and take him for a walk above deck?"

That suggestion met with a great deal more enthusiasm. As the children scrambled to their feet, she turned to Will. "Would you like me to help you back to bed?"

He shook his head. "I can make it that far on my own,

when I get ready. Right now I believe I'll stay up and read for a bit."

"At least let me fetch your book for you."

He smiled. "Very well. My books are in the brown trunk there in the corner. Look for Cooper's *The Pilot.*"

As Maggie searched for the book, she spied tomes by Milton, Shakespeare, Cervantes, and Irving, as well as works of poetry, treatises, and biographies. Will certainly had eclectic taste.

Finding the book he'd asked for, she brought it to him. "That's quite a library you've assembled."

Will smiled. "That's just some of my favorites. The majority of my books are being crated and shipped along with other items from my residence." He raised a brow and smiled. "Feel free to help yourself to any that interest you."

The thought of having access to an extensive library sent an anticipatory shiver through Maggie. She had always loved to read, as had her parents. Their home had been filled with all sorts of books and periodicals, most of them well-worn.

They had been lost in the fire that took her home and her father. Since then, books had been a luxury she couldn't afford. Even when she married, Joseph had thought them frivolous, so she limited her purchases to educational materials for the children, along with an occasional book suitable to read aloud to them.

"Thank you." She gave Will's arm an impulsive squeeze. She'd already benefited in so many ways from marrying him.

She only hoped he was as happy with the bargain as she.

Will watched her go, pleased to think it was he who put that smile on her face, that spring in her step. It seemed she was adjusting to her life as his wife quite pleasantly.

As long as he didn't try to touch her with his scarred hand.

Although, when Beth and Owen had questioned him about it, he'd sensed no distaste or withdrawal from her, only concern for the children's lack of tact. Surely that was a good sign? Perhaps, in time, she could learn to tolerate his touch.

It was something to hope for.

"Check."

Will leaned back and watched Maggie's brow furrow in that fetching way it did when she concentrated. She studied the chessboard with a determined, I'm-not-beaten-yet frown.

That was one of the things he admired about her. She approached obstacles as if they were only temporary impediments, something to either overcome or go around.

And more often than not, she succeeded. During the three days they'd already spent aboard ship, she'd managed to give the connecting cabins a warm, nest-of-a-home feel.

Part of it was the routine she'd established. In the mornings, she helped the children with their lessons. While they exercised their minds, Will exercised his body. Pacing in the cabin was monotonous, but he felt stronger, and could manage more activity with each passing day.

After the mid-day meal, the youngsters pulled out toys or books to amuse themselves, and Maggie turned her attention to him. As they played chess or cards, she chattered about the children's accomplishments or recounted stories from her forays outside the cabin.

He enjoyed listening to her as much as watching her competitive streak emerge as they played. She hadn't succeeded in beating him yet, but she'd come close a couple of times, and he'd had to work harder for each of his victories.

"Ah-ha." She bent over the board with a triumphant flourish.

To his surprise, rather than sliding her bishop in the defensive move he'd expected, Maggie countered with her rook, both defending her king and placing his in jeopardy.

She leaned back and folded her hands primly in her lap. "If I'm not mistaken, that's check and mate."

Frowning, he studied the board. She had him neatly cornered, right enough. How the devil had he missed that possibility?

Perhaps he'd spent too much time focusing on his opponent and too little on the game itself?

"Well," she said with what sounded suspiciously like a hint of gloating, "do you concede or did I misread the board?"

He raised his hands, acknowledging defeat. "I bow to your prowess. The game is yours." Seeing her little-girl excitement over her victory eased the sting to his pride at having lost.

She stood and made as if to put the game away.

"Surely it's not time for your afternoon stroll already?" That was the part of the day he disliked, when the four of them went out to enjoy the fresh air, leaving him behind. He wondered how big a battle he'd have on his hands if he told her he was ready to leave this prison of a room. Maybe he should find out.

"Actually," she said, her dimple coming out of hiding, "I thought, since you bore your defeat so well, the least I could do would be to reward you with a stroll up on deck." She paused, a teasing glint in her eyes. "Unless you don't feel up to it."

It was about bloody time. "Just try to hold me back."

She gave him a stern look. "Promise you'll let me know if you feel the least bit strained."

Will felt a prickle of irritation. Did she ever think of him in any other light than that of her patient?

A few minutes later, they stepped out into the passageway. "You go on ahead, with Tully" she instructed the children. "Just make sure you stay within sight."

Maggie's hand was cradled in the crook of his arm and he knew she was braced to support him if he should need it. But he was determined not to take advantage of her this time.

When they reached the open deck, Will turned his face to the sky and inhaled deeply of the fresh air. By the saints, it felt good to finally be out in the open again.

"You must be Maggie's Mr. Trevaron."

He lowered his gaze to find himself facing a turban-crowned dowager with a no-nonsense air about her.

He sketched a bow. "At your service, madam. And you must be Lady Maude."

"Maggie spoke of me, did she?" She eyed him speculatively. "You're Lynchmorne's grandson. The one who created all that stir a few years back when you left the country after the Radwin chit broke it off with you."

Will stiffened. It was starting, and they hadn't even set foot in England yet. "The same."

# Chapter Fifteen

"No need to get your back up. What happened is no business of mine. I prefer to judge a person for myself." She flashed an arch smile. "Truth be told, I raised quite a few eyebrows, myself, in my own day."

Lady Maude pointed an imperious finger. "Since you haven't gotten all stiff-necked over your bride's desire to practice medicine, it predisposes me to approve of you."

The air of largesse with which she made this pronouncement appealed to Will's sense of humor. "Thank you," he said solemnly. "Though, I fear your praise is undeserved. Once Maggie decides on a course of action, not even I can deter her."

"Really, sir," Maggie protested.

Lady Maude, however, grinned approvingly. "Since you said that last with a smile in your voice, I am even more impressed with your ability to recognize a woman's worth."

Will couldn't quite hide the quirk to his lips. "I'm pleased to have your approval, madam. However, before we go much further, I'm afraid I must correct you on one small matter."

The woman arched a brow. "And that is?"

"Due to a series of unhappy circumstances, I now find myself in the position of my grandfather's heir."

"Ah, so you're Lord Rainley now, are you? My condolences on the loss of your uncle and cousin."

Before Will could respond, she turned to Maggie. "You should have said something right off. Can't have me calling you Mrs. Trevaron when you should be addressed as Lady Rainley."

Maggie smiled. "I'm afraid all this talk of lords and ladies is still new and somewhat confusing to me. Besides, I'd much rather you just call me Maggie."

"Very prettily said, my dear. You are forgiven." Then the eccentric aristocrat turned back to Will. "You have the look of your grandfather. Probably share his obstinate streak, as well."

That raised Will's eyebrows. "You know my grandfather?"

She gave an inelegant snort. "Know him? Why, he courted me all through my first season."

The normally stiff-backed woman actually preened. "I cut quite a figure back then. Had a whole stable of young bucks mooning over me. Lynchmorne was the best of the lot, I'll give him that. Tall, handsome, intelligent, courtly."

Trying to picture his grandfather in the role of a "young buck" pursuing and being pursued by a bevy of debutantes was quite a stretch for Will. Had that seemingly all-powerful figure ever set his sights on something he hadn't attained?

Lady Maude shook her head. "A bit too much stiff-necked pride for my taste, but that was no doubt due to the kind of father he'd had. Probably would have offered for me if I hadn't made it clear I wasn't in the marriage mart."

Her words drew him out of his musings. "What do you mean, 'the kind of father' he had?" It bothered Will that

# Winnie Griggs

this stranger knew more about his family's history than he did.

But Lady Maude waved a hand dismissively. "No point resurrecting old gossip." Then something behind Will and Maggie caught her attention. "Abigail, where's your shawl? You know how prone you are to chills." With a nod, she excused herself and marched purposefully toward her cousin.

"Are you ready to return to the cabin?" Maggie asked solicitously.

Will reined in a sharp retort. Now that he'd gotten a reprieve from his sick room, he wasn't about to let her return him to invalid status. "I'm fine, Maggie."

The look of concern didn't go away entirely, but she nodded and strolled on, stopping occasionally to exchange pleasantries with the other passengers. After Lady Maude, however, the people to whom she introduced him seemed quite tame.

Until they encountered Simon Cassidy. As soon as Will heard the name, his senses went on full alert.

"You are looking particularly lovely today, Mrs. Trevaron," the lothario remarked as he bowed over Maggie's hand. "That gown complements your coloring most becomingly."

Will decided on the spot that he didn't much care for this smooth-talking American.

"Why thank you, sir." Maggie gave the flatterer a smile that soured Will's mood.

Didn't she realize the man was flirting with her?

Didn't the oaf care that her husband stood next to her?

"It's Lady Rainley," Will said stiffly.

Simon blinked. "Beg pardon?"

"My wife is a marchioness," he explained through gritted teeth. "She is to be addressed as Lady Rainley."

The man had the gall to look amused rather than set in his place. "I see." He turned to Maggie. "My apologies,

Lady Rainley. I hadn't realized your elevated station. Of course, one such as yourself would grace the arm of a king with ease."

Will had had enough. "If you'll excuse us, it's time my wife and I gathered the children and returned to our cabin."

Maggie gave him a solicitous look, then excused herself to gather the children.

As she returned to Will's side, she took his arm again. "I hope we didn't over-tax you today."

"Not at all." Will already regretted the impulsive excuse he'd used to pull her away from Simon Cassidy. It didn't do much to restore his non-invalid status in her eyes. "I'm just a trifle tired. Tomorrow will be better."

"I'm sure it will." She cut him a sideways glance. "I assumed you must have felt some discomfort. It's the only reason I can think of to account for your rudeness to Mr. Cassidy."

Rude—hah! He'd merely made it clear to the blighter he wouldn't countenance any dallying with his wife—whether his wife knew what was going on or not.

And Mr. smooth-as-glass-Cassidy better have understood the message or he would get a taste of what rude really meant.

Over the next few days, Will steadily increased the amount of time he spent up and about.

Not surprisingly, he discovered Maggie was popular with the other passengers. Her air of quiet dignity, mixed with that teasing streak of mischief, was irresistible. She invariably found inventive ways to relieve the tedium of shipboard life. The time she and the children spent up on deck turned into playtime enjoyed by adults and children, alike.

Today she had engaged the group in a word game she called "Mrs. Pennywhistle packed a trunk." A dozen or so passengers had accepted her challenge to participate. The others, including Will, watched, enjoying the entertainment.

The game was well underway—they were on their fourth pass through the alphabet. To Will's annoyance, the only players still in the game were Maggie and Cassidy. The American currently had her undivided attention as he recited a litany of items.

". . . quirt, a rug, a shawl, a teacup, a veil, a—"

"Foul!" yelled Calvin. "I don't know what you missed, but you skipped right over the letter 'U.' That means Mother wins."

Will felt smug satisfaction over Cassidy's loss.

"Not so fast," the boor argued with mock-severity. "Lady Rainley has yet to take her turn this round."

"Agreed." Maggie picked up the challenge with alacrity. She looked Will's way before she started her recitation, and he winked, letting her know he had confidence in her certain victory.

Maggie began her litany of items in a singsong chant. She went through the list, pausing only for an occasional breath. Will enjoyed that sparkle she always got when facing a challenge.

Cassidy might as well admit defeat and be done with it.

He smiled as she neared the end of the list.

". . . a teacup, *an urn*," she grinned saucily as she pronounced the item that Cassidy had missed, "a veil, a wick, a yoke, ashes, *and* some beeswax." She added her own final item with a flourish.

"Well done." Cassidy kissed her hand theatrically. "The entire list without hesitation. I hereby concede the victory."

Maggie curtsied coyly, and Will was surprised at the stab of jealousy he felt to see her elusive dimple aimed at another man.

"Thank you, kind sir, you made a most worthy opponent." Then she turned to Will, who was already pushing his way through the small crowd to her side.

He bowed. "My compliments on your victory."

"Thank you." A becoming shade of pink colored her cheeks.

The American nodded Will's way. "You're a lucky man to have such a bride. She's done much to keep our trip entertaining."

Will's eyes narrowed. There'd been just a hint of something in the man's tone that lent a second, less-than-innocent meaning to those words. This pretty-faced dandy bore careful watching.

Maggie turned at a hail from Owen. She had only taken a few steps, though, when she stumbled and fell.

Will was by her side in an instant. A small crowd had gathered, but he ignored them. Brushing the hair gently from her forehead, his heart lurched painfully in the split second before her eyes fluttered open.

"Lie still," he managed to say calmly. "Tell me if it hurts anywhere."

"What happened?" The children pushed through the crowd.

"I fell, just like a henwit. But I'll be fine." She turned a reassuring look Will's way. "Just a small bump on the head." Her voice reflected self-reproach. "I'm sorry if I worried you."

"Easy." Will offered her a hand up, then frowned as Cassidy did the same.

Maggie gave him a stern look. "You're not at full strength yourself, yet." She took Cassidy's hand with a grateful smile.

Will swallowed an oath. That smile should be his. But her well-being was more important than quibbling over his recovery.

When Maggie stood, however, she sagged, as if disoriented. The American steadied her by placing his arm around her waist.

She gave a weak smile. "I guess I'm shakier than I thought."

Will moved to extricate her from the bold American, to support her himself. But the oaf was quicker.

Cassidy scooped her up, facing Will with an innocent air. "If you're up to it, you can go on ahead and open the door."

Will's anger mounted. How dare this would-be Romeo handle Maggie so familiarly? His mood didn't improve when her arm snaked around Cassidy's neck. No wonder the man looked so smug.

There was nothing for it now, though, but to do as he'd requested. Fuming silently, Will gathered the children and marched to their cabin. The fact that the dratted cat trotted at his heels, causing a fit of sneezing, did not improve his temper. But he understood the children's need to be near their mother, so he suffered that indignity, as well. Thankfully, when they reached the cabin, Cal took Tully into the children's room.

Maggie had said the boy was perceptive.

Will threw open his and Maggie's door with a bit more force than was absolutely necessary. He took satisfaction in noting how winded Cassidy was. Will stood quietly as the American made a fuss over settling her in, though he itched to toss him out.

It proved too much, however, when he bent to remove her shoes. "I believe I can take care of any further ministrations *my wife* may require." Will didn't try to hide his irritation. If his glare made Cassidy uncomfortable, so be it.

"Of course, just trying to be of service." The bloke didn't seem at all discomfited. "If there's anything else I can do, seeing as you're not at full strength yet, just give me a yell."

The man was actually whistling as he exited!

"Well, you certainly were rude," Maggie said after the door closed. "He was just trying to be helpful."

*Like hell.* Will held his peace as he knelt at her feet. "Are you still feeling faint?" he asked, unfastening her shoes.

"No," she said unconvincingly. "I just have a headache."

He caressed her feet as he slipped her shoes off. Her foot felt so small and fragile in his hand, her skin so soft and warm.

Her eyes widened and he distracted her with a teasing smile. "So, is it my turn to feed you gruel in bed and lecture you whenever you try to overexert yourself?"

She gave a suspicious sniff. "I do believe that you are enjoying this bit of role reversal."

"Madam, you wrong me!" He rose, theatrically raising a hand to his heart, hoping she didn't realize exactly *how* he was enjoying it. "I assure you, I have the deepest of sympathies for your plight and am only eager to be of what service I can."

"Wretch!" she accused with a smile. "But you shall not have your revenge." She lifted her chin. "I'll do quite nicely with a little rest, so you may just go about your business."

He pulled a long face, and she laughed outright. The sound was music to his ears—and his soul.

Who would have thought he would enjoy such teasing banter? They had settled into a comfortable friendship, one where they shared laughter and conversation, where they could debate issues for hours without incurring hard feelings, where they respected each other as individuals.

It was the closest connection he'd ever shared with a woman.

So why did he want more?

Will put his book aside as he finally heard her stir. "How are you feeling?" he asked, moving to her bedside—his bed until today. In the soft lamplight, she looked ethereal, fragile.

"The headache and dizziness are gone." She made as if to sit up. "The children—"

He gently pushed her back down. "The children have had their supper and are safely tucked in bed."

"In bed? How long did I sleep?"

Will pulled out his pocket watch. "It's nearly ten o'clock."

"Ten o'clock," she echoed with a grimace. "And you tended the children all afternoon and evening."

Will was warmed by the light of appreciation in her eyes, but shrugged nonchalantly. "It wasn't much of a chore. They're rather self-sufficient youngsters."

"Still, I thank you."

"Are you hungry? I saved a bit of cold chicken from supper."

She nodded. "That sounds good." She started to sit up again, then paused with a startled look on her face.

Will watched her surreptitiously take stock of her situation. He'd removed the pins from her hair and partially unfastened her gown to make her more comfortable, but that's as far as he'd taken it. Not that it hadn't been tempting to go farther.

She gave him an uncertain look. Was she feeling some of what he had when she had ministered to him?

"I think I'll prepare for bed while you get the food," Maggie said, her voice unusually hesitant.

"Of course." Will made a fuss over gathering the meal as she scurried to gather her things and step behind the screen. When she'd made her ablutions and donned her unorthodox night clothes, she stepped out, pausing uncertainly in the center of the room.

"Back to bed with you," he said with mock sternness. "And no arguments. Tonight, I'm the doctor."

Maggie smiled, and started toward the bed.

"And by the way, as of tonight, we're switching beds."

She turned back around with a frown. "But—"

"I said, no arguments. Even though I'm 'not at full strength,' I *am* capable of climbing into that upper bunk."

Her expression remained mutinous for a second longer, then she gave in. Without another word, she climbed into the bed he had formerly occupied and slid under the covers.

She propped a pillow at her back and flashed a breezy smile that almost hid her disquiet. "Where is this food you promised?"

He carried the plate across the room and sat on the edge of her bed. Her eyes widened, but she made no move to evict him.

"Now, if I remember how this is done, the doctor feeds the poor, listless patient." Careful to use his left hand, he raised a small piece of meat to her lips.

"Will, really," she protested, "that's not—"

"Tut, tut," he admonished. "No arguing with the doctor." He waggled the morsel in front of her face.

She sighed, but her lips twitched tellingly. She dutifully opened her mouth and he deposited the morsel between those tempting lips of hers.

He watched her chew, then swallow. "Very good." When he lifted the next bite, Maggie parted her lips without hesitation. It seemed she was going to go along with his bit of play acting.

Feeding her with his fingers was a sensual experience— at once intimate and exotic. Not to mention arousing. But Will was feeling quite pleased with his control.

Until halfway through the meal, when her lips closed on the tip of his fingers. Heat sizzled through him in a lightning flash, hardening his body to an almost painful extent. It took all his energies to keep his breathing even and retain his smile.

She'd felt it, too. He could tell by the catch in her

breath, the flush of her cheeks. Withdrawing his fingers slowly, he barely swallowed a groan as her lips gave gentle resistance.

*Dear, sweet Maggie, what are you doing to me?*

"Let me get you something to drink." Will moved to the table, needing to put distance between them before he acted on impulses she wasn't ready to deal with yet.

He poured her a cup of cider, taking his time, getting his raging emotions back under control. He finally turned, only to find her watching him with a solemn, unreadable expression.

Had she guessed how close to the edge he was?

Maggie watched him approach with the cup, trying to read the emotions behind the hooded expression on his face. She had come to the conclusion that she was nothing short of a wanton.

Heaven help her she *wanted* him. Wanted him so bad she thought she would burst from sheer need. Being in his bed, enveloped by echoes of his presence, didn't help. She inhaled his scent—spicy, masculine, heady.

Little tremors of desire rippled through her.

And he wanted her, too. Even she had been able to read the passion and desire flaring in his eyes. All it would take would be for her to give him a sign that she was willing . . .

But wanting him to make love to her, and being able to act on those desires were two different things. At least in her case.

She was beginning to realize how unfair she'd been to him by accepting his offer. What would he think when he discovered her secret? Would he feel betrayed, turn away in disgust?

She didn't think she could bear to experience such a thing.

Somehow, she had to find a way to make this right.

# Chapter Sixteen

Maggie was up and about by the next day. Their normal routine resumed, as if nothing had happened to interrupt it.

Her emotional state was a different matter. She tried to keep that frailty of spirit hidden, and was convinced she did a creditable job.

There was no repeat of their intimate late-night feast, but that didn't mean the tension, the nearly irresistible tug of desire for physical contact between them lessened. She could feel the crackle and spark of electricity whenever they were alone together, especially at night.

But somehow, she made it through each day, keeping to the routine they'd fallen into, making sure the children and Will were thrown together enough so that they could grow accustomed to each other, but not so much that they chafed at the closeness.

About a week after her accident, during a stroll on deck, the children came clamoring to her and Will.

"Tully's slipped his leash," Owen reported breathlessly. "He ran off and we can't find him anywhere."

Maggie wasn't very concerned. Tully was a typical cat—curious and wily—but he was smart enough to not jump ship. "Why don't we make a game of it—see who can find him first."

The children were immediately taken with the idea, and a few passengers volunteered to help, as well. Will cautioned them on what sections of the ship were off limits, promising to send crewmen to check those if the searchers didn't have any luck.

Twenty-five minutes later most everyone was ready to admit defeat. Will had already asked the captain to have the crew check various areas of the ship the passengers didn't have access to, and Maggie was beginning to feel a pinprick of alarm.

Then Beth cried out, "There he is!"

Looking to where the girl pointed, Maggie's pinprick turned into full-blown anxiety.

Tully crouched on the mast at the very top of the rigging.

"How in the world did the animal get up there?" Mr. Cassidy stood beside her, looking up in amused disbelief.

Maggie groaned. "The question is, how do we get him down?"

She looked back up, her insides lurching as the mast swayed. *Dear God, please watch over that wretched beast a little longer.*

"I'll go after him," Owen volunteered. "I'm a great climber. Just watch, I'll have him back down in no time."

Beth chimed in at once. "I'm good at climbing, too."

"You can't come, you're a girl." Owen's voice dripped scorn. "Everybody knows girls can't climb worth a fig."

"Can too. Bet I can climb higher and faster than you."

While they argued, Maggie spotted Cal with a foot already on the rigging.

"Cal, get back here at once," Maggie commanded. "And you two, stop that bickering." She took a deep breath. "It's wonderful of you to be so brave, but it's too dangerous."

Mr. Cassidy nodded. "Your mother's right. I'll speak to

the captain and ask him to send someone to get the animal for you."

Maggie placed a hand on his arm. "Thank you, but the captain said pets were allowed only if they didn't become a nuisance. He threatened to have any animal who bothered the crew or passengers locked in the hold. I can't let him do that to Tully."

"It's only a cat," he shrugged. "If you must curtail the animal's activities, so be it."

Maggie narrowed her eyes as she met his gaze. "Mr. Cassidy, I'm sure you mean well, but Tully is more than just a cat. He's a very cherished part of our life." She nibbled at her lip. "I've got to find Will. He'll know what to do."

Mr. Cassidy raised a brow. "Splendid idea. Perhaps he can talk some sense into you."

The American's comment brought a smile to Will's lips. "You ask a lot of me, sir," he said as he joined them. He wasn't at all displeased to have discovered the two were at odds, for once.

Maggie cast her companion a disgruntled look before turning to Will.

So Cassidy *had* fallen from grace. Will's mood improved significantly. "Would someone care to explain what's going on?"

"Mrs. Trevaron's pet has climbed up on the mast," Cassidy answered. "I want to ask the captain to send someone to fetch the beast, but she's latched onto the notion that he'll incarcerate the animal in the hold if I do." He quirked a brow as if he fully expected Will to share his view of the situation.

Maggie shot him another glare, then shifted her gaze back to Will. "Captain Lucien said he would do just that if Tully caused any trouble, and I won't have it."

Will noted the worried, vulnerable expression lurking just below the surface of her calm demeanor, and the anxious expressions on the children's faces. With a shake of his head, he peeled off his coat and turned to Calvin. "Fetch a sack. I don't think Tully will be particularly grateful for my rescue, and I don't fancy fighting his claws on the way down."

Maggie's brow wrinkled. "You can't mean you're going after him yourself. You hate cats."

"I don't intend to be in contact with the beast for long." Not any longer than it took to stuff the troublesome feline into the sack, at any rate.

"But your shoulder," she protested, "it may not be—"

Not that again. "Maggie, I know what I can and can't handle. It's not idle boasting when I say I'm up to this. I've made this sort of climb before, and I know what it takes."

He handed her his coat. "Hold this. I won't be long." With that he took the sack from Calvin, and strode across the deck.

Maggie watched, fascinated, as Will jumped to the rigging and climbed with an air of ease and confidence. His movements were surprisingly agile and graceful for such a large man. The exertion caused the muscles in his arms and back to strain against the fabric of his shirt.

The resulting display was not lost on her.

He was doing this for *her*. As much as he hated cats, he was putting his own life at risk to rescue an animal he proclaimed to detest. Maggie felt a strange fluttering in her chest, a hitch in her breathing.

Captain Lucien arrived at her elbow just as Will reached the midpoint. "What's going on here?" he demanded.

"My husband is rescuing my cat." Maggie kept her eyes focused on Will. She'd never forgive herself if he made a misstep and caused himself serious injury.

"Your cat is in the rigging!" The captain was obviously concerned about an entirely different matter. "Mrs. Tre-

varon, I warned you what I would do if that animal became a nuisance."

Maggie turned to face his glare with an offended frown.
"Tully is *not* a nuisance. He's just stranded on your mast."
Maggie forced herself to adopt a placating tone. "None of
your crew or passengers has been bothered by this."

Will had reached his quarry now. With a quick, deft
motion, he threw the sack over the hunkered-down feline.

Maggie was impressed with Will's athletic prowess. Not
to mention his kindness. This act meant more to her than
all the dresses and titles he could ever bestow.

In no time at all, Will had his feet back on the deck.
He swaggered over, bowed, and handed her the sack. His
cock-of-the-walk display was only slightly marred by the
inelegant sneeze that escaped from him as he straightened.

"Thank you so much." She gave him a one-armed hug.

Will frowned at the furiously twitching sack in her
other hand. "Just wait until I'm well away before you open
that thing." His statement was punctuated by a second,
louder sneeze.

Maggie reluctantly released Will and turned to hand Cal
the squirming sack. "Take Tully, along with your brother
and sister, to your cabin. Don't release him until you're
inside and the door is closed. He'll likely shoot out like
his tail's on fire."

The captain stepped forward. "Mr. Trevaron, a word
please."

Maggie's impulsive hug had made Will feel like king of
the world and he wasn't about to let the captain spoil
things. Retrieving his coat, he turned with a cool smile.
"My apologies for not getting permission before I climbed
the rigging. Terrible breach of protocol. However, it was
a situation that called for quick action. I'm sure you understand."

The captain seemed only slightly mollified. "Of course,

sir. But there's still the matter of the commotion that cat caused."

Will clapped him on the back. "While the cat is an irritant for me, I don't see where he's been a problem for your crew. I'm sure you wouldn't care to make more of this than is warranted." He smiled, but made sure the hint of steel was still there.

Captain Lucien finally backed down. "No, of course not. Madam, please keep a closer eye on your pet in the future." And with a curt bow, he left them.

Maggie placed a hand on Will's arm. "Thank you, again. I believe you've just rescued Tully a second time."

"Good. That makes us even. Couldn't stand being beholden to a deuced cat, of all things."

"On the contrary, that puts you one up on Tully." She flashed a wicked grin. "I'm sure he'll want to find a way to even things up again."

Will raised an eyebrow. "You strike terror to my very soul."

As he slipped his coat back on, Will winced inwardly. That bit of derring-do had cost him, but it had been worth it.

He would swear he'd displayed no outward sign of discomfort, but Maggie immediately turned solicitous. "Is your shoulder paining you? Perhaps I should take a look at it, just to make sure you haven't done any additional damage."

"Yes ma'am." He took her arm, allowing her to escort him to his cabin. Would she give him another hug?

Will caught Cassidy's gaze as they passed. The American offered him a you've-won-this-round salute. Will nodded acknowledgment, smug in his victory. His triumphant exit was spoiled only by another sneeze.

Maggie squeezed his arm in sympathy and moved a bit closer to his side.

Yes, it had definitely been worth it.

\*     \*     \*

The next several days brought inclement weather that kept them from spending time up on deck. Maggie was thankful it wasn't a full-blown storm, just steady rain from gloomy skies.

So why did she feel so edgy, so jumpy?

The third evening of their confinement, her restlessness became nearly unbearable. The children were tucked in bed and Will sat at the table with his nose in a book, as he did most evenings. She had put aside her piecework and pulled a book from his trunk in an attempt to lose herself in another world. But the words seemed like jumbled nonsense.

Finally she shut the book with an irritated thump.

Will looked up. "Is something wrong?"

She placed her elbows on the table. "Talk to me."

Will set his book aside, an agreeable smile on his face. "Very well. What shall we talk about?"

Maggie watched his right hand absently caress the spine of the book. "Tell me about the carriage accident, the one where you injured your hand."

Surprise flashed in his eyes, then they darkened from silver to gray with some other, deeper emotion. Suddenly, she was appalled at her insensitivity. "I'm sorry. I shouldn't—"

He held up a hand, a calculating cast coloring his expression. "Don't apologize. I'll tell you about that night if you answer an equally personal question for me."

Maggie shifted in her chair, not at all sure she wanted to play this game. "What question is that?"

His head tilted and he gave her an assessing look. "You speak of your parents with affection, yet you told me once that your father had let you down. I want to know what happened."

Maggie's stomach clenched at the thought of recounting

that tale. She couldn't do it, couldn't relive that time. Better to withdraw her question.

But that would be cowardly.

She had started this—it was only fair she reveal something of herself to him. "Very well, I agree."

Will flexed his scarred hand, staring at it as if reading a story there. "I was fourteen at the time. My father had been dead for two years, so I considered myself man of the family."

He gave a tight smile. "The way Calvin does, only more so."

Then he looked back at his hand. "Mother, Jenny, and I were returning from a family gathering—I don't even remember what, anymore. The roads were wet, but the sky was clear when we set out. It was getting on to dusk and we were only a few miles from Briarwood when it happened—a wheel broke. The carriage careened about a bit before it came to rest at an odd angle."

Maggie watched his face. Something terrible had happened. And she was forcing him to relive it. She opened her mouth to tell him he didn't have to say more, when he began talking again.

"I wasn't hurt, except for a scratch or two. Jenny was bawling something fierce. She was only three then, and it took me a few minutes to discover she was more scared than hurt.

"One door was wedged shut, the other almost above us. The driver opened the upper one and I handed Jen out to him. It was when I turned to help Mother that I realized she was hurt."

His jaw clenched. "Her leg was broken. It wasn't easy getting her out. I could tell she was in a great deal of pain, but she bore it without complaint. When we finally had her out, we set her on a lap blanket the driver had placed near the carriage. Some of the dampness from the road seeped through, but I was afraid to move her for fear of hurting her even more."

He met her gaze briefly, as if asking her to understand.

"I instructed the driver to take one of the horses and go for help. Then I sat down to watch over Jen and Mother, and wait."

His finger traced a circle on the table. "Jen fell asleep, which made my job easier. Then, about ten minutes after the driver left, it happened. I don't know if it was because the road was wet, or because something else on the carriage failed, but the whole thing began to tilt, to fall on top of Mother. It happened so fast, I didn't have time to move her."

Maggie felt his horror, his helplessness. She reached over and took his free hand between both of hers.

"I grabbed the axle, trying to keep the full weight off her. I succeeded for a time. But she was pinned and couldn't slide out, and I couldn't let go to help her."

She knew what was coming and her heart bled for the boy he'd been. She squeezed the hand she held, offering comfort.

"I held on for what seemed an eternity. She kept telling me over and over, that whatever happened, I wasn't to blame myself. It's as if she knew I would fail." He swallowed. "Eventually, my strength gave out and the carriage crashed down on her. My hand was caught under it, as well."

He met her gaze. "About three minutes later, help arrived."

"Your mother was right," Maggie managed to say. "It wasn't your fault. You did all you could."

It was as if he hadn't heard her. "If I'd moved her away from the carriage to begin with, or if I had just been able to hold up a few minutes longer, she would likely be alive today."

"You don't know that."

But he refused to be absolved. He gently withdrew his hand. "So, now you know my story. Let's hear yours."

Maggie took a deep breath, still trying to absorb the horror of his experience. Her story, by comparison, seemed trivial.

"Very well." She gathered her thoughts. "I've already told you about the broach," she touched it briefly, "so you know my parents loved each other very much. Almost obsessively so. Shortly after my sixteenth birthday, Mother and I caught a fever. I recovered, but despite all Father's efforts, my mother died."

Maggie shivered, remembering that awful time. "It was as if Father's whole world crumbled, as if something inside him died with her. He locked himself in his room for days after the funeral, refusing to see anyone, barely touching the food I laid at his door. I could hear him in there, alternately raging and smashing things, and sobbing uncontrollably.

"When he finally came out, he wasn't the same man. He continued his practice for a while, but he no longer cared as he once had. And he began to drink. I went from assisting to assuming more and more of his work, with him merely looking on."

Maggie smiled, though it took an effort to do so. "That's where I gained most of my medical experience."

This time, *he* took *her* hand. The sympathy in his face nearly undid her. But after another deep breath, she continued. "The drinking got worse. He blamed himself—I understood that. He felt his medical skills had failed him.

"Then, after six months of this, a girl came to our door saying her mother had gone into labor and something had gone wrong. I tried to send her to the local midwife, but she'd already tried that and the woman was busy tending another.

Maggie swallowed hard, forcing herself to finish the

tale. Will had bared his own pain to her—she owed him no less.

"I sent her back to her mother, promising that we'd be right behind. But father was drunk, almost incoherent. He was looking at this." She touched the broach again. "He kept saying over and over that he'd let her down, that he'd failed the only person who had ever meant anything to him."

Her hand tightened around Will's. "He said that while looking straight at me, as if I meant nothing at all to him."

She could still remember the pain of that moment, the realization that he would have preferred to see her die rather than her mother.

"When I tried to explain that someone needed his help, he threw the amulet across the room and told me to help her myself, if I cared so much. Then he poured another glass of whiskey."

Maggie realized her voice was unsteady, but she couldn't seem to get it back under control. "So I picked up the amulet and his medical bag, and left. I saved the woman and her baby. When I returned home, I found the house in flames. Father was still inside. It was so far gone, I couldn't get close enough to save him or anything else."

She met Will's gaze and forced herself to say the words that she'd held deep inside all these years, the truth she hadn't dared admit, even to herself. "The most horrible thing about this is, a part of me was glad to see it wiped away, to not have to face the man he'd become or painful reminders of what I'd already lost."

She lowered her head. "That's the woman you married."

Will released her hand and she thought for a moment he'd withdrawn from her, repulsed by what she'd confessed.

But a second later he knelt beside her chair. Placing a finger under her chin, he turned her face toward his. "The woman I married is kind and generous and strong and resilient. And I wouldn't have her any other way."

Maggie saw the honesty and compassion in his eyes, and her composure crumbled. Burying her face in his shoulder, she sobbed uncontrollably, mourning the father she'd lost even before his death, crying for the girl she had been, crying all those tears she hadn't been able to shed seven years ago.

Will silently cursed her father for his self-centeredness, for the hurt he'd inflicted on the child Maggie had been.

He let her cry, wishing there was more he could do to comfort her. Her wracking sobs tore at him. She was caught up in her pain—so much so that he didn't think she realized when he gathered her in his arms and carried her to the bed. He sat there, cradling her, until she finally seemed spent.

As she stilled, he carefully withdrew his right hand and pulled a handkerchief from his pocket. He rested his scarred palm on the bed, continuing to support her with his left hand wrapped about her shoulder.

No point upsetting her further.

Maggie wiped her face with the cloth, and blew her nose, sliding him an abashed, apologetic look.

"Feel better?" he asked.

She nodded. "Yes, thank you. I'm sorry. I didn't intend to fall to pieces on you."

"No need to apologize." In fact, it felt good to know she had let down her guard in front of him. It took them one step further toward completing the bridge of trust he wanted to forge.

She gave him a watery smile. "I managed to turn our evening into quite a cheery interlude, didn't I?"

He returned her smile, itching to draw her to him and kiss away her hurts. At least she'd made no move to withdraw from his embrace. "You *did* ask for a distraction."

She smiled. "That I did."

She shifted and Will tensed, unable to control his

body's reaction to her soft derriere pressed so intimately into his lap.

Maggie stilled, as if she had just realized where she was. Her eyes darkened, turning from liquid shamrocks to shadowed moss. He could almost see the desire build, and held his breath, waiting for her to make the first move.

"Will, I . . ."

The words seemed to escape from someplace deep in her soul, a place that snatched them back before she could get them all out.

"What is it?" The answer was important, he knew that as well as he knew he wanted her. After the painful histories they'd just shared, would she trust him with whatever troubled her now?

When her hand crept to her broach, he knew he'd lost again. He commanded his shoulders not to sag under the weight of his disappointment

She shook her head. "Nothing. I'm tired—I think it's time I prepared for bed." But as she made to rise, she paused and pressed two fingers to his lips, as if in a kiss. "Thank you," she said softly, and then was up and across the room.

Will didn't move for several minutes, just listened to her movements. She felt the attraction between them, too—all the signs were there. So what held her back? Was it something about him? Or another secret she had yet to share?

Only five months left before their platonic truce was at an end. It seemed an eternity.

Once more he'd given his word without understanding the high cost of keeping it.

# *Chapter Seventeen*

As Maggie stepped on deck, she sensed the excitement, the anticipation, from passengers and crew alike. After weeks at sea, they would be able to disembark in a matter of hours.

Will was having a word with the captain. The children were down in their cabin, dutifully packing the last of their things. Her own packing had been completed hours ago. Now she felt restless and somewhat at a loss.

She would miss this ship. Though restrictive, it had felt more like home to her than any place since her mother died. Mainly because she'd had people she loved around her. It had also served as a cushion, a rest stop of sorts, between her old life and her new one.

Now she would leave this cocoon behind and attempt to make the transition to butterfly in Will's world. Could she do it?

"Lady Rainley."

Lady Maude bore down on her, her cousin in her wake.

"Good day, ladies."

"Just wanted to say my farewells and wish you luck. The Trevarons are a formidable lot, but I imagine you'll hold your own with them." She gave a bark of laughter.

"I wish I could see Benjamin's face when he learns his heir married an American."

As usual, Maggie wasn't sure how to respond to the woman's bluntness. She decided to address the most innocuous of her statements. "I wish you and Miss Landry luck, as well. Will you be setting out on another adventure soon?"

Maggie let the elderly adventuress prattle on about her plans, making an occasional non-committal sound to indicate she was listening. But her mind was occupied elsewhere.

What had Lady Maude meant about the Trevarons being a formidable lot? Were they all like Will?

Heavens, what had she gotten herself into?

In a remarkably short time after they docked, they were ushered into a luxurious room at London's elegant Boxwood Hotel.

"This room is yours," Will said. "That door near the vanity leads to the room where the children will sleep."

He moved aside as the first of their bags arrived. "Freshen up, rest, take your leisure as you please. We'll sup at eight, if that is acceptable?"

"Yes, of course." Did that mean he wasn't sharing her room?

As if he'd read her mind, Will waved toward the corridor. "My room is across the hall." Then he pointed to a cord near the door. "If you require something from the hotel staff, such as hot bathwater, pull this and someone will come to assist you."

A bath! With fresh steaming water? Maggie felt as if she'd been offered a precious jewel.

Will met her gaze and grinned. As another load of baggage arrived, he handed the porter a coin. "Have bathwater brought up for Lady Rainley, please."

"Of course, m'lord. I'll see to it at once."

Will turned and pointed to the other end of the room. "You should find what you need behind that screen. Enjoy." With a smile, headed toward his own room.

Maggie tossed her hat on the bed. Peeking behind the screen, she found a large brass tub. Situated beside it, a small table held a pair of wonderfully soft-looking towels.

Making certain the children were settled comfortably, Maggie searched eagerly through her trunks. As steaming buckets of water were carted in, she laid out a fresh change of clothes.

Digging deeper, she gleefully retrieved a vial of bath salts, a wedding gift from Madame LeBlanc. When the bath was ready, she dismissed the servants and cautioned the children not to venture outside their suite. Then she eagerly stepped behind the screen.

Swirling the salts into the water, she inhaled the floral scent with approval. Then she undressed and gingerly eased herself into the deliciously hot water.

In the process, however, she bumped the table and the towels slid in after her.

Drat—what now? Then she remembered Will's instructions. Feeling a bit like royalty, she instructed Cal to pull the cord and ask whomever answered to bring fresh towels.

Then she leaned back to enjoy her soak.

Ahh—how decadent to lie here, head lolled back, arms hanging over the sides, soaking in pure pleasure. She could hear Beth humming softly, and the pleasant sound relaxed her. She might just spend the whole afternoon right here.

The sound of a knock revived her just enough for her to warn the children to hold Tully when they opened the door.

Beth's humming blended with the murmur of voices in the hall.

Footsteps approached. "Place the towels over the screen."

"I'm afraid I didn't bring towels."

The sound of Will's amused voice snapped Maggie out of her dreamlike state. She sat up, banging her arm painfully as she scrabbled for a towel to cover herself.

"Are you all right?" Will asked.

"Yes, thank you . . . it's nothing," she stammered. "I . . . that is, was there something you needed?"

"I wanted to inform you I'm going out. I need to speak to my solicitor. Is there anything I can do for you before I go?"

Was that amusement in his tone? The cad! He was enjoying her discomfiture. "No, thank you. Don't tarry on our account."

"Very well. I'll see you for dinner."

Maggie exhaled in relief as he left. She leaned back, but the serenity that had cradled her earlier was gone. Blast the man—why did he have such power over her state of mind?

After supper, Will escorted Maggie and the children to their rooms. "I'd like a word with you after you settle the children down, if you don't mind," he said as she opened her chamber door.

She met his gaze, a question furrowing her forehead. "Of course. We'll only be a few minutes."

Will followed her inside and turned up the lamps.

All afternoon, images of what Maggie must have looked like lying in that tub had tormented him. He could picture it—her skin wet and glistening, the steam painting it a rosy hue and teasing wisps of hair into damp curls to frame her face. Her lusciously long legs, bare and crooked at a tantalizing angle to fit in the confined space. And her breasts—they would have been—

Will ruthlessly clamped down on that line of thought.

He needed his wits about him for the discussion ahead.

He smiled at the sounds from the other room—the rustle of fabric, settling in noises as the children crawled into bed, a goodnight kiss and soft word for each of them. He'd grown accustomed to the ritual, could no longer imagine an evening without it.

"Now," she said, closing the door to the children's room, "what did you wish to discuss?"

He handed her into a chair and then took the one beside her. "I've taken steps to hire a nurse-governess for the children."

Maggie stiffened militantly—just as he'd known she would. "Don't you think you should have discussed this with me first?"

"I'm discussing it with you now." Will leaned forward. "You must understand. In the world you're entering, it is what's expected. Children, for the most part, are relegated to the schoolroom until they are in their teens. They seldom take meals with the adults, and their days are strictly regimented."

"But—"

"I'm not saying it must be that way at Briarwood," he said. "But it is what will be expected when we visit others."

Will settled back. "Even when we are at Briarwood, you will have various duties to perform. Mrs. Peprick will be there to watch the children when you are otherwise occupied."

"Mrs. Peprick?"

"Yes. She's a fine woman—quite good with children. She maintains discipline without being harsh, imbues an interest in learning, and allows children time to enjoy their childhood."

He smiled. "I speak from experience. She had charge of the schoolroom with both myself and Jenny. She stayed on as Jenny's governess until a few years ago. I think you'll like her. I've invited her to Briarwood so you may meet

her. The choice, however, is yours. If you don't feel she'll
suit, we'll find someone else."

"I don't like the idea of someone else raising my children."

"You have my word, no one will try to build walls between you and the children. All I ask is that you give this
a chance."

"And it is my choice?"

"Absolutely. If you don't think Mrs. Peprick is the right
person, we'll send her packing and keep looking until we
find someone you feel comfortable with."

She gave a reluctant nod. "Very well. But I won't have
the children made to feel like outcasts."

"Of course not." He ran a hand through his hair, glad
to have that over with. No point burdening her with the
rest of his news. It could wait until later.

"What is it?"

He glanced up. "I beg your pardon?"

"What are you not telling me?"

Cal wasn't the only member of this family who was too
perceptive for his own good. "It's nothing. I—"

"Don't!" she said sharply. "Tell me it's none of my business if you like, but don't lie to me."

That drew him up short. "Very well. I learned another
ship from Crane Harbor docked here four days ago. It
brought rumors that I hadn't survived the stabbing. My
family has been trying to verify the story ever since."

Will's concern over what Jenny must have felt still
burned in his gut. "I've sent word that I'm alive and back
in England."

"Oh Will, I'm so sorry. Your family must be frantic."

"Jenny, at least. As for the others . . ." Will shrugged.

Maggie frowned. Was his family as indifferent to him
as he believed? "Tell me about your grandfather."

He raised a brow. "You know how this works. I answer

a personal question for you, and then you answer one for me."

Her chin raised a notch. "I could just wait a few days and find out firsthand."

"If that's your choice." Will made as if to rise.

"Oh, very well. I agree to your terms."

Will smiled. He'd known she couldn't resist. "Grandfather is an excellent horseman, and quite a sportsman, in general. He's nearly as tall as I am and rather fierce-looking. Last time I saw him he still had a full head of silver hair and a ramrod straight posture, despite his sixty-two years."

Maggie frowned. "That's a physical description. What's he like?"

Will spread his hands. "He's more kind-hearted than he'd have you believe. Family is important to him, and he was very good to Jenny and me after our parents died. He also has a strong sense of fair play and lives by a strict code of honor."

Trying to shake off the memories that evoked, Will moved on. "But that's not to say he isn't intimidating," Will said with a crooked smile. "He's gruff and can be quite autocratic. He's very much accustomed to his word being law."

Sounded very much like someone else she knew.

Will leaned back. "If that's satisfied your curiosity, I believe it's my turn."

Maggie tensed as she nodded. What would he ask?

He studied her, as if weighing and discarding any number of questions. With each passing second she felt a building urge to squirm, to demand he get on with it, but she held her peace.

Just when she thought she couldn't stand it any longer, he spoke up. "Tell me why you still wear the broach."

Maggie's breath caught and her hand flew to the broach. But she met his gaze levelly. "To remember."

"To remember what?"

"To remember the lesson behind the legend," she answered.

"That you must always hold a piece of yourself apart."

She nodded, hating that she had put that heavy weariness in his expression.

He stood with the easy grace that was always so surprising in a man his size. "It's late. I'll bid you goodnight."

Maggie stared at the closed door long after he exited, wishing it could be different—that *she* could be different.

The problem wasn't that he didn't understand her.

It was that he understood her all too well.

"We've just crossed onto Briarwood lands." Pride colored Will's voice. "You'll see the manor in a few minutes."

Maggie peered out the window as eagerly as the children. They passed from neatly tended farms to a well-established orchard. A few minutes later the carriage topped a hill and rounded a curve, and the main house came into view.

Maggie studied her new home with keen interest. Briarwood Manor sat amidst a vast, sweeping lawn of lush green, dotted with majestic shade trees.

The three-story building had walls of weathered gray stone and a low-pitched tile roof. The imposing, long main structure faced the drive squarely. Two wings angled obliquely from each end. Rounded bushes, punctuated by an occasional spear-like fir, softened the facade, giving the place a warm, inviting feel, despite its size.

"Golly, would you look at that?" Owen gave a low whistle. "It's bigger even than Clover Ridge." He elbowed Cal. "Wouldn't Uncle Henry be green as sour apples to learn we're living *here*?"

Cal grunted an assent.

"You mustn't speak disrespectfully of your uncle," Maggie remonstrated.

"Yes ma'am."

She didn't detect any repentance in the boy's tone, but let it pass. The carriage was already slowing to a halt.

"Sir?" Beth said, turning to Will, "why is it so big? Do other people live here, too?"

Will gave her question serious consideration. That's one of the many things Maggie admired about him: He never talked down to the children—or to anyone else, for that matter.

"Well, poppet," he explained, "there are quite a few servants who live on the premises. And we need extra chambers for guests who come to visit."

He gave her a conspiratorial smile. "And, of course, there's the children's wing. Besides bedchambers, there's a schoolroom, and a large playroom, which probably still has some games and toys from when my sister and I were your age." He quirked a brow. "I seem to remember a rocking horse Jenny was particularly fond of."

Beth's face lit up and Owen's eyes had a glint of interest.

Will spread his hands. "Then rooms such as the library, music room, and ballroom all take up a great deal of space."

A liveried servant opened the carriage door, let down the steps, and executed a deep bow. "Welcome home m'lord, m'lady."

Will indicated Maggie was to precede him. A moment later, she took her first step onto the grounds of her new home.

Was she truly up to the role of mistress of such a place?

An imposing gentleman stood at the entrance, awaiting their approach. Nonplussed by his formal pose, Maggie turned to watch the children and Will step down.

Owen immediately darted around to speak to the coachman. "How is Tully?"

"Your cat is fine, Master Owen," the man replied, handing the carrier down. "Although, I fear he is tired of his confinement." A yowl from Tully confirmed the coach-man's assessment.

Owen peered into the carrier. "Can we let him out now, Momma, please? This is his home, too, isn't it?"

Maggie smiled apologetically. "I think we should let Tully grow accustomed to his new home before we let him run wild."

Will turned to the footman, "What is your name?"

The young man gave another bow. "It is James, m'lord."

"James, would you be so kind as to take the children for a short walk so they may exercise their pet? Then es-cort them to the kitchen and have a bowl of cream pre-pared for the animal. Afterwards, you may show all of them, including the cat, to Lady Rainley's room."

"Very well, m'lord." The footman never blinked, as if the request was nothing out of the ordinary.

"And Calvin," Will turned to the boy, "make certain you keep Tully on his leash, at least for now."

"Yes sir." Cal retrieved the leash and clipped it on Tully's collar. Then, with a casual wave to Maggie and Will, the children followed along behind the footman.

"Shall we?" Will extended the crook of his arm.

Maggie took a deep breath, placed her hand on his arm, and moved with him to the polished marble steps.

The austere gentleman standing at the door executed a deep bow, then gave a broad smile. "Lord Rainley, this is a most happy day. I can't begin to say how pleased we are to see you in good health, sir."

Maggie spied members of the household staff gathered in the doorway, beaming excitedly at them.

Will raised a brow. "So, rumors of my demise reached Briarwood, as well."

"Indeed, sir. Most distressing. We were quite relieved to receive word that the rumors were false."

Will stepped slightly to the side, extending the arm

where Maggie's hand rested. "Richards, this is my wife, Lady Rainley."

He turned to Maggie. "My dear, this is Richards, who's served as butler at Briarwood since I was in short pants."

"M'lady," Richards said with another deep bow. "It will be my pleasure to serve you as I have served his lordship in the past. I hope you will excuse my precipitous greeting. It is only that we are so pleased to see his lordship returned to us."

Maggie smiled. "Thank you, Richards. It is good to know my husband is so well thought of among his people."

Will drew her back to his side. "Allow me to escort you into your new home."

Richards pushed the doors fully open and then stepped aside.

As they crossed the threshold, Maggie took a look around. Her initial impression was one of elegance and taste. Her attention was immediately drawn, however, to a long line of servants, all standing at attention as if awaiting inspection.

Good heavens, were they expecting something from her?

# Chapter Eighteen

As if sensing her uncertainty, Will gave her hand a quick squeeze. "Richards, would you do the honors, please?"

"With pleasure, m'lord."

Richards began introducing the servants, starting with the housekeeper, then the cook, and on down the line. After the first dozen, Maggie knew she would never remember all the names.

"This is Emma, my granddaughter," Richards said when they were about halfway down the line. "If it is not too presumptuous of me, might I suggest she serve as m'lady's personal maid? Just until you find someone to fill the role permanently, of course."

Maggie studied the girl who rose from a deep curtsey. She was young, probably no older than seventeen, with dark hair and a pleasant face. She was petite and had eyes that looked at her with the open innocence of Beth's.

But whatever was she to do with a lady's maid?

Realizing everyone waited for her response, Maggie bowed to the inevitable. "Of course. I would be quite pleased to have Emma's assistance, if she is willing."

The girl's eyes lit up and she bobbed another curtsey. "Oh, yes, m'lady. Thank you, m'lady."

With a bow, Richards continued down the line until at last the introductions were complete.

"Lady Rainley and I thank you for the warm welcome," Will said, assuming the lord of the manor air as if he'd been born to it. Which, of course, he had.

Richards dismissed the staff and turned to Will. "Your rooms have been made ready for you, m'lord. I assume you and your lady wish to retire and freshen up after your long journey."

"Yes, thank you. And please have Mr. Croft join me in my study in about two hours time."

"As you wish. However, there is someone waiting for you and Lady Rainley in the small parlor."

*Visitors already? And why had Richards waited until now to let them know?*

Will raised a brow. "And who might that be?"

"Mrs. Peprick, m'lord. She said you were expecting her."

*The governess was already here?*

"Of course. I didn't expect her until later. Please see that she has refreshments and anything else she requires, and let her know Lady Rainley and I will be down to see her shortly."

"As you wish."

Will took Maggie's arm and moved toward the stairway.

"But don't you think we should see her now," Maggie protested. "If she's already been waiting—"

"Mrs. Peprick is almost like family here," Will said with a smile. "I'm sure she has her knitting with her, as always, and the servants will see that she is well taken care of."

He took firmer hold of her elbow as they stepped onto the lower stair. "You, on the other hand, look like you could do with a bit of a breather before tackling this interview."

Maggie allowed him to lead her up the gracefully curving staircase without further demurral. When they reached the top, Will guided her to the right and stopped in front of a door near the end of the hall. "This is your room," he said. "My chamber is the next one down."

So they wouldn't share a bedchamber. Maggie told herself that it was for the best, but deep inside she felt a pang of disappointment.

Will stood back, allowing to her to enter, then followed. "Should you need me for anything, however, anything at all—"

The look he gave her, and the emphasis he put on those last three words, set a fluttering in her chest.

He opened a door set in the wall next to the bed, "you can reach me through here."

So, there was a connecting door. How . . . *convenient*.

"And this door leads to your private dressing room," he said, moving to the other side of the bedchamber.

Curious, Maggie walked over and looked inside. To her surprise, Emma was already there, busily putting away her things.

The room was larger than she'd expected. It had a vanity and chair, a highboy, and an ornate cheval glass. A brass tub peeked from behind a beautifully carved screen. And most impressive of all, an enormous wardrobe was built into one entire wall.

Had this set of rooms belonged to Will's mother?

Turning back to the bedchamber, she studied the room with something akin to awe. Several shades of rose silk draped a canopied bed. The large fireplace had wood already laid, ready for the flame. A pair of comfortable-looking chairs, padded in a fabric designed to match the bed coverings, flanked a small table set into one corner.

She turned to Will. "This is so lavish, so grand. I could fit my room at Clover Ridge into this one three times over. I feel like a queen."

"Only a marchioness, I'm afraid." He moved toward his own room. "I'll leave you to freshen up. Rap on my door when you're ready and I'll introduce you to Mrs. Peprick." With that, he disappeared into the adjoining room and closed the door.

Slowly, Maggie shed her hat and traveling cloak, and moved into the dressing room. She nodded to Emma, then turned to the washbasin, where a fresh cloth and pitcher of water awaited her.

"Which dress does m'lady wish me to lay out?" Emma asked.

Maggie smiled ruefully. "Whichever is least crushed. I'm afraid my things have been stuffed into trunks so long it will likely take several days to hang all the wrinkles out."

"But m'lady," the girl protested, "you have all these other gowns to choose from."

Maggie turned as Emma opened the doors to the wardrobe. The number and richness of the gowns displayed there took her breath away. Her first thought was that these had belonged to Will's mother. But then she realized these were too new, the style too modern, for that to be true.

Will!

She couldn't find it in her to get angry. This was the man she had married—arrogant and certain he knew best. But generous and thoughtful, as well. She could not have one without the other—and she was no longer certain she cared to.

With a smile, Maggie pointed to a simple poplin day dress of a pretty sky-blue color. "I believe that one will do nicely."

Maggie made quick work of her ablutions and with Emma's help, slipped on the pretty new frock. She wasn't surprised to find it fit perfectly. As Emma turned to pull out matching slippers, Maggie heard a knock, and instinctively moved to answer it.

"Please, m'lady, allow me," Emma insisted.

Having a personal maid was going to take getting used to.

When Emma opened the door, the children swarmed in, bouncing with excitement.

"Isn't this a grand place?" Owen asked. "It'll take days to explore it all. And James says there's a huge stable. Do you think it's anything like the one at Clover Ridge?"

"Cook gave us teacakes while Tully had his bowl of cream," Beth added. "They were sooooooo scrum-shish."

Even Cal had something good to say. "We passed a room filled with shelves and shelves of books. I don't think it would be possible to read all of them in an entire lifetime."

Maggie smiled at the footman. "Thank you for taking such good care of the children."

"My pleasure, m'lady." With a bow he closed the door, presumably leaving to perform more orthodox duties than acting as her children's squire.

"Now," she said, "come and tell me all about your adventures while I tidy my hair."

She ushered them into the dressing room, but when she sat at the vanity and reached for the brush, Emma again stepped forward. "If m'lady will allow me, I am quite good with dressing hair."

Looking at Emma's eager-to-please expression, Maggie sighed and handed the girl the brush. "Emma, I would like you to meet my children. This is Calvin, Owen, and Elizabeth. Children, this is Emma. She'll be helping tend to my things."

Emma curtsied and exchanged greetings with the children, then turned to Maggie. "Does m'lady have a preference in how her hair should be styled?"

"A simple bun will suffice, thank you."

The girl seemed disappointed, but nodded and went to work, removing the pins from Maggie's hair.

While Emma worked, Maggie listened to the children

chatter about the things they'd seen and done since their arrival. It appeared they already knew much more about Briarwood and its staff than she did.

Finally, Emma stepped back. "I hope m'lady is pleased."

Maggie glanced in the mirror, her eyes widening in surprise. Emma had arranged her hair in a bun, right enough, but it was not in the prim style Maggie was accustomed to. The roll of hair was situated up on her head rather than at her nape, and it was puffed into a loosely shaped ball rather than a tight knot. Several wisps tumbled free to tickle her ears and frame her face.

Just looking at this image of herself made her feel younger.

She had a momentary bout of panic. First Will had stripped away the protective guise of her matronly gowns with his gifts of fancy clothes. Now, this girl was stripping away the last of her mask, exposing her youth, enhancing her femininity.

Was she ready for this?

She saw Emma's hopeful smile falter as the silence drew out, and gathered her wits. "Thank you Emma, you did a fine job."

Maggie stood. "Now, if you don't mind, Wi—Lord Rainley and I have a visitor. Would you be so good as to escort the children to their rooms and help them settle in until I can join you?"

"Of course, m'lady."

"Cal," Maggie cautioned, "Mind that Tully doesn't stray beyond the children's suite."

"Yes ma'am."

Maggie smiled as she heard the eager-to-please Emma extol on the many delights that awaited them. Once they'd gone, she turned and stared at the door that connected her room with Will's. Taking a deep breath, Maggie gave it a tentative rap.

A few seconds later, Will open it, an apologetic smile

on his face. "It seems you are quicker with your toilette than I. Come in, if you wish. I won't be but a moment longer."

He turned back into his room, and Maggie followed. She had been curious about his room, but for the moment she couldn't tear her gaze away from her husband. Apparently Will had ordered a new wardrobe prepared for himself, as well. Though he had not yet donned his waistcoat or jacket, he was otherwise fully dressed.

But this was not how she was accustomed to seeing him. She was glad he had turned away—she couldn't stop staring.

The white linen shirt he wore was finely tailored, crisp and pristine. But it was the lower half of his body, forbidden territory for a lady's gaze, that snagged her attention. His buckskin pants fit like a second skin, showing his muscular thighs to such advantage that her mouth went dry. His black boots, which reached mid-calf, supple and firm as the leg they hugged, were polished to a mirrored shine.

She forced her eyes back upward as he slipped into a gold-striped brocade waistcoat, and watched with fascination as he buttoned it across his broad chest. When he lifted a length of white cloth and wound it about his neck, she finally forced herself to drag her gaze away and look about her.

The room was slightly larger than hers, it's furnishings heavier, more masculine in feel. But the bed dominated the room.

It was massive in both size and design. The mahogany headboard nearly touched the high ceiling, and had been intricately carved to resemble two trees with overlapping branches shading a sleeping stag. The workmanship was remarkable, the effect striking.

"Impressive, isn't it?"

Maggie turned to find Will watching her, a glint of amusement shining in his eyes.

"Quite." *But no more so than you.*

"I believe it must have been constructed along with Briarwood. There's no way it could fit through the doors."

He shrugged into a burgundy tailcoat, completing his transformation from prosperous American businessman to proper English nobleman. He extended his arm. "Shall we?"

"Of course."

As they stepped into the hall, he gave her a sideways glance. "You look quite fetching in that dress. I don't believe I've seen you wear it before."

Was that a hint of trepidation in his tone? No doubt he was trying to gauge her reaction to his extravagant gift.

"Thank you for the compliment." Then she gave him a wide-eyed, ingenuous smile. "I've discovered something marvelous."

A hint of wariness crept into his eyes. "Have you now?"

"Oh, yes. Did you know that the wardrobe in my dressing room has magical properties? It's true. One has merely to wish for a new gown, and then open the door to find it already there."

"Amazing." Will's tone still reflected uncertainty.

"Yes, I thought so as well." Maggie decided she had teased him enough. She squeezed his arm and flashed a more genuine smile. "It was a nice surprise. Please tell whatever fairy godmother is responsible that Cinderella is most appreciative."

Will patted her hand as they descended the stairs, his smile echoing her own. "I'll be sure to pass the word along."

Then he escorted her into a warmly furnished parlor. A slender woman with steel gray hair sat on the settee, comfortably knitting what appeared to be a scarf. Maggie's first impression was of a rather homely, horse-faced matron with a forbidding expression and an unbending posture.

Will expected her to turn her children over to *this* woman?

Mrs. Peprick put aside her work and stood to greet them. The smile she turned on Will softened her features considerably. And now that Maggie was able to view her more fully, she saw warmth glinting from the woman's eyes and crinkle lines around her mouth that could only come from frequent smiles.

"Master Will." Mrs. Peprick beamed in pleasure. "It has been much too long since I saw you. You are as fit and handsome as ever. And now I hear you are not only returned from your adventures, but have been elevated to a marquess."

The woman's speech seemed overly familiar, until Maggie remembered she had known Will as a small boy, had been an integral part of his young life.

Maggie envied her those memories.

Will took Mrs. Peprick's hands. "It was good of you to come on such short notice."

"Pshaw. As if I would refuse the opportunity to be here again. Besides," her gaze looked past Will to Maggie, "how could I resist the opportunity to meet the woman who finally captured your heart."

Maggie's cheeks heated, as Will drew her to his side.

"Of course. How remiss of me. Maggie, this is Mrs. Peprick, or as Jenny and I used to call her, Mrs. Pepper. She knows enough about my childhood to embarrass me mightily if she were given to gossip.

"Mrs. Pepper, this is my wife, Lady Rainley."

Mrs. Peprick nodded deferentially. "Lady Rainley, it is truly a pleasure to make your acquaintance."

"If you will excuse me," Will bowed, "I will leave you to get better acquainted."

Maggie felt a momentary panic. What was she supposed to say?

*You might be the most wonderful governess in all of England, but I don't want you to take my place with my children* seemed a bit inappropriate.

With what she hoped was a confident smile, Maggie pointed to the settee as she moved to an armchair across from it. "Please, do take your seat again."

Mrs. Peprick settled back down and folded her hands.

Maggie decided the direct course was the best. "As you no doubt deduced from my speech, I'm American by birth. The use of nursemaids and governesses is not common in the circles I moved in. And it is not a concept I fully agree with."

She took a deep breath. "My stepchildren and I have a very close relationship, and it is one that I value. It is not something I am eager to delegate to another."

Mrs. Peprick nodded. "That is a commendable attitude, Lady Rainley, one I wholeheartedly approve of. It always pleases me when my charges' parents take an interest in their daily lives as well as in how they perform their lessons."

The woman tilted her head to one side. "Since you have done me the honor of being frank, may I do the same?"

Maggie nodded. "Please do."

"Whether you hire me or someone else is not important. What *is* important is that you can more effectively dispatch your other duties if you have someone you trust to see to the children's welfare when you are otherwise occupied. Please understand, that doesn't mean you will not be able to spend time with your children. Rather, it means you will be assured that the time you do spend with them is relaxed and as free from other distractions as you can make it."

Maggie leaned back and mulled over those words. "I hadn't thought of it in quite that manner."

Mrs. Peprick smiled. "I know this is all new to you. But remember, this is the manner in which your husband was raised, and I think you will agree that he turned into a fine man."

Did she know what Will had done six years ago, the reason he had exiled himself to America?

"You make a convincing argument, Mrs. Peprick," Maggie responded, "but of course I would want to see how you get on with the children. Perhaps we could give this a trial of sorts. Try it out for say, a month, and then make a final decision."

But Maggie knew the decision had already been made. If she were to entrust her children to the care of a governess, she could not ask for a finer person. Despite her qualms, she had taken the first real step toward her new life as Lady Rainley.

What else would she be called on to do in the coming weeks?

# *Chapter Nineteen*

Will watched Maggie descend the stairs, a wistful look on her face. "Has Mrs. Pepper made the acquaintance of the children?"

Maggie nodded. "Yes, she is reading to them from the *Adventures of Robinson Crusoe* as we speak."

"I'm sure they'll grow to like her in no time at all. She never fails to gain the affections of those in her care."

For some reason this didn't reassure Maggie as he'd hoped it would. He decided to offer a distraction. "I thought we could take a stroll around the grounds. Unless you're too tired?"

Maggie perked up. "That sounds lovely."

"Good. We'll start with the terrace." Will tucked her hand in the crook of his arm and escorted her to the drawing room. Crossing the parquet floor, he opened a pair of tall glass doors and let her precede him onto the tiled terrace.

Maggie stepped out and seemed to drink in the view of lush, lovingly trained greenery, meandering paths, and gently splashing fountains spread out before her. The sparkle of appreciation in her eyes drew a satisfied smile from him.

She moved to the balustrade that encircled the terrace, and stared at the sight without a word. Then she turned to face him. "I can understand why you love this place so much."

"I hope you will come to love it as well, that you will one day think of Briarwood as home."

Something at once primal and bittersweet flared in her eyes. "It *is* my home—*our* home."

"Will!"

He turned as a blond female bolted through the doorway.

"I had to come see for myself." She squealed. "It *is* you!"

Realization hit just as she flung herself into his arms. "Jenny!" He tightened his hold. Without releasing her, he set her far enough away to study her appearance.

Saints above, he'd missed her entire adolescence. "What's this?" he asked in mock-horror, hiding the bitter taste of regret. "I leave a pigtailed hoyden behind and return to find an *almost*-refined, saucy young lady in her place."

"I *am* seventeen." Jenny preened haughtily. "Practically ready to come out. As you would know quite well if you bothered to read the letters I sent." Then her expression sobered and her eyes grew moist. "Oh, Will, we heard you'd been—"

He put a finger to her lips, hating that he'd caused her such distress. "I know, and I'm so sorry, pet. But as you can see, I'm as healthy and feckless as ever."

Jenny gave his waist another squeeze, then turned toward Maggie. "And married as well, I hear."

Following his sister's not-too-subtle cue, Will took Maggie's hand and drew her closer. "Jenny, I'd like you to meet my wife, Maggie. Maggie, this pert child is my sister Jennifer."

Jenny curtsied. "I'm honored to make your acquaintance, Lady Rainley."

"Please," Maggie said with a smile, "call me Maggie. And I'm pleased to meet you, as well. Will has told me so many wonderful things about you."

"Then you have me at a disadvantage." Jenny cut her gaze toward Will. "He hasn't told me *anything* about you."

Will saw the assessing glint in Jenny's eyes, remembered how her quick mind worked. She'd never thought any woman good enough for him. "On the contrary, if you'd bothered to read *my* letters, I told you a great deal about Maggie over five years ago."

Both women looked at him with startled expressions.

"You did?" Jenny's pretty forehead puckered.

"Yes. When I wrote about the accident I had shortly after I arrived in America, and of the ministering angel who rescued me."

Jenny whirled around to face his now pink-cheeked wife. "You're *that* Maggie?" She took Maggie's hands in each of her own. "But this is wonderful. And we're sisters now. I always wanted a sister." She spared Will a quick, teasing look. "I'm certain they're ever so much more fun than brothers."

Will smiled as he watched his sister link her arm through Maggie's. He'd known the two would get on well.

"Tell me," Jenny asked, "was it love at first sight or did his domineering tendencies put you off initially? Has my brother courted you for all of those years? When did you get married?"

Will rolled his eyes. It seemed Jenny hadn't outgrown her ability to talk without pausing to breathe. Nor had she tamed that artless inquisitiveness of hers.

He was spared the necessity of rescuing Maggie from the barrage of questions by the appearance of a four-legged fugitive.

"Tully!" Maggie scooped up the cat. "How did you escape?"

Jenny turned to Will, her eyes wide. "You have a *cat*?"

Will shrugged, glad he was several paces back. "Not I. The wretched animal belongs to Maggie and her children." He waved a hand. "You may as well let the beast down. He won't go far and he's been penned up in one fashion or another since we set sail."

"But—" Jenny halted whatever observation she had been prepared to make, and turned back to Maggie. "Children?"

Maggie set Tully down. "Stepchildren. Three of them."

Jenny linked arms with them. "This is extraordinary. Will has learned to tolerate cats, and I've become a sister and an aunt all in one day. Come along, you two, tell me everything."

*Maggie stepped into the library, looking for a book to take her mind off of the storm. The moon and stars were hidden by the heavy clouds, but the frequent flashes of lightning provided enough illumination for her to find her way through the familiar room. She reached up to one of the higher shelves, then let out a squeak of surprise as a hand fell on her shoulder.*

*Spinning around, she sighed in relief. "Mr. Peabody, sir, you startled me. I—"*

*His hand slid from her shoulder to her breast. Shock held her frozen in place for a heartbeat of time, then she jerked away. "Sir! You have no right—"*

*"Such a fiery little temptress." His words were slurred and she inhaled the stench of sour whiskey on his breath. "Always flaunting your wares in front of me, trying to fool others with your prim ways. But I know better." His other hand joined the first and she felt him push open her wrapper, tear her shift.*

*Thoroughly frightened now, she pushed at him, pounded him with her hands. "Mr. Peabody, please, let me go." He had her backed against a bookcase, trapped with his flabby bulk pressed firmly against her.*

*His hands were everywhere, tearing at her clothing, pawing at her flesh. When his face came down to hers, she screamed.*

*He backhanded her across the face, setting off an explosion of pain, blurring her vision. "Scream all you want, no one will hear you."*

*He mashed his mouth against hers and it was all she could do not to retch. Then she was pounding and flailing and kicking, begging him to stop, but all he did was laugh and hit her again and again. Maggie closed her eyes to blot out the sight of his leering face. Worse than the pain was the feel of his hands and mouth on her, violating her, like loathsome insects crawling on her skin, leaving slimy poison and stinging bites in their wake.*

*"Let me go! Let me go!"*

*She shot upright and opened her eyes. He was there, looming over her, his hands trapping her wrists, calling her name.*

"Stop touching me, you monster!" she sobbed. "This is vile, wrong. Please, just let me go."

He released her at once, and Maggie blinked, confused. She heard the thunder rumbling outside, blending dream and reality. Her mind was sluggishly starting to function again. Her old nightmare had returned. But why had it ended differently?

Then her heart thudded as she saw the shadowy form seated on the edge of her bed. She drew back, ready to scream again. But it wasn't Edwin Peabody—it was Will.

He stood with slow deliberation. "My apologies for the intrusion." His voice was cold, remote. "I meant only to rouse you from your troubled dreams. It won't happen again." He made his exit, closing the adjoining door with a click of finality.

Maggie buried her face in her hands. What had she done?

How much had he witnessed, what had she said aloud?

She threw off the bedcovers, with hands that still trembled. It was past time she told Will about that terrible night, no matter what he thought of her afterward. She should never have allowed it to come to this.

Slipping a wrapper over her thin nightdress, Maggie fought to shake off the aftermath of the nightmare. She had to think coherently, had to be able to explain.

Her courage wavered as she lifted a hand to knock at Will's door. Could she do this? Would he welcome her intrusion?

No! She would not allow herself to falter. Grasping the knob, she quietly opened the door, just wide enough to peek inside. Several lamps were still lit, illuminating a vast expanse of unoccupied mattress.

"What do you want, Maggie?"

The weary question came from her left. She opened the door wider and stepped inside. Will stood at a small table, swirling honey-colored liquid in a glass, staring at it as if reading tea leaves. His silk robe, a rich burgundy, was loosely tied, displaying a deep V-shaped portion of his chest.

She dragged her gaze up to his and was surprised by the icy flatness there. Was he so repulsed by what he had witnessed?

"If you've come to apologize," he took a swallow from his glass, "then please don't bother. I understand perfectly."

"You do?" Had he learned so much from her incoherent ramblings?

"Of course. You're not the first woman to be repulsed by the touch of my hand."

*Repulsed by*—Maggie stared mutely at him for a long moment, appalled by his interpretation if what had just happened.

Will watched her cross the room in long-legged strides. She certainly didn't look ready to apologize for anything. As she passed the bed, she scooped up a pillow without even pausing.

Will set the glass down. "Maggie, what—"

"You big oaf!" She swung the pillow with all her force,

hitting his shoulder. "You should know me better than that. How *dare* you think so little of me? Didn't I nurse your worthless carcass not once, but twice? Did I ever once show any sign of being repulsed by your wounds? Fresh wounds, ragged and bleeding and inflamed? No! Why would I treat your hand differently?"

She hit him with the pillow again. "Of all the conceited, self-absorbed, addle-pated fools—what makes you think what happened in there was about *you*?"

And she swung the pillow a third time.

"Enough of this!" he bellowed, catching the cushion in mid-swing and tossing it aside. What the devil was she fuming about?

He searched her face and what he saw there bewildered him further. There was fury, certainly, but something else, too, something he was afraid to believe.

"Maggie, I don't understand. I—"

Before he could finish, she took his right hand in hers, and slowly lifted it to her face, brushing her cheek softly with it, her eyes never leaving his. "Then try to understand this."

Very deliberately, she kissed the top of his hand, then uncurled his fist, bringing his scarred palm to her mouth, anointing every inch with her warm, soft lips. Still holding his gaze with her own, she placed seductively lingering kisses on each finger, even the scarred stump.

Watching her take a finger into her moist, warm mouth, Will almost stopped breathing, had to lock his knees to keep them from buckling. Did she have any idea how thinly his control was stretched? He had to stop her before things got out of control.

But for the life of him, he couldn't pull his hand away.

By the time she'd done with his fingers, sweat was beaded on his forehead and his arms trembled with the effort of not reaching for her. But she wasn't finished. She held his hand to her cheek, nuzzling it, her expression as appreciative as if it were the rarest of silks.

She opened her eyes, staring deep into his. "This hand is a part of you and as such it could never disgust me. I would feel the same, regardless of how it came to be as it is."

She rested her other hand on his cheek. "But knowing that you lost a finger and acquired those scars trying to save the life of another makes it a symbol of the courage and goodness that is such a part of you, and only endears it to me more."

"Oh, Maggie." He trapped her hand in his. Heaven help him, he had to have her, or he'd burst with the longing for it.

But Will forced himself to wait. He had to understand what had happened earlier, and there would never be a better time.

He gently drew Maggie to the bed and settled her on the edge. He sat beside her and tilted her chin up, capturing her gaze with his. "Tell me about your nightmare. It has something to do with why you fight my touch at every quarter, doesn't it?"

Maggie lowered her gaze and he saw something akin to shame shadow her expression. "Yes."

She was quiet for so long he thought she would refuse to speak of it.

But then she pushed a lock of hair from her face with a trembling finger. "It happened when I first went into service."

As Will listened to her story, his chest tightened, his whole being filled with rage against the beast who'd done this to her. His heart bled for the pain she'd been made to suffer, for the innocence that had been torn from her.

"I was spared the final humiliation of actual . . ." she halted, then swallowed with difficulty, "deflowering only because the butler thought he'd left a window open in the downstairs hall."

She lifted a hand, then let it drop back in her lap. "Mr. Peabody blamed me, said I'd tried to seduce him for weeks, and that I'd lured him into the library that night. I was dismissed without references, without a place to go. I carried bruises and bite marks for weeks, could barely move my left arm for days."

Will's blood boiled and his hands itched to wrap themselves around the neck of the man who'd done this to her. She'd only been sixteen at the time, a mere child. So help him, he would track down this Edwin Peabody and make him pay.

Maggie shook her head, as if to clear away the memories. "Reverend Matthews and his wife took me in, allowed me to clean the chapel for my keep until I was able to find another position. It was they who taught me to disguise my appearance, control my wanton ways, so I would be less likely to tempt another man."

Devil's teeth, even the local minister had made *her* feel responsible for this atrocity? No wonder she so distrusted men.

He ached to pull her into his arms, this time to comfort her, to ease the pain and wipe away any traces of blame she felt. But he understood now that he would have to move slowly.

With a jolt, he realized how extraordinarily brave she had been to accept his proposal after the confession he'd made. Why had she accepted him, knowing what she did? Dare he hope there was some part of her that believed in him, trusted him?

"Maggie, look at me." Again he placed a finger under her chin. "What occurred that night should never have happened. It was vile, brutal and unforgivable. But it was *not your fault*."

"But I—"

He put a finger to her lips. "No arguments. It was not your fault. You have no cause to feel even a jot of blame." He raised a deliberately imperious brow. "I refuse to allow it."

That high-handed comment earned him a timorous smile, as he'd known it would.

"Much better. Now, if you'll allow me, I'm about to put my arms around you, because I will explode if I don't hold you within the next few seconds. But if you feel uncomfortable at any time, tell me and I'll let you go." *Even if it kills me.*

She nodded, and leaned against him. As she nestled into his chest, her hair tickled his skin, her breath blessed it.

Sweet heaven above, he could almost feel those moist lips of hers on him. Forcing himself to move slowly, to hold her loosely, Will wrapped an arm around her shoulder and stroked her hair. Lord, but he loved the feel of it, so silky, so sensuous.

Her softly whispered "thank you" squeezed a band around his chest, making it difficult to breathe.

When one of her hands crept up to rest above his pounding heart, the skin-to-skin contact almost shattered his control. Sweat beaded on his forehead.

*Gently. You must go gently.*

*Let her feel in control of the situation.*

"Stay with me tonight?" The words escaped of their own volition.

Maggie stilled, and he gave her shoulder the tiniest of squeezes. "I won't ask you to do anything you aren't ready for." He glanced toward the window. "But the storm hasn't died down yet, and I don't want you to be alone tonight."

He shifted, staring deep into the shimmering pools of unborn tears that were her eyes. "I don't want *me* to be alone tonight."

She returned his stare a heartbeat longer, then gave him a shy smile. "I would like that very much."

Will couldn't hold back his triumphant grin. His dear, sweet, courageous Maggie. Tonight she would sleep beside him for the first time—but not the last. If he could be patient, could bear the agony of waiting, he knew he could gradually woo her into his arms one day soon. There he would make her forget the ugliness that had happened to her, would show her how delicious the passion between a man and a woman could truly be.

Standing, he took her hands and tugged her to her feet. With only a whisper of hesitation, she untied her wrapper and let it fall to the floor.

The vision she presented nearly brought him to his knees. Her chaste white shift was all but transparent. It revealed tantalizingly veiled images of all her womanly secrets—her proud breasts with their dusky peaks, her trim waist and flaring hips, the legs that were long enough to wrap around even a man of his size. And that dark triangle at the juncture of her thighs—

Heaven help him, his body was hard as stone, and burning.

She was the most beautiful, desirable woman he'd ever seen.

And she was his.

He dragged his gaze back to her face, and her look of trepidation helped bring his raging desire back under control.

"You won't ever have to fear me, Maggie," he promised, his voice husky. "Yes, I want you, in every sense of the word. I want you so much I ache with the need. But I can wait until you're ready—for as long as that takes." He brushed a strand of hair from her face. "*You* are in charge here. Nothing will happen that you don't want to have happen."

He bent and placed one hand behind her legs, the other behind her back, and lifted her onto the bed. "Now, make yourself comfortable while I turn down the lamps."

Maggie slipped under the covers, feeling swallowed whole by the enormous bed. She watched Will move around the room.

What had she ever done to deserve such a husband? Others who knew her story had treated her with contempt or pity, as if she were little more than a harlot. Yet Will's reaction was to absolve her, to offer her comfort, to show outrage on her behalf.

She had seen the heated passion in his eyes as he looked at her, had felt the raging wildfire threaten to consume him from within. And it frightened her.

Not because she doubted his promise or ability to keep it.

But because, heaven help her, she felt something of that same wildness. And she couldn't bear to think she might let him down.

The room was shadowy now, the only remaining light coming from a lamp on the bedside table. Will shrugged out of his robe, watching her, his form a darker shadow against the gray. Then, as he moved toward her, a flash of lightning provided a brilliant backdrop of illumination.

Maggie sucked in her breath. He was naked. Totally, gloriously, magnificently naked. This was how the Greek gods would look were they flesh and blood.

She felt, more than saw, him climb into bed. He slipped across the vast expanse until he was within a hand's breadth of her, but he made no move to touch her. He lay flat on his back, staring at the ceiling. Still, the heat from his body reached across to her, enveloped her, connected her to him like a gossamer web.

"You can put your head on my shoulder if you like."

Maggie decided that yes, she would like that very much. Sliding across the few inches that separated them, she curled against his side and rested her cheek on his shoulder.

*Uhmm, that felt nice.* He was so firmly muscled, so supple. Yet something didn't feel right. Will's arm extended under her, but rested flat on the bed.

Why didn't he hold her as he had earlier?

He'd said she was in charge—did he expect her to ask him?

Perhaps a hint . . . Gathering her courage, Maggie draped an arm across his chest, letting her fingers slide through the mat of fine hair there. She felt his muscles bunch and ripple under her fingers, heard a low intake of breath.

Had she touched his scar? Was his shoulder bothering him again? "I'm sorry." She lifted her hand. "I didn't mean—"

He captured her hand and placed it back on his chest. "Don't apologize, and don't stop on my account."

Maggie stroked his chest again, raising her head to see his face. Fire blazed there, the same tightly leashed passion she'd seen earlier.

And like a moth, it mesmerized her, drew her ever closer, until her mouth found its way to his.

This kiss was different from the one they'd sealed their wedding vows with. There was nothing chaste or tentative now. She pressed her lips against his hungrily, confident he wanted this as much as she. And he responded with an intensity that set her on fire. Her hands moved from his chest to his face, cradling his cheek, twining in his hair, drawing him closer. He teased her lips, nibbling, pressing, parting them. Then his tongue entered and weaved a sorcerer's spell that had her breathless and yearning for something more.

But still he didn't reach for her. Finally she pulled back, frustration dueling with the passion building in her. She saw the corded tension of his arms, followed the muscled lines to the clenched fists digging into the mattress, and finally understood.

"Maggie?" Will's voice seemed almost too controlled. "Is there something you'd like from me?"

"Hold me." she answered with conviction. "Hold me and kiss me. Make love to me until yours is the only touch I remember."

With an animal-like growl, Will wrapped his arms around her and turned until they faced each other. Maggie's heart pounded—not with fear, but with anticipation.

His lips took hers greedily. But he didn't limit his kisses to her lips. He kissed his way across her face—her cheeks, the tip of her nose, her eyelids. When he nibbled at her earlobes, Maggie felt the delicious shiver all the way to her toes.

Her own hands and lips were busy, as well. She kissed any part of his face she could reach, massaged his broad back, reveling in the feel of his warm, firm flesh under her hands.

The sensations were almost overwhelming—the wonderful abrasion of his raspy face against hers, the feel of her breasts straining against her shift to rub his chest, his hands tangling in her hair, cupping her face, sliding down her back.

Murmuring sweet endearments that set her heart singing, he trailed kisses down her neck to the hollow of her throat. She shifted, lifting her neck into the kiss, rubbing her hands along his back and shoulders. His rumble of satisfaction vibrated through her with delicious echoing tremors.

Before she quite realized what he was about, Will's hand slid between them, massaging her chest through her shift, circling one breast and then the other, but never actually touching them.

Maggie squirmed, an urgent need growing inside her. Like a candle with a low-burning wick, her insides turned warm and soft, threatening to melt at any moment. Finally, she could bear it no longer. Placing a hand over his, she firmly nudged his palm onto her breast, now straining and heavy with need.

It was all the encouragement he required. His hands caressed and kneaded, his thumbs teased the rigid peaks. The sensation set her pulse racing, blurred her vision. She couldn't keep still. Squirming, she raised her hands to his chest, imitating his movements, reveling in his inhaled-breath reaction. But her frustration rose. She wanted more!

His right hand moved to the ribbon at the neckline of her shift, while the other continued to build sparks in her chest.

*Yes!* That's what she needed—his hands on her skin. Surely, that would ease her ache. The candle flame inside her flared at the thought, turning the wax to molten liquid, heating her blood.

But he didn't loosen the tie. His hand just rested there, still except for the slight trembling of his fingers on her skin.

She looked up to find his gaze waiting for hers. "May I?"

She wanted to bless him and kick him at the same time. He was holding to his promise, giving her the opportunity to stop him at each point of the way.

But she didn't want him to stop. Just the opposite.

His free hand still weaved magical patterns over her bodice, playing havoc with her emotions, making it impossible for her to lie still. Not trusting herself to speak, she gave an emphatic nod. A heartbeat later, her chest was as bare as his.

He held perfectly still, his eyes drinking in the sight of her. "Sweet mercy, Maggie, you're so beautiful." His voice was thick, husky. Gently, he spread her hair about her like a cape.

Then he moved like a man possessed—covering her face with greedy kisses, pulling her close, rubbing her sen-

sitized nipples against his chest. His lips left hers to trace
her neck again. She arched her neck and back, giving him
freer access to her throat, pressing herself tighter against
him.

But this time, his kisses didn't stop at her throat.

When he began to gently suckle at her breast, the molten wax inside her bubbled and expanded, sending wave
after wave of sensation shimmering through her.

She tangled her fingers in his hair, trying to draw him
closer. His hand moved to her other breast, teasing the
peak with his knuckles, intensifying her pleasure.

Crying out his name, she slid her hands from his hair,
down to his neck. Moving them lower still, she kneaded
and stroked his sensuously warm and muscled back as
she tried to join more fully in this primitive ritual. Her
hand skimmed from his waist up his side and then down
again. His shiver in response to her touch set the molten
wax in her veins flowing in a steamy path from her chest
to her abdomen and lower still.

Her hand skimmed his buttocks, and he groaned, lifting
his mouth from her breast and leaning his forehead
against her chest.

"Maggie, please." His voice was hoarse, ragged, his jaw
worked. Then he looked up. "If you don't want to finish
what we've started, tell me now and I'll stop. It will be the
hardest thing I've ever done, but I gave my word and I'll
honor it."

He squeezed her hand. "But if you don't ask me to stop
now, by morning you'll be my wife in more than name."

# Chapter Twenty

Maggie stared into his beautiful sorcerer's eyes and knew, without question, she wanted this. She twined a lock of hair from his forehead around one of her fingers. "Don't stop."

He searched her face, his expression strained, intense. "Are you absolutely certain? Do you understand what you're saying?"

She nodded.

"Say it," he insisted.

Maggie returned his look, and from deep inside the words came, words she had no recollection of forming. "I want to wake up tomorrow and know that I am finally and truly your wife, in every aspect. I want more of the sensations you made me feel just now, and I want to make you feel the same." Her hands stroked his sides as she spoke. "I want you to plant your seed inside me, and I pray it grows to be a beautiful babe for us to cherish and raise together. I want you to teach me how to please you in the most intimate of ways."

Will's expression changed to a exultant smile and he began his tender assault anew, whispering endearments, working the magic with his lips and hands that drove all reason from her, that had her breathy and squirming and wanting . . . *more.*

His hand lowered, tracing a tingly trail along her stomach to her thigh, and Maggie's fingers dug into his shoulders. The tension built inside her, an unbearably sweet ache, a simmering pressure that made her feel she would shatter at any moment.

When his hand moved between her legs, the wax candle inside her evaporated and all that was left was the flame, flickering wildly, threatening to consume her entirely. His lips moved to tease at her ears, while he whispered words of heated passion and his hand continued to stoke the flame.

The friction of his flesh against hers in that most intimate of places wrested throaty cries from her. She arched and squirmed, desperate to find the release she knew he could bring her if she could only get close enough.

When he stopped, she cried out. It couldn't possibly be over—there had to be more.

"Patience, my sweet Maggie. Let me join you for the final lap of your journey."

He settled between her thighs, his manhood nudging its way into her, stretching her, heating her from within. Her arms wrapped around him, kneading his back, trying to draw him closer.

Then he stopped. What was he waiting for? Maggie squirmed, wanting more of that heavenly friction, the lucifer-strike that sent those exquisite sparks coursing through her.

"Maggie, please, don't move."

She stilled, confused, wondering what she had done wrong.

"The first time for a woman is usually . . . uncomfortable." She saw the tightness of his jaw, the corded tenseness of his neck and arms. "I would spare you the pain if I could, but—"

Maggie decided nothing could be more painful than stopping now. Besides, if there was to be pain, it should not come through his action. Stealing herself, she slid her hands to his buttocks, pulling him to her as she thrust her hips upward. There was a moment of tearing pain, a feeling of being too full, unable to contain him all.

With a smothered oath, he bent down to kiss her, to stroke her cheek with his, to whisper words of comfort and endearment. And in a short time her body adjusted, accepting him.

A wiggle brought a strangled laugh from Will. "All right, my impatient wife, now comes the fireworks you've been wanting."

With that he began to move rhythmically within her, stroking her, teasing her with his body, until she moved with him, arching into him, crying for the release he'd promised her.

When it finally came, the flame exploded into a shower of sparks, firing through her in wave upon wave of sensation.

Spent, Will settled on his side, cradling Maggie to him, listening to the pounding of her heart, the ragged pace of her breathing. He had guessed she had a sensual nature, but even he hadn't suspected how magnificently she would express it.

He should have known she would never do anything by halves—whatever she set her mind to, she did fearlessly and wholeheartedly.

He tugged a damp curl away from her forehead, taking smug satisfaction in her lazily contented look. "Such a wild display of passion," he teased. "Who would have thought the proper Lady Rainley had the soul of a tigress?"

Maggie sputtered an indignant protest, but he placed a finger on her lips. "That, my dear, was a compliment. I count myself lucky to have such a sweet wanton for a wife." He kissed the tip of her nose, then drew her head onto his shoulder. "Settle down now, and get some sleep. You must fortify yourself—tomorrow you meet the rest of the Trevaron family."

"Such a tyrant," she sighed, brushing his cheek.

He frowned as a discolored patch on her arm caught his eye. "What's this?"

She looked at the bruise and then colored prettily. "It's nothing. I banged it against something yesterday."

She sounded too evasive. "When?"

"If you must know, it was while I was bathing."

Will recalled the flailing he'd heard from behind the screen, and his lips curled in a smile, picturing her pretty body wet and glistening. "So, a part of the blame is mine." He pressed his lips to the bruised flesh. "You have my most sincere apologies."

"Apology accepted." Maggie shifted, nestling her head more comfortably on his shoulder, snuggling her body against his like a soft kitten. Her sigh washed over him like a prayer. He stared in wonder as she took his hand— the maimed one—in both of hers, and cradled it against her chest.

His Maggie—the most spirited, courageous, generous person he'd ever known. Making love to her left him both sated and hungry for more. His wonderfully lustful wife was an addiction, was a woman who cried out to be savored, again and again.

And it wasn't only the physical pleasure. That she gifted him with her trust touched him in a way he hadn't known possible. After all she'd been through in the past, after all he had told her about his own past, she still wanted his touch, his embrace.

He hoped he had done what she asked—made her forget that bastard's foul misuse of her, replaced the ugly memories with smile-inducing ones.

He stroked Maggie's hair, absorbing into his very soul

the feel of it, the breathy sound of her slumber, the beat of her heart against his side. This was how contentment felt. It had been a long time since he'd experienced that particular emotion.

He hadn't realized how much he'd missed it.

Maggie stared at her reflection in the vanity mirror. How could she not look different this morning? She was not the same person she had been last night—her perceptions of herself, of her marriage, of her world, had changed so drastically.

She'd never dreamed she could feel such wild abandon, such freedom to fly without fear of falling. And she had Will to thank.

Her always arrogant, sometimes infuriating, deliciously sensual husband. She knew just how difficult it must have been for him to subjugate his own needs to hers, to give *her* control over every step forward in their lovemaking.

She would cherish that gift her entire life.

Was this what love felt like?

Maggie stilled, her smile fading. That was a dangerous thought. Not that she couldn't love Will, she already did. But that didn't mean she must give over her whole self to him.

She couldn't let herself forget. No matter how good and honorable he was now, he had done something truly awful to a woman once.

She truly loved the man he was today, but how could she turn all of herself over to him? If he ever lost control again, as he had with his fiancée, she would have nothing to keep her going.

Emma bustled in, providing a welcome distraction from Maggie's brooding. "Has m'lady decided what she wishes packed for her stay at Lynchmorne Hall?"

Maggie turned to the impossibly full wardrobe, choosing several items at random. "As for the rest, Emma, I will trust to your judgment."

Emma's face lit up. "Yes m'lady. I'll see you are properly outfitted to meet His Grace."

Maggie mentally grimaced. The duke was planning a "small" houseparty at the end of the week in honor of Will's homecoming.

Whether she was ready for it or not, Maggie was going to get her first taste of English society.

Will whistled as he knotted his cravat. He'd wakened to the sweet feel of Maggie curled trustingly against him, had shared a drowsy smile with her when she woke, had watched a rosy blush warm her cheeks as she remembered their night's activities.

He devoutly hoped it was the first of many such mornings.

And nights.

Will quickly slipped into his jacket, straightening the cuffs as he strode across the room. His knock brought Maggie to the door with pleasing alacrity.

"Good morning, Lady Rainley," he said with a theatrical bow. "I have come to fetch you for breakfast."

"That is well, sir." She gave a regal toss of the head. "I find I am quite famished this morning."

With that teasing glint in her eyes, she looked good enough to feast on herself. If Jenny hadn't been here, he might have been tempted to find a more interesting way to spend the morning.

He stepped into her room and offered his arm. "I—" Will stiffened, the smile freezing on his face. Nestled in the lace of her bodice, the hateful amber broach stared balefully, as if a hag had turned her evil eye on him.

He lifted his gaze to hers, looking for answers. Had she donned it out of habit? Had he read too much into the gesture?

She met his look resolutely. The message there was unmistakable. That amulet represented a wall she had deliberately erected, one she would not allow him to breach.

Will's jaunty mood turned to ashes. They stared at each other for what seemed an eternity. She never flinched, never blinked, just waited for him to accept or refute her.

Finally, he stirred, offering his arm again. "Shall we?"

She released a breath and relaxed slightly, though her smile held a touch of nervousness. "Of course." She placed her hand on his arm and they exited the room as if nothing were amiss.

As if his world hadn't just lost its color, its sparkle.

When they reached the dining room, he had no recollection of what they had chatted about on the way down. It was a relief to see Jenny already seated at the table.

"There you are." His sister waved a fork in their general direction. "I've been waiting forever for you to come down."

Will glanced pointedly at her full plate. "Unless you are on your second helping," he said dryly, "I very much doubt that."

"Oh well," she said cheerily, "it felt like forever."

Getting through the meal was torture. He wanted to throw Maggie over his shoulder, carry her somewhere private, and demand she tell him why she'd re-armored herself with that broach after all they'd shared last night.

But he couldn't do that.

He was too afraid of what her answer might be.


As the carriage carried them away from Briarwood, Maggie only half listened to the conversation around her. They bounced along at a comfortable pace.

There were two vehicles in their little cavalcade. This first carriage was shared by her, Jenny, the children and Tully. The one behind them carried Emma and Mrs. Peprick, along with most of the luggage.

Will had chosen to make the two-hour trip on horseback.

Maggie stared out the window, hoping to catch a glimpse of him. But he rode ahead of the carriage, just out of her view.

She'd hurt him, she knew that, had known it as soon as he'd spied the broach and she saw it leach the warmth from his eyes. Would it have been better to keep her feelings hidden, to lock away the broach and not flaunt it in front of him? She was just so tired of keeping secrets—especially from Will.

For good or ill, it was done.

Jenny, who sat next to her facing the children, reached over and unobtrusively squeezed Maggie's hand. Startled, Maggie glanced at her sister-in-law.

"Whatever it is," Jenny said softly, "I know you two will work it out. Don't give up on him."

A quick glance showed the children occupied with Tully, oblivious to Jenny's gesture. Then, before Maggie could form a response, Will's sister turned back to the children, quizzing them on what it was like to sail across the ocean.

Maggie leaned back. There was more to Jenny than the flighty chatterbox she appeared. Did Will know how perceptive his sister was?

"Is Lynchmorne as grand as Briarwood?" Owen asked.

"Oh, much grander," Jenny boasted. "It's nearly twice the size and a hundred years older. And," she said, leaning forward conspiratorially, "it has its own ghost."

"A ghost!" Owen's eyes gleamed.

"She's bamming you," Cal scoffed. "Ghosts aren't real."

"Not true," Jenny insisted. "Lynchmorne does have a ghost. But Rosebud's not at all scary."

"Rosebud." Owen sounded disgusted. "What kind of name is that for a ghost?"

"I think it's a fine name," Beth declared. "Have you ever seen Rosebud, Aunt Jenny?"

"No, I'm sorry to say I haven't. Not that I haven't tried. I've spent many a night camped in the gallery, hoping to get a glimpse of her. But so far I haven't had any luck."

"See, I told you there was no such thing." Cal's voice bordered suspiciously on smug.

"Just because I haven't seen her doesn't mean no one has. Aunt Robbie told me that she saw her once, a long time ago."

"What does Rosebud do?" Beth asked.

"The legend says she comes out to warn members of our family when they are in danger. She mostly appears to women, though."

Beth hugged her doll. "She sounds like a very nice ghost."

Owen grunted. "Are there any ghosts at Briarwood?"

Jenny shook her head. "I'm afraid not."

Before Owen could interrogate her further, Will drew even with the carriage window.

"Lynchmorne is less than ten minutes away," he informed them.

He looked directly at Maggie, giving her an encouraging nod. Another bit of the tension coiled inside her eased. He might not like the situation, but it appeared he didn't resent her greatly for it. Perhaps there was hope for their future after all.

Now all she had to worry about was facing Will's family. Somehow, she didn't think the others would accept her as readily as Jenny had.

Maggie studied Lynchmorne Hall as they turned up the long drive. It seemed nothing short of a storybook castle. Built of a pinkish-colored stone, it stood a massive four stories high and had a crenellated walk on the roof leading from a rounded tower.

The structure looked as if it had stood there for centuries, seeming as natural a part of the landscape as the trees and hills that formed its backdrop. The lawn was scrupulously groomed, and tall firs lined the drive at precisely spaced intervals.

As soon as the carriage stopped, Will was there to hand them down. "Make sure the leash is secure before you let that undisciplined feline out of there," Will warned, looking past Maggie. "It won't do to turn him loose on Lynchmorne just yet."

Jenny grinned. "I can't wait until Grandfather learns you've brought a cat with you." She smoothed her skirt. "Oh, Alex and Aunt Edith were supposed to arrive yesterday. So you should have a full complement to welcome you home."

"A much anticipated reunion for all involved, I'm sure."

Will's tone was dry, Maggie noted, but not particularly worried. Was he truly so unconcerned about what sort of reception he would receive?

Jenny gave him a stern look. "Everyone was so worried when we heard the rumors. Even Grandfather aged a bit. The one good thing to come from this is, I think it has him more amenable to a true reconciliation."

As they drifted toward the house, Will tucked Maggie's hand securely on his arm. Her heart lightened at this further sign that he had come to terms with the boundaries she'd set.

They were met at the door by a tall stick of a man with wispy, white hair. "Good day, m'lord. And may I say, welcome home."

"Thank you, Thomas. Let me present my wife, Lady Rainley."

"M'lady, I'm honored." Thomas greeted her with a low bow.

Will gestured to the children. "And these are Calvin, Owen, and Elizabeth."

"Don't forget Tully," Beth chimed in.

"Of course." Will made a half-bow to Beth, then turned back to the butler. "Tully is the children's cherished pet. Make certain the staff understands he is to be treated as such during our stay."

Thomas seemed nonplussed, then his training took over. "Of course, m'lord." He held the door open. "His Grace requests your party join him and the others in the sitting room, sir."

Thomas led them along a broad hallway, richly appointed with tapestries and beautifully polished floors. Maggie felt dwarfed by the sheer size and grandeur of the place.

Reaching their destination, Thomas threw open the doors. "Lord Rainley's party has arrived, Your Grace."

Before they entered the room, Will turned to Beth. "Thomas will mind Tully for you."

Maggie swallowed a grin at the sight of the rigidly formal butler accepting the leash from Beth as if it were a viper. Then she faced forward as Will led her into the sitting room.

She took in the circle of faces quickly and then focused on the elderly gentleman standing near the fireplace. Will's grandfather stood ramrod straight, his hands clasped behind his back. The expression on his face was unreadable.

Tall and athletically built, he had the same firm chin as Will, the same aquiline nose, and steely gray eyes. Will was several inches taller and a bit broader of shoulder, perhaps. The duke's eyebrows, too, were bushier and drawn together, giving his countenance a fierce appearance.

Despite Will's relaxed stance, Maggie felt the tension in him. His gaze locked to his grandfather's with an intensity that seemed almost explosive. Whatever was being communicated in that look did little to relax either man.

The silence drew out for a long moment, with no one

in the room speaking or even seeming to breathe.

Will deserved a better reception than this. Incensed, Maggie raised her chin and squeezed his arm supportively.

Her movement drew the duke's attention. With a nod, he finally spoke. "Welcome back to Lynchmorne, William. Do you plan to introduce us to your newly acquired family?" His tone was polite but not warm.

Will's jaw tightened almost imperceptibly. "Of course. My dear, this is His Grace, the duke of Lynchmorne. Grandfather, this is my bride, Margaret. And these," he waved the children forward, "are my stepchildren, Calvin, Owen, and Elizabeth."

Maggie felt a jolt of surprise. This was the first time Will had claimed the children as his own. Was it because he had formed an attachment with them, or for his grandfather's benefit?

Determined to do Will proud, she executed a deep curtsey. "Your Grace." The children followed her lead, the boys bowing and Beth dropping a prettily executed curtsey.

Will's grandfather nodded, acknowledging their greeting. "Welcome into the Trevaron family, and into my home."

"I thank you, sir, for your welcome." Maggie matched the formality of his tone. "I look forward to acquainting myself with my new family."

"Then let me continue with the introductions." He indicated a willowy woman seated to the left of him. Her hair framed her face in a silvery nimbus, her skin was a translucent alabaster and her eyes were the crystal blue of a mountain lake.

"This is my sister, Lady Roberta Trevaron."

"Lady Roberta," Maggie said with a curtsey. She understood now what Will had meant when he said she had a fey quality to her. There was an ethereal, distracted air surrounding her.

Maggie found it quite plausible that this woman had seen the Lynchmorne ghost.

"You must call me Aunt Robbie, my dear." Her smile was friendly, but her eyes studied Maggie with a strange intensity, as if she tried to read Maggie's mind, tried to determine some intimate secret locked away there. When Will's great-aunt turned to the children, Maggie felt as if she'd been freed from a spell.

Lady Roberta motioned the three over with a bright smile. "Let's have a look at you. Yes, I see you all have a great deal of spirit. Especially *you*," she said, wagging a finger at Owen. "It will be delightful to have young ones at Lynchmorne again."

Will's grandfather waved toward the other lady in the room. "This is my daughter-in-law, Lady Osgood Trevaron."

Will's Aunt Edith was an imposing woman. Not tall, but big bosomed and with a chin that jutted out militantly. She glared at Will with an expression of resentment. When she faced Maggie, her expression turned distinctly superior.

"Lady Osgood." This time Maggie did not curtsey, but merely gave a polite nod.

"Lady Rainley." Will's aunt returned her nod, her tone coolly polite. She made no gesture at all toward the children.

Thankfully, the duke moved quickly on to the room's final occupant. "And this is my grandson, Alexander."

Alexander looked as if he'd rather be anywhere but in this room, which immediately won him Maggie's sympathy. Though athletically built, a trait apparently common among Trevaron men, he was slimmer than Will and a jot shorter. He also lacked the distinctive gray eyes. His were a warmer shade of brown.

He eyed Will with loathing, but smiled as he turned to Maggie with a bow. "It is my pleasure to welcome you into our family. Please feel free to call on me if ever you should feel the need."

Maggie noted another difference between the cousins. Controlled and reserved by nature, Will wore his assurance and composure as if they were part of him. Alex, on the other hand, wore his passions for all the world to see. One would never doubt what he felt about any person or subject under discussion.

He looked at her now as if he thought she might immediately take him up on his offer. When she merely murmured a polite, "Thank you," he seemed almost disappointed.

With the introductions over, Maggie felt the tension thrum through the room. It seemed everyone waited for the moment of confrontation between Will and his grandfather.

# Chapter Twenty-one

Maggie refused to take part in their drama. "What I have seen of your home thus far is truly magnificent, Your Grace," she said lightly.

The duke nodded. "Lynchmorne Hall has stood for nearly three centuries. Of course, it has been added to and refurbished in that time, but parts of the original still remain."

"That's longer than your country has been in existence, is it not?" The question had come from Lady Osgood.

"Quite true," Maggie answered, smiling sweetly. "Isn't it amazing how far America has come for all its youth? Why, even our upstart armies have bested some of the most established in the western world."

Lady Osgood drew up in a huff, and the duke stiffened with a frown. Maggie dared not look at Will, fearing she would see censure.

But at least the focus was on her rather than Will now.

"If you will allow me," Jenny said quickly, "I'd be happy to escort the children to the schoolroom. I'm certain Mrs. Peprick is already awaiting them there."

Maggie nodded, trying not to be jealous that the four were escaping. "Of course, Jenny. That is most kind of you."

"Sir," Beth asked Will, "may we let Tully loose now?"

"Not until you have him safely in the schoolroom. You can take him for a walk in the garden when Mrs. Pepper is ready for you to do so."

"And who or what is Tully?" Will's grandfather asked.

Beth dipped another curtsey. "Tully is our cat, Your Grace."

"Cat!" The duke turned to Will. "You brought a *cat* into Lynchmorne Hall?"

Beth's mouth pursed sympathetically. "Do cats make you sneeze, too?"

The duke sputtered an affronted *harrumph*.

Cal took his sister's hand. "Come along Bethy. I think the adults want to talk without us."

As soon as the door closed behind Jenny and the children, Will turned to his grandfather. "Tully is a cherished family pet. He goes wherever the children go. If he is not welcome here, I will be glad to return to Briarwood with my family."

The challenge hung in the air between the two men, stretching tauter and tauter until Maggie was certain it would snap.

Finally, the duke waved a hand. "Just keep the nasty creature away from me."

Will gave a short bow. "Of course. Now if you will excuse us, my wife and I would like to freshen up after our journey. I assume you still dine at eight."

"Yes. Your former room has been prepared for you, and the adjoining one for your wife."

Will nodded and took Maggie's arm. "Aunt Robbie, Aunt Edith, if you ladies will excuse us." And with that he led Maggie through the door and up a wide, graceful stairway.

Maggie had thought Briarwood wonderfully luxurious, but it was nothing compared to Lynchmorne. Everywhere she looked were the trappings of inherited wealth.

Will led her to a room midway down the corridor, opened the door and stood aside for her to enter. He moved across the room to an inner door, similar to the one in her room at Briarwood. "This leads to my room, if you should need me."

Was he going to leave her already? "I apologize if I insulted your family," she blurted out.

He paused, hand on the knob, and turned with an amused smile. "Actually, I rather enjoyed the show of backbone. If I'd wanted a timid, simpering wife I would have looked elsewhere."

Maggie wasn't certain if that was a compliment or not, but decided to take it as one.

"And regardless of his reaction," Will added, "Grandfather will respect you the more for your standing up for yourself. As for Aunt Edith," he shrugged, "let us just say that it is well to let her know from the outset that you refuse to be cowed."

He leaned against the door, and crossed his arms. "So, now that you've met the family, what do you think?"

"They are an intriguing lot," Maggie said, searching for a judicious way to phrase her response.

Will laughed outright. "Well said. They are also—with the possible exception of Aunt Robbie—stuffy, provincial in their view of the world and not overly fond of me at the moment."

His light tone didn't fool her. "Which only proves them an unperceptive lot."

Will smiled crookedly. "Always ready to come to my defense."

Something colored his tone that she couldn't quite decipher.

He straightened. "Rest now. You still must face the ordeal of dinner. Knock when you're ready to go down." And with a short bow, he was gone.

Though she stretched out on the bed, Maggie's mind

refused to allow her to rest. Finally, she decided to go in search of the children. Should she ask Will for directions? She stared at the forbiddingly closed door, knowing it was his company she craved more than his assistance.

Then she tossed her head. She was quite capable of locating someone to help her. Stepping into the hall, the first person she spied was Jenny.

"Oh, well met," she said. "I was hoping to find someone to show me the way to the nursery."

"Of course." Jenny linked an arm with hers, then gave Maggie a contagious smile. "I knew Grandfather would like you."

That wasn't the impression she had left with. "Did he say that?"

Will's sister waved that away as inconsequential. "Not in so many words, but I could tell, nonetheless."

Skeptical, Maggie turned the subject. "Your aunt Edith and cousin Alex don't seem to bear much affection for Will."

Jenny shook her head. "Aunt Edith never forgave Will for being Grandfather's favorite when we were growing up." She paused. "I suppose, because of his injured hand, Will always tried harder than Thomas and Alex. He strove to be the best at everything he attempted, and usually succeeded."

The girl sighed. "It seemed the only thing he couldn't do was forgive himself."

"For your mother's death, you mean?"

"He told you about that?" Jenny's tone was incredulous. Maggie nodded.

Jenny stared at her with new respect. "He *never* speaks of that awful night—not even to me."

Maggie felt a tingle of warmth shimmer through her. But she tried to steer the conversation back on course. "Why would your aunt still feel such animosity?"

"Will is now titled and Grandfather's heir—Alex is neither. Did Will tell you our father and Uncle Osgood were twins?"

When Maggie shook her head, Jenny added, "Except for a small accident of timing, Alex would now stand where Will is."

"And is that why your cousin also dislikes Will?"

"The title? Not at all. Growing up, Will and Alex were like brothers. I think Alex looked up to Will, though he'd never admit it. Then Will got engaged to Lilly." Jenny's tone made it plain she hadn't cared for her brother's fiancée.

"The thing was, Alex had formed a tendresse for Lilly, himself. But neither Grandfather nor Will ever knew this" She cut Maggie a sideways glance. "You'd be surprised the things a curious nine-year-old hears."

Thinking of Cal, Maggie had no trouble believing Jenny had been privy to secrets her brother and grandfather had not.

"At any rate, Alex kept his feelings to himself, but he distanced himself from Will. Then, when he learned what happened—" She threw a questioning glance Maggie's way.

"Will told me about the incident." What a tame word for such a horrid affair.

"There was an awful shouting match in Grandfather's study—I think Alex wanted to track Will down and demand satisfaction. But Grandfather forbade it, said it would only bring further dishonor to both the Trevaron family and to Lilly, herself."

Maggie could picture a younger Jenny with her ear to the door. "And did Alex pursue Lilly once the way was clear?"

Jenny shrugged. "He tried. But she went into seclusion, then became engaged to someone of more lofty rank than Alex."

Maggie felt some sympathy for Will's cousin, even

though she could not like his display of animosity.

"And here is the schoolroom." Jenny threw open a pair of double doors, effectively ending their discussion.

Maggie had a pleasant visit with the children, then made her way back to her bedchamber, only losing her way once among the labyrinth of corridors. Emma was already there, waiting for her.

The maid was visibly disappointed that Maggie had dressed on her own, so Maggie allowed the girl to style her hair.

When she was ready, she tapped on Will's door. He opened it at once and his manner made it obvious there would be no lingering in his room today.

"You look quite handsome this evening," she said as she took his proffered arm.

Will gave a short bow. "Why thank you, madam, and may I return the compliment."

"You may." They were being pleasant, but their banter lacked the sparkle it had held before. Would they ever return to the place they had been before this morning?

She smoothed the soft green fabric of her skirt. "Emma assured me this is the right attire for dinner at Lynchmorne."

"Emma was right." He placed his free hand over hers and gave it a light squeeze. "But don't let such matters worry you over much. You are Lady Rainley and may set your own style."

They entered the room to find Alex, Jenny, and Lady Osgood already there. Will's grandfather strolled in behind them.

"So, Will," demanded his cousin with something of a sneer, "tell us about this near-fatal injury. Receive it in some drunken brawl, perhaps?"

Maggie stiffened. How *dare* he take that tone with Will?

\*     \*     \*

Will felt Maggie brace herself to jump to his defense and squeezed her hand in silent warning. He was gratified by her impulse, but he was quite capable of fighting his own battles.

He seated her beside Jenny, then casually moved to lean on the piano. "Actually, I let a cutpurse catch me unawares in an alley." He gave a self-deprecating shrug. "Careless of me. Not only did he steal my wallet, he left a knife wound in exchange."

"Oh Will! How awful!" Jenny raised a hand to her throat.

Will bowed toward Maggie. "I have my resourceful wife to thank for saving me. Not only did she stumble on my unconscious carcass, but she patched me up and nursed me back to health."

The duke turned his piercing gaze full on Maggie.

"My father was a physician." Maggie appeared charmingly flustered. "He taught me something of his craft before he passed away. I did what I could while we waited for the local doctor."

Will shook his head at that paltry description of her efforts. "My wife is too modest. She took charge of the situation, cowed everyone into doing her bidding, and cleaned, stitched and bandaged me up."

He grinned wickedly. "She also bullied me into curbing my natural exuberance and vigor so I could recuperate properly."

Will leaned back and smiled as Maggie became the center of attention. The duke studied her with guarded approval. Jenny, placed a hand over Maggie's and offered a soft, "Thank you." The look Alex gave her was unreadable.

Trust Aunt Edith, however, to find fault. Her nose wrinkled. "I must say, such behavior seems most unladylike." She smiled condescendingly. "I suppose standards are different in America."

Maggie stiffened and Will waited in amused silence to

hear what set-down she would use to put his aunt in her place.

Aunt Robbie choose that moment to make her entrance, however, and the opportunity was lost. A few moments later, Thomas regally announced dinner was ready.

The duke took his place at the head of the table, and Aunt Robbie, as always, sat opposite. Will found himself next to Jenny, with Maggie across from him, between Alex and Aunt Edith. Now this was going to be interesting.

Aunt Edith turned to Maggie as the first course was set. "I hear America is still a rather savage country."

"Parts of it are," Maggie agreed with perfect composure. "There is an inherent beauty and nobleness in what has not yet been spoiled by so-called civilized influences, don't you agree?"

Maggie smiled apologetically. "Oh, I'm sorry. You have no idea of what I mean. England is bereft of such natural wonders, isn't it?" Then Maggie turned to engage Alex in conversation.

Will's lips twitched as he looked from the sharp expression on his aunt's face to the guileless one on his wife's. Aunt Edith would soon learn that the rose he'd brought to Lynchmorne had rather sharp thorns.

As if reading his thoughts, his aunt turned her attention his way. "It was a stroke of luck for you to find such a . . . *singular* woman to bring home as your bride. It saved you the need to see how you would fare on the marriage mart here at home."

"I count myself the lucky one." Maggie had a militant look about her as she answered for Will. "I'm certain there will be many English maidens who think I took unfair advantage by snaring Will before they had an opportunity to try for him themselves."

As she turned to him, Will felt the warmth of her smile clear across the table. "But I count their loss to be my gain."

# Winnie Griggs

"And how well do you know my nephew?"

"Mother!" Alex protested. "You are turning Lady Rainley's meal into an inquisition."

"I meant no offense," his mother said in feigned apology. "I merely wished to get better acquainted. Please, Lady Rainley, do continue with your meal if my questions make you uncomfortable."

"Not at all." Maggie's smile was equally polite. "I met Will nearly six years ago. Our paths crossed several times since then, and I always found him to be charming and generous. He helped me settle my first husband's estate and assisted me in other matters over the years. Before we became engaged he told me the reason for his leaving England and for his desire to return. Shortly after our engagement, I nursed him through near-fatal injuries. After we married, we shared a small shipboard cabin on an extended voyage where we had little to do except share family histories."

She raised a brow. "So I would say that I know my husband quite well. Does that answer your question?"

Will nearly choked at the resounding silence that greeted her full and quite personal answer. That was Maggie, never one to mince words, especially when her back was up.

"Well!" Aunt Edith straightened. "I've heard Americans are a forthright lot, but I never—"

Maggie's smile would have done a queen proud. "It is true we value openness and honesty." She made a small movement with her fork. "Given the nature of your questions, I'd assumed it was true of your countrymen, as well. I apologize if I was mistaken. I have yet to become fully attuned to your customs."

Jenny coughed and reached for her glass. Will met her gaze and saw her eyes brimming with the effort not to laugh.

He sympathized.

His grandfather cleared his throat and signaled one of the servants. "I believe we are ready for the next course."

After supper, the ladies withdrew to the parlor while the men retired to the library to enjoy a drink.

Jenny attempted to draw Maggie with her to the settee, but her Aunt Roberta forestalled her. "Do you play piano, my dear?" she asked Maggie as she took out her needlework. "I do so enjoy music, but neither Jenny nor I play well. Alexander, on the other hand, is quite talented, but the men may be a while."

Maggie gave a small nod. "Yes ma'am, though I don't do well with complex passages. I would be more than happy to play a few simple tunes for you if you like."

In truth, Maggie was pleased to occupy herself this way, effectively erasing the need to make polite conversation.

The men didn't tarry long, and she was still at the piano when they entered the room.

"Very nicely done," Alex announced when she completed her piece. "My cousin has been as lucky in marriage as in everything else he attempts."

Maggie returned his smile but shook her head. "You flatter me, sir. I'm well aware that my playing is passable at best."

He grinned. "Ah, but you haven't heard Jenny's or Aunt Robbie's attempts. In comparison, your playing is inspired."

"Wretch!" Jenny pursed her lips in a pretty pout. "It's true, but you should be more gentlemanly than to say so."

Maggie stood. "I understand you are the virtuoso of the family. Please, do take my place."

Alex bowed. "I am yours to command."

As Alex began to play a classical tune, Maggie drifted across the room, intending to steer clear of Lady Osgood. Not that she was afraid of Will's sharp-tongued aunt. She just didn't want to get into another verbal sparring match with the woman.

But Jenny intercepted her and drew her down to the settee, placing Maggie in arm's reach of her self-appointed inquisitor.

Things went smoothly for several minutes. Jenny had an unending litany of questions about life in America, and Maggie relaxed as she answered the eager queries.

"I've never met an American," Lady Osgood commented during a lull. "Your accent is so charmingly provincial."

"Why, thank you, madam," Maggie answered, vowing to hold on to her temper. "I find the British accent equally charming. It brings back fond memories of my parents."

"Your parents were from England?" The duke frowned. "Why didn't you mention this sooner?"

Maggie directed a tilted-chin look his way. "Because I didn't consider it important. It doesn't change anything about who I am."

"Immigrants seeking their fortune, no doubt." Lady Osgood's voice dripped condescension.

"Actually, they were escaping the displeasure of their families. My mother was the daughter of a vicar and granddaughter of a baron. My father was a younger son of the earl of Whitehaven."

Lady Osgood's mouth dropped open, but it was Will's raised brow that caught Maggie's eye. She realized guiltily that she had failed to mention that bit of family history to him.

"Impossible." Lady Osgood had apparently found her voice again. "The earl of Whitehaven has only one son."

"Not the current earl," Will's grandfather agreed, "but his father did, by his second wife. I seem to remember some scandal or other associated with the lad, and that he dropped out of sight years ago." He eyed Maggie in a more approving light. "So you are Whitehaven's cousin?"

Maggie waved a hand. "As I said, that is neither here

nor there. I was born and raised an American, and I make no claims otherwise." She spared another glance for Will. "Although, I am quite pleased to be the wife of an Englishman."

"But this is marvelous," Jenny exclaimed. "An attractive, plainspoken American, married to an English nobleman, who actually is only one generation removed from English nobility herself. You will be all the rage in London next season."

*Now that thought is truly terrifying.* Maggie's hand went to her broach as she contemplated facing a whole roomful of women like Will's aunt Edith.

Lady Osgood excused herself then, claiming a headache.

The mood in the room immediately seemed lighter. Jenny turned to Maggie. "Do you play whist?"

When Maggie nodded, the girl organized a game, recruiting Alex and Lady Roberta to complete the set. That left Will and his grandfather to amuse themselves, which, Maggie suspected, had likely been Jenny's strategy.

If so, it met with only limited success. Rather than open a discussion, the duke challenged Will to a game of chess.

Maggie made a poor partner for Jenny. Her mind was focused more on her husband than on her cards. Luckily, the girl was not the least competitive and took their loss well.

When the game ended, Lady Roberta excused herself. Maggie, Jenny and Alex strolled over to watch the chess players.

The duke studied the board with a frown of concentration. "It seems you have learned some new strategies since last we played," he told Will.

"I've learned quite a bit more than that in the interim, sir," Will replied dryly.

*Good for you!* Maggie barely restrained herself from saying the words aloud.

Jenny linked her arm through Maggie's and her cousin's. "Alex, why don't we show Maggie the conservatory. These two are liable to be at this game all night."

Jenny, hopelessly transparent, was still trying to force her grandfather and Will to talk to each other. Maggie met Will's gaze, and he gave her a slight nod, indicating she was to go on.

Reluctantly, she let Jenny lead her and Alex from the room. But she stopped once they entered the hallway. "I believe I'll postpone this little tour for another time. I'd like to look in on the children before it gets too late."

"Do you need me to show you the way to the nursery?"

Maggie shook her head. "Thank you, Jenny, but I believe I can find my way this time."

With a pang of regret, Maggie found the trio already sound asleep. Tully was the only one who stirred at her entrance. She placed a soft kiss on each head, snugged the covers under their chins, and made a silent promise to do better in the future.

Then she returned to her room, where the tireless Emma awaited her.

"There's truly no need for you to wait up on me every night," Maggie protested. "I'm capable of preparing for bed on my own."

"It's no trouble at all, m'lady," Emma assured her. "And I aim to be a proper lady's maid to you, just like the ones the other ladies in this house have."

Ah, so it was a matter of pride for the girl. Resigned to her fate, Maggie allowed Emma to help with the fastenings to her gown and then carefully put it away. The girl, who was as efficient as she was enthusiastic, had already laid out Maggie's nightclothes. As Maggie stepped behind the screen, Emma busied herself with turning down the bed.

Maggie tied a wrapper over her filmy nightshift, then pulled the pins from her hair. Emma was immediately at her side.

But Maggie demurred. "Brushing my hair relaxes me and helps me to sleep better," she explained

The girl nodded agreeably. "As you wish. Is there any other way I can assist you tonight?"

"No, thank you. You've been most helpful."

"Good night m'lady." And with a curtsey, the maid left, and Maggie found herself blessedly alone at last.

She drew the brush through her hair in long, rhythmic strokes. How long would it be before Will returned to his room? Would he want her in his bed tonight?

She realized they had not had more than a moment or two alone together since he'd spied the broach at her throat this morning.

Stars above, had it only been this morning?

Maggie studied the door joining her room to Will's with an uncertain frown. Finally she walked over and opened it as wide as it would go.

There, that invitation could not be misinterpreted. When Will returned to his room, he could either walk through and join her, or close it and leave her to her own lonely bed.

Which would he choose?

Maggie awoke from a light sleep to the soft sound of activity from the adjoining room. She was instantly wide awake.

Turning toward the door, she waited to see what he would do as the tension coiled in her chest. She had left a lamp burning low beside her bed and a soft light came from Will's room as well, so she had a clear view of the opening.

After an intolerably long wait, there he was, filling the doorway, standing there without moving.

Was he afraid to disturb her? Or just deciding whether he wanted to enter?

Finally she could stand it no longer. "You'll be warmer here under the covers with me."

He gave a startled bark of laughter. "No doubt. But say we use my bed. It's larger."

*He still wanted her!* Happily, Maggie threw off the covers and sat up. But before her feet touched the floor, he had lifted her in his arms. Then he paused. "Are you all right?"

She nodded, wrapping her arms around his neck. "More than all right. I feel tingly." She couldn't believe she'd said that. He brought out a boldness in her that was most indecent. Only it didn't feel indecent when she said such things to Will.

He laughed again as they entered his bedchamber. "My sweet, eager Maggie. What a delight you are." Then he gave her a fierce frown as he shed his robe. "Before we get to any more of this tingling business, however, you have some explaining to do."

"I do?" Maggie wet her suddenly dry lips as she studied his magnificent body.

"Stop that," he commanded, a strangled laugh in his voice, "and pay attention."

She brought her gaze up to his own. "Yes?"

He slipped under the covers beside her. "I want to know why I had to learn about your impressive connections at the same time the rest of my family did. Don't you think you might have apprised me of that little detail earlier?"

She shrugged. "I didn't think it was important. Besides, I did tell you my parents came from England." Then her eyes widened. "Do you think I married you under false pretenses?"

She sat up, "I vow, it would never have occurred to me to solicit help from these people. I doubt they even know I exist. They all but booted my parents out of their respective families."

"Settle down." He stroked her hair. "I was only teasing. I have no regrets whatsoever over marrying you. In truth,

I'm glad you had that option—it proves I wasn't your only choice."

"Oh." She gave his chest a little shove. "Well, that is quite too bad of you to tease me so." She tossed her head. "You know how fragile my emotions are."

He grinned. "Fragile, are they? Come here, madam, and let us test just how fragile they truly are."

Maggie pulled a face, then snuggled comfortably in his embrace. His hand slid up and down her side, skimming her breast each time it passed in a way that left her breathless. But she wasn't ready for this yet. She wanted to talk some more, while she could still think coherently.

"My turn to ask a question," she announced.

His hands paused their movement for a heartbeat and then resumed. "And what question would that be?"

"How did it go with your grandfather tonight?"

"He professed himself willing to overlook my past indiscretion, consider it a one-time aberration, as long as I continue to prove myself reformed." His tone was matter-of-fact. Too much so. Had he expected more?

"The party at the end of this week," he continued, "is to show the world I am truly welcomed back into the bosom of my loving family and all is right with the world once more. And to introduce you into polite society, of course."

Will raised up on one elbow, loosening the tie on her night shift. "He approves of you, by the way—and not just because of your connections. He said you had both mettle and intelligence."

Will drew the garment off her, sliding it down her sides and over her hips and legs, his hands trailing hotly along with it.

His gaze never left hers. She found herself squirming both inside and out, aching for his touch in other places.

"Grandfather also said marrying you was perhaps the smartest move I'd made since I left England. On that point

I'd have to agree with him." Without another word, Will crushed his lips to hers while skimming his hands up to her breasts.

And Maggie had no further interest in conversation for quite some time.

# Chapter Twenty-two

"Quite a grim looking group, don't you think?"

Will was giving her and the children a tour of Lynch-morne. Jenny trailed along, adding spicy tidbits of gossip and family lore that provided a delightful counterpoint to Will's more pedantic tendency to lecture.

They'd already strolled through a remarkable assortment of rooms and heard enough Trevaron history to leave Maggie's head spinning. This latest room was long and narrow, with portraits and various battle trophies lining every inch of available space.

"Who are all these people?" Beth asked.

"They are my Trevaron ancestors."

"Would you look at this?" Owen stared in awe at a battle-ax that was twice his size.

Cal seemed more interested in foils. "Sir, do you fence?"

Will nodded.

"His fencing master said he'd never had a more skilled pupil than Will," Jenny said with obvious pride.

"Monsieur DuPlantis was given to exaggeration." Will dismissed his sister's praise. Then he raised a brow at Cal. "Is fencing a sport that interests you?"

Cal nodded slowly. "Yes sir, I think it is."

What was this? Bookish, intuitive Cal—interested in such an inherently violent pursuit?

"Well then, if you apply yourself to your studies, I could be persuaded to hire you a fencing master come spring." He smiled. "In the meantime, I could teach you a few basics myself."

Maggie stiffened. She wasn't at all certain she wanted Cal to take fencing lessons. How could Will make such a promise without consulting her first? They would definitely discuss this later, when they didn't have an audience.

"Can I learn, too?" Owen looked at Will hopefully.

"Of course," Will answered agreeably.

This was too much. Audience or no—

"*When* you are Cal's age," Will continued, "and *if* you apply yourself to your studies as well as he has."

Maggie snapped her mouth shut. At least the man had that much sense.

"Over here, Maggie," Jenny called. "This is a likeness of Grandfather's father."

Maggie stared at the portrait in astonishment. The man gazing haughtily back at her looked eerily like Will. It was only when one studied the eyes that a real difference emerged.

While perhaps a flaw in the painter's interpretation, the eyes of the man in the portrait were cold and flat, carrying none of the warmth and passion she'd seen in Will's so often.

Of course, she had experienced a certain amount of ice from his stares as well, but never with such chilling deadness as she saw here. Maggie gave an involuntary shiver.

"Well," Jenny asked, "what do you think?"

"A striking resemblance." *But it's only superficial. That man is nothing like Will.* "What sort of man was he?"

"He wasn't one of our more illustrious ancestors," Will replied. "He fell down a flight of stairs in a drunken stupor, breaking his neck. That's one reason Grandfather feels as he does about excessive drinking."

*An intemperate drinker. That probably accounted for the deadness in his eyes.*

Will led the way out of the gallery and guided them to the conservatory.

Maggie turned around slowly, taking it all in. "This is wonderful!" The domed glass ceiling let in an abundance of sunlight. Inside this bubble, a wondrous variety of plants flourished in exotic abandon.

A large pool stood in the middle, shaded by strange looking trees and filled with aquatic plants. Water trickled in from an unseen source, the sound peaceful, soothing.

"It's like a jungle," Owen exclaimed. "Can't you just picture headhunters hiding in here, waiting to pounce on you?"

Maggie rolled her eyes. Would Owen ever outgrow this bloodthirsty phase?

Will pulled out his watch. "I believe Mrs. Pepper is waiting for you in the schoolroom about now," he told the children.

Maggie smiled at the chorus of groans. "No long faces. We'll do more exploring this afternoon."

"I'll escort them," Jenny offered. "I'm certain there's more Will wants to show you."

"Excellent idea," Will answered quickly. Then he smiled at Maggie. "I thought you might enjoy a horseback ride."

Twenty minutes later, Will escorted Maggie to the stables. Her riding habit, a rich shade of dark blue, sported a matching hat adorned with a jaunty feather. She felt quite dashing.

The stables, like everything else here, were large and well managed. Grellson, the head groom, had two horses saddled and ready. One was a large brown gelding who pranced about, eager to be off. The other was a trimmer, dappled gray mare.

"Meet Comet and Cinder." Will handed her the mare's bridle.

"What a beauty you are, Cinder." She rubbed the mare's nose appreciatively. "Such a mannerly lady, too. I think you and I will get along wonderfully."

Will handed her up, then mounted Comet. They left at a leisurely pace, Maggie letting Will set their direction.

"Are we going anywhere in particular?" she asked after a few minutes.

Will nodded. "There's a place I'd like to show you. It's not too far, no more than fifteen minutes or so."

He refused to elaborate, even after some not-so-gentle prodding on Maggie's part, so she satisfied herself with just enjoying the ride and the scenery.

They soon turned onto a smaller trail that cut through a wooded area. It was obviously little used, overgrown in places, but easy enough to maneuver. After a while, though, the track narrowed and grew rockier, until they were forced to travel single file.

Not that Maggie minded. It gave her a chance to watch Will unobserved. My, but he sat a horse well.

Just as she began to wonder if the trail would disappear entirely, it abruptly emptied into an open, treeless area. This in turn was edged by a sheer drop into a rocky, roughly bowl-shaped basin. The cliff face opposite soared higher than the one they were on and was striated, rough hewn and ruggedly beautiful.

"It's breathtaking. What is this place?"

"A rock quarry. Stone's been mined here for ages, though it's not used very much anymore. The stone to build Lynchmorne Hall, itself, was taken from here."

Will dismounted while he talked, and now helped her down as well. "My father sometimes took us here for picnics. It had been a favorite spot of his in his younger days."

As they reached the edge, Maggie held tightly to Will's

arm and gingerly peered over. "Mercy, it's a long way down."

He nodded. "Spectacular, isn't it? After Jenny and I moved to Lynchmorne, I would sneak away here whenever I wanted to be on my own or felt particularly adventurous."

"I can see the appeal this place would have for a boy. It has a sort of adventurous mystery to it." She shot Will a warning glance. "Which means, of course, that Owen must not learn of this place for several years yet."

He held his hand out. "You'll get no argument from me. The boy would likely try to scale these cliffs just to see if he could."

Maggie shuddered at the thought, then rounded on Will again. "Speaking of which, what did you think you were about, promising Cal fencing lessons?"

Will frowned. "The boy was interested and he is old enough."

"Don't you think you should have discussed it with me first?"

He stiffened. "Are you saying you don't trust my judgment?"

Maggie gestured impatiently. He was twisting her words. "Of course not. But fencing is dangerous."

Will took her hands and his smile melted some of the starch from her resolve. "Cal won't stay a little boy forever. If he is interested in swords, he will eventually pick one up."

Maggie knew he was right, but part of her resented him for pointing it out.

"I thought it best it be under some responsible person's tutelage." He released her hand and took a half step back. "Now, if you would prefer that person be a someone other than myself, I can arrange it so."

"No, of course not. I trust you. It's just . . ."

He smiled. "I know. But you have to let him grow up."

Will watched Maggie absorb what he'd said, watched her struggle with the idea, and finally nod in acceptance.

She squeezed his hand. "The children are lucky to have you in their life."

Will's chest tightened as she stared trustingly up at him. She made him feel like the hero of her own personal fairy tale.

It should have been enough—but it wasn't.

If only that blasted broach wasn't stubbornly guarding her heart from him. Like the dragon in the figurine, it had become his nemesis, a beast he must slay or perish in the trying.

"So, Maggie, where did my cousin take you this afternoon?"

Will watched Alex make small talk with his wife, and wondered how he had ended up across the table from her again.

At least the final course was being laid, and the meal would end soon. Thankfully, the conversation had been much tamer this evening than it had yesterday. Perhaps Aunt Edith had learned to tread carefully around his difficult-to-intimidate wife.

"I'll wager I can answer that," Jenny offered. "The quarry."

Maggie smiled. "How did you know?"

Jenny cut Will a teasing look. "He's so predictable. That was always the first place he'd visit when he came home from school term."

"So, William." The duke claimed Will's attention. "How soon do you plan to move your family to Crestview?"

"Actually, I plan to make Briarwood my primary residence."

"But Crestview is such a beautiful place," Aunt Edith protested. "Much grander than Briarwood. And it is, after all, entailed to you with the title."

"Briarwood is my home. Besides, Aunt Charlotte, Chloe, and Thomas's widow are still in residence there. I see no need to turn them out."

He turned back to his grandfather. "I will, of course, take over the management of the Crestview holdings."

"Oh, m'lady! I am so sorry." A maid had tipped over Maggie's wine glass while serving her plate, and now stared aghast at the spreading stain.

"There's no harm done," Maggie said, excusing the girl with her usual grace.

"But your gown—"

"Only the sleeve is wet."

"Tizzy," Aunt Robbie commanded. "Please get Lady Rainley a fresh place setting."

"Yes, madam." The flustered maid dropped a curtsey and made a quick exit.

"Here, let me help." Alex took his napkin and patted Maggie's hand and wrist.

"Thank you," Maggie protested, "but I can—"

"Bloody— What's this?"

Will pushed his chair back at the shocked expression on Alex's face. What was wrong? Had something happened to Maggie?

But she seemed unconcerned. "Oh, that. It's only a bruise. Nearly healed—nothing to worry over."

But Alex was not to be put off. "How did this happen?"

Will tightened his jaw as he felt all eyes in the room focus on him—all but Maggie's. It was as if he were some odious insect pinned to an entomologist's board.

It took Maggie a heartbeat longer to realize what was happening, to see every pair of eyes clouded by accusation or doubt. Then she exploded out of her chair.

"No!" Maggie jerked free of Alex's hold and glared around the table. "How *dare* you even consider such a thing?"

The relief on Jenny's face rubbed salt in his wound.

"Such theatrics," Aunt Edith protested. "Hardly proper behavior for a lady of breeding."

Maggie tossed her napkin down. "But I'm American, remember?"

Her outrage was magnificent to watch. Gratifying to know it was on his behalf. Of course, she had the advantage of being privy to the truth—it required no test of faith from her.

Maggie raised her arm, displaying the bruise for all to see. "Since you are so interested in how I acquired this, I'll tell you. I banged my arm against the tub while I was bathing three nights ago."

She tilted her chin. "If that is too indelicate a topic for polite conversation, I suggest you don't question me on insect bites or pinpricks you may notice on my person in the future."

She was magnificent when she got this passionate— defending him like an avenging goddess, an Amazon warrior. If only he could tell her the truth. The need burned in his gut, threatened to incinerate his soul. But of course, he couldn't.

Then her gaze sought his. "I find I no longer have an appetite. Would you escort me to my room, please?"

She was giving him a graceful way to make an exit, and he was happy to take it. Circling the table, he took her arm, and they stepped into the hall without another word. Once the door had closed behind them however, Maggie began her tirade all over again. "And they call themselves civilized! How—"

Will touched a finger to her lips. "Hush. Come with me."

Rather than move to the stairway, he led her to the conservatory. "I thought you might enjoy the view by starlight."

Maggie stared at the stars and soft moonlight shimmering in through the glass dome, and some of the stiffness in her stance was softened by her smile of appreciation.

Will seated her by the pool. Stars reflected on the water like iridescent fish. He stroked her face, loving the soft feel of her skin, the way she nuzzled her cheek into his caress, the understanding in her eyes. "Thank you for that heated defense." He smiled crookedly. "Though I'm not sure my family will ever recover from your speaking in mixed company of taking a bath."

She laughed with him, then covered his hand with her own. "Will, I'm so sorry. If I'd realized how they would react I would have gone to greater pains to cover—"

"Stop taking the blame, Maggie. At least now I know where everyone stands." *Except for you. If you had not had proof, would that look of doubt have shadowed your eyes as well?*

She wiggled her fingers in the water, studying the ripples. "There's nothing to hold us here. We could return to Briarwood."

"I'll not run from this. Not again. Besides, we don't want to set the gossips' tongues wagging before they've even had a chance to meet the outrageous Lady Rainley."

She smiled. "I've never been one to run from a challenge either."

"So I've noticed." His dry response drew a laugh from her.

"Was I so terrible?" she asked.

"Absolutely fearsome." Then he pulled her into his arms, pressing his lips to hers, trying to erase the old feelings of anger and stung pride and betrayal that had been resurrected tonight.

Maggie seemed more than willing to help him forget. When he finally pulled his mouth from hers, he was aching with need.

He stood, drawing Maggie up with him. "Come along, Lady Rainley. I think perhaps we should retire early tonight."

*   *   *

Maggie heard a knock just as she put the last pin in her hair. A moment later, Emma admitted Jenny.

The girl wore an uncertain smile. "I saw Will ride out. I thought I'd join you for breakfast."

"That was thoughtful." Maggie kept her tone noncommittal. "But I plan to check on the children before I go down."

"May I join you?"

"Of course." Maggie knew Jenny wanted to talk about last night, but she had no intention of making it easy. Will would never admit it, but he had been hurt last night. His pain had resonated deep within her own heart.

"How is Will this morning?"

Maggie escorted Jenny into the hallway, making the girl wait on an answer. "He seemed in perfect health when he left."

"That's not what I meant."

Maggie gave her a direct look. "I know. How would *you* be if your family stared at you as if you were a fiend?"

Jenny bit her lower lip and Maggie saw tears well in her eyes. "I didn't mean to hurt him. I *do* believe what you said, Maggie. I know Will wouldn't ever hurt you."

"It's Will you should believe in, not my words."

Jenny nodded. "You're right. It was just, for only a moment, I remembered the last time. . . ."

Those self-recriminating words gave Maggie pause. What would she have done, have thought, had she been in Jenny's place?

She linked an arm through Jenny's. "Just let him know how you feel." Then she gave her an arch look. "So, what happened after we left? Am I henceforth banned from polite company?"

Jenny gave a watery giggle. "Aunt Edith nearly had an apoplexy. Alex clenched his jaw and didn't say another word. Aunt Robbie, of course, went on as if nothing had occurred."

"And your grandfather?"

Jenny grimaced. "Grandfather doesn't care for scenes. But he didn't say much." She gave Maggie a sideways look. "And how will you greet everyone this morning?"

Maggie had wondered that herself. "I shall mind my tongue, I suppose, as long as everyone else does. I don't want to make this more difficult for Will than it already is."

Maggie was as good as her word. An undeclared truce seemed to be in force. All through the day, everyone made a point to be scrupulously polite to one another.

Maggie even had a surprisingly pleasant conversation with Lady Osgood. She encountered Alex's mother on the terrace, feeding bits of teacake to a condescending Tully.

Lady Osgood spared her a glance before turning back to the cat. "This is your Tully, I presume."

"Yes, ma'am."

She held up another pinch. "I hope you don't mind my treating him to a share of my cake."

"Not at all. I'm certain Tully is enjoying it immensely."

"Will must be fond of you if he allows you to keep your pet."

That sounded like an olive branch. "Will is a generous man."

Lady Osgood looked inclined to disagree, but said instead, "Tully is a noble-looking feline. I have three of my own. My Osgood did not suffer the adverse reaction to cats that afflicts most Trevaron men, and neither, thankfully, does Alexander."

Maggie made a noncommittal response. Then, with Lady Osgood's attention focused on Tully, she managed to drift away without further comment.

It seemed she and Will's aunt had finally found something they could agree on. Perhaps there was a caring person under Lady Osgood's abrasive exterior after all. She smiled to herself. It only stood to reason that a person with such a fondness for cats couldn't be all bad.

By the next day, some of the tension had lifted from the household. While not exactly convivial, the atmosphere was at least relaxed. After the midday meal, most of the family gathered in the drawing room. Conversation among the women revolved around the upcoming house-party, while the men discussed matters of politics and the appearance of a poacher in the area.

Maggie found herself itching to join in the men's debates, though there was no graceful way for her to do so.

At one point Will caught her glance, and gave her a knowing wink. Maggie guiltily turned her attention back to Lady Roberta. Had anyone else noticed her ill-mannered lack of attention?

A moment later, Will stood at her side. "If you ladies will excuse my wife, I promised her a ride to Eiderdown today."

Maggie tried to keep the startled look from her face. She recalled no such promise.

"What fun!" Jenny turned eagerly to Will. "Why don't we make an outing of it? Alex, you will join us, won't you?"

"Have you forgotten the fitting for your new gown?" Lady Roberta asked.

Jenny's face formed a pretty pout. "Oh, that's right. I guess I'll have to pass."

"As will I," Alex added. He seemed as disappointed as Jenny. "I have an errand to run in Cromfold this afternoon." He sent Maggie a pointed look. "Why don't you hold off until tomorrow when we can all go together, perhaps have a picnic as well?"

Was he implying she shouldn't go out alone with Will? Maggie smiled just as pointedly. "Oh, but I'm so looking forward to the ride. Perhaps the four of us can plan a picnic for another day."

Alex bowed. "As you wish."

As they exited, Maggie cast Will a sidelong look. "My memory must be failing. I don't recall you making any such promise."

"Oh, did I fail to mention it?" Will's brow furrowed, though she saw the dry twinkle in his eye. "How remiss of me."

It was one of those rare summer days when a gentle breeze whispered through the trees and the sky was a cloudless, robin's egg blue. The trail they were on, though bound by trees on either side, was wide enough for them to ride side by side.

Will was glad he'd been spared the necessity of uninviting Jenny and Alex. He enjoyed Maggie's company too much to want to share it this afternoon.

"So," she said, "Eiderdown is not a village or town, and it is not an estate or a ruin. It's not manmade and it's not a lake or an island. It is on Lynchmorne property, however."

"All true." For most of their ride, she'd quizzed him about their destination, but he'd given her only dribs and drabs of information. He knew she enjoyed the challenge of guessing.

And it was fun to watch her mind at work.

"I've got it—it's a cave. And inside this cave lies a treasure, the source of the Trevaron wealth. This treasure is guarded by a grumpy dragon whom the Trevaron men pay homage to by feeding it any cat who dares intrude on their domain."

Will laughed outright. "No, my imaginative and ghoulish wife, it is not a cave. And your time is just about up."

Maggie's face puckered in a moue of disappointment.

# Winnie Griggs

"And I was so looking forward to meeting a real live dragon."

As the trail twisted around a bend, a large, flower-strewn meadow opened before them, a brook passing through the far end. Will pulled Comet to a halt. "This is it—Eiderdown Meadow."

"It's lov— Oh, Will, look!" Maggie lifted up in her saddle, pointing. A doe and fawn had paused at the stream for a drink.

Will smiled at her delight. He was learning to throw out his old notions on how to please a woman. *This* woman found more joy in this natural beauty than in all the extravagances he'd showered on her since their engagement. Tomorrow he would—

Something hissed passed his ear and stung his cheek a split second before Cinder reared.

Maggie was thrown to the ground with a sickening thud.

# Chapter Twenty-three

Will leapt from the saddle, his heart lurching painfully as he raced to her side. The sweetest sight he ever saw was the rise and fall of her chest as she took a shuddering breath.

"Don't move," he commanded, wishing he had her medical skill. "Just tell me where it hurts and what to do."

Maggie smiled wanly. "I just had the wind knocked out of me for a bit."

Will wasn't convinced. "You took a bad fall. Are you sure you didn't hit your head?"

"My head is fine," Maggie protested. "My arm feels a bit sore, though."

"Hold still and let me check."

He saw the protest form on her lips and gave her a stern look. With a martyred sigh, she settled down.

He brushed the hair from her forehead, searching for signs of injury. Finding none, he placed his fingertips above her ears, and gently explored her scalp, removing pins as he went.

When she protested again, he shushed her. Finally, he sat back. "There don't seem to be any bumps."

"Just like I told you. You unpinned my hair for nothing."

# Winnie Griggs

"Oh, not for nothing." Will gave her an unrepentant smile. "I rather enjoyed the chance to muss it up."

"Oh!" She looked startled and then amused by his confession. "You truly are incorrigible, you know."

"I know," he agreed. Then he sobered. "Which arm hurts?"

"This one." She gingerly lifted her left arm and examined it with her right hand. She grimaced. "It's not broken, only banged up a bit. Might be a sprain, but I don't think so."

Then she looked past him with a frown. "I wonder what spooked Cinder. Poor baby, she still looks shaken."

Will glanced over his shoulder. The mare stood several paces off, tossing her head and trembling. "I'm not certain. I—"

"Will! You're bleeding." Her hand touched his cheek. Only then did he feel the sting, remember the earlier whirring.

"Devil's teeth!" He stood and strode toward Cinder, calming the mare with soothing words, until he was able to reach for her bridle. It took only a minute to spot the droplets of blood oozing from the tip of her ear.

Will stroked the mare's nose as he studied the lay of the land, remembering where Comet had been, where Cinder had stood.

"Will, what is it?"

"I'll tell you in a minute." He waded into the tall grass. If he was right, someone would pay dearly for this day's work.

A few minutes later he found what he'd been seeking. Pulling the arrow from the ground, he marched back to Maggie. "This is what spooked your horse, and what scratched my cheek."

Maggie's face paled. "But who— The poacher!"

Will nodded stiffly. "He no doubt disliked our being between him and a prime bit of venison. This time he's

308

gone too far." Will's gut clenched at the thought of what might have happened to Maggie. "Let's get you back to Lynchmorne so we can have that arm properly cared for."

"It's not bad, truly. Your cut looks to be more serious."

"It's only a scratch. Can you stand?"

"Of course."

He helped her up, studying her closely. But her color had returned and she showed no signs of dizziness.

"Stay here." He tied Cinder's reins loosely to her saddle, then returned to Maggie.

"Why did you do that?"

"She's still too skittish to ride, but she'll follow Comet back to the stable tamely enough. You're riding with me."

She studied Cinder, then nodded. "If you think that best."

Will settled into Comet's saddle then reached down a hand to Maggie. With little effort he soon had her seated snugly in his lap. He wrapped an arm around her waist, holding her securely, then set Comet in motion.

She peered over his shoulder, apparently making certain Cinder followed. Then she swiveled back around to study his cheek. "The bleeding's stopped. It doesn't look too deep."

"I told you it was nothing, Maggie."

She frowned. "And just who is the doctor in this family?"

He laughed. It just wasn't in her to back down. "You don't suppose it will scar, do you? After all, you *did* marry me for my handsome face as well as my charm."

Maggie rolled her eyes at his teasing. "Men—such vain creatures." She sighed. "If worse comes to worse, I suppose we can work on enhancing the charm."

At least he'd distracted her from what had just happened. Not that he had forgotten. The man who did this would be captured within the week, if Will had to track him down himself.

Maggie fidgeted again, settling more comfortably in his lap. Perhaps a bit *too* comfortably. "Maggie, sweetheart, would you mind not squirming quite so much?"

"I'm sorry." She looked up contritely. "Am I hurting you?"

"Not hurting me. Let's just say, I'm experiencing discomfort of another sort." He held her gaze for several heartbeats, waiting for his meaning to sink in.

Her face turned red as a cardinal's robe. "Oh!"

"Exactly."

For the next few minutes, Maggie held perfectly still, barely even breathing. At last Will laughed, and gave her a squeeze. "Relax, Maggie, lean against me if you like. Just don't wiggle your sweet little bottom in my lap unless you want me to carry you straight to my bedchamber when we reach Lynchmorne."

With a shy smile, Maggie did as he said, easing her tense muscles and resting her head against his chest.


"We're here."

Maggie raised her head with a start to see they were nearing the stables. She must have dozed off. And no wonder. Will's heartbeat against her ear was as sweet and soothing as a lullaby. She glanced back, relieved to see Cinder following behind them.

Alex, who appeared to have just returned from his errand in the village, frowned as he spotted them.

"Help Maggie down," Will called out. "And careful with her left arm—it's been hurt."

"What happened?" Suspicion vibrated in Alex's tone.

Maggie wasn't about to go through *that* unpleasantness again. "Alex Trevaron," she warned as he helped her down, "if you say one word against Will, so help me I'll forget I'm a proper lady and tear your tongue out with my bare hands."

That won her a startled look from Alex, and a shaky-sounding cough from Will.

She fought the urge to shake a finger at Will's overly suspicious cousin. "We crossed paths with that nasty poacher, and my horse threw me. Will's been hurt, too."

"Poacher? On Lynchmorne lands?"

"Out by Eiderdown Meadow." Will held up the arrow he'd retrieved. "This nicked both me and Maggie's horse."

Alex gave a low whistle. "This is the first sign the bounder's crossed onto Lynchmorne lands. He's a cock-sure devil to be out in broad daylight." Alex's lips twisted in a wicked grin. "Grandfather is going to have someone's head over this."

"He isn't the only one." Will's tone carried a steel edge.

Maggie was gratified see the cousins discussing a common enemy for a change, even if in this bloodthirsty manner.

One of the stable boys hurried over to gather the reins of both horses. Will nodded to the lad. "Have Grellson look at the mare's ear—she had a little accident."

Then he gently took Maggie's right arm. "Come along, let's get you inside."

Though Maggie's arm was only badly bruised, Will insisted she take it easy for the rest of the day—which included having supper in her room.

She frowned up at him. "I recall you mentioning something about not caring for doctors who mollycoddled their patients."

He arched an unrepentant brow. "And I seem to recall you telling me I was no doctor."

She made a face, which drew a smile but no reprieve.

"I'm not going until I have your word you won't leave your room this evening."

Maggie tossed her head melodramatically. "In that case, I refuse to give you my word." She laughed at his startled reaction. "I want you to stay, silly. After all, you were injured, too. We can have a nice, quiet supper together."

"Now that is a tempting offer. Very well, I'll arrange it with Cook." He pointed a finger firmly toward the bed. "While I'm gone, I expect you to rest."

"Yes, sir." She gave a salute, then flounced onto the bed.

That night, Will held her while she slept, her sweet, firm body snuggled tightly against his own. He had suggested she might be more comfortable in her own bed, in deference to her bruised arm. To his immense satisfaction, she demurred, saying she liked falling asleep to the sound and feel of him nearby.

Her hair tickled his nose and he softly blew it aside. Thinking about what had happened today, about how tragically it could have ended, he tightened his embrace.

He'd already spoken with his grandfather, setting plans in motion to capture the poacher. He wasn't just motivated by a thirst for vengeance. Will wanted to make certain there wasn't something else at work here. Could the string of "bad luck" that dogged him before he left Crane Harbor have followed him to England?

He would never forgive himself if he'd put Maggie in danger.

She mumbled something unintelligible, squirming in a way that set his pulse afire, then settled back to sleep.

He forced himself to loosen his hold, to not wake her with the hot, passionate kisses and intimate caresses his body craved. Instead he checked that her arm was still cushioned protectively, and settled for a chaste kiss to the top of her head.

He couldn't contemplate life without her. Somehow, in the time since she'd reentered his life, Maggie had become all-important to him. He would do anything to keep her safe.

Even lay here and hold himself painfully in check while he let her sleep in peace.

* * *

# A WILL OF HER OWN

"I'm so glad you planned this picnic, Jenny. I've missed having time with the children." Maggie squeezed the girl's arm. Cal, Owen, and Beth raced ahead of them, across the field to a large oak with spreading branches. Behind them, Will and Alex tended to the carriage and horses.

Jenny grinned as she shifted the hamper she carried. "With the houseparty only two days away, I thought it best we get away before we were recruited to assist with some last-minute chores."

Alex caught up with them. "Here, let me take that." He confiscated the hamper from Jenny, hefting it as he did so. "Hmm, feels a trifle light. Didn't you tell Cook you had a couple of healthy males and three active children to feed?"

Jenny tilted her head with a haughty sniff. "What makes you think I plan to feed you and Will? As I recall, the two of you invited yourselves along on this picnic."

"Aw, now Jen—"

Maggie smiled. "Don't worry Alex, there's another hamper in the carriage. Will's fetching it."

"Did I hear my name?" Will took Maggie's right arm.

Alex eyed Will mournfully. "It seems our presence here is merely being tolerated by the ladies."

"Is that so?"

Jenny laughed. "Oh, I'll allow, now that you're here, you have your uses. Why don't you spread the blanket under the oak?"

Will met Alex's gaze over the ladies' heads. "I see what you mean. We've been relegated to the role of hired help."

"Go along with you now," Jenny said, making shooing motions. "Earn your meal while Maggie and I watch the children."

"Play with the children is more like it," Alex grumbled.

As the two men walked away, sharing pointed observations about bossy women, Jenny linked her arm with Maggie's. "It's good to see them on friendly terms again."

Maggie nodded, though she knew things were not as smooth between the two as it seemed. Will still held part of himself back, and Alex hadn't completely let go of his suspicions. But they apparently had called a truce for now, and that was a start.

Maggie thoroughly enjoyed the afternoon. The children romped across the field as if they were back at Clover Ridge, while Jenny, Will, and Alex spoke of their own childhoods spent here.

Despite Alex's earlier protests, there was plenty of food to go around. And even after they'd eaten, no one seemed in a hurry to end the outing. Will found some stout, supple branches and he and Alex decided to give the boys their first fencing lesson.

At first, Owen was excited to be included. But once he discovered they would only cover the basics of how to hold the foil and proper foot movement, his interest waned.

Maggie grinned when she saw him discard his "sword" in favor of studying a toad that had the bad luck to hop across his path.

Beth plopped down beside Maggie. "Tell me a story."

Maggie patted her lap, letting Beth lay her head there. "Let's see. Once upon a time, there was a princess with long golden curls, bright blue eyes, and a smile that could charm a robin from its nest."

"What was her name?" Beth's question ended in a yawn.

Maggie stroked the girl's silky curls. "Princess Daffodil. Now, the princess had a very special pet, a cat named Scamp."

Beth's eyes drooped, and Maggie lowered her voice to a monotone. "What made Scamp special was that he could talk, just like you or me. But he would only talk to the princess . . ."

Two minutes later, Maggie stopped her rambling story.

Beth didn't open her eyes, merely turned with a drowsy mumble.

Maggie leaned against the tree at her back, and smiled when she noticed Jenny had nodded off as well. She could still hear the sounds of wooden swords clacking together, hear the rich rumble of male voices, but turning to watch them seemed too much effort. She closed her eyes, thinking how wonderful it was to feel part of a large family, to truly belong somewhere again.

Maggie opened her eyes, guiltily wondering how much time had passed. Beth still slept on her lap, but Jenny was sitting up—though she wore a dazed, freshly wakened look.

"The fair maidens awaken. And it didn't even require a kiss from the handsome prince." Alex and Cal grinned down at them.

"It's a good thing," Jenny said. "Because from where I sit, I don't see a handsome prince anywhere around."

Alex placed a hand to his heart. "You wound me most grievously, cousin."

Maggie ignored their theatrical byplay. There were more clouds in the sky, some of them seeming ripe to deliver a summer shower. "Where are Will and Owen?"

Alex shrugged. "Owen wandered off—Cal thinks he headed down the path. Will's gone to fetch him back."

Maggie nibbled at her lip, feeling a pinprick of anxiety. Owen had a knack for attracting trouble.

Alex smiled reassuringly. "Don't worry—Will is quite familiar with this wood—he'll find him."

Beth stirred, rubbing her eyes. "Is the picnic over?"

"I think so, Sunshine." Maggie pointed toward the sky. "It looks like we might get a shower soon."

Jenny stood and dusted off her skirts. "Then we'd best pack up so we'll be ready to go when Will and Owen return."

Maggie fingered her broach, staring at the wood a moment longer. It might only be a reaction to yesterday's near catastrophe, but she couldn't shake the feeling that something was wrong.

"If you don't mind cleaning up without me," she said, keeping her tone light, "I think I'll see what's keeping our truants."

"Is something wrong?" Cal frowned at her in concern.

"No," she assured him. "I just want to hurry them along."

"I'll join you," Alex said. "Wouldn't want you to get lost."

Maggie started to protest, then saw the firm set of his jaw. Was that protective streak bred into the Trevarons? Not wanting to waste time arguing, she nodded, then looked past him to Jenny.

Without her having to say a word, Jenny nodded, and smiled at the children. "It looks like it's up to the three of us to get things packed and stowed away. Let's see if we can get it all done before they return, shall we?"

As they stepped onto the tree-shaded path, Maggie glanced at Alex. "You're not concerned about my getting lost, are you?"

He shrugged. "It's a nice day for a stroll. Besides, I never did care much for cleanup duty."

Maggie wasn't fooled by his lazy smile. She set a fast pace, calling Will and Owen's names occasionally. The path they were on twisted and turned back on itself so many times, she wasn't quite certain what direction she was facing anymore. After about ten minutes, the path abruptly ended at crumbling stone wall.

"This is what's left of an old abbey," Alex told her. "This and a pile of stone on the other side."

This was just the sort of thing to fire Owen's imagination. "Why don't you follow the wall that way, and I'll go this way? If we don't spot them by the time we reach the ends, we'll meet back on the other side."

"I don't know—"

"This will allow us to cover more ground and I'll be all right. I'll stick close to the wall. Please."

He looked doubtful, but nodded. "Very well. But if you encounter any problems, back away and come find me."

So, he *was* worried. Maggie headed off without another word.

A few minutes later, she heard a cry of pain.

*Owen!*

Ignoring Alex's orders, she lifted her skirts and sprinted in the direction of the cries.

"Stop! You're hurting me. Let me go!"

Someone was hurting her baby! Maggie's heart thudded painfully, her mind conjuring images of the poacher or some other villain with his hands on her brave little adventurer.

She crashed through the underbrush, then stopped in her tracks.

There, bent over a sobbing and struggling Owen, was Will, holding the boy down.

# Chapter Twenty-four

Will's eyes met hers across the few yards that separated them, and for an eternal moment she couldn't move, couldn't think past the fact that he had Owen pinned to the ground.

*What was he doing? Had she been wrong to trust him?*

His jaw tightened as he watched her, his face assuming that hooded expression. He didn't say a word, leaving it to her to break the silence.

Everything else receded—there was no movement, no sound—only her and Will silently communicating in a test of trust.

Then Alex crashed through the brush, breaking the spell. Suddenly, the world righted itself, and she saw past Will's closed expression to the pain and resignation buried in his eyes.

"Maggie, what—" Alex checked at the tableau before him. "You bastard! What are you doing to the boy? Let him—"

Maggie swung out her arm, halting Alex as he tried to brush past her. "Stop! Will is trying to help Owen, not hurt him."

Freed from her momentary paralysis, Maggie hurried

to Owen's side, trying to communicate a wordless apology to Will. A more complete apology would have to wait.

"It's all right sweetheart," she crooned, "Momma's here now. Just lie still and let me have a look at you."

"It's his leg," Will said tersely. "He must have been on the wall and it gave way. One of the rocks landed on his left calf."

Maggie nodded and gently probed the leg, her heart breaking at the cries of pain from Owen, and at what she found. She looked at Will. "It's broken. We'll need to set it before we can move him."

*Please God, let it be a clean break.*

"What do you need me to do?"

"Find something we can use to fashion a splint. And I'll need your and Alex's cravats to secure it."

Will was already unfastening his neck cloth as he stood.

She swallowed hard. "And find a stout twig he can bite on."

In short order the men had gathered the necessary materials.

Now came the hard part. Maggie gently wiped Owen's brow. "Listen to me carefully, sweetheart. I need you to be very brave. I must set your leg, and it's going to hurt something fierce. But we can't move you until I do or it'll just make it worse."

Owen's eyes were wide with fright, his face ghastly white, but he nodded.

"Now, I'm going to put this stick in your mouth and I want you to bite down on it. And if you want to scream, you scream just as loud as you can. All right?"

Again he nodded, and Maggie stroked his forehead once more, trying to steel herself for what was to come.

Fighting the roiling in her gut, she sought Will's gaze, gaining courage from his compassion and support.

Then she turned to include Alex. "You hold his ankle. Will, take his thigh. When I tell you to, I need you both to pull, firmly but slow and steady. I'll work to ease the broken ends back into proper position as you do. This must be done just right if the leg is to heal properly."

She took a deep breath. "All right, slow and easy."

Owen's cries of pain wrenched at Maggie, but she forced herself not to waver, to finish what had to be done.

When she finally sat back, she found her sweet, brash young avenger had tear tracks on his face and was clutching the twig between his teeth with whimpering, heartbreaking intensity. She shifted so she could hold his head in her lap, offering him the comfort of her touch as she instructed Will and Alex on how to apply the splints properly.

As Will lifted Owen in his arms, Maggie turned to Alex. "Please, go on ahead and let the others know what happened. Then ride back to Lynchmorne and have someone send for a doctor right away. You'll have to take Cal up on your mount with you—we'll need extra room in the carriage for Owen to stretch out."

Alex nodded, and sprinted off.

Will and Maggie moved at a slower pace, careful not to jar Owen's leg. Maggie held on to Owen's hand, crooning words of comfort, commending him on how brave he'd been. She was also keenly aware of Will, and of how terribly she'd failed him.

And not just in this. That eternity between one heartbeat and another, as they'd stared at each other over Owen's writhing body, had been an epiphany for her. Her mind had played back in a flash of vivid detail the story he'd told her about brutalizing his fiancée. And just like that, the answer she'd been looking for had materialized, become crystal clear. She understood, because now she realized the one telling thing he'd *not* said.

She couldn't say any of that to him now, though, no matter how much she wanted to. Owen's hurt demanded all her attention.

But soon. Very soon.

# A WILL OF HER OWN

*    *    *

Will leaned against the doorjamb, half in his room, half in Maggie's. She'd insisted Owen be carried to her room rather than the nursery. He knew she wouldn't leave the boy's side until she was certain he was on the mend.

Silently he watched her fret as Dr. Clemmons examined the boy, watched her confer with the physician on the course of treatment, watched her hover by the bedside until her son drifted off to sleep.

She should get some sleep, too. The circles under her eyes were a testament to how much strain this afternoon's activities had placed on her. But he knew better than to suggest it.

Maggie was amazing. She'd held herself together with a composure that was nothing short of miraculous. He knew she'd felt every ounce of pain Owen had endured, and then some.

Will tried to be as selfless, to block out the memory of that dark moment when she'd looked at him with doubt in her eyes, with a sick dread that he might have done something reprehensible.

*But she chose to believe in me at the end. Hold onto that thought. It was more faith than most offered.*

Emma entered with a fresh basin of water, and Maggie motioned the girl over. "Please sit with my son until I return. If anything changes—if he wakens, or starts thrashing about—anything at all, send for me at once."

"Yes, m'lady."

What was this? She was going to leave Owen to the care of a maid. What was so pressing that—

To his surprise, she walked toward him and motioned him inside his room. Following him, she closed the door and leaned against it. "I owe you an apology for ever doubting you."

Will felt a jumble of emotions—admiration for her courage in facing him, hurt that by voicing her moment

321

of suspicion she made it more real, gratitude that she no longer felt that doubt.

"I understand, Maggie. I know how it must have looked."

She stepped closer and took his hands in hers. "I don't mean just this afternoon. I mean I'm so sorry for *ever* doubting you."

What was she talking about? When had she doubted him before?

She stroked his jaw, her eyes tender and filled with a light he hadn't seen there before. "I have more to say, but not here."

Still musing over what he'd seen in her eyes, Will let her lead him to the drawing room.

"Good," he heard her murmur. "Everyone is here."

What was she up to?

"How is Owen?" Jenny asked anxiously.

"He's sleeping now," Maggie answered. "He's going to be in some pain for several days, and the doctor is not sure whether the leg will heal properly. We'll just have to wait and see."

"Oh Maggie, I'm so sorry."

Maggie acknowledged Jenny's concern, then squared her shoulders. "However, I didn't come down here to speak of Owen. I have an announcement to make and I want you all to hear it."

Was she planning to make a public apology? Did she truly think that would solve anything?

There was a militant, challenging cast to her stance. "Will did not commit the reprehensible acts his fiancée accused him of six years ago."

Will's head shot up, and everyone else in the room froze in mid-movement.

The duke frowned forbiddingly. "That is not a subject we speak of in this house."

"You're wrong, sir." She ignored both the duke's affronted *harrumph* and Will's utterance of her name. "You speak of it in the accusing stares and subtle cuts you send his way. We *will* speak of it now, though in a more honest and forthright manner."

Will could not believe what he was hearing. Did she mean it? How could she know? But she wasn't looking at him—she kept her gaze firmly focused on his grandfather.

"I will make allowances for the fact that you are upset by your son's accident." The duke's tone was steely. "But I warn you, I will *not* be spoken to in such a manner."

Undeterred, Maggie speared him with her most imperious glare. "I'm sorry if I seem disrespectful, Your Grace, but I will not allow you to continue with these misconceptions about Will. You must take a few minutes to *really listen* to what I have to say."

"This is preposterous." Aunt Edith's words came out as a sputter. "I refuse to sit here and listen to such rubbish."

"Sit down, Edith," the duke commanded. "Let's hear what she has to say."

Maggie took a deep breath. "You may not know me well, but I am *no one's* willing victim. I have made my way on my own before, and am fully confident I could do so again if need be. If Will treated me or my children in the manner you seem anxious to accuse him of, I would leave him forthwith, regardless of my financial options. I most definitely would not protect him."

She tossed her head. "As for what happened six years ago, ever since Will first told me the sordid tale of his exile, I had difficulty picturing him doing what he was accused of. The man I knew was too honorable, too kind, to commit such an atrocity. But I had to believe it, because he admitted to doing it."

She placed a hand over his in a gesture of support, and Will covered it with his own. He wasn't sure what she intended to say, but he would stand by her as she said it.

"Then today, when I saw him in a compromising position, I, too, had my moment of doubt. But something else happened. I realized Will was falsely accused not just in this past week, but six years ago as well—I *know* it, as surely as I know my own heart."

Will felt that now-familiar band tighten around his chest. He wanted to believe her words but didn't dare do so yet.

She turned to Will, her gaze asking for his trust. "I want you to answer some questions for me."

He nodded.

"First, are you responsible for the bruise on my arm or for the injury I received at Eiderdown?"

"No." What did she hope to accomplish with this?

"Did you attack Owen today?"

"No."

"When I tended to you before we sailed to England, did you strike me in your delirium?"

Will felt a slap of betrayal at that question. Why would she ask him to incriminate himself this way? But her gaze begged for his trust. "Yes," he bit out.

She took a deep breath. "Can you deny you attacked your fiancée six years ago?"

Will's jaw clinched. He was going to let her down. He could not give her the answer she wanted. "No."

"Aha!" Alex pounced on Will's admission.

But Maggie ignored his outburst. She placed her hands on Will's, and he saw the unshakable faith there. "Well then, can you admit to having attacked her?"

Will's tension eased as comprehension dawned.

She understood!

Somehow, she knew what had bound him to silence all these years. A wry smile touched his lips and his eyes saluted her for the clever preciseness of her words. "No, I cannot."

She squeezed his hands as she turned to his grandfather. "You see. This is what I realized today. Will never admitted to having attacked that woman, he only refused to deny the charge. At least, that's how it was when he spoke of it to me, and I'll wager it was the same when you confronted him six years ago."

Will saw his grandfather struggle to remember.

"You're playing with words," Aunt Edith said impatiently. "What difference does it make if he won't admit it? His refusal to deny it marks him as guilty."

"Hush, Edith, let her finish." Will's grandfather stared at Maggie with a fierce scowl of concentration.

She shot a quick look at Will, then faced the others. "For whatever reason, Will refuses to call his accuser a liar. That doesn't mean she isn't one. No matter what anyone else chooses to believe, *I* will always know in my heart Will is as innocent of those charges as he is of the ones leveled at him this week."

She lifted her chin. "He would not defend himself to those on whose faith he should be able to rely. That doesn't make him guilty, only deeply, and perhaps foolishly, trusting. He was the one who was let down by us, not the other way around."

She tucked her arm through Will's. "I've said all I plan to. If you will excuse us, I plan to escort my husband somewhere more private where I may apologize properly."

And with that outrageously provocative statement, she tugged Will out of the room.

Minutes later, they were in the conservatory, and Maggie's eyes glistened with remorse. She pushed a stray lock from his forehead. "I'm so sorry I doubted you. Can you forgive me?"

Will gathered her to him in a crushing embrace. "There's nothing to forgive." How could he ever convey to her what a precious gift she'd just given him? And she'd handed it to him, with that sweet, humble smile, asking for forgiveness.

It no longer mattered what the rest of his family

thought. Maggie knew the truth—without him having to tell her, she'd seen into his heart and discerned his integrity. "I wish I could—"

She touched a finger to his lips. "I know you have reasons for your silence, and I would never ask you to compromise that. I don't need words. I know *you*—and that's all that matters."

He pulled her to him in a long, control-shattering kiss. Several minutes later he tried to catch his breath as he nuzzled her neck. Heaven above, how had she done this to him? Broken through every carefully erected defense he had, and laid him bare so that he no longer felt whole without her.

He moved his head far enough to look into her eyes. "Maggie, I no longer want us to be partners in some business arrangement." He took a deep breath. "I love you. Forget the pompous things I said when I proposed—the person who said all that doesn't exist anymore. I want to see you cradle our children in your arms. I want to stand beside you and watch them grow. But most of all, I want to love you and laugh with you and cherish you."

He searched her eyes. "Please say you want those things, too."

He'd said he loved her!

Maggie felt as if her heart had grown too big for her chest. She raised a trembling hand to his cheek. "I love you, Will Trevaron, have loved you for a very long time. I want all of those things and more. I want to entwine my life with yours."

He melded their lips with another long, body-tingling kiss.

After a while, Maggie reluctantly pulled back and pressed her cheek against his shoulder. "I need to check on Owen."

He massaged her back. "I know."

"I plan to sit up with him tonight."

She felt his smile as he kissed her head. "I know."

She looked up. "You don't mind?" The mother in her would not be appeased until she was certain Owen passed a restful night, but a part of her resented having to leave Will. They'd just declared their love for each other and she very much wanted to express those feelings in a most intimate, primal way.

"If you're asking if I'll miss having you in my bed, the answer is yes. But I understand, and we'll have other nights." His eyes darkened hungrily. "A lifetime of other nights."

Maggie smiled softly. Surely, she was the luckiest of women.

"However," he added with a crooked grin, "if you don't stop looking at me like that, I may drag you off to a secluded corner of this very conservatory and plant a seed or two of my own."

Maggie laughed, even as her cheeks warmed. His scandalous words conjured images that had her longing for his touch.

He gave a deep, satisfied chuckle. Then he tucked her hand on his arm. "Come along, my oh-so-tempting wife, we'll both sit with Owen for a while."

But the duke met them at the foot of the stairway, his expression solemn, troubled.

"I'd like to have a word with you," he said to Will.

Maggie felt Will's hesitation, sensed his stiffening.

She squeezed his arm. It was past time the two of them talked. "Go on. You know where to find me when you're done."

Will studied her, then nodded. "I won't be long."

She watched the two men, so alike in bearing and pride, walk side by side to the older man's study. As she climbed the stairs, she sent up a silent prayer that they would begin to heal the breach that had separated them for six years.

Will followed his grandfather into the study, the room that held such painful memories. To his surprise, rather than take his accustomed seat behind the enormous desk, his grandfather stood in front of it, hands clasped behind him.

The duke cleared his throat. "It seems I've done a terrible injustice. I regret it bitterly, more than you'll ever know. I can't make up for what my lack of faith cost you, cost us."

He drew himself up. "However, there's something I must tell you, something that may help you understand how I could have been guilty of such an error in judgment." He paused, then asked abruptly, "What do you know of my father?"

Will frowned. "Just that he was overly fond of spirits and died in a fall one night when he was too far gone in his cups."

His grandfather nodded. "That's all I intended any of you to know. But I was wrong. You should have been told the full story before now."

Will wondered at the grim set of his grandfather's jaw.

"When he was sober, Father was the most civilized of men, charming, witty, gracious. But when drunk, he became bullying, aggressive. He regularly beat my mother."

Will bit out an oath.

His grandfather picked up the miniature from his desk. "Mother was a recluse. She didn't go out and rarely received visitors. It was how she kept her bruises, her shame, hidden." A tic fluttered below his left eye, then stilled. "She tried to keep us out of harm's way, but she wasn't always successful. Robbie was so helpless, so vulnerable. I'd see the bruises, hear her crying, and I'd hate my father enough to kill him."

Devil's teeth! Will's fists clinched at the thought of what his fragile aunt had endured.

"After I got older," the duke continued, "and had gained

some size and muscle, it got better." He set the miniature down and moved to the window. "I knocked him out once when I caught him going for Mother. After that he pretty much avoided us, spent much of his time in London. I made it a point to always be close to hand, though, when he was at Lynchmorne."

He let the drape fall and turned around. "One evening I arrived home to find he'd returned early. He had Mother and Robbie cornered in the upstairs hallway. Mother was on the floor bleeding from a cut lip. He was yelling obscenities at Robbie and his arm was pulled back to strike."

What must it have been like to live such a nightmare?

"I charged up the stairs and grabbed his arm. But I misjudged his strength. He sent me sprawling next to Mother."

The duke rubbed his forehead. "He'd let go of Roberta when I attacked, but now he stalked her, catching up with her near the head of the stairs. Before I could do anything, something extraordinary happened. He stared past Roberta's shoulder, his expression turning to horror. Then he screamed. When he turned to run, he tripped and fell down the stairs."

His grandfather shrugged. "Roberta swears Rosebud appeared, but it was likely just a drunken vision. Whatever it was, we were rid of him, and not one of us shed a tear."

The duke finally met Will's gaze. "I've long feared that one of my sons or grandsons might inherit, through me, a tendency to be what my father was."

Will straightened. "Grandfather—"

The duke raised a hand. "Let me finish. When that Radwin girl came along with her tale, and you refused to call her a liar, I felt my worst nightmare had come true. I despised you for becoming what my father had been, and I despised myself for having passed this depravity on to another generation."

He stopped speaking. He stood straight, as always, but

somehow he seemed older, more fragile than he had before today.

Will crossed the room. "I believe, sir, there is need for pardon and understanding on both sides." He held out his hand.

His grandfather clasped it, then grabbed Will in a fierce hug. "Thank you. And welcome back home, my boy."

Will had no sooner exited his grandfather's study, than he encountered a solemn-faced Alex.

"I owe you an apology," his cousin said. "I've been a fool and insulted you beyond repair. I may not be able to make it up to you, but I want you to know I'm going to try."

Will mentally shook his head. It seemed his bulldog of a wife had made another convert.

Alex stood straighter. "For now, I think it best I put some distance between us. I'll leave first thing tomorrow."

Will gave his cousin a long, hard look. Alex had been like a brother at one time. Yet he'd shined the light of accusation on Will over and over this past week.

Why had he needed Maggie's words to bring him around?

But Will could not find it in him to hold grudges today. He'd learned through experience how poisonous that could be.

He held out his hand and offered Alex a crooked smile. "You may have been a tactless jackanapes, but you thought you were defending my wife and her son. For that, I can forgive a good many things. Don't feel you must leave on my account."

Some of the tension left Alex, and he took Will's hand. "Thank you," he said thickly. "That's better treatment than I deserve. I'll see you don't have cause to regret it."

Clapping his cousin on the back, Will moved to the stairs, taking them two at a time as he headed up to join his wife.

# Chapter Twenty-five

The next morning Owen felt somewhat better. He was still in pain, but Maggie and Will carefully described how courageous he'd been to anyone who came to visit, and the boy enjoyed being the hero of his own story.

By midday, Maggie finally agreed to move him back to his own room, though she didn't entirely relinquish him to Mrs. Peprick's tender care. While Will and his grandfather rode over the estate, she spent time playing quiet games with the children.

Maggie couldn't wait to return to Briarwood. Funny how it already felt like home. She would not keep the children so separate from her life there. If she had her way, they would leave the day after the houseparty.

Will headed up to his room, stopping a footman along the way to order a bath be drawn. His grandfather had led him through some of the boggier sections of the estate, and Will felt the need for a bath and change of clothes.

A satisfied smile tugged at his lips. Owen was back in the nursery. That meant he would have Maggie to himself tonight.

Crossing his room, he paused as he spied a note

propped prominently on his desk. His smile broadened as he read it.

*After last night I feel we need a little time to ourselves. I've slipped away to your favorite spot by the quarry and have a very special surprise planned. Please hurry to join me. Maggie.*

A very special surprise, was it? Just the two of them in that starkly beautiful, isolated spot. The thought of possible ways they could pass the time brought a wide grin to his face.

This would be a very quick bath, indeed.

Forty minutes later, as Will neared the quarry his mood had turned pensive, wary. Something about the note niggled at him, though he couldn't put his finger on just what. But it was the same sense of wrongness he'd had about that series of accidents just before leaving America.

Will pushed his horse to a faster pace. An urgent need to see Maggie, to make certain she was unharmed, built inside him.

Clearing the trees, the first thing he saw was her mount, tethered to a bush and peacefully grazing. A blanket was spread out, with a hamper and a pair of ladies gloves sitting on top.

But Maggie herself was nowhere to be seen, and his hail received no response. The whole area was eerily quiet.

Then, snagged on a scraggly bush at the very lip of the cliff, he spied the perky blue hat from Maggie's riding habit.

A fist of fear slammed into his chest. Calling her name, he raced forward. "Maggie," he yelled again, more desperately this time as he peered over the edge and scanned the area below.

A prickling at the nape of his neck was the only warning he had, a split second before he felt the shove that sent him pitching forward.

\* \* \*

Entering her room, Maggie went to the adjoining door, eager to see if Will had returned. Getting no answer, she opened the door and peeked inside. She smiled indulgently at the sight of Will's dirty clothes scattered on the floor.

He'd obviously been in a hurry, and he hadn't been gone long—the tub of dirty bath water still stood untended. As soon as she freshened up she'd go look for him.

Before she could turn back to her room, a gust of cool air raised gooseflesh on her arms. Was another storm brewing?

She stepped inside to check, but the windows were all shut. Where had the breeze come from? It came again, this time ruffling a slip of paper on the edge of his bed, wafting it to the floor. She saw a movement from the corner of her eye, but when she turned there was nothing there.

Maggie frowned uneasily as she retrieved the fallen paper. Then she paused—why was her name on the bottom of this note?

As she read the missive, her blood seemed to freeze in her veins. Maggie tossed the paper aside and raced to her wardrobe.

As she pulled out her riding habit, she heard a knock on Will's outer bedroom door, then heard it open.

Her heart slammed in her chest. Had the author of that note returned? She sagged with relief at the sound of the maid's off-key humming.

Maggie finished dressing in record time, then stepped to Will's doorway.

"Excuse me, m'lady." The girl bobbed a curtsey when she saw Maggie. "I was just cleaning up after Lord Rainley's bath."

Maggie tried to compose herself. "That's quite all right." She tried to pull her thoughts together. Dear Lord, Will was in danger and she didn't even know the source! "Tell me, how long ago did Lord Rainley leave?"

"No more than ten minutes, m'lady. I'm awful sorry I didn't come sooner, but—"

"No need to apologize, I'm sure you're doing just as you should. I was just curious."

Ten minutes! She devoutly hoped Will had set a leisurely pace. She had to catch him before he reached the quarry.

And she had to go alone.

Until she knew how things stood, she wouldn't trust anyone.

Alex met her at the head of the staircase. "Hello, Maggie. Going riding, are you?"

*God, please help me to not fall apart.* "Yes. I thought I'd get some fresh air after being cooped up all day."

He frowned. "Is something wrong? You look a bit pale."

Were those worry lines for her welfare or for his own schemes? She forced a smile. "I'm fine."

"Care for company?" Alex still blocked her way.

Was he trying to keep an eye on her for some reason? "No." Then, fearing she'd been too abrupt, she added, "I wouldn't be good company just now." She stepped around him and all but fled down the stairs, relieved when he didn't follow.

It seemed to take ages for the stable boy to prepare her horse. Finally climbing into the saddle, she set a brisk pace, breaking into a full gallop as soon as she was well away.

*Please let me be wrong.*

*Please let me be in time if I'm not.*

She held that punishing pace until the terrain made it too dangerous. Still, she pushed her mount as much as she safely could until she reached the clearing atop the quarry. Icy horror gripped her throat as she took in the scene.

Alex's mother stood near the cliff's edge, pistol in hand.

As for Will, only his hands and the top of his head were visible. The rest of him dangled out of sight over the side. He gripped a small bit of brush growing precariously at the lip of the cliff. It seemed woefully inadequate to support his weight, and would almost certainly give way at any moment.

If he didn't lose his hold first.

As Maggie slid from her horse, Lady Osgood kicked viciously at Will's hand. Maggie screamed his name as she ran toward them.

"You!" Lady Osgood turned and spat out the word. "Come any closer, and I swear I'll shoot him and end it right now."

Maggie halted mid-step.

"Maggie!" Will's cry was edged with desperation. "Leave here, now!"

The woman's eyes narrowed. "Listen to him. There's nothing you can do, so get back on your horse and ride away."

"Surely, we can talk through this, work something out." Maggie tried to keep her voice even.

"Don't speak to me as if I were a simpleton." Lady Osgood made a sharp movement with the gun. Then she frowned. "How did you know to come here? Who else knows where we are?"

Maggie had a burst of inspiration. "Rosebud told me, of course. She sent me here to help Will."

"Rosebud!" Lady Osgood's eyes glinted with superstitious fear for a moment, but then she drew herself up. "Preposterous."

Had she found the woman's weakness? "Rosebud always shows up to help when a Trevaron is in danger." Maggie took a small step forward. "If you do this, she'll haunt you forever."

Again, Alex's mother shifted uneasily. "Stop it. I won't

listen to that kind of talk. Besides, it doesn't matter. I have to finish what I've started."

Maggie took another half step, spreading her hands. "But why? What reason can you have for doing this?"

"For Alexander, of course. The title should be his. He is a better man than William will ever be. Their fathers were twins, barely five minutes apart. Who is to say my Osgood wasn't really the senior twin?"

Maggie changed tactics. "We'll go back to America if you like. Will can denounce his rights to the title."

The woman's lips turned up in a sneer. "You Americans really are an uneducated, uncivilized lot. He can't just disown the title. No, this is the only way. If that inept assassin I hired to take care of things in America had done his job, none of this would be necessary."

"Assassin!" Maggie's hand flew to her chest.

"Of course. He's the one who stabbed Will, and before that he set the fire. He had a hand in several other so-called accidents. But the incompetent fool bungled it all, so now I must finish it."

Maggie's eyes widened. "That arrow at Eiderdown—"

"That was me." The woman actually seemed proud of herself. "I'm quite good at archery. I can't imagine how I missed."

Lady Osgood's eyes narrowed. "Actually all of this—the attacks in America, the attempts here—it's all your fault."

From the corner of her eye, Maggie noticed Will's knuckles whiten and his head rise slightly. He was gaining ground. If only she could keep Lady Osgood talking.

Maggie shifted her weight, taking another small step forward. "How can it be my fault?"

"None of this would have been necessary if you hadn't intervened six years ago. You've turned me into a murderess."

Maggie continued her silent prayers. So far, the woman had not noticed Will's progress. She had to keep Lady

Osgood's gaze focused on her and away from him.

"Even then, I thought luck would go my way," Alex's mother continued in an injured tone. "My son had everyone convinced Will was a barbarous villain, until you exonerated him. No one but Jennifer would have mourned his loss, or looked too deeply into the cause. Now he's welcomed like the ne'er do well prodigal, while the faithful grandson is ignored."

Maggie felt a sinking sensation in the pit of her stomach. "Alex is part of this?"

Lady Osgood seemed genuinely affronted. "Of course not. My son is too noble to take part in such sordid matters. It's up to me, as his mother, to look out for his interests."

The gun came back to rest on Will. "So now we come to this. At this range I can't miss. Unpleasant, but I have no choice."

Maggie tried to draw her attention away again. "But you're not fast enough to kill both of us."

"That remains to be seen. And it doesn't really matter. Only Alexander matters. And with Will dead, my son will be his grandfather's heir, no matter what happens to me." There was a glitter of madness in Lady Osgood's eyes.

Maggie realized no amount of reasoning would get through to her. Her mind scrambled for ideas.

"There's something you don't know," she blurted out. "Even if you kill Will, it's possible Alexander won't become the next duke. I'm carrying Will's child. If it's a son, *he* will succeed to the title instead of Alex." There was no way Lady Osgood would know that she had been a virgin up until a week ago.

Her plan worked. Lady Osgood spun back to face her. "Slut!" The women's face contorted with rage. "I won't let you ruin things this time. You and that whelp you're carrying will die as well." And she raised the gun, pointing it at Maggie.

But she never had a chance to pull the trigger.

Will, drawing on a strength powered by sheer desperation, lunged up and forward, managing to grab his aunt's ankle.

Screaming, she lost her footing and plunged over the cliff.

He tried to catch her, did in fact snatch a piece of her dress. But he didn't have the strength to hold on for long, and the handful of scrub that was his lifeline started to pull away from the rock face.

Lady Osgood's dress tore from his grasp, just as Maggie threw herself down on the ground above him, reaching a hand to help him up to solid ground.

Then he was sitting beside her and she collapsed in his arms, sobbing uncontrollably. "You're all right! Oh Will, I thought I had lost you!"

The tears poured out of her in an unstoppable flood.

Will held her tightly, rocking her, stroking her hair, soothing her with words that welled out of his heart. He didn't think he would ever be able to let her go. Dear Lord, he'd aged ten years when he saw his aunt turn the gun toward Maggie.

When her sobs had quieted to a final hiccup, he loosened his grip just enough to tilt her chin up.

"Are you all right?" he asked, searching her face.

She nodded wetly, sniffling a bit. "I should be asking you that. Oh, look, your hand is bleeding. Will, you're hurt."

"It's nothing that can't wait. First, I want to tell you what a wonderfully brave lady you are."

"Brave!" she squeaked. "I'm surprised my legs held me up, they were trembling so much."

He smiled. "But you faced up to her, kept her talking and gave me the time I needed. How did you find me?"

"I found the note that lured you here."

"And so you naturally came running to my rescue all on your own. You saved my life today, Maggie my heart."

338

"And you, mine. Oh Will, she would have shot me if you hadn't stopped her."

Will shuddered at the memory. That had been the worst moment of his life, when he'd seen his aunt turn her gun toward Maggie and level it with every intention of pulling the trigger. He still felt the sickening lurch in the pit of his stomach.

"Your ability to keep your wits about you constantly amazes me." He was trying to lighten the mood, to help ease some of the tension he still felt in her. "To concoct that story about being with child, and the allusion to Rosebud, was quick thinking. It kept her distracted and off balance just long enough."

"I'm not so sure I *was* lying about Rosebud."

Will leaned back. "What do you mean, you're not sure?"

Maggie met his gaze earnestly. "I found the note because it caught my eye when it fluttered off your bed. But Will, the window was closed, and nothing else stirred. There was nothing to cause it to move."

Will raised an eyebrow. "Maggie, you don't really believe a ghost sent you a message, do you?"

She lifted her chin stubbornly. "You didn't feel that cold breath of air. It *could* have been Rosebud."

But then she looked uncertainly toward the quarry. "I don't suppose there's any chance—"

Will squeezed her shoulder. "She's dead, Maggie," he said firmly. "No one could survive such a fall. We'll send someone for the body. Right now, I want to get you back to Lynchmorne."

Will kept an arm around her as they moved toward the horses.

"What are we going to tell Alex?" Maggie's voice held a world of pain and sympathy. "None of this was his doing."

"I know." He was so proud of her, so touched that she could think of his cousin's feelings after what they'd just been through. "We'll have to tell him and Grandfather the truth. But as far as the rest of the world is concerned, we need say no more than that she fell from the cliff."

Two days later, the funeral was held and Alex departed immediately thereafter. Maggie's heart bled for him as he tried to come to terms with what had happened, but she knew the only things that could help him now were time and distance.

The next day, Maggie breathed a sigh of relief as she climbed the steps of Briarwood. This already felt like coming home.

Will carried Owen up to the children's wing in grand style while Maggie helped Mrs. Peprick settle the other two children in. By the time she returned to her own room, Emma had finished putting her things away. Maggie dismissed the girl with a smile. Then she quickly freshened up, retrieved something from her vanity, and went in search of Will.

She found him in his study, looking over a ledger. "Am I interrupting anything important?"

Will closed the ledger with a smile. "You are always a most welcome interruption."

Maggie wandered closer. This was the first time she had been in his study. It was a very masculine room, sparsely furnished with heavy, comfortable-looking wooden pieces. There was a clean, elegant feel to it. A large globe stood in one corner and several leather-bound volumes filled a bookcase next to it.

A table flanked the other end of the bookcase, near his desk. On it, she spotted an object that would suit her purpose nicely.

She moved toward her target, assuming a leisurely pose. "I see you've given your wedding gift a position of honor." She stroked the figure of the dragon fighter, so reminiscent of the man who now stepped up beside her.

"I like to keep it close." He snuggled his face in her hair.

Maggie felt a shiver flutter through her, but she refused to be distracted. "I've always thought it lacked something," she said thoughtfully.

Will peered at the figurine over her shoulder. "It looks perfect to me." He nuzzled her neck. "Just like something else in this room."

He certainly wasn't making it easy for her to maintain her focus. "Don't you think he should be fighting *for* something? Not just battling for battle's sake?"

Will rested his chin on her shoulder, wrapping his hands around her waist. "Oh, I don't know. It looks to me like he *is* fighting for something—his life."

"But that seems a bit . . . unworthy of such a valiant knight. He should have a nobler goal, be protecting something precious."

"Such as?"

Maggie opened her fist and placed the amber broach before the beleaguered figure, under the protection of his upraised sword. "Such as the heart and spirit of his lady fair, freely given for him to cherish and protect."

She heard Will's indrawn breath, felt the tightening of his hands around her, a heartbeat before he spun her to face him.

His eyes burned with a fire so intense it ignited a thousand firefly sparks inside her. "Are you sure, Maggie?"

She placed a hand to his cheek. "I've never been so certain of anything in my life. I have you—my own sweet Will—and that is all I'll ever need."

He stilled, absorbing her words. Then he squeezed her to him, exultation singing through his veins. When he let her go, he gave her a tender kiss. Nuzzling her ear, he whispered, "I love you, Maggie. My heart is yours, guard it well."

He lifted her in his arms and headed for the door.

"Will," she protested. "Put me down. Will, it's the middle of the day, you can't mean to—"

"Is that a challenge, my dear?" He raised an eyebrow, delighting in the way her cheeks flushed so prettily.

"Of course not," she said hastily. "But, oh my, what if someone sees us?"

"Then they will think I am the luckiest man on earth." And with a joyous laugh, Will pushed open the study door and carried his blushing bride up the stairs to their room.